Readers love the
Kildevil Cove Murder Mysteries
by J.S. COOK

Dark Water

"…Cook fills every page with the sounds and sights of Kildevil Cove, the diverse crew of characters, and the increasingly disturbing secrets that begin to surface with the washed-up-bones of a long dead teenager."

—Paranormal Romance Guild

"…the murder/mystery was engaging, there is plenty of character building, the backdrop was fascinating to me, and the slow romantic development matched the mood of the book perfectly."

—Rainbow Book Reviews

Dark Mire

"Cook outdid herself with the second installment in Kildevil Cove Murder Mysteries series. Psychological, twisted, dark, emotional, suspenseful, and at times just plain scary!"

—QueeRomance Ink

By J.S. Cook

But Not For Me
Come to Dust
As JoAnne Soper-Cook: The Eye of Heaven
Famous Last Words
A Little Night Murder
The Lovely Beast
My Man Walter
Oasis of Night
The Quality of Mercy
Sixteen Songs About Regret
Skid Row Serenade
Stranger at the Door
The Winter Dark

Published by DSP Publications
Because You Despise Me

KILDEVIL COVE MURDER MYSTERIES
Dark Water
Dark Mire
Dark Tide
Dark Souls
Dark Vows

Published by DREAMSPINNER PRESS
www.dreamspinnerpress.com

DARK VOWS

J.S. COOK

DREAMSPINNER
PRESS

Published by

DREAMSPINNER PRESS

5032 Capital Circle SW, Suite 2, PMB# 279, Tallahassee, FL 32305-7886 USA
www.dreamspinnerpress.com

Trade PaperbackISBN: 978-1-64108-513-7
Digital ISBN: 978-1-64108-512-0
Trade Paperback printed February 2023
v. 1.0

Printed in the United States of America
∞
This paper meets the requirements of
ANSI/NISO Z39.48-1992 (Permanence of Paper).

PROLOGUE

THE ROAD in front of his house was empty, a bare space of crumbling, pitted asphalt dotted with deep holes, some still holding water from the previous night's rain. A lone seagull circled above, calling endlessly, its white wings outstretched to catch an upwards-tending thermal that would eventually bear it out to sea.

The boy on the bike circled too, sketching a series of concentric rings on the wet pavement, vague shapes that expanded outwards as he moved farther away. *Maman* had told him to stay nearby. She was going out, but he was a big boy now, big enough to see to himself while she dashed to the shop to purchase milk. *Maman* had made him promise to stay in front of the door and not go riding off down the harbour or over to the Point where the land fell suddenly away and all that was beneath was the roaring maw of the North Atlantic. "*Cette terre maudite,*" she often said. This cursed land. This cursed land seemed to be the sum and total of her woes. She hated it, hated that they'd had to come here, despised Papa and his inability to stay rooted in one place. *Maman* feared and hated the sea and believed it would one day eat them up if they weren't careful. "*Cette terre nous dévorera.*" This place will devour us.

There was no one else about; all his friends had gone to school, but that morning *Maman* had felt his forehead and said he wasn't well enough to attend and had better stay in bed. Staying in bed was boring because his bedroom had only a tiny window set high up in the wall, too high to see anything interesting. Around nine he said he was feeling better and could he go outside to ride his bike a little in the fresh air. *D'accord,* but only if he stayed where she could see him from the window. That goddamned window. He tried the word aloud: "Goddamn." He liked the shape of it in English, the way his tongue curled around the first part, holding it, until the second half exploded like a bomb. "God*damn.*"

He expanded the outward radius of his latest circle, pushing past the Apostolic parsonage and towards the abandoned school. A glance back over his shoulder told him *Maman* was nowhere in sight, so he pedalled a little farther, his small legs pumping hard, driving the bike forwards. At the intersection where the main highway met Secretary Road he stopped, looking up and down both ways, like he'd been taught, but there was nothing to impede his progress, and he took this as a lucky sign. It was safe. Nothing bad was going to happen. Just for luck he crossed himself the way he'd been taught and started across the road. All he saw was the road in front of him, the abandoned schoolhouse, the tantalising ditches on either side, full of interesting bits of rubbish. The white pickup truck, its windows tinted dark, drew close to him, its driver peering unseen at the small boy on the bike.

The truck pulled to a stop just as the child's house exploded behind him in a roar of flame.

CHAPTER ONE

Monday

INSPECTOR DEINIOL Quirke—Danny to his friends and intimates—was waiting in an examination room for the arrival of his doctor, who was probably bringing news he didn't particularly want to hear. For the past two or three years he'd endured ever-increasing pain in his knees, coupled with a loss of flexibility, and it had gotten to the point where he could no longer ignore the toll it was taking. It was his husband, Tadhg, who'd forced him to make the appointment, after growing tired of hearing Danny complain about the agony in his joints.

"Go and see the doctor," Tadhg had insisted. "Get some X-rays taken. It's not normal, Dan, the way you're always in pain." Although they'd been married less than six months, Tadhg had slipped far too easily into the role of nagging spouse.

There was a rustle outside the door of the examination room, and Dr. Roman St. Croix was there. "Danny! Good to see you. You're looking well." St. Croix was about thirty years old but looked much younger, tall, thin, and with the dark eyes and olive skin that suggested a Mediterranean ancestry. Danny had been seeing him for the past five years, ever since his previous doctor had retired and moved back to Hong Kong. "Wish I could say the same about your X-rays." He sat down at the desk and touched a key to bring the computer out of hibernation, then another to retrieve the X-ray images from the digital bank where they'd been stored. "I'm afraid the news is not good."

"Oh?" Danny's gut tightened in anticipation. St. Croix wasn't one to beat around the bush. If he said something was bad, it was definitely that and possibly more.

"Take a look at this." The doctor pointed to the image displayed on the screen. "This is your left knee. Now normally there would be a significant space between the two ends of the bone—right here."

Danny leaned forward to gaze at the monochrome images on the screen. "Okay."

"But the space between your bones has all but vanished, and the X-ray picked up several osteophytes—bone spurs—growing where there should be healthy cartilage." He sat back and drew a deep breath. "You have advanced osteoarthritis in both knees, with subsequent breakdown of the cartilage. This would explain the pain you've been feeling, especially at the back of the knee. The loss of cartilage means the tendons back there are working overtime to take the load that the knee cartilage would normally handle."

Danny knew enough about arthritis to know it wasn't fatal, but neither was it a cause for celebration. "So what should I do?" Surely there was some prescription St. Croix could give him. He wasn't expected to live like this. Was he?

"You are going to need both knees replaced. I would recommend sooner rather than later. The degree of deterioration is significant, and I don't want to wait to get this remedied."

Knee replacement? That was major surgery, wasn't it? With a long recovery time, months off his feet, and even when he was able to stand unassisted, he'd be using a walker or crutches. "How long will that take?"

St. Croix peered at him over the tops of his glasses. Danny had long suspected the doctor didn't actually need spectacles but simply wore them to give himself a certain air of gravitas. He was ridiculously young. "Depending on what we find when we go in there, as well as other factors—lifestyle, how well you respond to physical therapy—it might be up to six months."

Danny felt like a bridge had fallen on top of him. "Six *months*?"

"For each knee."

"I don't have a year. I can't just…." He laughed, even though there was nothing funny. "Good God! I can't take a year off work. That's mental. You can't expect me to…." He fell silent, aghast at what St. Croix was proposing.

"Danny, this is serious. If you don't take care of this problem, eventually you are going to lose function in both knees. When that happens, you're looking at joint fusion surgery. Your knees will never move again."

"If you're trying to scare me," Danny said dryly, "it's working." He scrubbed a hand over his face and drew a deep breath. The examination room air was dry and smelled like antiseptic soap. "Is there anything we can do in the meantime, until I'm able to have the surgery? You wouldn't do both knees at once, would you?"

"It depends on the surgeon," St. Croix replied, "but no, they're usually done one at a time. Until you have the surgery, there's not much I can offer you except NSAIDs and physiotherapy."

"I can't take NSAIDs. They tear up my stomach."

St. Croix sat back in his chair and tapped his pen on the edge of the desk. It was a beautiful September day outside, with the sun shining and a light breeze from the northeast. For once the weather was nice; there were no gale-force winds or lashing rain. Danny had made plans for a picnic lunch with Tadhg near Single's Bridge, a local swimming spot. Now he wasn't in the mood for anything of the sort. "There is one other alternative."

"Oh?"

"We can inject your knees with hyaluronic acid, otherwise known as viscosupplementation. This can potentially give you up to six months' relief." St. Croix saw Danny's hopeful expression and quickly countered with, "but it's not a cure, and you will eventually require joint replacement."

"I'll have that viscose stuff," Danny said, getting to his feet. "Can you make the appointment?"

"No need," St. Croix replied. "I can do it in the office. We don't currently have any on hand, so I'll have to order it in. It will take a week or so." He wrote something on a prescription pad and tore off the sheet, which he handed across to Danny. "That's for Tylenol 3. Codeine. The pharmacist will have to give it to you from behind the counter. Use it only when you absolutely need it. I don't need to tell you it's habit-forming."

Danny had thanked him and was on his way out the door when his mobile phone rang. It was Cillian Riley. "Bad situation," Riley told him. "We've got a house explosion and fire. No word on casualties, but the fire department's currently on-site." Riley's warm Newcastle accent did nothing to mask the concern he obviously felt.

"Witnesses?"

"None that we know of, although a fair-sized crowd has gathered. The usual gawkers and rubberneckers."

"Thanks, Cillian." Danny had reached the parking lot by now. "I'll be there as soon as I can." He unlocked his car and slid in, grimacing as his painful knees protested. The car was lower than the battered antique Land Rover he'd been driving the previous year, and getting in and out of the driver's seat was proving to be quite the feat. He remembered the old Rover with a wistful fondness, wishing he'd never sent it to the scrapyard. But it represented a dark and difficult time in his life when his accidental entanglement with the criminal Martin Belshawe had almost ended his career. All that was over now. The new Royal Newfoundland Constabulary head, Adrian Molloy, had reinstated him, and Danny and Tadhg had married in Inverness on Danny's birthday in April. Things were finally looking up.

The neighbourhood where the explosion occurred was within sight of the police station, not unusual in a village as small as Kildevil Cove, but Danny had to park farther down the block to avoid the volunteer fire department's equipment. Inspector Cillian Riley, still limping from a badly broken leg incurred the previous winter, was waiting when Danny arrived at the scene. In deference to the warm weather, Riley was wearing a short-sleeved shirt and pressed chinos, but the beard he'd taken such pains to grow was nowhere in sight. Riley looked odd without it.

"Who called it in?" Danny asked.

"No idea, at least not yet," Riley replied. "Anonymous call to the station. We tried a preliminary trace, but it came back as an unassigned mobile number. When we called it—"

"Let me guess. Nobody answered."

"Out of service." The Englishman shook his head. "I seriously hope we haven't got a firebug."

The local vegetation was exceptionally dry, owing to an unusually hot summer with very little rain. A stray spark, even an unintentional one, and the whole place would be ablaze. It was hardly the desired outcome for a town that had burnt nearly to the ground back in the early 1960s. Danny nodded towards the house. "Anyone at home?"

"Nobody as far as the fire department can tell. The house belongs to a young couple living there with their lad." He glanced back at the smouldering heap of embers that had once been a house. "Gerard Caron, his wife, Amalie, and the boy's name is Joseph."

"Caron," Danny remarked. "French?"

"Just moved here from Quebec a few months ago," Riley replied. "The husband was in the Armed Forces for a while. Got a job with Newfoundland Power as an electric linesman when he got out. He's at work right now, actually; I've just called and notified him. He's replacing poles on the Old Perlican barrens, though, so he might be a little while."

According to the neighbours, Riley explained, the marriage was not a happy one, and the couple could often be heard fighting, shouting at each other in French, sometimes late into the night. The boy, six-year-old Joseph, went to the local elementary school just up the shore in Winterton and was sometimes seen playing with some of the boys from the Cove.

"So where is the boy? Wouldn't he be at school today?" Danny asked.

"I called the school," Riley replied. "According to the secretary, his mother signed him off sick today. Some of the neighbours said they saw him riding his bike in front of the house around nine this morning. He hasn't been seen since."

"All right." Danny glanced around at the assembled crowd, noting the presence of a few familiar faces, the usual curtain-twitchers and rubberneckers he'd expect to see. "Get someone to photograph and video the crowd."

"Already done." Riley smirked. "Downloading to your computer as we speak."

"Aren't you a busy little bee," Danny said, but there was no insult implied. Riley was very good at his job; that was the simple truth of it.

"Nice to know I'm appreciated," Riley said.

"All right," Danny said finally. It appeared that Riley had everything well in hand. "I'll leave you to it. I need to organise a search immediately for the boy and his mother. What about the mother—Amalie, is it?—what's she do? Is she at work?"

"I've heard conflicting reports. One woman said she works in a shop in Carbonear while someone else said she doesn't work outside the home." There was a collective shout from the assembled spectators as the outside wall of the house collapsed in a shower of sparks. Two firefighters immediately ran forward with a hose to douse any remaining hot spots while Constables Sarah Avery and Dougie Hughes struggled to hold back the crowd.

"Hughes, Avery!" Riley shouted to them. "Get those people out of there." He turned back to Danny as the constables began working to disperse the crowd. "Apparently the Carons don't really mix with anyone else in the Cove. Keep themselves to themselves."

"Language barrier?"

"No. From what I've been told they speak better English than you and me." This was the case with most Quebecois Danny knew: they spoke both official languages fluently and were able to switch between them with enviable ease. He'd taken French classes all throughout school, but his own mastery of the language was barely adequate.

"Do you want to go back to the station and run the Carons through the database?" Danny asked. "Get off that bad leg. Put out an Amber Alert for the missing boy while I organise the search."

Riley nodded gratefully. "Thanks. It's been aching like a bastard all day." He'd shattered the leg in several places the previous winter, the result of a high-speed chase on slippery roads and an untimely encounter with a moose. Surgery had pieced the bone back together, but he would never be the same.

"If the Carons are originally from Quebec, we should probably contact the *Sûreté*," Danny said. "Oh, by the way, how's the application for law school going?"

Riley smiled. "Suspended," he said, "indefinitely." He pocketed his notebook, and Danny knew not to pry any farther. Perhaps Riley's law school aspirations had succumbed to the demands of his injured leg—or maybe his relationship with Sergeant Kevin Carbage had matured to the point of mutual contentment and he was reluctant to leave.

"Sorry to hear it," Danny replied automatically. He wasn't, not really. Riley was an extremely capable cop, and over the two years he'd been posted to Kildevil Cove, he'd become a close friend. Danny would have been sorry to see him go. The Cove's small RNC detachment didn't really need two inspectors—Chief Inspector Adrian Molloy had promoted Riley the previous year—but as long as he was useful, Danny saw no reason for Riley to leave.

Riley shrugged. "I think I'm better off as a copper," he said. "See you back at the station."

Danny moved closer to the site once Riley left and the constables had dispersed the crowd of onlookers. He wondered if it was merely luck that nobody had been at home when the explosion occurred or if the arsonist had planned it that way. It wasn't unknown for someone to destroy their own property in the hope of recouping greater value from the insurance money. In a larger city, he could see how that might be the case, but Kildevil Cove was tiny, and most houses were not worth much more than the cost of the land.

Danny pulled out his mobile phone and put a call through to RNC headquarters, asked to speak to Adrian Molloy. The acerbic Irishman had been tapped to replace disgraced former Chief Moira Fraser after her involvement with a human-trafficking ring had necessitated her removal from the police force. Molloy was in his late fifties with sixty riding hard on his heels, and he looked it.

Molloy answered immediately. "Quirke."

"Good morning, sir. I've got a situation here, and I need your help." Danny knew not to waste Molloy's time in small talk. The Chief Inspector had no time or tolerance for it. "Local house firebombed and burned. I need an arson investigator."

"Do ye?" Molloy's voice crackled with impatience. "And what am I supposed to do about that?"

"Sir, there's no one here qualified."

"Listen here, fella, we've had a rash of unexplained house fires in the downtown core overnight. Twelve houses—do ye hear me?—twelve of them, completely gutted. Now I don't know if we've got a firebug or if some young arseholes are having themselves a laugh, but every single man I've got is busy." *Too busy to bother with your little problems* was the unspoken coda to the sentence.

"Well, what am I supposed to do?" He tried for calm but heard the desperation in his own voice. "We don't have an arson investigator, and I—"

"Can't you do it?"

The question brought him up short. "I'm not an arson investigator."

"But you are an investigator, last time I checked." Molloy could be heard shuffling papers. "So do some investigating and let me know what you find." A final, decisive click and Danny was listening to dial tone.

"Found something you might be interested in." Danny looked up as Alan English, the volunteer fire chief, approached.

"Oh?" Danny shoved his mobile back into his pocket. "Your guys found something?"

"Not what I was expecting," Alan replied. He was holding a length of scorched wire with a metal apparatus attached to one end, the whole thing badly charred. "This wasn't any ordinary fire. The house was rigged to explode."

So it *was* arson. "Are you serious?"

"It was attached to the doorbell. Whoever rigged it knew what they were doing. It might look simple, but something like this requires advanced electrical knowledge." He pointed to the metal apparatus. "Ringing the doorbell would trigger it, but this sort of thing could be activated remotely using a mobile phone."

"So this fire wasn't an accident," Danny said. "This was deliberate."

"Yep."

The idea of someone rigging a house to explode and then simply walking away appalled him. "Nasty." He fished around in his pocket until he found a plastic evidence bag. He dropped the device in and sealed it. "Thanks, Alan. Will you let me know if you find anything else?"

The fire chief nodded. "Absolutely."

"I'll leave Constables Hughes and Avery here to keep the locals out. I don't want that site disturbed until we can get in and have a look around." He suspected the "we" would probably be him. "I'll be in touch if anything changes."

Danny got back into his car for the short drive to the police station. The Kildevil Cove RNC detachment was located in a former Loyal Orange Lodge building across from the Pentecostal church. It housed the Criminal Investigation Division, of which Danny was the head. The CID was responsible for investigating any serious crimes that might occur. There was a time when crime in Kildevil Cove was confined to fishery violations: taking too many cod during the recreational fishery, selling undersized lobster. With the arrival of hard drugs like methamphetamine and fentanyl, however, crimes like murder and human trafficking were on the increase, and the influence of organised-crime syndicates reached into even the smallest coastal fishing villages around the island.

He had just begun to turn into the parking lot at the station when a small red car screeched to a halt in front of him, missing his vehicle's front fender by mere centimetres. The driver's side door flew open, and a man in his mid-thirties tumbled out, nearly falling in his haste. He stared wide-eyed at the remains of the house, then started forward, a look of horror etched on his features. At the cordon he was stopped by Dougie Hughes.

"Sir, you have to stay back."

"*Où sont-ils?*" he shouted. "Where are they?"

Danny parked and shut off his car, then hurried over to where Hughes stood. "Constable, what's going on?"

At Danny's approach the distraught man turned. "I am Gerard Caron. This is my house. My wife—" He broke off on a sob. It was almost predictable, but Danny was cynical about such things.

"Mr. Caron." Danny laid a hand on his shoulder. "I'm Danny. Will you come to the station with me and have a cup of tea? We can talk in my office." He retrieved Caron's car keys and had Sarah Avery move the distraught man's car out of the road and then return the keys to Caron.

"Why are you taking me to the police?" Caron asked. He pulled away, dislodging Danny's hand from his shoulder. "I have done nothing wrong!"

"You're not being arrested," Danny replied, "but I would like to talk to you. I'm in charge of the police here. I want to talk to you about your wife and son." They had crossed Secretary Road by now, and Danny reached out to open the door to the station for Caron. He waited while the man preceded him into the building, then directed Caron down the hall towards the back where Danny's office was. A call to Marilyn, the station's desk sergeant, produced two cups of hot tea and a tray of biscuits, neither of which helped to calm Caron down.

"Where is my wife?" he asked, ignoring the tea in front of him. "Where is my son?"

Danny drew a deep breath. He was a career cop with many years in the profession, but Caron's barefaced anguish touched a raw nerve in him. He would be frantic if his own house had exploded, especially if he thought Tadhg and Lily were still inside. "According to the fire department, there was no one in the house, but we won't know for sure until an investigator can get in there."

Caron shuddered, a violent spasm that seemed to erupt from deep within his core. "But you don't know! You are just talking. All you have to offer me is talk—nothing more."

"Mr. Caron, I promise I will do everything I can to find out. We're in the process of organising a search party to locate your wife and son." There was nothing else he could offer Caron, and it frustrated him. He turned to his computer and opened a blank report form. "Would you mind answering a few questions? It would help with our investigation." He was careful to keep his tone neutral; it wouldn't do for Caron to think he was under suspicion, not when he was so overwrought.

Caron blinked at him, confused. "Investigation?"

"The process of trying to find your wife and son."

"*D'accord.*" He sipped his tea cautiously, then looked into the cup.

"When did you last see them?" Danny asked.

Caron gazed blankly at him. "*Quoi?*" Then, "Oh. Yes. Uh, early this morning, before I left for work." He leaned to the side, evidently trying to see what Danny was typing. "I work as a linesman for Newfoundland

Power since seven months ago. We came from Mont-Tremblant, and my wife, she came with me, and the boy. Joseph. He is six years old."

"Where did you train as a linesman?" Danny asked. "Here or in Quebec?"

"In Quebec I trained as an electrician," Caron replied, "and here as a linesman."

"Electrician?" Danny swivelled in his chair to look at him. "Your house was rigged to explode by someone who knew what they were doing, using a sophisticated triggering device that would require extensive electrical knowledge." To hell with going gentle on the man. If he'd done this, he'd damn well answer for it. "Is that something you'd know how to do, Mr. Caron?"

Caron stood up abruptly and moved for the door. Danny started after him. "Wait!" But Caron was younger than him and faster on his feet, and by the time Danny reached the station's front door, the Quebecois was out on the road, making for his abandoned car. He watched as Caron got in, started the engine, and peeled away without putting on his seat belt. The bastard would be halfway to Carbonear before Danny or anyone else caught up with him.

"What's going on, sir?" Sergeant Kevin Carbage drew up beside Danny, his arms full of file folders. Carbage was working on a cold case, the disappearance of a young girl back in the 1980s. It had recently been reopened in the wake of new evidence, and Carbage had jumped at the chance to pitch in. The first time Danny had met Carbage, he'd dismissed the younger man, assuming his youth, coupled with his upbringing in a particularly strict brand of Protestantism, marked him out as a dullard. Nothing could have been further from the truth. Carbage was bright, astute, excellent with facts and numbers, and so naturally intuitive it bordered on witchcraft.

"Mr. Gerard Caron," Danny said, "lately of Mont-Tremblant." He relayed the morning's events, the explosion and fire at Caron's house, and Caron's possible part in it. "Get that bugger and bring him back here right now. We need an official statement from him, and I'm not convinced he had nothing to do with this," Danny said. "Gerard Caron is our chief suspect, and we need to find out what he knows."

CHAPTER TWO

Monday

INSPECTEUR BLAISE Pascal, *Sûreté du Québec*, was standing over a corpse in the middle of a forest, somewhere in the Laurentians near Mont-Tremblant. A grey-haired man in a flannel shirt lay on his back, his eyes wide and unseeing, a huge wound in the centre of his chest. Pascal gazed down at him, his expression inscrutable, while several constables and the local wildlife officer stood nearby, watching him closely. No one said anything. Pascal walked around the body, peering at it, then suddenly crouched on his haunches and leaned forward, close to the dead man's open mouth. A young constable, unable to contain himself, asked, "What do you think, *Monsieur l'inspecteur*? Is it murder?"

Pascal glanced up at him sharply, shook his head. "Hunting accident," he said. He dug a hand into each of the dead man's pockets, muttering to himself, then pulled out a battered leather wallet. "Herbert Landry," he pronounced, holding up the driving licence for them to see. "From Beauceville. Sixty-three years old and an organ donor. Also a fucking idiot. When you find the other one, charge him with hunting moose out of season." He spoke quickly and in French, but the French of downtown Montreal, with its elongated vowels, not the clipped accent of the Laurentians. Pascal didn't belong here. Or anywhere else.

"The other one?" the constable asked. "*Inspecteur*, I don't understand."

Pascal glared at him. "Well, he didn't shoot himself in the chest with a rifle." He stood up and walked away, but the wildlife officer dogged his heels, walking so close behind that Pascal was forced to acknowledge him. "What?" he barked, turning. They were standing in front of his pickup truck now, a powerful Ford crew cab emblazoned with the *Sûreté* du Québec logo. "What do you want?" This was simply too much bullshit for a Monday morning, and Pascal had had no coffee yet. *Tabarnak*, he'd need a pot of the fucking stuff the way things were going.

"Are we just to leave him there?" the man asked. He was small, in his mid-fifties and close to retirement. He had dealt with *Inspecteur* Pascal before, knew that he could be harsh and plainspoken and that he always seemed to be angry. Up here, away from the hectic pace of Montreal, it was easy to assume that crimes never occurred, but both Pascal and the wildlife officer knew different. During the busy winter ski season, the small village was thronged with tourists, many of whom were careless, didn't speak French, or were simply stupid. Some drank too much, wandered out into the snow, and froze to death. Others fought with strangers or people that they knew and ended up dying of their injuries. While some took unwary journeys into the wilderness alone or in questionable company and ended up stabbed to death or shot. The picture-postcard prettiness of Mont-Tremblant hid a darker, seamier side that might easily compete with Montreal when it came to crime.

"*Non.* I'll send a recovery team." At the wildlife officer's expression of dismay, he added, "Don't worry. He's not going to get up and walk off anywhere. Maybe he'll be food for the wolves before too long." Pascal yanked open the driver's side door, got in, and drove off.

He was aware of his reputation in the town and did nothing to mitigate the unfavourable impression *les habitants* had of him. It was good that they were a little afraid. People ought to respect and fear the police; respect for the law encouraged citizens to behave appropriately. If only everyone behaved appropriately, there would be so much less chaos in the world and fewer idiots running around in the forest getting themselves shot out of season. He smirked grimly. *Calisse*, people nowadays had their heads up their asses.

His mobile phone rang, and he tapped the button on the truck's steering wheel to answer it. "*Oui?*"

The call came from Sergeant Louis Prud'Homme, one of the few people who could stand to work with Pascal for any length of time. "*Inspecteur*, there is a telephone call for you, concerning a missing woman."

"What missing woman?"

"*Pardon*, a missing family. The Carons, if you remember."

The tiny hairs on the back of his neck rose. "I do." It wasn't a situation he relished revisiting, but he knew that the case had never really been closed.

"And Tachereau wants to see you. She said *immediatement* and not to try and escape."

"*Mon Dieu*," Pascal grumbled. "What the hell is it this time, eh?" He pondered his options for a moment. Autoroute 55 South would take him out of the province, out of the whole country. He could be in Vermont inside of four hours. Vermont was lovely this time of year. By the time Céline Tachereau—his immediate superior—caught up with him, he could be anywhere in the United States, living under a false name. Maybe he'd dye his hair, get cosmetic surgery to change his face, learn to speak American English with an accent....

"*Inspecteur*," Prud'Homme said, breaking into his reverie, "where are you?"

For Christ's sake, Pascal thought, it was like Prud'Homme's only job was to monitor him. "About five minutes away from you." He glanced in the rear-view mirror, saw the tandem transport truck that was bearing down on him, and pressed his foot harder on the gas pedal. His vehicle surged forward, and he grinned at the truck driver in his mirror. Eat shit, *salaud*.

"I'll tell her you're on your way." Prud'Homme paused. "And there is a personal message as well, from the—" He paused, the soul of delicacy. "—hospital."

"*Oui*. I'll see to it." He closed the connection, unwilling to continue the conversation. Prud'Homme was a good man but tended to concern himself with aspects of Pascal's personal life that were none of his damned business. On top of that, he had a predilection for the kind of solicitousness that rightly belonged to someone's *grandmère*. He constantly reminded Pascal to button his coat, put on a scarf, what about gloves? Had he eaten that day, and perhaps *monsieur l'Inspecteur* didn't need another cup of coffee. Besides, he was smoking too much. If Pascal didn't know better, he'd swear he was married to the man.

PASCAL'S ARRIVAL back at the small police station in Mont-Tremblant coincided with news that the national police database had flagged an inquiry from a police force in Newfoundland about a missing woman, Amalie Caron.

"This is what you called me about?" Pascal peered over Prud'Homme's shoulder at the computer monitor, practically leaning on him. He was glad something interesting had come up to keep him occupied, most especially because it would keep Céline away, at least for a little while. Lately she'd taken to following him, showing up in the break room and in the corridors, and once she'd appeared at his side in the men's toilets while he was trying to take a piss.

Céline Tachereau was a career officer who'd started in Montreal as a member of the *Service de Police de la Ville de Montréal*, familiarly known as SPVM, when she was barely out of school. Céline was fair, decent, and honest, and had managed to carve out a career for herself without falling prey to institutional favouritism or corruption. She held her officers to the same high standard, which was why she insisted Pascal meet with the *Bureau des Enquêtes Indépendantes*, BEI, representative who'd been dogging his heels for the past three months. This was probably why she wanted to see him now.

"I didn't do it," Pascal had told her when the accusation had first been levelled against him. "Any of it. This is bullshit, and you know it." He had a fair idea who might be behind the charges and wasn't surprised that it had taken her this long to lash out at him. When it came to revenge, that bitch played the long game.

"All the more reason to meet with investigators," Céline said, "and clear your name."

It wouldn't be that easy, of course. The BEI was the provincial police oversight body, charged with investigating allegations of officer misconduct towards members of the public. Pascal had had a standing appointment to meet with them ever since the allegations had been made, but so far he'd managed to dodge it. Part of him worried that the investigating officers would find some way to make the charges stick, ending his career. He knew his personal slate was hardly clean. But neither was anyone else's. With his luck, the BEI would turn up some sordid chapter from his younger years, and that would finish him.

"*Oui*," Prud'Homme said now, pulling Pascal out of his reverie. "You remember she went missing some years back after an argument but returned to her husband, Gerard."

He'd met her in Montreal, where Pascal had worked before relocating to Mont-Tremblant. She had reported her husband for domestic violence on four separate occasions, and Pascal was in the process of investigating when she, the husband, and their young son all disappeared. He'd spent many months and a lot of *Sûreté* resources looking for them, but the search ultimately uncovered nothing. Rather, it had brought to light something that Pascal had never divulged.

"Has she turned up?" he asked.

"She did, *Inspecteur*, and now she is gone again." Prud'Homme turned in his chair to look up at Pascal. "The message is on your desk. They asked that you call back as soon as is possible."

"*Bon.*" Pascal clapped the younger man on the shoulder as he straightened. "Bring me some coffee."

His office was in the basement of the building, a small windowless room with a vent directly above his desk that showered overheated air on him in summer and cold air in winter—and also formed a conduit for conversations from the floor above that frequently interrupted his thought processes. He had repeatedly appealed to building maintenance, but to no avail. Getting anything done was a lengthy process that involved far more paperwork than was strictly necessary and usually resulted in the request being rerouted back to him because he'd overlooked some miniscule detail that needed to be filled in. It was like they did it on purpose.

Several message slips were waiting for him on his desk, arranged in three separate stacks according to their perceived importance, courtesy of Prud'Homme's tidy administrative mind. One—he assumed it concerned the Caron family—sat in the middle of his desk blotter. He picked it up and glanced at it. "Terre-Neuve," he remarked. And the national database had flagged this. Interesting.

A constable passing by in the corridor asked, "*Quoi, Inspecteur?*"

Pascal shook his head. "*Rien.*" Nothing. He checked the clock, calculating the time-zone difference between Quebec and Newfoundland. They were half an hour later than Atlantic, weren't they? He stuck his head out into the corridor, looking for someone to ask, but he was alone except for the janitor. "What time is it in Newfoundland?" Pascal asked the man, who merely shrugged and went on his way. He dialed the number, listening to the rings going out, then someone with an Irish accent took the call. Yes, they knew who he was. Yes, his call was expected. They would transfer him immediately to Inspector Quirke. Pascal identified himself in English, indicating that he'd received the message and knew of the Caron family. Why had this Quirke felt compelled to call the *Sûreté*?

"Their house exploded and burned," Quirke told him. "Just this morning. We have located Gerard Caron, but his wife and son are unaccounted for. We've issued an Amber Alert for the boy, but we've also been doing some background checks on the parents. When we ran Gerard Caron's name through the database, it returned several hits. I understand he was arrested on four separate occasions for domestic abuse. You were the arresting officer."

"Correct."

"The Caron family were living in Montreal at the time," Quirke continued. "I understand you then lost track of them for a while—"

Pascal stopped him there. "I did not lose track of anyone," he snapped. "The investigation is ongoing. I am still looking for the Carons."

There was a lengthy pause on the other end, and Pascal wondered if Quirke had disconnected. Finally he heard a sigh and "Then you had better pack a bag and come to Newfoundland," Quirke said. "Until today they have been living here in Kildevil Cove, but Mrs. Caron has vanished, and her son is gone as well."

Pascal's curiosity was piqued. "You've spoken to Gerard?"

"Yes."

"And?"

"It's something best discussed in person. I'd be grateful if you could take a look at the scene and tell us what you think."

"About Madame Caron, or about the fire?" Pascal snapped.

"About anything," Quirke replied testily. "Could you come and stay for a few days? At our expense, of course."

Pascal considered this, leafing idly through the message slips on his desk. There was nothing keeping him in Mont-Tremblant now, and Prud'Homme could handle the dead hunter on his own. The busy summer season had ended, and the skiers wouldn't arrive until at least the end of November. The town was likely to be quiet and uneventful, and perhaps he could be of some use to this Newfoundland police inspector. Besides, the lack of resolution in the Caron case irritated him, and here was a chance to finally put it to rest, along with one other matter that was still on the books. "Okay. I have some arrangements to make, but I will come to you at the earliest convenience." He thanked Quirke and closed the connection.

Maybe it would be all right. The trip would give him an excuse to continue avoiding the BEI, and they would hardly send the Newfoundlanders a laundry list of his supposed crimes. Would this Quirke or any of his people ever know or wonder? Of course not. He was a blank slate to them and to a lot of others.

As for the other incident, no one outside of the *Sûreté* knew about that, or its outcome, so no one was likely to cast aspersions or question his capabilities on the island. The incident in question was several years behind him, and there was much even the *Sûreté* didn't know. Nor was he ever going back to that dark emotional place he'd occupied for far too long afterwards. He couldn't go back there. He wouldn't survive. Not this time.

The abduction of Caprice Gilles was the sort of crime that was usually resolved quickly, with the stolen child returned home and those responsible taken away to jail. Children were kidnapped—five thousand of them a year in Quebec, sixteen a day—for a variety of reasons, and the majority of cases involved a disgruntled non-custodial parent. Stranger abduction was rare, but occasionally a vulnerable child would disappear from their school or be taken from their home in the middle of the night and whisked away.

Pascal was still a member of the SPVM in those days, working permanent nights and renting cheap accommodations on the 4000 block of Avenue Henri Julien. Caprice Gilles was nine, and he lived two doors down with his mother, four brothers, and his mother's boyfriend, a recent immigrant from Algiers who spent an astonishing amount of time not working. Pascal knew him—the entire SPVM knew him—and was aware that he had a string of arrests for various offences, many of them serious. Whenever the man saw Pascal leaving for work or returning home, he'd call a greeting, usually something offensive, which Pascal ignored. He liked to sit on the front steps, roll a spliff in plain sight (before it was legal), and taunt the regular police patrols that came by. *Eh, what you going to do to me, monsieur flic? You want a smoke of this?*

His friends were no better, a group of ragged men without any visible means of support who hung around the front of the building at all hours, playing loud music on their car stereos and shouting at each other. One in particular stood out because he was so different from the rest: short, quiet, slender, with a smooth, doll-like face and round blue eyes that never seemed to blink. He affected old-fashioned three-piece suits paired with shiny black wingtip shoes, smoked cigarettes in a long black holder, and liked to approach people on the street, shake their hands, and formally introduce himself as "Jimmy Cashmere."

At first Pascal dismissed him as a harmless eccentric, albeit one with poor taste in friends, but he soon noticed that Jimmy Cashmere seemed to pay an inordinate amount of attention to Caprice, bringing him expensive gifts and talking to him as if he were an adult. It made Pascal very uneasy.

One day Jimmy Cashmere disappeared, and so did Caprice Gilles. A long and complicated search for the boy ensued, and it wasn't until fifteen days later—

Non. Je refuse d'y penser. Don't think about it. The horrific memory was easier to bear that way.

By the time Pascal's team had tracked Jimmy Cashmere to a flophouse on Rue Saint-Urbain—literally metres from police headquarters—he had long since fled. An anonymous tip the next morning led Pascal to an abandoned sugar plant near the Lachine Canal, where he found the dismembered body of Caprice Gilles locked inside a chest freezer.

The blame landed squarely on Pascal, the detective in charge of the search for the missing boy. An internal investigation was launched to try to determine how, in the name of God, and with the entire police force at his disposal, he'd failed to find Caprice until it was far, far too late. The board of enquiry determined negligence, and he was disciplined, demoted, and placed on administrative leave for eighteen months. It was no less than he deserved. He was also required to submit a written apology to the boy's mother, outlining all the ways in which he had failed in his duty. The hardest punishment of all, however, was the knowledge that a young boy, an innocent, died because Blaise Pascal had failed him. He would never erase the image of Caprice's horribly mutilated body, and it drove him literally insane. Six months after the enquiry's verdict, he was living in a black hole of depression, addicted to painkillers, and about to be evicted from his apartment. This was when Louis Prud'Homme found him.

Prud'Homme was a new hire from Lachine looking for a senior officer to assist him with a frustrating fraud case. That Pascal was no longer a cop didn't bother Prud'Homme. No one else at headquarters was interested in lending a hand, and if Prud'Homme couldn't bring the case to a satisfactory conclusion, he would lose his job. So Pascal helped him, guiding the younger officer through the necessary steps to locate the guilty party and bring him in. As much as Pascal hated to admit it, he liked Prud'Homme, and soon they were an inseparable team. Pascal made a lot of noise about Prud'Homme being a pain in the ass, but he understood exactly what he owed him. He was determined never to forget.

Prud'Homme appeared at his elbow. "Your coffee, sir. I hope it is satisfactory."

"Pascal!" The salutation came from the corridor outside his office. Céline Tachereau. And she was much too close for him to even think of fleeing. *Tabarnak*....

"I am here." He nodded at Prud'Homme, stood up, and followed her into her office. Céline's space was much larger and better equipped than his, with an enormous desk and a high-backed leather chair dominating the room. That was the extent of the luxury, however. Tachereau wasn't interested in creating a cozy retreat or a workplace oasis; there were no lush green plants hanging from the ceiling and no motivational posters. There was barely anything at all, except the necessary desk and chair, and a coat tree, which he'd never seen her use.

"Don't sit down." He'd been about to sink into a chair when she stopped him. "You won't be here that long." She plopped ungracefully into her seat and shuffled some file folders to the side, clearing a space in which to put her clasped hands.

This didn't look good, Pascal thought, with a sudden sinking feeling. Did she call him in here to fire him? Place him on suspension? The top half of her office space was clear glass, and he caught sight of Prud'Homme passing by in the corridor. *Come in*, Pascal silently begged. *Pretend you have something to do and come in here right now!* But Prud'Homme simply nodded at him and carried on his way. Useless goddamn *crétin*....

"I've had a phone call from our contact in the government."

Oh. This was unexpected.

"As you're aware, we've been trying to track our target, and until recently, it was as if she'd vanished into the air." Tachereau picked at a hangnail on her thumb, worrying the small tab of loose flesh. "That is no longer the case." She raised her head and looked at Pascal. "Our contact advised that she has been communicating with someone in Newfoundland for several weeks now."

It felt to Pascal as though someone were pouring cold water down his spine. "*Vraiment?*"

"Yes, really." Tachereau sighed and pushed a strand of curly red hair out of her face. "Her location is still unclear, but she might be heading towards the island, or she may already be there."

"Fuck," Pascal said in English. "Is the intelligence good?"

She nodded. "It seems so, yes. I assume you are heading to Newfoundland regarding the Caron case?"

"I... yes," he said, wondering how she always seemed to know everybody's business almost before they did.

"Good. You can follow up. Intercept her, then hold her in custody until the Europeans can get here."

"You want me to arrest her?"

"Yes."

He nodded. "Can I take Prud'Homme?"

"No. I need him here, and two *Sûreté* officers might attract the wrong kind of attention."

"*D'accord*," Pascal agreed. "I'll give him the bad news myself." He turned to go, but Tachereau called him back.

"Be careful," she said. "You know these people as well as I. Be discreet." She waved a hand at him, and he understood he'd been dismissed.

He went back to his desk and drank some of the coffee Prud'Homme had made. It was still hot and tasted good. Sorting through the piles of phone messages, he located the one that Prud'Homme had said was from the hospital and picked it up, even though he already knew what it would say. There was no way around it; he would have to go there, and the thought of the four-hour drive ahead of him wasn't a pleasant one. It was just after nine in the morning. If he left now, he could arrive there by one at the latest, perhaps earlier if he took Autoroute 40 East and ignored the posted speed limits.

On the other hand, it probably wouldn't matter if he didn't go at all. That was the ugly truth of it. He knew better than to expect any last-minute breakthrough or reconciliation. The patient blamed him, Pascal, for what had happened to him, and today's visit would be just like the last visit—and the one before that, and the one before that—a futile attempt to communicate something he didn't feel to someone who had long ago given up listening to him.

Tabarnak, why even bother?

Because he hated loose ends, hated leaving any one particular stone unturned. Because he was someone who always made his bed in the morning. Because he'd been raised a good Catholic who always did what was proper and expected. Because today would likely be the very last time he ever went.

WHILE KEVIN Carbage was out pursuing Gerard Caron and the rest of the station personnel were searching Kildevil Cove for his wife and son, Cillian Riley had spent the morning tracking down information on the Caron family by phone, speaking to their nearest neighbours and anyone else with whom they'd had dealings. As he told Danny, it was as if the Carons existed in their own little bubble, only venturing out into the larger world when necessary. Caron went to work and came home and didn't appear to have any friends. Riley had gotten hold of his supervisor at Newfoundland Power, who had nothing much to offer. Caron was a good worker, an excellent linesman who showed up on time and stayed until the work was done, then went home. He had no qualms about working in inclement weather, and his experience of many Quebec winters appeared to shield him from the cold. He didn't socialise with his coworkers and appeared to go nowhere except home and to church. It seemed Caron was trying to keep his nose clean after his previous brushes with the law, working a full-time job and living a quiet married life—so far. Riley wasn't surprised Caron had been arrested for domestic violence; he'd seen it before with men of Caron's type who got themselves discharged from the army or the navy and didn't know where to spend their pent-up aggression.

"He was always very energetic," Caron's former commanding officer said when Riley contacted him at the armed forces base in Bagotville, Quebec. "Ready at a moment's notice to go, no matter what the mission was." Caron had joined up when he was eighteen, fresh out of high school, and had enjoyed a twenty-year career in the forces before his 4C—completion of service—discharge. His reputation was good. He was quiet but seemed to enjoy the company of his fellows and rarely complained. "Beyond that, I don't know what to tell you. Nobody here knew him very well."

The woman he spoke to at the office of the *Directeur de l'état*, Madame Vachon, didn't have much to add either. According to their files, Gerard and Amalie had been married in Montreal early in 2012 in a civil union at the palais de justice, witnessed by two court clerks. Neither the bride's nor the groom's family had been present at the ceremony. She expressed surprise that Amalie was using Caron as a surname as this was not permitted in Quebec due to marriage alone. Her records did not show that Amalie had petitioned for a formal name change, but—and Danny could almost hear the woman shrug over the line—what Amalie chose to call herself outside legal affairs of the province was her business.

What Gerard Caron did immediately after the wedding—if he took Amalie for a meal or on a lavish honeymoon to some tropical destination—was unknown. There was so little information available on the man that he might as well be a figment of someone else's imagination.

His missus was even more of an enigma and was only ever seen in the company of her son, who went to elementary school in Winterton but who, according to his teacher, was off sick a lot. Once a month they closed up the house and went away for several days at a time, always returning in the dead of night without any baggage or other belongings, and even when they were in residence, the curtains were always firmly drawn across the windows, leaving neighbours to wonder what exactly was going on inside the house. Wanting privacy wasn't a crime, Riley reflected, but perhaps it was a little unusual nowadays, where the world and its wives seemed to be on social media, everyone rushing to their computers to report what they'd said and done that day, and what they'd eaten for all three meals and snacks. The boy, Joseph, was always clean and dressed appropriately for the weather, and the Carons kept their drive and walkway clear of snow in the wintertime, even laying down rock salt if there was ice.

None of this was particularly significant, but the families living on either side of the Carons seemed to think them strange. The neighbour on their immediate right, a Mr. Harry Letto, said that Gerard Caron burned garbage in an empty oil drum in his yard, and Mrs. Caron never hung out her washing. Letto had greeted Caron over the fence one morning, but the man had stared brazenly back at him while feeding something into the fire out of a black plastic rubbish bag. "He was burning it," he told Riley. "I seen it."

"What did you see?" Riley asked. Letto had turned up at the police station of his own accord, wanting to speak to a police officer and ready and willing, he said, to give a witness statement. "What was he burning?" Riley reached for the cup of tea he'd forgotten about and took a sip, pleased to discover it was still piping hot.

"Looked like animals."

"Animals." *For Christ's sake....*

"Dead ones. Rabbits and cats."

Riley duly noted this down, even though it was probably rubbish. "Earlier you said that you noticed someone around the Caron property during the night. Can you tell me about that?"

"I got up to get a drink of water."

"What time was this?"

Letto paused. "Might have been three o'clock. I'm not sure. I went to bed early with a bad headache. I haves awful headaches, almost like migraines they are, except I don't get them flashes, what do you call 'em, when you gets them flashes in the corners of your eyes?"

"Auras?"

"Yeah, I don't get that."

Riley waited. Letto gazed at him expectantly. "You got up to get a drink."

"Yes, I did, so." He told Riley he'd seen someone around the house, fiddling with something under one of the bedroom windows.

"How did you know it was a bedroom window?" Maybe Letto was the type to go sneaking around other people's houses in the dark, hoping to get a glimpse of the forbidden.

"I... well, t'was at the back of the house. That's where the bedrooms is." He'd flushed a deep, angry red, and Riley could tell by his tone of voice that he resented the question. "Am I being charged with something?"

"I don't know," Riley said evenly. "Have you done something?" Letto didn't reply. Riley continued, "So you were inside your house when you saw this other person doing something to one of the bedroom windows."

"Yes. I never goes out at night."

"The person you saw." Riley flipped back through his notes. Letto was the third witness who'd come forward with something supposedly vital to contribute, but so far none of the statements added up to anything significant. "Man or woman?"

"I don't know. They had one of them sweatshirts on with the hood up over their face. Big and baggy, it was. Couldn't see their hands or nothing."

"You're wearing glasses," Riley said, gesturing at the man's face. "Do you wear them all the time?"

Letto indicated that he did. "Sure I'm as blind as a bat."

"Were you wearing your glasses when you got up to drink some water?"

"No, I don't think I was." Of course not. Even if he was seriously myopic, the man could probably find his way around his own house at night.

"So you can't be entirely certain that what you saw behind the Caron property was in fact a person. It might have been a moose."

"Listen, I knows what I seen!" Letto angrily insisted Caron was up to no good, but Riley put this down to a general distrust of outsiders. He thanked Letto for his time and told him he could go.

The neighbours on the other side of the Caron property weren't much better, accusing Amalie Caron of being involved in dark satanic practices meant to corrupt the fine upstanding men of Kildevil Cove. Bessie Bailey, who lived with her husband, Arch, said that twice she'd spotted Amalie sunbathing in the nude on the roof of her house, something that seemed highly unlikely. The Caron house was a biscuit box with a steeply pitched roof that rose at the back and was constructed to shed snow in winter. For anyone to sunbathe on it, naked or otherwise, they'd need to employ supernatural means. But Bessie insisted it was true.

"I seen her, the hussy. Up there all sprawled abroad and showing everything she got. Night before last she was out in the yard, dancing around a bonfire. It's not right what they're at, the two of them."

"Where were you when you saw Mrs. Caron on the roof?"

"I was hanging out me clothes on the line. I always hangs out me clothes, I do. Not lazy like some." She said this with an air of self-righteousness, no doubt convinced of her own virtue. Riley suspected she was a pillar of the local church who involved herself in her neighbours' business whether they wanted her there or not.

"Where is your clothesline located in relation to the Carons' house?"

"At the back, so I gets the wind off the water. Arch put it up for me."

"How far away from the Caron house would you say the clothesline is?"

She thought for a moment. "About five fathoms."

Riley did the math. A fathom was roughly six feet, so perhaps about thirty feet away—a good distance from the house, then. In metric it was about ten metres, but he couldn't be bothered to do the calculations. He'd worry about that when he wrote up the witness reports. Still and all, if Bessie Bailey had been standing at her clothesline looking up at the backwards-sloping roof of the Carons' biscuit-box house thirty feet away, her chances of seeing anything were nil.

"Does your husband ever hang out the washing?"

Her eyes widened. "For the love of God!" she barked. "That's women's work."

"So he wouldn't have seen Mrs. Caron sunbathing on the roof?"

Her eyes narrowed, and her features hardened as if her face was closing in on itself. "He wouldn't be at the likes of that. Not with the likes of she."

"This bonfire you mentioned." He seriously doubted there'd been a bonfire or anything like it. "When did this allegedly take place?"

She must have picked up on his tone of voice. "Are you saying you don't believe me?"

"Not at all." He smiled at her, realising too late that the gesture might be misinterpreted.

It was. "You friggin' little bastard!" She leapt to her feet, slammed her purse down hard against his desk, and stormed away.

Ultimately, he gained nothing of substance from the Carons' neighbours. Only that they were universally disliked in the Cove, and those living around them wanted them gone. Maybe, he reflected, the Carons' neighbours were to blame for Amalie and Joseph's disappearances. It wouldn't be the first time a small, insular community had driven out those they saw as undesirables.

He was just about to take an early lunch break when he received a call from Mrs. Caron's boss at the local library. Amalie Caron had been working there for two months, the librarian reported, and was seconded to the bookmobile on Wednesdays. That previous Wednesday she hadn't reported for work, and no one had seen or heard from her since. He called Danny and relayed this information; Danny suggested they both go and pay a visit.

"Any trace of the woman or her son?" Riley asked while he still had the boss on the phone.

Danny had joined the searchers in the hills behind Kildevil Cove after speaking with Gerard Caron and making some calls, but he seemed to think it unlikely they'd find anything useful. Riley wondered at the wisdom of Danny tramping around uneven ground for hours when he had trouble even walking properly. Riley had seen him struggling to get upstairs from the basement, and the pronounced limp he had developed had been commented on by several of the station personnel.

"Nothing so far," Danny replied. "If she and the boy are still alive, I don't see them hiding in the woods. She doesn't know the land around here, and some of these bogs are dangerous." It was all too easy, Riley knew, to step into a sinkhole and be swallowed up, or to lose your way in heavy fog.

There was no fog today, however. A bout of warm weather had persisted since the previous week, a long parade of sunny days with temperatures reaching into the low twenties and cooler nights perfect for sleeping, so Riley welcomed getting out of the police station for a while. September on the island was glorious, the one time of year Riley didn't pine for the UK.

"I'm not doing anything useful out here," Danny continued. "I'll meet you at the library."

"Yes, sir," Riley said. He left his desk behind and signed out one of the unmarked patrol cars for the short trip to the library.

Ever since his accident and the surgery that followed, Riley had been overly cautious. If things were going well—his work, his relationship with Kevin—he tended to worry, wondering when the other shoe would drop. He'd landed in Kildevil Cove after his impromptu departure—some would say "flight"—from the UK several years previous, and his tenure under Danny's direct supervision had been satisfying. Until the accident that shattered his thigh, he'd been planning to apply to law school, but his recovery had taken longer than anticipated, so he'd missed this year's intake, which was a bitter disappointment. He'd agreed to stay on in the Cove but wondered if this wasn't a mistake. The small RNC detachment didn't need two inspectors, and Riley was under no illusions about his position there. Danny was still relatively young, with perhaps another fifteen years left in his career, so it wasn't realistic to expect his spot would be opening up anytime soon. That left Riley overqualified for what was essentially a sergeant's position, without the authority or independence to conduct his own investigations. He and Kevin had already discussed his options and concluded there weren't many.

"If you go back home," Kevin said, "I'll go with you. I'm pretty sure I can find a job in the UK."

But Riley could never go back. There was a reason why he'd left the UK, an ugly reason arising from a set of unfortunate circumstances that he'd tried his best to forget. For better or worse, Newfoundland was home now. He hadn't shared this with Kevin; it wasn't a conversation he was eager to have, although he knew he might have to eventually. For now, he thought it best to let sleeping dogs lie.

THE KILDEVIL Cove Public Library was located in one of the few remaining historical buildings left standing after a fire swept through the village in the mid-1960s. It had originally belonged to the Catholic Church but was sold to the province in the late 1980s, after allegations of abuse surfaced and the Church was obliged to pay compensation to the victims. The Cove's small Catholic population had worshipped in another church building it had acquired on the cheap some years later, although the discovery of the body of a murdered girl there and the apparent involvement of a young assistant priest in sex trafficking had further depleted the congregation. The events and fallout of that case were things Danny preferred not to think about.

The library building was in the shape of an octagon, three storeys high, the exterior decorated with Victorian "gingerbread" moulding and other similar embellishments. It ought to have been singularly ugly, but it wasn't, and there was a curious elegance in its silhouette that Danny had always admired.

"It's a bloody monstrosity," Tadhg had said once. "Who the hell builds something that shape around here?" Tadhg, a property developer, maintained that the complicated baroque structures of the past embodied a grotesqueness out of step with the modern world, and the glorious sparseness of Nordic design was clearly superior. Until last year, Tadhg and his teenaged daughter, Lily, had lived in a huge Scandi-modern house on the island of Eigus, in Conception Bay, but a dishonest accountant with ties to organised crime had driven him out of business and into bankruptcy. He was only now getting back on his feet, thanks in large part to Danny. Eigus, along with the rest of his assets, was sold. It was a crushing blow for a man with more than the usual amount of pride.

"You've found your way back before," Danny had told him. "You will again." Tadhg's resilience was one of many things Danny admired and loved about his husband.

"The Amber Alert we put out for her son hasn't turned up anything," Riley said as Danny met him in the library parking lot. "I'm thinking wherever she went, the boy went with her."

Danny nodded. "Hopefully we'll get a hit before the end of the day. I can understand someone fleeing the site of a fire, but not disappearing immediately afterwards. It doesn't make sense."

The librarian was expecting them and indeed met them at the door. She was a tall, extremely thin woman with bright red hair that she'd had permed into an impossible pouf. Her wire-rimmed glasses caught the light from the stained-glass windows in the foyer as she greeted them.

"I'm Michelle Froude," she said. "Wouldn't think this needed two policemen." She looked them up and down, her pale green eyes appearing small and mean behind thick corrective lenses.

Danny ignored the implied slight. "Is there somewhere we can talk in private?" he asked.

She glanced behind her, into the circular room that housed the library's fiction collection. Even at this early hour, just after 9:00 a.m., several people were walking about, looking through the stacks and searching the DVDs for popular movies and box sets of television shows. "I suppose," she said with obvious reluctance. "Follow me."

Riley shot a look at Danny behind her back, and Danny resisted the urge to roll his eyes. He'd met her kind before, little tin-pot dictators who, having gained a tiny measure of authority, believed themselves to be all-powerful. He could just imagine what working for this woman would be like. She'd insist on controlling every aspect of an employee's life, and nothing they did would ever meet her lofty standards.

In all fairness, though, Danny had known other librarians who were kind and helpful, passionate about books and eager to share that passion with others. In this case, it was the person, not the job.

"Right this way," Michelle Froude said officiously. She led them through the main room and down a small side corridor lined with doors, all of them closed. At the end of the hallway, she ushered them into a large, well-lit office located in one of the building's two wings. The ceiling was a vaulted dome of clear glass some twelve or fifteen feet in diameter, with fourteen individual panels of leaded glass set into the walls below, each portraying a different Station of the Cross in a gothic style. Between the panels were small niches or shelves built into the wall, some of them containing houseplants exploding out of their containers in a profusion of green.

"Please, have a seat." Ms. Froude—Danny couldn't imagine addressing her as Michelle—waved at two chairs set in front of a gigantic oak desk, and Danny and Riley sank into them. "I think you'll agree the décor is beautiful." She bared her teeth at them in what Danny assumed was a smile. "Boss's prerogative, but I insisted on taking this office for myself." She clapped her bony hands together in front of her face. "Now! Amalie Caron is fired, of course. I can't possibly have someone so unreliable working here. Doesn't show up for work. Doesn't bother to call."

Riley ignored this and took out his notebook. "We're wondering how long Amalie Caron has been employed here."

Her lips thinned into a disgusted expression. "*Was* employed here, Constable."

"Inspector," Riley corrected her.

She drew an appointment book to her and flipped through its pages. "Of course," she said conversationally, "I didn't want to employ her in the first place. They're always coming here and taking jobs away from local people, getting what they can for free and living on our dime."

"Who?" Danny asked.

"Immigrants." She looked up from the book. "Nothing works in their own country, so they decide to hop on a boat and come here. Oh yes, Amalie Caron started here at the end of July. July thirtieth. Should have never hired an immigrant."

"Amalie Caron is from Quebec," Riley said. "Last I checked that was part of Canada."

"Not to my mind it's not," she retorted.

Oh, for Christ's sake, Danny thought. *Next she'll be calling them frogs.*

Riley made a note. "July thirtieth."

"Yes, that's correct."

"What sort of work did she do here?" Danny asked.

"She was a low-level library assistant. Shelving books, checking out materials for patrons, just general tasks. On Wednesdays she was assigned to the bookmobile."

"Where does the bookmobile go?" The bright blue bus—Danny remembered it fondly from his own childhood—was literally a library on wheels. When he was small, it stopped at the end of Southwest Path once a week, and he and his grandmother would walk out to meet it. Climbing the three metal steps into the bus was like stepping into a dreamscape: tall walls lined with books of all sizes and shapes. Even thinking about it now gave him a little tingle.

"I can give you a map of the route." She rustled around in a drawer, then finally pulled out a sheet of printed paper and handed it across to Danny. "Every red star is a stop."

He glanced over it, noting that the route had deviated very little from when he was a boy. The bus halted in most communities up and down the peninsula for at least half an hour, which would have made for a very long workday. He wondered how much Amalie Caron was being paid for what she did.

"Was there anyone else on the bus with her," Riley asked, taking the map as Danny passed it to him, "or did she drive the bus herself?"

"We have a driver, Tony Blake, but he's off today. You can try contacting him directly. He's in the phone book." It wouldn't have killed her to offer Blake's phone number, Danny thought, but it probably pleased her to make him search for it. What a horrible bitch.

"Do you know if Amalie was friendly with anyone along the route?" Riley handed the map back to Danny. "Would she have stopped in at anyone's house for a cuppa and a biscuit?"

Ms. Froude's thin eyebrows arched alarmingly. "What are you suggesting?"

Danny leaned forward in the chair and gazed directly at her. "Was she having an affair?"

The sudden distillation of blood into her pale cheeks was alarming to watch. She flushed violently to the roots of her hair and drew back as if she'd been slapped. "It would have meant her job. I don't allow my employees to carry on that way. This library is an important institution here. We have a certain reputation to uphold."

"I'm not interested in your reputation. A woman is missing, and so is her son. I need to find them," Danny said coldly. "I would like a list of anyone who checked out books from the library bus in the past two weeks."

"I couldn't do that! The privacy of our patrons—"

He cut her off. "I repeat, I am not interested. Everyone who checked out books from the bookmobile in the past two weeks, as soon as possible, or I will be back with a warrant for this information." He got to his feet.

"I heard her threaten to kill her husband." Her statement drew them both up short.

"What?" Riley had been in the act of tucking his notebook into his pocket, but he took it out again. "What do you mean?"

"Just what I said." The smirk looked particularly unappealing on her. "They've been having problems ever since they got here. She didn't want to leave Quebec. And he dropped her off to work one day and she swore bloody murder at him when she got out of the car."

"In English?" Danny asked.

"No. In French. And before you ask, no, I do not speak that language. But when a person draws a finger across her neck as she screams, it is obvious what she means."

"Did anybody else see this?" Riley asked.

"I don't know. I certainly did."

"Thank you for bringing it to our attention." Danny drew himself up. He couldn't wait to get away from her. The woman was everything he despised in a public servant: preening, self-important, critical of everyone, and far too eager to wield the speck of power given to her. He turned to go, catching Riley's elbow to hurry him along.

"Ask anyone!" she called after them. "They'll tell you the exact same thing."

"Ugh," Riley said once they were back in the car. "I'd hate to have to work for her." He glanced across at Danny as he fastened his seat belt. "What do you think? Is there anything in it, or is she just talking a load of bollocks?"

"She's revolting," Danny agreed, "but that doesn't mean we should discount what she said. I think the bit about them not getting along rings true. After all, the neighbours complained about hearing them fight all the time."

"That's so," Riley said grudgingly, "and he's got form for domestic violence."

Danny was about to reply when his mobile phone rang. It was Sergeant June Carbage, Kevin Carbage's sister. "Sir, we just had a call from an autobody shop in Heart's Desire. Amalie Caron dropped off her car there yesterday morning at ten fifteen to have the tires rotated. She was supposed to pick it up today, but she never did."

"Oh?" Maybe this was significant. But…. "The shop was open on a Sunday?"

"I got the impression the owner is happy to take on work at any time."

"I see," Danny said. It wasn't unusual. People who owned their own businesses often worked long hours in the struggle to make ends meet.

"There's something else, sir," June said. "The back seat of the car contained blood. It's soaked into the upholstery and carpet."

"Thank you, Sergeant." He rang off. "Amalie Caron's car is in Heart's Desire," he told Riley. "There's blood in the back seat."

CHAPTER THREE

Monday

THE DRIVE from Mont-Tremblant to Quebec City ought to have been a pleasant one. Quebec in September was gorgeous, with blue skies and the golden sunlight of late summer slanting through the trees, but Blaise Pascal saw none of it. Normally he was someone who enjoyed the outdoors, sometimes hiking many kilometres through the Laurentians in the spring and autumn and snowshoeing in winter. But now his mind contained only one thought. He was dreading what waited for him in Quebec City, and every additional kilometre that ticked over on his odometer only increased his sense of unease.

He reached under the collar of his shirt and touched the ridged landscape of his left shoulder, fingertips tracing every bump and hollow of the thick scar tissue there. It didn't hurt—not anymore. It hadn't really hurt when it was happening, except for the first few moments, and then the painful destruction of tissue had vanished as the nerve endings were seared into silence. He still had dreams about the fire—screaming nightmares that woke him from even the soundest sleep, dragging him into a wakefulness littered with dangerous shadows. A glass of whiskey taken half an hour before bed was usually sufficient to let him rest for at least a little while, but on those nights he didn't drink, he lay awake for hours, his muscles rigid with fear.

He could still see the tiny apartment on rue Saint-Jacques in downtown Montreal, the place he'd returned to early every morning after the punishing night shifts that kept him permanently exhausted. If she was waiting for him, there would be a smile, a kiss, and a cuddle in bed before the boy woke them up, demanding to get in with Papa and *Maman* and be tickled.

Sometimes the boy slept late, and then she would be waiting for him to climb in with her, and they would make love as the sun rose over the city. "Don't get me pregnant again," she would say. She made him promise. "I'm not going through it again, not even for you, Blaise."

She had been bedridden for most of her high-risk pregnancy, which was rife with dangerous complications, and the boy was born eight weeks prematurely, with underdeveloped lungs and a hole in his heart. But he was so beautiful, with a head full of dark hair, huge dark eyes, and a look of preternatural knowing. So beautiful and with such promise, it was easy to believe the lie that all would be well.

Pascal approached Quebec City via Boulevard Champlain, driving parallel to the St. Lawrence with all the windows down, breathing in the warm, clear air. Several times during the journey he'd felt nauseated, but now, passing Anse Saint-Michel, he was forced to pull over onto the narrow shoulder and stumble out of his vehicle to vomit. Several cars slowed to look, probably wondering if he was drunk and whether they should contact the *Sûreté* to report him as he stood there, bent double, voiding the contents of his stomach onto the grass. He was shaking, off balance, so dizzy that he had to sit down in the passenger seat for ten minutes before he felt well enough to move. A drink of water helped to rinse the nasty taste from his mouth, and he lit a cigarette to steady his nerves. He drew on it hard, which started a coughing fit, so he tossed it away and ground it under his heel before climbing back into the driver's side of his car and pulling into traffic.

There was no point in rehearsing what to say. Anything he said would be met with absolute silence. Nor was there anything to be gained by trying to breach the silence, which was impenetrable. He might as well try to burrow through the ramparts of Old Montreal using only his nails and teeth. One of them in that room would be talking, and one of them would be listening, and when he said what he'd come to say, he would leave. For the last time, he would leave.

He made a left turn onto Côte Gilmour and climbed the leafy hill towards the Plains of Abraham, where the final decisive battle in the Seven Years War was fought between the armies of Wolfe and Montcalm. The battlefield was now a public park, the site of soccer games and Sunday afternoon picnics and Frisbee matches, and the names of the eminent generals were now relegated to the history books. The eighteenth-century cannons stationed around the field seemed like quaint set pieces, props from a motion picture rather than genuine artillery used to kill opposing forces.

Pascal turned onto Avenue Wolfe-Montcalm, passing the regal church of Saint-Dominique underneath an over-arching canopy of trees still clinging to their leaves. The city had changed since the last time he'd been here, with old buildings taken down to make way for new ones and construction barricades everywhere. For a city as old as this, it seemed always on the verge of transforming itself, hurrying forward, looking towards the next new thing.

Rue Saint-Luc terminated in a double barricade set in front of an imposing Georgian building, the Centre for Child and Adolescent Psychiatry. He parked in the designated visitors' area, went inside, and showed his badge to the security guard at the reception desk, a skinny boy with the beginnings of a beard spotting his cheeks and chin.

"Wait here, *Inspecteur*," the boy said.

Pascal stood by the wall, next to a large poster with photos of smiling children and teens engaged in various activities and the slogan *Nous avons tous un rôle à jouer*—We All Have a Part to Play. The youngsters in the photographs looked suspiciously happy; Pascal doubted they were actual patients of the hospital.

After about ten minutes, a nurse arrived, dressed in street clothes, and introduced herself as Anne. "*Bonjour, monsieur.* We had a bad night last night." She caught hold of his elbow and steered him onto the elevator, her fingers clamped around his arm like a vise. Her hand was cold, the chill burning through his sleeve, and he found himself wondering if she was ill.

"I've driven four hours," he told her. "I want to see him."

"He will not respond, *monsieur.*" The elevator dinged, and the doors slid open.

"I am going away for a while," he said. "I must speak with him."

He followed her down the corridor, the rubber soles of her shoes squeaking on the immaculate tile floor. She was wearing dark slacks and a blue sweater over a white blouse, the sort of outfit a nun might wear on business outside the convent if she chose not to be recognized. There was a puff of pale lint on the left shoulder, cotton wool or cat hair—*la pure laine*, Pascal thought sourly. The pure wool, a designation favoured by those Quebecois who could trace their ancestry back to the first true French settlers in the area. He'd always viewed this with derision. His family had never been anything but mongrel French with plenty of competing DNA mixed in.

"Here." The nurse stood to one side of the door. Pascal hardly needed her to lead him to his son; he had been here many times over the years and could find the way in his sleep. "Shall I accompany?"

"No." He stared at her in silence, watched her gaze playing over his face, knowing how he probably looked to her: pale, fatigued, his eyes as dark and cold as an empty barrel.

"Very well." She inclined her head and went away.

The boy was sitting on the bed with his back against the wall. He was seventeen years old, thin to the point of emaciation, his features eaten away, his eyes hidden by a long fringe of dark hair, greasy and unkempt. He wore jeans and a band T-shirt, but his feet were bare, and what Pascal could see of the soles were black with dirt. The sight of his hands was as disturbing as ever: The flesh was as pale and rippled as melted wax, and the abbreviated fingers had no nails. He didn't look up when Pascal stepped inside but continued staring straight ahead, presumably at some vista only he could see.

"I came to tell you I'm leaving," Pascal said.

There was no reply, but he hadn't expected one.

"I may be gone for a while," he continued. He moved closer, one hand outstretched, but stopped short of actually touching the boy. "That doesn't bother you, hm?" The boy's forearms were scored with red marks, scratches and cuts, dark bruises. "Why are they not looking after you in here? I told them to attend to you properly. I was promised you would be looked after." He allowed his fingertips to rest lightly on the scarred flesh, but there was no movement from the still figure, and after a moment Pascal stepped back. "Has your mother been to see you? Did she bring you anything?" No, of course not. That wasn't possible. He sighed. "Théodore." At the door of the room, he stopped and looked back. "I won't come here again." There was no sign of recognition from the boy.

In three months' time he would be eighteen, and then he would be moved to a long-term adult facility, a much harsher place without any of the considerations he currently enjoyed. The province's government preferred to house adults in group homes that provided a family-like setting, and there was no way Théodore could ever be left on his own. It would be like turning an infant out into the street to starve. Perhaps Pascal could have him moved closer to Mont-Tremblant, where at least he'd have access to his father. Except he knew that Théodore couldn't care less if he saw Pascal or anyone else ever again. He had been this way ever since the incident all those years ago, and even though the doctors had tried with everything at their disposal to make him well, nothing they did affected him. The boy might as well have been made of stone.

"All right, I am going."

Silence. He walked away.

TWO HOURS later Pascal was walking down the Jetway to board his flight to Newfoundland. Up until the last moment, Prud'Homme had been on the phone, pestering him. "You should let me come with you. I might be able to help, you never know." The younger man's wide-eyed insistence that Pascal needed him was cute—irritating, but cute. He seemed to think Pascal required handholding on his very dangerous trip to Terre-Neuve.

"There is nothing for you to do there." Pascal was still talking as the made his way onto the aircraft, tossed his small suitcase into the overheard compartment, and sank into his seat. "Now I have to turn off my phone."

"*Inspecteur*, I think I might—"

"*Au revoir*, Prud'Homme." Pascal disconnected and stowed the phone in his hip pocket. He was looking forward to some uninterrupted time, possibly for a nap, before the flight landed and he was forced to get back to work. Looking for Amalie Caron had occupied a significant amount of his time with the *Sûreté*. Now he was perhaps closer to finding her than he had been in a very long time. And the other woman, the subject of yet another long and arduous investigation, would he find her as well? Céline Tachereau had instructed him to "intercept her," but to do that he needed to pinpoint her exact location, and so far she'd been devilishly difficult to find.

For months, Pascal had liaised with officers in several different jurisdictions, from Canada to Colombia and back again. There were repeated sightings of several of her associates, but she herself was never seen, and earlier attempts to accost her in public places met with failure. She'd been seen in a casino in upstate New York and approached by a member of American law enforcement, but the officer had been careless and she'd slipped away. Then a surveillance camera picked her up standing on a street corner in Toronto, waiting to cross, but before detectives could apprehend her, she disappeared into the crowd. There were reports of her being everywhere: Honduras and New Mexico, Atlanta and Australia. For the most part, these were mistakes, errors in judgement. Someone saw a woman who looked like her, or who was seen in an area she was known to frequent, and made unfortunate assumptions. If only 1 percent of the reported sightings turned out to be genuine, then she would have to have mastered teleportation. Either that or she was a witch.

Lately she had been in contact with someone in Newfoundland, someone whose telephone number was encrypted and whose email address changed daily. Attempts had been made to try to track her interlocutor, but all methods failed. Whoever his target was in contact with, they were exceptionally proficient in the art of concealment.

He closed the window shutter and leaned against the bulkhead, bunching up his jacket and using it as a makeshift pillow. A couple hours' sleep would make a world of difference to him now, and he was exhausted. The long drive from Mont-Tremblant and the uncomfortable meeting at the psychiatric hospital left him feeling as if he'd been dragged through a knothole backwards, so tired he could "*cogner des clous*" as the saying went—"bang nails." Settling into the seat, he allowed his entire body to relax, the fatigue flowing through him like water. At the very edge of sleep, his mobile phone buzzed and he started up, cursing. The flight was about to depart; he should have turned it off.

The call originated from an unknown number. He swiped a finger across the screen to unlock it and saw there was a text message in French.

Ne me cherche pas. Don't look for me.

CHAPTER FOUR

Monday

THE AUTOBODY shop was located on a dirt road at the back of Heart's Desire, a small fishing village of some two hundred people strung out along the shores of a shallow harbour. June Carbage drove slowly, afraid of damaging the patrol car's undercarriage on any one of the several dozen potholes in the road. Danny had delivered a lecture on the necessity of caring for the vehicles assigned to the Kildevil Cove station after Chief Superintendent Adrian Molloy had complained about the condition of the fleet. It was fine for Molloy, June thought. He didn't have to drive over these roads. No trouble to tell he wasn't a Newfoundlander, or he'd have understood the difficulty of maintaining a twenty-first century car on roads left over from the eighteenth century.

She pulled up in front of a weathered sign decorated with a smiling puffin and the legend Tom's FixIt. Time and climate had done their worst on both the sign and the attached premises, both of which could have done with a lick of paint. The building was vaguely barn-shaped, with one bay door now open to reveal a late-model Toyota Corolla and a second, smaller door, which presumably led to the office. June knocked on the door and a young woman, heavily pregnant and wearing cut-off jean shorts and a T-shirt, answered.

"What do ye want?" she asked, grimacing when June showed her badge. "That's Tony. I'll tell 'un to come down to ye." She disappeared into a dim interior, from which June could hear small children shouting at each other. After about five minutes, a man appeared. He was in his mid-thirties and perilously lean, with a dirty baseball cap and grease-stained hands.

"Come here, I shows ye," he said. He stepped through a door into the adjoining vehicle bay and June followed. "Dis been here for ages," he said, and although June wondered if twenty-four hours qualified as ages, she stayed silent. "Missus wanted the tires rotated, but I never done it after I seen the back seat."

June pulled out a pair of nitrile gloves and slipped them on, then opened both back doors. The scent of blood—a rank, meaty smell—assaulted her nostrils, and she drew back. "When did you first notice the blood?"

The man—Tony—approached and investigated the car's back seat. "Well, she dropped off the car and give me the keys. Told me she wanted the tires rotated. I never looked in until later on that evening. I told my missus I was going out to do the tires. Must have been after supper, maybe about half past six." He leaned over June's shoulder as he looked into the vehicle.

"Did you touch anything?"

"No, that I never. I don't want nothing to do with the likes of that." He backed away. "She was supposed to come back and get the car, but I never seen her no more."

June stepped away, stripped off her gloves, and closed both doors. "Did anyone else touch the vehicle?"

"No." He shook his head emphatically. "I don't allow anyone in here except myself. The wife wouldn't bother coming in here, and the youngsters knows better."

"What time was the car dropped off yesterday?" She already knew but asked anyway; sometimes people contradicted themselves or misremembered details they had supposedly been sure about.

"Quarter after ten on the dot." That tallied with what he had already told them.

"Was she with anyone? Did you notice anyone else present in the car?"

His mouth fell open and stayed that way for several long moments. Then, "Like who?"

"Like another human being."

"No, it was just her."

June nodded. "So you didn't notice a child in the car, a boy."

"Nope."

"Where did she go after she left the car?" There was a local bus service that ran every day, taking passengers to and from St. John's, but it left much earlier in the morning. If Amalie Caron dropped the car off at 10:15 a.m., she would have missed it.

"I never seen her. I told her I'd get the tires done. She said okay, and I went in the house. Last I seen of her." He gestured angrily at the vehicle. "Listen, someone got to take that car. I can't get no work done with that in the way."

"All right," June said. "I'll contact someone to have it towed."

"I wants it gone." He assumed a hostile posture in front of her, arms crossed on his concave chest.

"The sooner you get out of my way," June told him, "the sooner I can call the tow truck." She turned her back on him and took out her mobile phone, punched in Danny's number. When he answered she said, "There's blood in the car, sir, just like he said. We need to have this towed back to the station so Bobbi can get a proper look at it." Bobbi Lambert was the station's forensics chief, a nurse practitioner with the medical examiner's office.

"I'll send someone out right away," Danny said. "Stay with the vehicle until they arrive. I don't want to risk contamination."

"Will do, sir." She rang off and turned to Tony. "The tow truck should be here in a few minutes. You can go about your business. I'll stay here until he arrives."

June waited until he had left before pulling out a fresh pair of gloves and slipping them on. The car was unlocked, the keys still in the ignition. She located the release handle underneath the driver's seat and pushed it back, feeling around on the floor but finding nothing. The passenger seat likewise yielded nothing. She was loath to disturb the blood in the back seat, so she confined her efforts to a visual inspection. The stain appeared to originate from one concentrated source, perhaps two to three feet above, and the blood had pooled on the seat and dripped to the floor from there. She wondered whose it was. Amalie's or the boy's? Probably not Amalie's. Surely Tony would have noticed if Amalie was wounded. Forensics would have to answer these questions.

But all that aside, why would anyone leave a car with fresh blood in the back seat at a repair shop?

The glove box was full of the usual things: fast food napkins and condiment packets, plastic spoons, tissues. She found a broken lipstick and a half-eaten child's lollipop stuck to its wrapper, as well as a receipt from Udell's, a clothing store in Carbonear. Near the back of the narrow compartment, she found an iPhone, presumably belonging to Amalie Caron. A touch of the screen revealed it was unlocked and not password protected, so she scrolled through the list of recent calls. There were only two, both of them made to a number in the 819 area code, most likely somewhere on the mainland. She dropped the phone into an evidence bag and sealed it, then jotted her initials on the front and went back into the glove compartment. At the very back, hidden under a stack of discarded napkins, she found a flash drive, which she sealed into its own bag. Then she closed the doors and left the car as she'd found it. Bobbi's team would make a thorough examination of the vehicle, and hopefully they'd find something to provide a clue as to where Amalie Caron—and her little boy—had gone.

June left the garage and did a slow walk-through of the area in front of the building. Footprints on gravel were difficult to detect, and the recent spate of warm, dry weather ensured no clear impressions appeared on the shoulder of the road. The asphalt itself was unremarkable. Amalie Caron might have gone in any direction at all. She might have hitchhiked; someone could have picked her up and driven her anywhere. Whatever trail she'd left behind—if she'd left a trail—ended here.

June climbed back into the patrol car to wait for the tow truck, knowing it would take about twenty minutes for it to arrive from Kildevil Cove. The iPhone and the flash drive would go to Bobbi Lambert, but June's natural curiosity won out. Still gloved, she plugged the flash drive into the laptop in her patrol car and brought up a list of the files. They were all .mov or .mp4 format—videos—so she double-clicked on the first one and waited for it to load.

The first thing she saw was a close-up of somebody's carpet. Then the camera panned up to reveal a small boy sitting on a wooden rocking horse. A man's voice spoke: *"Dis-moi ce que tu as dit à ta mère!"* June's French wasn't the best, but she thought he'd said *Tell me what you told your mother.*

The boy shook his head, his long, fair hair falling into his eyes. The man repeated his question. Again the boy refused. He began rocking back and forth, urging the wooden horse on violently. The angle of the scene shifted as the camera fell onto the floor. Then June saw the backs of a man's legs, clad in jeans, advancing towards the boy. The man yanked him off the horse and struck him while he screamed.

June reached to shut the video off, appalled. Was this why Amalie had disappeared?

THE AIR Canada jet carrying Blaise Pascal had entered Newfoundland airspace, and he opened the window shutter to look down over the landscape. He saw ragged cliffs, their sheer sides gnawed by the North

Atlantic, and low, scrubby trees twisted into surreal shapes, and always the glimmer of dark water both near and in the distance. What would these Newfies expect from him? Did they think he possessed some special insight about Amalie Caron, an elusive piece of information that would recall her from wherever she had gone? How well did he know her, after all? How well did anyone know Amalie Caron?

That wasn't even her name, not when he met her during his time at SPVM. Back then she called herself something else and made her living gyrating to the beat at Sexe Plus on rue Ste.-Catherine in Montreal. He'd gone in there one night with some coworkers, eager to see what all the fuss was about, and Amalie was on the pole. "Don't fall in love," they'd teased him. He was younger then, much more susceptible to the charms of a beautiful *femme de nuit*, but he didn't wish to see himself as that sort of man.

It was the night before he'd married his wife, and the boys took him to the place and paid for lap dances, which embarrassed him. A beautiful girl grinding herself against him left him unsure where to look or what to do. He pretended to appreciate it, drank the watered-down booze they bought for him, tipped the girls, and tried to act like he did this sort of thing on the regular. But he didn't.

Still, after that night, things changed. In the beginning, he would drop in at Sexe Plus after work by himself, just to drink a bottle of beer before heading home to Louise and their tiny apartment, and Amalie—she had given him her real name by then—would sit with him, and they'd talk about nothing much. In those days, you could still smoke in clubs, and he'd light her cigarette for her, ask about her family. She told him she was from Trois-Rivières in the Mauricie, and she had an older sister who had married and moved away to Montreal. It was no matter; they never did get along as sisters should. She wanted to be a nurse, she told him, which was why she was on the pole at Sexe Plus, but it could have been worse. She could have been earning her living on her back.

Much of what she told him then were lies, but it was a while before he knew that. He believed her sad tale and found her warm and kind. Eventually she invited him home to her apartment. He should have refused, but he did not. Her husband, she told him, was working in Alberta for months at a time, and it appeared he was neglectful. The apartment was a dump, the cupboards and refrigerator bare. It was clear that what she earned at Sexe Plus was not enough to sustain her.

"Where is he, really, your husband?"

When he questioned her like this, she confessed the truth. Her husband, Gerard, had left six months ago, walking out the door one night after they had an argument, and she hadn't seen him since. Pascal asked if she considered him missing. No, he was in Alberta; she was sure of it. Or perhaps British Columbia. One of the provinces out west, most certainly. Did she want to charge him with abandonment? No, there was no need for that. She didn't want to be vindictive or make him angry. He would come home again. He always did.

Pascal drove her to a Provigo supermarket and bought groceries for her. He found her landlord and lambasted him about the state of the apartment. Then he made an appointment for Amalie to see someone at the employment office so she could find a better job. She wept when he told her what he'd done for her. "You are too good to me, Blaise. I don't deserve it."

He said nothing about any of this to his wife, Louise, consoling himself with the lie that it was business; he was doing his duty as a police officer by helping a vulnerable woman. But it became harder to convince himself as his relationship with Amalie grew more complicated and he learned who she was beneath her seductive wiles.

When she left—and hadn't he always known she would?—he came to her one night to find her apartment cleaned out and her nowhere to be found. He didn't look very hard, knowing it would be futile. Even so, when he saw her again years later, he was drawn to her as strongly as ever. By that time he was a different man and would have ended things differently if he'd had the chance. She disappeared again before he could. She was very good at disappearing.

THE AIRCRAFT dropped, the sudden decrease in altitude jarring him out of his reverie. The pilot announced they were beginning their descent into St. John's. Pascal reached to check that his seat belt was still securely fastened and his tray table in an upright position. A steward came through the cabin with a plastic bag, asking if there was any garbage. The entire flight had taken a little over two and a half hours. When the plane landed, he waited until the other passengers had disembarked before standing up to retrieve his one bag from the overhead baggage compartment. His mobile phone buzzed, vibrating his inside pocket. He pulled it out and looked at the screen: Céline Tachereau.

"*Oui?*"

"We believe she's on the island."

As quick as that. "I'll take care of it."

He collected his rental car at the airport and set the navigation system for Kildevil Cove, trusting that the vehicle knew how to get there even if he didn't. So much of his career had been spent finding what was lost and bringing home the missing. Amalie Caron was merely another loose end that needed tying up, and he would deal with her as he had dealt with her before. As for her missing son....

He mentally thrust the memories that thought awakened away from him. He didn't need to revisit that dark time. If he ever wanted to remember, it was right there, waiting for him, laid out in exquisite detail, each line engraved on his consciousness like a catechism.

The message—"*Ne me cherce pas*"—that he'd received on his mobile phone was from Amalie Caron. He was sure of it. She was very clear that he should abandon any attempt to find her, which probably meant she had decided to leave Gerard for once and for all. She wouldn't have left him easily. Those two didn't have a marriage. They had mutual Stockholm syndrome, both locked together in a covenant of hatred. She depended upon Caron's income to care for herself and the boy, so she'd stay in the marriage out of economic necessity if nothing else.

He also realised he himself was not entirely objective when it came to her. "Don't fall in love," his friends had told him all those years ago, the night before he married Louise. Their advice was ignored. Despite his discomfort, all it had taken was for Amalie to slide one slender leg over his and settle her perfect derrière into his lap, and she owned him completely.

IT WASN'T until after seven that same evening that Kevin Carbage managed to catch up with Gerard Caron. There was a great deal of empty landscape between the Kildevil Cove station and the northern tip of the peninsula, and just as much going the other way. It was impossible to traverse on foot, considering that much of it was bog, and they simply didn't have the time or the manpower to launch a full-scale search—which meant Kevin was forced to make a wide sweep of an area some

600 kilometres square and hopefully see something. If he couldn't find
Caron, the delay would allow him ample time to disappear, and even if
the APB would inform the public that police were looking for him, there
was no guarantee he'd turn up. It would have been easier if Caron had
taken flight in a densely populated urban area.

Fortunately for Kevin, extreme measures weren't necessary. Caron
had driven to Bay de Verde and taken refuge at the home of a friend.
Kevin recognized the small red car parked in the driveway of a saltbox
house at the water's edge. "Fucker," he muttered. He'd already decided
on Caron's guilt. People didn't run from police unless they had something
to fear. He pulled the patrol car in behind the smaller car, blocking Caron
in, then got out and straightened his uniform jacket before reaching back
into the vehicle to retrieve his cap. He hoped that Caron would agree
to come into the station to answer questions without too much trouble.
However, if the Quebecois wanted a struggle, Kevin was well prepared
to give him one. Either way he wasn't leaving here without Caron, so it
was in Caron's best interest to put up and shut up.

He rapped smartly on the door and waited. The warm sunshine of
earlier had been replaced with clouds, gathering in dark ranks along the
southeasterly side of the peninsula, and a chill breeze had sprung up. It
might seem like summer lingered during daylight hours, but the evenings
were cool, and Kevin wished he'd thought to bring a warm sweater to put
under the light windbreaker he was wearing.

He could hear a radio or TV playing inside the house, so he knocked
again, harder this time. "Royal Newfoundland Constabulary," he said. "I
would like to speak to Gerard Caron. I have reason to believe he is in
this dwelling." He said it twice and repeated it again in French. Kevin's
French was perfect, the result of summers spent working on farms in
the Eastern Townships during his high school years. "Monsieur Caron, I
only want to speak with you. You are not under arrest."

The front door swung open suddenly, and a middle-aged woman
was there, wearing a shabby sweater and a pair of slacks that had
obviously been at their best many years before. Her badly dyed reddish
hair was pinned on top of her head, but several strands had fallen down,
obscuring one eye. Her feet were bare and very dirty, the toenails painted
a bright pink. "What?"

Kevin showed his badge. "Sergeant Kevin Carbage. I have reason
to believe Gerard Caron is here. I would like to speak to him."

Her gaze flickered over him head to toe, taking him in. "He never did anything." Her accent wasn't local, but neither was she from the mainland. She sounded like she came from the French shore near Stephenville, on the island's west coast.

"He isn't in any trouble," Kevin repeated. "I just need to speak with him."

She turned around and shouted "Gerry! You better come here!" Glancing back over her shoulder at Kevin, she added, "Pass me down the stairs my smokes, eh?"

Gerard Caron, when he appeared, looked like he'd been trapped between two heavy objects and pressed flat. His hair was sticking up at the back and flattened on one side, and his eyes were red-rimmed. He wore a ratty flannel shirt with the top three buttons missing and a pair of navy-blue work trousers that seemed in danger of falling down. "What you want?"

"Inspector Quirke requests that you accompany me to the station."

"Station?" Caron asked, blinking. Clearly, he had been asleep upstairs.

"The police station in Kildevil Cove. We would like to ask you some questions regarding your wife's disappearance."

He nodded dully. "They find the boy yet?"

"I'm afraid not, sir." Kevin wasn't prepared to divulge any more than this.

Caron peered at him, his gaze playing over Kevin's face as though he were committing his features to memory. "Are you real?" he asked.

"What?" An odd question.

"Can I touch?" Caron reached out and captured a fold of Kevin's sleeve between his fingertips. Then, apparently satisfied that Kevin was fully corporeal, he released it and stepped back. "I'll come. Let me get my coat." Nodding, he turned and started back inside the house.

Kevin followed him. The interior was dark and musty smelling, as if the place had been shut up for months or even years. A narrow, claustrophobic hallway opened into a small kitchen, with a chrome-and-plastic dinette set against the wall by the window, two chairs, and a small electric stove along with a bar-sized fridge. Some of the cupboards were missing doors, and several didn't close properly. There was a pervasive smell of old food and rotting garbage, possibly from several overfull bin bags set against the opposite wall. The linoleum underfoot was an old-fashioned design, cracked and stained from many years of hard use and sporting numerous cigarette burns. Caron plucked a padded flannel shirt off the back of a chair and slipped into it. As he did so, he pushed away an ashtray full of what looked like several plump spliffs. He saw Kevin looking and frowned.

"It's legal," Kevin said, nodding at the ashtray. "What you do in your own home is your business."

"It's not my home," Caron said. "I am only visiting. I have a cabin in the woods. I go there sometimes. It's fine to stay."

They made their way out to the patrol car, where Kevin helped Caron into the back seat. He could have allowed him to sit up front, but he didn't want to risk Caron bolting, and there were no locks or door handles in the back. "You're not under arrest," Kevin repeated.

"Then why am I behind a barrier in your patrol car?"

"For your own safety," Kevin lied. He got in the front and started the engine. "Someone will drive you back here to claim your vehicle later."

"*Bon*. I'm too fucking stoned to drive anyway." Caron fell silent, gazing out the side window at the passing vista. Now and then Kevin glanced at him in the rear-view mirror, but Caron seemed to be sunk deep in his own thoughts. When they arrived back at the station, it was fully dark outside. Cillian Riley had already left for the day, but Danny was in his office.

"I found Gerard Caron," Kevin told him.

Danny glanced up from a report he was reading, his glasses balanced on the end of his nose. "Put him in Interview Room 1," he said. "I'll talk to him in there."

"Do you mind if I sit in?" Kevin asked.

Danny appeared surprised. "Won't Riley be expecting you home?"

"Yes, but in this case, I think he'd understand."

"This won't be a casual interview," Danny informed him. "Right now, he's our number one suspect, and he'll be questioned under detention. Are you okay with that?"

Kevin bristled, a little insulted that Danny considered him such an amateur. "Perfectly."

"Is he in a cell right now?"

"Yes, sir. Hughes brought him down."

"Have Hughes fetch him back and take him to Interview 1. You go in and get everything set up, then leave him for a while." Danny turned back to his reading.

"How long will I leave him?" Kevin hated having to ask, worried that it suggested he was inept, but he'd learned not to assume anything where Danny was concerned.

"Long enough to get uncomfortable."

"Sir, he's not been charged with anything," Kevin protested. "Surely we should see to his comfort."

Danny laid aside the report and took off his reading glasses. "The family home exploded and burned to the ground, Sergeant." He gazed at Kevin and shook his head. "Under suspicious circumstances, no less, and a detonator device was found at the scene, one that would require significant knowledge to construct. Caron has that knowledge. We've heard firsthand from witnesses that Caron and his wife weren't getting along. How much more do you need?" He put the glasses back on. "For God's sake, I'm going to question him, not subject him to medieval torture."

"Of course, sir." Privately Kevin wondered if Danny's tactic of leaving Caron to stew for a while was truly ethical.

"Look, Kevin." Danny sighed. "I've had Bobbi's crew all over the site. They found traces of gasoline in every room of the house. Every room. Whoever set this up was determined to make a proper job of it."

"I know, I know. Motive, means, and opportunity."

"Right. Go and get the interview room set up. I'll join you there."

AT HALF past eight Kevin was in the interview room with Gerard Caron, who still seemed sleepy and out of sorts and who didn't respond to Kevin's offer of tea or coffee but stayed slumped forward, his head resting on his folded arms. Forty minutes later, Danny arrived with a notebook and pen and a file folder. He took the seat opposite Gerard Caron and gazed at him for a moment, then reached over and started the tape recorder. "Gerard Caron, you are not under arrest. It is my wish to inform you that you have the right to private legal counsel at any time, twenty-four seven. We can give you access to a telephone if you wish to call a lawyer. Do you wish to retain legal counsel?"

Caron shook his head.

"For the benefit of the recording," Danny said, "Mr. Caron shook his head, indicating no." He flipped open the file folder and paged through some documents inside. "Mr. Caron, before you came to Newfoundland you lived in Quebec. Is that correct?"

"Yes." Caron's gaze slid from Danny to Kevin, who sat beside him. Kevin returned the gaze.

"When we ran your name through the database, we discovered you had been previously charged with domestic violence." Danny glanced up from the folder. "All of these offences occurred in the province of Quebec."

Caron raised his shoulders and let them drop.

Danny narrowed his eyes. "Is that a yes or a no?"

"If it says it there on the paper you have, then I suppose it must be."

"You and your wife, Amalie, would you say you enjoyed a happy marriage?"

"What is it you call happy?" Caron laughed mirthlessly. "Kissing and hugging, all that business? No, Inspector. We were not happy."

"Yet she dropped all the charges against you," Danny continued, "and remained in the home."

"Are you asking me something?"

"Mr. Caron, did you rig the family home to explode?" Danny laid aside the copy of Caron's criminal record and pulled out a photograph. Kevin recognized the timing device recovered from the ruins of the Caron house. "Firefighters found this in the front foyer. What was left of it. According to the local fire chief, this is a sophisticated electrical incendiary device, designed to be activated by a mobile phone."

"If that is what you say it is, then you must be correct, *non*?"

Danny shifted in his chair, a signal that he was becoming irritated. "Mr. Caron, your wife and child are missing. Your family home is in ruins. Did you construct this device to deliberately destroy your house?"

"No. I had no reason."

"You were in an unhappy marriage with a woman who, according to witnesses, once threatened to kill you. Several times the two of you were seen fighting in public. Did you ever raise a hand to your wife?"

"Did you?"

It was as if someone had sucked all the air from the room. Kevin risked a quick glance at Danny. He was outwardly calm, but the colour had drained from his face. Like most others at the Kildevil Cove detachment,

Kevin knew that Danny's wife, Alison, had died several years before—a horrible, lingering death from fatal familial insomnia.

"Did you," Danny said carefully, "ever hit your wife?" He flipped through the printed copy of Caron's record. "Because according to this, you did."

"Perhaps you should ask Amalie about domestic violence." Caron straightened his spine, sitting upright in his chair. "Take a closer look, Inspector. Isn't that what you get paid for?"

Danny started to say something but was interrupted by a tap at the door, which opened to reveal Constable Sarah Avery. "Sir?"

"Is something the matter, Constable?"

"A word, sir."

Danny rose from his chair and went to the door, where he conferred with Avery for a moment. Then he returned, holding a sheet of paper. He sat and slid the sheet across to Kevin. It was a medical report from Old Perlican Hospital, dated the previous year. Caron had been admitted to the hospital after complaining of severe nausea and vomiting, as well as muscle cramps, tremors, and profuse sweating. Although blood tests were inconclusive, the attending physician believed Caron had been suffering from acute organophosphate poisoning, possibly administered in food or drink.

Kevin handed the sheet back to Danny, then said, "You were taken to the hospital last year, and the doctor thought you were poisoned. You didn't file a police report?"

Caron smirked. "There would have been no point."

"Why?" Danny asked. "If someone poisoned you, that's grounds for criminal charges. Why didn't you—"

Again a tap on the door, but this time it was an unknown man. He was about Danny's age, dark-haired and dark-eyed, with a faint growth of stubble along his cheeks and chin. He pointed at Gerard Caron. "Stop questioning this man immediately."

Danny raised his eyebrows. "And you are…?"

The man fumbled in his pockets, produced a badge. "*Inspecteur* Blaise Pascal, *Sûreté du Québec*. I will now take charge of this investigation."

CHAPTER FIVE

Monday Night

IT WAS close to ten o'clock that night when Danny finally made it home. He slumped wearily against the wall in the front porch, needing a moment's rest before he bent to slip off his shoes. Easter, Lily's dog, heard the door open and came bounding out to meet him. "There's my girl." Danny caught her up in his arms and snuggled her, accepting several enthusiastic licks from her broad pink tongue.

"It's about frigging time," Tadhg said. Easter leapt out of Danny's embrace and bounded away. "Jesus, Dan, ye looks like death warmed over, my son." He stepped forward and enfolded Danny in a hug, and they stood like that for several long moments. "Bad day?" He stepped back to gaze at Danny, his dark green eyes filled with love and sympathy.

"Oh Christ, ye don't know the half," Danny lamented. "I didn't mean to be so late." He'd texted Tadhg earlier in the day with a brief outline of the situation, stressing that it was complicated and he'd explain later. "Can I just fall asleep out here in the porch? I don't think I've got the energy to make it up the stairs and that's the God's truth." Not to mention that his knees were giving him absolute hell. They should probably get one of those chair lift things installed, like the ones used in old age homes, he thought sourly.

Tadhg knelt and tapped one of Danny's feet. "Lift up." Danny did as he was told, resting his left shoe on his husband's knee while Tadhg untied the laces of his sturdy Doc Marten oxford and slipped it off, then switched to the other. "Did ye eat anything the day, or are ye full of nerves and strong coffee?"

"The coffee wore off hours ago," Danny confessed. "And my nerves are shot to hell." His knees were aching too, but he kept this to himself.

"I kept a bit of supper for ye." Tadhg took Danny's briefcase from him as he straightened up. "Nothing fancy, just soup that Lily made."

"What kind?"

"Turkey vegetable," Tadhg replied. "Mind you, she's not back on the meat again herself. I don't know what the hell she lives on, to be honest."

"The soup sounds really good." Tadhg's sixteen-year-old daughter, Lily, was proving herself as much of an adept in the kitchen as her father, turning out soups and stews, pies and buns, in rapid succession. "I'll just run a washcloth over my face," Danny said, forcing himself upstairs to the bathroom.

He ran the hot water, doused a facecloth, and scrubbed his face roughly. Maybe if he rubbed hard enough, he could erase the Carons and their exploded house, along with that ignorant frigging *Sûreté* officer.

Danny dried his face and draped the wet cloth over the shower rail before descending to the kitchen. Tadhg had set a place for him at the island, with a plate of soup, fresh bread, and a big glass of water. "Where's Lily?" Danny asked. He sank into the chair and picked up his spoon to taste the soup.

"Doing homework in her room," Tadhg replied, "or that's what she says. I think she's got a boyfriend, truth be told." He sat down opposite Danny. "Or a girlfriend. She's always up there with the door closed. So what's this about some Frenchman?"

"Oh, he's from the *Sûreté*. I contacted him because the database tossed up Gerard Caron." He spooned up more of the soup, which was hot and delicious, fragrant with rosemary and summer savoury. "Domestic violence in Quebec. This Pascal character was the investigating officer. I got the sense the Carons are a pet project of his." He explained how the Carons had come under *Sûreté* scrutiny back in Quebec owing to their ongoing domestic troubles. "*Inspecteur* Pascal—Blaise—was investigating Gerard Caron fourteen years ago in Montreal when he and the missus abruptly disappeared off the radar. When the database turned them up here, I decided to do him the courtesy of letting him know." Danny wished he could rewind the clock and go back to undo that decision.

"Blaise?" Tadhg was grinning. "*Blaise* Pascal? I suppose he's good at mathematics, is he? Ask if he's made up any new theorems lately."

"He'd probably bite my head off. This fella isn't your usual happy, friendly Quebecois." Pascal had impressed Danny as one of the angriest men he'd ever met. "If he saw Bonhomme outside of Winter Carnival, he'd probably shoot him dead in the street."

"Do you think he's going to be any help?" Tadhg asked.

Danny scoffed. "I think he's going to be a pain in the arse." He reached for the water and took a long drink. "He's a queer hand. I can't pick him out at all." He'd already taken the precaution of surveillance, enlisting Kevin Carbage to follow Pascal at a discreet distance and keep Danny informed of anything unusual. Carbage was good at remaining under the radar, and he had sense enough to stay out of Pascal's way.

"Send him back to Quebec."

"Yeah, like I would. Molloy would have my arse in a sling. He wants us to get along with other regional police forces." Danny tilted the soup plate towards him and drained it, then emptied his water glass. "That," he said, with satisfaction, "was good."

Tadhg collected the dishes and stacked them in the dishwasher, then shut off the kitchen lights. He extended a hand to Danny. "Come on," he said. "Upstairs. I'm gonna run ye a nice hot bath. That and a little drink'll send ye right off to sleep."

A few moments later Danny was cradled in Tadhg's arms and surrounded by hot water, a generous dram of Glenfiddich in a glass at his right hand. He sighed, surrendering to the creeping lassitude that the warm bath and Tadhg's presence created. "I love you," he murmured between sips.

"Of course ye do," Tadhg said. "I gives ye whiskey." He kissed the side of Danny's neck and tightened his embrace. "I love you too."

"How is the project coming along?" Danny asked. "I drove past the day before yesterday. Ye got the walls up, I see." The restoration of Danny's grandfather's old house had taken much longer than expected, with various setbacks springing up to knock everything off course. First there were problems finding enough skilled tradesmen to do the work. Then a crooked accountant had absconded with the entire budget, driving Tadhg into bankruptcy and forcing him to sell his beloved island, Eigus. When he pursued the accountant to Ireland, he found himself up to his eyeballs in corruption and organized crime, and only the help of a private detective, who was an old friend of Danny's, and a young Garda sergeant had kept him from more serious consequences.

"Got the walls up and the insides are framed," Tadhg replied. "Gypsum board is going up tomorrow, and then next week it's the plasterers. The cottages will be ready the first week of December." It had long been Tadhg's dream to rebuild the site where the house Danny had grown up in had once stood. The house, a traditional Newfoundland biscuit box, had burned to the ground two years previous, and the setbacks Tadhg had endured were enough to try the patience of a saint. "I'm hoping to offer them to people for Christmas vacation rentals, if they're done in time."

His tone was light, but Danny could detect an undertone of worry. This project had been Tadhg's baby for the past two years and counting. Please God there were no further delays, nothing to prevent the development from coming to its full fruition. The universe or God or the cosmos—whoever—owed Tadhg a favour.

"Christmas?" Danny said. He leaned his head back onto Tadhg's shoulder. "You're well away, my love."

"It gives us a little over three months." Tadhg ran his fingers through Danny's wet hair. "D'ye fancy going away for the holidays?"

Danny hadn't thought that far ahead. "Where do you have in mind?"

"Ever been to Quebec City for Christmas?"

He opened his mouth to say something derisive about their recently arrived *Sûreté* detective but thought better of it. Maybe he was misjudging Blaise Pascal. After all, he knew nothing of the man. Maybe Pascal was one of those people who weren't good at first impressions. "I have never been to Quebec City any time of the year."

"Oh, Danny, you'd love it. Absolute magic. We'll take Lily and Easter, get the ferry across to Nova Scotia, and drive up from there." Tadhg hugged him. "Finished with your whiskey? It's nearly eleven thirty."

"Christ," Danny exclaimed, draining his glass. "I better get out of this and go to bed or I won't be able to get up in a minute." Between the whiskey and the warm water, his knees felt better as he stepped out of the tub. Too bad he couldn't stay half-drunk in warm water all the time. He stood aside to allow Tadhg to get out of the bath, then swiped a towel off the rail and wrapped it around himself. Pulling down the duvet seemed like an insurmountable task, and when he finally sank into the mattress, sleep came almost immediately.

THE SIGN on the door to his room said No Smoking, but Pascal really didn't give a damn at that moment. The motel manager—a fat, lazy-looking man in his late forties with greasy hair and a neck beard—

was probably asleep by now, and it wasn't as if there were any other inhabitants of the motel around to complain.

Pascal should have been asleep, but sleep didn't come easy for him. It never had. Even as a young man, he'd lie awake for hours, his eyes tracing the cracks in the ceiling, his ears straining at even the slightest of slight sounds. This motel room was like all the other motel rooms he'd stayed in over the stretch of his career: small, tacky, with ugly wallpaper on the wall and an out-of-date television set that received one local channel and nothing else. There wasn't even any pay-per-view or live-streaming porn if he wanted it. He didn't.

Pascal stubbed out his cigarette in the lid of a jar he'd found underneath the bathroom sink. Clearly the room's previous inhabitants had used it for this purpose too, judging by the numerous burn scars. The thin, dirty carpet on the floor boasted its share of cigarette burns as well, and the shabby bed with its papery blankets smelled of body odour and stale booze. It was the kind of room you might find at the end of the world, he thought, or the kind of room where you'd go to kill yourself. Even opening the door and all the windows did little to relieve the musty smell of despair.

He propped a straight-backed chair against the open door and sat in it, smoking with all the lights off and only the illumination of a dim streetlight some distance down the road. Thinking was easier in the dark, without the distraction of unnecessary light, and night had always felt intimate to him, whether he was alone or with another. Amalie and Gerard Caron had vanished from the province of Quebec some fourteen years ago, only resurfacing now in Newfoundland. Why? What were they running from? Had Gerard Caron's intemperate habits finally caught up with him? Probably not, judging by the lack of criminal charges on the provincial record. Clearly he'd been behaving himself, keeping his hands away from Amalie and the boy, or at least making it seem that way. So it wasn't him who was to blame. The Newfies weren't as stupid as he'd heard, but he doubted they understood the truth about Amalie Caron. They didn't know her like Pascal did. She and her idiot husband had occupied innumerable hours of his time for the past fourteen years. Truth be told, he wasn't surprised she'd turned up in Newfoundland. She'd been just about everywhere else—and wherever Amalie went, Gerard was wont to go as well.

His questioning of Caron at the Kildevil Cove police station had been unsatisfactory. The man had answered most of Pascal's questions with a flat "*aucun commentaire*"—"no comment." Pascal's attempts to draw him out with either reason or threats all failed. His promises of judicial leniency were likewise ignored. It was infuriating, but Pascal wasn't yet ready to tip his hand. What he knew about Caron's lady wife could keep until later. Maybe there were certain truths Caron didn't need to know about.

Pascal drew on his cigarette and tossed the butt out into the parking lot, where it subsided against the gravel in a shower of sparks. He leaned forward, easing his lower back on the uncomfortable chair. He was still too keyed-up to sleep. Amalie and Gerard Caron had apparently invented new lives for themselves here, which was both admirable and entirely expected. What was it the younger *officier* had said? They were "well camouflaged." That was accurate enough. But why here instead of anywhere else? Why flee to the far eastern end of the country when you had nothing to fear, when none of the charges brought against you in Quebec could be made to stick? True, the charges against Caron himself were minor, in most cases amounting to little more than a warning: domestic assault, public drunkenness, being a common nuisance.

It was Amalie who had always interested Pascal. Now that one... she was something other. He knew her very well, and she possessed him in ways no other criminal had done before or since. She was beautiful, wildly intelligent, and very strange, with tastes that ran the usual gamut and descended into the truly sordid. In the years he'd known her, she had always managed to escape capture, and her crimes were such that she received only minor penalties. He suspected, was almost certain of, her guilt in other, more serious matters but had never been able to find the kind of evidence to make the charges stick.

The problem with the house both intrigued and annoyed him. If Caron and his family had made a life for themselves here, why blow up the family home? Had he intended to kill his wife and son, he could have taken a hunting rifle to them both. Why fire, and why now? No doubt Quirke would examine the available evidence and come to the incorrect conclusion—that Caron had planned the whole thing to destroy his wife and son. He would arrest Caron, there would be a trial, and a jury of Caron's peers would deem him guilty. Case concluded.

Except the odds were strongly against it being Gerard Caron who had rigged the house with a detonator. Pascal would know more once he'd been to the site and had a look at the scene. He intended to do that first thing in the morning. He doubted Quirke would volunteer to take him. It was the kind of task Pascal himself would have fobbed off on a subordinate. Besides, he could tell his impromptu arrival in the middle of Quirke's interview had immediately soured the Newfoundlander's view of him.

Pascal's mobile phone buzzed. He held it up and looked at the screen: Prud'Homme. *Tabarnak.* No, he wasn't going to take the call. Likely it was some small problem that Prud'Homme could well solve on his own. But as soon as he'd dismissed it, the call came through again, lighting up the screen.

"Fuck, Prud'Homme, what is it?"

"*Pardon, Inspecteur,* but I have information."

"Yes?"

"Madame Tachereau has received further intelligence about that ongoing matter."

And she couldn't have sent it via encryption? No, Pascal decided, this was an opportunity for Prud'Homme to check up on him. "Ah, oui?"

"An image of the subject was captured by cameras at the ferry terminal in Nova Scotia. She is traveling under an assumed name with false identification." Prud'Homme sounded as proud as if he'd uncovered this information himself.

"What name is she using?" Pascal asked.

"Charlotte O'Leary, monsieur. I am sending the images to you now."

So she was heading to the island. No surprise there, Pascal thought. Criminals often returned to the scene of the crime, but with this one, that could be anywhere in the world. The organisation she was involved with was especially far-reaching, a sex-trafficking ring with ties to the Sicilian mafia, the Camorra in Spain, the Japanese yakuza, and various Latin American drug cartels. There was evidence to suggest that the group had extensively infiltrated the highest levels of several European governments, influencing political decisions and paying off the police and military in exchange for the right to operate unhindered. There was nowhere their influence couldn't reach.

His phone chirped, alerting him that Prud'Homme's pictures had arrived. He opened the file and paged through them quickly. The quality wasn't the best, but the images were clear enough that he could make out her features. She'd aged since the last time he saw her, and she was wearing a wig and large sunglasses, but it was definitely her. He'd wager his badge on it.

"Is she traveling alone?" Pascal asked. It was unlikely. Her kind went nowhere without two or three heavily armed bodyguards doubling as hit men. There was never any worry about Customs and Immigration because they always flew privately, using small luxury jets they owned or had leased and landing at isolated airstrips in the middle of nowhere.

"She is, *Inspecteur*." A pause. "As difficult as that is to believe."

Certain disaster, Pascal thought. Either she was trying to escape—impossible—or she'd fallen from grace and was running like hell to save her miserable life.

"Merci, Prud'Homme. Contact me if there is additional information?"

"*Bien sûr*."

He disconnected the call and sat back in the chair. A car passing on the road slowed down, its driver leaning over to peer at him. He wondered if this was just another inquisitive local or if Quirke had someone watching him. Pascal resisted the urge to flip the bird. He had more important things to think about, like Amalie Caron and her missing son, and the viper who was even now crossing the Gulf of St. Lawrence, returning to the island of her birth.

The car that had slowed now sped away, leaving Pascal with a fleeting impression of its rear licence plate. Shivering a little in the sudden cool breeze, he stood, brought the chair inside, and closed and locked the door. The lock would never stand if someone decided to kick the door in, but this was a very small town, so it was highly unlikely Pascal would be assaulted in the night. He undressed and went into the tiny bathroom, flicked on the light. There was only one bulb set into the ceiling, inside a frosted glass globe spangled with dead insects, and it threw an uncertain illumination that made his reflection in the mirror look sickly. The burn scars, that eternal reminder of his past, seemed to glow in the wan light, their edges rippled like melted wax. He touched his left shoulder, tracing the margins of each scar, fingertips sliding over damaged flesh that no longer had the capacity to feel.

Caron hadn't rigged the house to explode. True, he had the knowledge to do so, but not the motive, and if he'd wanted to kill his wife and son—

You are thinking in circles, he thought, staring at his reflection. *Go to sleep. You know what happens if you don't.*

Tuesday morning

TONY BLAKE had driven the library's bookmobile for the past twenty years, according to him, and until Amalie Caron came along, he'd done a fine job of everything that needed to be done. Why the library board saw fit to add someone to his route he didn't know, and someone like Amalie Caron? Ridiculous.

"What did you not like about Amalie Caron?" Kevin asked. He was standing outside the garage in Brownsdale where the bookmobile was stored when it wasn't on the road. Tony Blake—a short, powerfully-built man about Kevin's age—had opened the bonnet and was standing on a stepstool, the upper half of his body buried inside the guts of the machine, which was currently running. This made conversation extremely difficult. Blake shouted something unintelligible from inside the engine.

"Mr. Blake," Kevin said, exasperated, "could you please shut off the motor and come down here? This is an official police investigation."

Blake hopped down off the stool and went into the cab. The motor died with a curious grumble that sounded like a large animal. "I figured you could hear me," he said apologetically. He wiped his hands on an oily rag as he came towards Kevin. "Now, what was ye sayin'?" He scratched his short blond buzzcut with filthy fingernails. "I couldn't hear yer in there."

Kevin repeated his question about Amalie Caron. "Why didn't you like her?"

"Lazy, my son." Blake turned to the side and shot saliva through his teeth at a spot on the ground. "Lazy as a cut dog, that one."

"In what way?"

"She was lazy," Blake repeated, like it explained everything. In what way was she lazy, Kevin asked, and could he be more specific? "She used to sit down the back of the bus, reading them romance books. We'd make our stops, and she'd ask me to see to everyone. She wasn't feeling well, she said. Had a headache or she was stomach-sick. Stuff like that."

"Can you show me where she would sit?"

Blake opened the bus door and ushered Kevin inside, where the smell of books saturated the air. On either side of a narrow aisle, there were shelves, specially constructed with wooden strapping across the front to prevent the books from slipping out if the bus was traveling over rough terrain. Since most of the roads on the entire peninsula were in a near-constant state of disrepair, this was a wise precaution.

"Down there at the end," Blake said. At the extreme rear of the bus there was a small fold-down seat that could be retracted and fastened into place with a leather strap.

"Amalie sat here?"

"That was her spot, sir. She never budged out of it unless she had to."

Kevin bent to examine the floor under Amalie's designated seat. "How often is the bus swept and mopped?" He turned to glance at Blake, who shuffled his feet and shrugged. "Has it been swept in the past several days?"

"I never got around to it. I will, though."

Donning a pair of nitrile gloves, Kevin picked through the usual balls of dust and dead chewing gum, finding nothing until he spied a tiny piece of cardboard no larger than his thumbnail. It was brightly coloured and appeared to be part of a label or some commercial packaging. He held it up so Blake could see it. "Any idea what this might be?"

"That got nothing to do with me," Blake said, backing away.

Kevin stood up, dropped the piece into an evidence bag, and sealed it. "You're not in any trouble."

"That's women's stuff. That got nothing to do with me." He turned and hurried outside, his boots clattering on the metal steps.

"Mr. Blake, do you know what this is? Did you see Amalie with it?" Kevin had followed him outside, something that apparently made Blake deeply uncomfortable given the shade of putty grey he was.

"That's woman's stuff." Blake picked up a wrench and climbed onto the stepstool in front of the bus's open bonnet. "She was always taking them things."

"What things?"

Blake turned around and gestured at the evidence bag. "Them candies. Said she had a bad stomach."

"Did she say why?"

"I don't ask nothing!" Blake waved the wrench wildly. "That's none of my business. That's woman's business."

Something occurred to Kevin. "Mr. Blake, you said that Amalie Caron mostly stayed in the back of the bus reading. Was there any particular place you stopped that she perhaps got out? Did she visit with anyone on the route?"

Blake leapt down off the stool so violently that Kevin was forced to jump back out of his way. "Dat," he said, "was the biggest hoor going." He stood so close now that Kevin could see the tiny red veins in his eyeballs. "I was ashamed to be on the bus with the likes of dat." When Kevin asked what he meant, he continued, "Gary Pretty, down the shore. Ask Gary Pretty about her. He'll tell ye something." He turned away to slam the bonnet of the bus shut with a resounding clang, like the bonging of an enormous bell. "Gary Pretty in Grates Cove. Go ask."

"Did this Gary check out any books?"

"From here? Oh yes." Blake laughed nastily. "Nothing you'd ever want to read, though. The Bible in Sanskrit, or a book about chess. That fucker don't even play chess. And she'd have to bring 'em in the house to 'un. He wasn't coming out to the bus to get 'em."

"But…." Kevin was momentarily confused. "What's so strange about that? It's a library bus. He'd want to check out books."

"There's no need in this earthly world for Gary Pretty to check out books," Blake said. He paused as if allowing the suspense to build.

"Why not?"

"Because he can't read."

DANNY DIDN'T bother taking his car to the burn site since the Carons' house was so close. He could do with the exercise. Ever since Dr. St. Croix's diagnosis, he'd been careful about his knees, acutely conscious of the pain that seemed to flare up at the slightest provocation. Even climbing the stairs in his house caused the tendons to twang painfully, and every step he took felt like a series of sudden electric shocks. His running days were over. In fact, anything more strenuous than a leisurely stroll was out of the question, and he resented it bitterly. The codeine-infused Tylenol pills St. Croix had prescribed helped with the pain, but he was cautious about using them too frequently. The last thing he needed was an opioid addiction.

He passed Strange Brew on the right and rounded the corner of Secretary Road where it ascended a gentle curve towards the old

Methodist church. The Caron house—what was left of it—stood on the opposite side. Even at a distance, the smoky smell of charred wood was in evidence. It reminded him of bonfires on the beach when he was young and long summer nights under the stars—but there was nothing pleasant or idyllic in the burned-out shell of what had been a family home. The explosion and fire that had reduced the building to ashes annoyed him. If the Carons wanted to leave, why not simply leave? Why go to all the trouble of rigging the house to explode unless the anticipated result was murder? It occurred to him that arson of this sort, so meticulously planned, required a darkness of mind and a seriously faulty conscience.

There was a flicker of movement to the left of him and he turned his head, convinced for a moment that he'd seen someone making their way on foot towards the road. There was nothing down that way except a fallow field, once used for growing potatoes, but lately overtaken with wild raspberry canes to the height of a man's waist. It could be that some late-season tourist had wandered off one of the usual routes and thought that a shortcut through the field was the quickest way to the beach. He stood looking, straining his eyes into the distance, but there was nothing of consequence. Then as he turned to go, a flicker of something yellow in his peripheral vision and the impression of movement.... But no. More than likely he'd seen the line of police tape marking off the boundary around the arson site. The remains of the Caron home were just ahead and across the road from where he'd been standing.

What you saw came from over there, Dan. His inner monologue liked to spring up at times like these. *You're not senile yet, bhoy.*

A car was parked in front of the house, just outside the fluttering line of yellow police tape the constables had erected earlier, and his annoyance returned. Who the hell was it? Had some nosy local made themselves free to go inside, thus contaminating the site? Bobbi Lambert's forensics team had already been through, but Danny hadn't, and he'd made it very clear that no one—absolutely no one—was to set foot inside the Caron house without his say-so. The police were responsible for preserving the scene, thus there was no need for anyone else to be in there.

He paused outside the gate to slip on a set of shoe covers, then stepped carefully into what had once been the front foyer. There was a strong smell of ash in the room, overlaid with damp, and the burned remnants of the floorboards squeaked under his feet. Even here the path of the fire was visible on the walls and ceiling, where it had raced into the main part of the house, devouring everything in its way. The fire had originated, according to Alan English, inside the doorbell, which had been wired to ignite, but whoever had started the blaze would have used a chemical accelerant. The evidence of this was easy enough to see in the concentrated burn patterns climbing up the walls and reaching across what was left of the ceiling where the roof had not yet fallen in. There were even splash marks where the accelerant had been applied, quite possibly by someone shaking it out of a bucket or can.

The Carons hadn't carried insurance on the house, which made the fire even more puzzling. Had someone besides them started it? They weren't especially liked by their neighbours, and it wasn't difficult to imagine someone torching the place to get rid of them. Whoever had done it hadn't intended any loss of life. According to Alan, the fire had most definitely started when none of the Carons were at home.

Danny stepped over the remnants of a wooden chair, passing into what would have been the kitchen. A man was crouching in the debris, examining the remains with his head down, both hands sifting through the ashes. Blaise Pascal. He glanced around at Danny's approach. "They didn't do this for the insurance," he said.

Danny suppressed a flare of anger. "Did I give you permission to be in here?"

Pascal straightened, pulling off his nitrile gloves. "I don't require your permissions." The ruptured ceiling allowed the daylight into what remained of the room. Pascal looked haggard and exhausted. "I am investigating this case."

Danny wondered what else Pascal was doing. So far, Kevin Carbage's surveillance of him hadn't turned up anything much, but it was early days yet.

"The *Sûreté* has no jurisdiction here. I invited you to be an observer only." Perhaps "observer" meant something different in Quebec, and indeed a recent conversation with Pascal's superior officer, Céline Tachereau, had indicated he was fiercely independent and preferred to work alone. That much was apparent; Pascal had basically barged into the investigation and demanded to be put in charge.

The Quebecois tilted his head to the side with an "oh please" expression. "Don't be ridiculous." He fumbled in his pocket for a packet of cigarettes and a lighter. "The Carons are my business as well as yours." He lit his cigarette with a flourish and fell silent, sucking smoke.

"Those things will kill you," Danny said. "How do you know they didn't do this for the insurance?"

Pascal looked at him as if he were patently stupid. "They didn't have any."

Of course. Pascal probably knew all the dirt. Didn't he say he'd been investigating the Carons for years?

"My constables have collected witness statements," Danny told him. "You're welcome to go through them once I've finished, if you like." This was something of an olive branch, but he also didn't want Pascal thinking of him as inept. The *Sûreté* officer struck him as arrogant and overly impressed with his own intelligence. He'd be damned if he'd let Pascal swan in and take over the entire investigation. *But you invited him.* Yes, to examine the scene and offer advice, nothing more. Pascal was acting like he owned the bloody place.

"I require the evidence of my own eyes," Pascal replied tartly. "I would like to get on with it, *s'il vous plaît.*"

They stood regarding each other for several uncomfortable moments. Finally Danny said, "All right. We'll work together."

Pascal bristled. "I do not require—"

"This is my crime scene, my jurisdiction." It came out as a savage hiss. "You were invited here to observe, out of courtesy, and because you have experience with the Carons. Nothing more."

"You are a nasty little man." Pascal threw his cigarette down and ground it under his boot, heedless to the trace evidence he was destroying. "Lording it over your stupid little town full of stupid little Newfies who know nothing." He came to where Danny was and stood uncomfortably close. "I have been a member of the *Sûreté* for thirty-five years, and I have more knowledge in my little finger than you have in your stupid little head." He leaned in, almost spitting the words. "*Calisse!* Get some sense, you." Without waiting for a reply, he turned and stalked off, fists clenched at his sides, his back rigid.

"And you can fly to fuck," Danny muttered. Arrogant bastard.

He put Pascal firmly out of his mind and turned to the task at hand. The concentrated burn marks on the walls and ceiling suggested the presence of an accelerant, but which one? Bobbi would have most likely taken samples from the scene, and her analysis might help determine whether the arsonist had used gasoline, kerosene, or something else. Most arsonists tended to favour whatever was readily available and plentiful, which in this case would be gasoline, but he couldn't be sure until Bobbi's results were in. It was significant that whoever had set the fire made sure the boy was out of the house before the explosion; it suggested they didn't want him hurt when the dwelling caught fire. Had one of the Carons torched the place, getting Joseph out just in time? Or was his absence merely happenstance? It was one thing to burn your own house down, for whatever reason, and quite another to use fire as a means of murder.

Danny passed under a sagging portion of what had been the living room ceiling. The plaster had apparently been decorated with the kinds of whorls and curlicues popular in the 1980s, but most of it was now on the floor. A chandelier had sprung loose from its mooring and dangled dangerously low, suspended by a single wire. All its bulbs had burst in the heat. The remnants of a green sofa still sat against the northeast wall, but the upholstery and cushions had melted, the synthetic fabric running together in curious-looking blobs and bulges, like a science fiction monster. The fire had burned with ferocious intensity in here, destroying not only the furniture and drapery but also the floorboards and wall coverings. It would have been hellish for anyone caught in it. Good thing no one was.

Danny went down the narrow hallway that led to the back portion of the house, where the bedrooms were. Most of the damage seemed to be concentrated at the front of the dwelling, which made sense, as the doorbell was the likely point of origin. It seemed as if several smaller fires, likely spawned from the initial conflagration, had burned here. There were scorch marks on the walls some four or five feet high, and in several places, the ceiling was charred and broken.

So who'd taken it upon themselves to torch the place? They'd have needed access, but the Carons kept to themselves, never entertaining company. Who hated them so much that they'd willingly burn them out of town? Apparently, the Carons had very few visitors. Danny had yet to go through the witness statements, but he doubted they'd shed any new light. The people of Kildevil Cove were notoriously clannish, regarding outsiders with suspicion and distrust. It was unlikely they'd have let the Carons into their tight network of extended family and lifelong friends, choosing instead to keep them at a distance. It was the way of things in tiny little villages like this one. Even Danny, who'd grown up in the Cove, had found himself ostracised when first he'd returned here from the city. It couldn't have been easy for the Carons, coming from Quebec and having to acclimate themselves to a culture not their own. Clearly more context was needed, not just on their lives here but also the details of their time in Quebec. He knew very little about them, and a thorough investigation into their background was necessary if he was to establish any pertinent facts about the case.

Arson, like any other crime, was composed of equal parts motive, means, and opportunity. Who had motive? In this case, it might have been anyone. The means? According to Alan English, the incendiary device was sophisticated and would have required thorough knowledge of electricity. The only qualified electrician in the village—besides Gerard Caron—was Dave Pitcher, and he'd been working on a building site in Carbonear for the past several months.

"There are no smoke alarms in here."

The sound of another voice amid the silence startled Danny, and he jumped. He recovered at once when he saw it was merely Pascal. "I thought you left."

"*Mais non.* Like you, I am intending to examine." He peeled off soot-stained gloves and turned them inside out before stuffing them into his coat pocket. "Have you found anything interesting?" His earlier fit of pique appeared to have exhausted itself; he was calm and almost civil.

"'Fraid not," Danny replied.

Pascal's brow creased. "You are afraid?"

"No, it's…. Never mind. No, I haven't found anything else." He turned to examine a charred window frame, the broken glass around its perimeter glistening like a set of jagged teeth. "I knew this couple once. Young people." He was still working in St. John's at the time, married to Alison and living on Bonaventure Avenue in the city's east end. "She was sixteen and he was a year or two older. Both of them came from really bad circumstances." He touched the wall next to the window lightly with his gloved fingertips. "Their parents didn't want them together. I think he was Catholic, and she was Protestant, something like that." In some other parts of the world, such a minor detail wouldn't matter, but there were still regions of the island where sectarian prejudices ran deep. "They made a promise to each other—vows, almost—that if they couldn't be together, they'd take their own lives." Danny had been called to the scene by firefighters after the bodies of the couple were discovered in the crawlspace of a burned house. "They drank drain cleaner and lay down together. We were never really sure how the fire started, but it was in one of those old wooden row houses downtown." The older part of St. John's had a tendency to burn; a major fire in 1892 had reduced much of it to ash. The rows of wooden houses, many of them without adequate fire protection, went up like tinder. "It was so sad. You don't ever think—" He turned to speak to Pascal and found he was alone.

DANNY WAS going over the witness statements from the fire when June Carbage put her head round his office door. Danny's office had no ceiling. Instead, the four walls stopped about ten inches short of the acoustical tiles. He always thought of the door in one wall as mere affectation. He could close it, but there was no true privacy, and even the slightest noise from the rest of the station would filter in. If he wanted genuine quiet, he had to wear a pair of noise-cancelling headphones Tadhg had bought for him.

"Sir, have you got a moment?" June asked.

"Of course, Sergeant. Come on in." He stood up to shift a pile of file folders off the chair nearest his desk. "Have a seat. What's on your mind?"

"Something weird at the Caron property." She fluttered a piece of paper at him. "Bobbi's team collected DNA from some of the personal belongings that escaped the fire."

"It wasn't burned?" Having been over the scene himself, he knew that the conflagration had been intense. There was very little in the house that hadn't succumbed to the flames.

"No, sir. The forensics crew are working with materials taken from the debris, and apparently there was a bathroom still intact. We found the boy's toothbrush in a ceramic cup under the sink, and a hairbrush in what was left of the master bedroom. I asked Bobbi to send them out for DNA testing."

Danny nodded. "Okay. Good idea to have their profiles."

"Well, a friend at White Hills RCMP owed her a favour, so he rushed it through in a couple hours." June laid the paper flat on his desk. "I suppose I shouldn't be as surprised as I am, considering." She shook her head. "In the old days we'd just assume he'd been born the wrong side of the blanket and leave it at that. There's a few people here in the Cove in that situation."

"In what situation?" he asked, completely nonplussed.

"Joseph Caron, the little boy?" At Danny's nod she continued, "Gerard Caron isn't his biological father."

"Who is?"

"No idea, sir."

This certainly threw a wrench into the proceedings. Danny wondered if Gerard Caron knew he wasn't the boy's father. That might have given him a motive to destroy the house and kill Amalie and Joseph, but so far the evidence indicated the arsonist had made sure the house was empty. "Is Caron still in custody?"

"No, sir. Inspector Pascal let him go."

Danny hissed through his teeth, directing his gaze at the ceiling. Fuck Pascal anyway. "How exactly did this happen, Sergeant? He has absolutely no jurisdiction in this area."

"Apparently he spent some time with Caron. Questioning him, I guess." June shrugged. "He told Dougie Hughes we didn't have sufficient grounds to hold him any longer, that we had to either charge him or release him." June stood up to leave. "I wasn't here, and Dougie didn't feel he had the authority to dispute it."

"Where is Inspector Pascal now?" He'd been with Danny earlier at the Caron house. He couldn't have gotten too far.

"Not sure, sir." She looked apologetic, as if it were her fault that Pascal was God knows where. Pascal's tendency to wander was another thing that irritated Danny. God alone knew what the *Sûreté* detective got up to when he was outside the station, and he certainly seemed to be outside a great deal. According to Kevin Carbage, Pascal had been down the shore as far as Bay de Verde, at the extreme northern end of the peninsula, and Kevin had also seen him lingering near the old swimming hole at Single's Bridge and pacing the shingle beach immediately adjacent. What the hell was he doing?

"Find him," Danny snapped. "Tell him to come back here immediately." He paused. "Please." None of this was June's fault.

"Will do." She left the DNA results on his desk and hurried off down the corridor.

Danny went to his window and pulled open the blinds to peer out at the road. It was another beautiful September day, with a stiff breeze from the northeast and whitecaps on the harbour and the gorgeous golden light of late summer. What the hell was Pascal at, anyway? He had insisted—no, bullied—his way into the investigation despite having no jurisdiction whatsoever. He was only in Kildevil Cove on Danny's sufferance and because Danny had invited him to come and assist in the Caron case. Pascal seemed to think that "assist" meant barge in and take over. Sure, he knew more about the Carons than Danny did, but that was hardly licence to assume control. Pascal was arrogant and bad mannered and seemed to think he was in a superior position. It was time someone showed him the error of his ways.

The scream of a siren snapped Danny abruptly out of his angry reverie, and he turned to see two constables running down the corridor. He caught a glimpse out the window as one ambulance streaked by, followed by a second.

"What's going on?" he called, stepping out of his office.

"Bad road accident." Cillian Riley was shrugging into a light jacket as he headed towards the front door. "Just outside the Cove on the main road. Transport truck, two or three cars, and a motorcycle."

PASCAL HAD no illusions that Deiniol Quirke would invite him to take part in the investigation, especially after their heated exchange earlier. Rather than wait for a member of Quirke's team to throw him a bone, he decided to hunt up his own leads in the search to find Amalie Caron. Maybe he could teach these people how real police work ought to be done. He pulled up a map of the town on his phone and used it to navigate. An exploration of the national database indicated Amalie had worked at the local library, so he went there first and spoke to an unpleasant woman who resented his questions and threatened to call the police. She assumed a sour expression when Pascal showed his badge, and told him that two other officers had already spoken to her about Amalie Caron, and she wasn't prepared to say any more about "that woman" to anyone. Next, he approached several shopkeepers, none of whom would say anything about Amalie except that she kept to herself rather than socialise with her neighbours. The last place Pascal stopped was the rectory of the local Catholic church. The parish priest had nothing to report except that Amalie Caron was a faithful attendee at mass.

"No sins, then," Pascal commented. This earned him a nasty look from the priest and several pointed questions about the state of his own soul.

He had just pulled out of the church parking lot when the sound of a siren—no, make that a lot of sirens—caught his attention. Two ambulances went by, followed by a police car, all with lights blazing. Pascal consulted the map on his phone. The town's main road linked up with the highway that ran from north to south on the peninsula. The emergency vehicles appeared to have been headed that way. Pascal dialled Quirke as he drove; Danny picked up on the first ring.

"Quirke."

"Inspector, is there an emergency?" He waited for Danny to tell him to stay out of it, that it was their problem and they'd deal with it.

"Yes, a bad motor vehicle crash. Preliminary reports say there are at least two cars and a motorcycle. On the highway leading into Kildevil Cove. Are you able to assist?"

"Absolutely," Pascal replied. His pulse accelerated, pounding violently at his wrists and temples as he hauled the car around, tires screeching on the main road's broken asphalt.

There was very little traffic, even in the middle of the morning, and no construction delays, so he arrived at the accident scene mere moments after speaking to Danny. The road leading into the small town was blocked by a transport truck, in flames and burning furiously. The remains of a motorcycle, smashed beyond recognition, were scattered across the adjacent intersection, where the unlucky biker had apparently collided with the truck. Pascal assumed from the vivid smear of fresh blood on the road that he was the still figure covered by a blanket. Two other vehicles, a passenger sedan and a pickup truck, were pulled off to the side of the highway, the sedan having been T-boned by the pickup, which showed relatively little damage.

Pascal parked his rental car in front of the pickup and set the emergency flashers, then hurried to the centre of the intersection where two paramedics were alighting from an ambulance just as the second one arrived. Three police constables in Royal Newfoundland Constabulary uniform were busy setting up a cordon around the scene while Quirke stood with a younger man in plainclothes, probably a detective.

The transport truck was burning furiously, the fire belching clouds of thick, foul smoke into the air. Spectators, having heard the sirens, had begun to gather, some on foot and others arriving by car. "Keep them away from here," Quirke called to the constables as Pascal approached.

"This is bad," Pascal said. They were several dozen metres away from the burning truck, but he could feel the heat on his skin. It was all he could do not to turn and run. "The driver." He gestured at the semi. "Where is he?"

"Not sure," Danny replied grimly. "Nobody can get close enough. I'm hoping he managed to ditch in time."

"That's not good." Pascal slipped out of his leather jacket and pulled it up to cover his head. "I am going to see. If I'm there more than thirty seconds, get the barbecue sauce, okay?"

Quirke started forward. "You are not going anywhere near that—"

"Just a quick look. I promise. I have experience." He was away before Quirke could object, sprinting towards the flames, wondering what in the name of *le bon Dieu* he was doing putting himself in harm's way. He gained the cab of the truck and reached for the door handle to haul himself up without thinking. The hot metal seared his palm, and he was forced to fold the sleeve of the jacket around it before he could open the door.

The driver had not managed to escape his burning truck and was slumped over the steering wheel. He was a big man, hefty as well as muscular, and although Pascal was tall, he lacked the sheer brute strength needed to pull him from the truck.

"Wake up!" he shouted. "You are still alive. Come on! Help yourself." He wound both hands in the fabric of the man's sleeve and tried to tug him down off the seat. The fall to the ground was considerable, but at least he would be somewhat safe and not burned to a crisp inside the cab. "Come on!"

The man stirred, opened his eyes a crack, and coughed. Pascal pulled harder and managed to move him a few centimetres, but the smoke was getting into his eyes and down his lungs, making him retch and gasp for breath.

"Move." He turned his head aside, coughing violently, wondering where the hell the fire department was and why these maudit Newfoundlanders were so goddamn backwards. "Come on, you fat fuck! Move it!"

With one gigantic heave of his shoulders, he pulled the driver clear of the cab, stepping away just in time as the man tumbled slowly to the ground. Pascal's eyes were burning, his head felt hot, and his fingers were full of sharp pains that felt like a thousand fiery needles. A woman ran towards him—pretty, with long dark hair and wide blue eyes—and threw a blanket over his head and shoulders. "You're on fire," she said. "Come with me."

He was led to one of the waiting ambulances and given a bottle of cold water to drink, and his burned fingers were dressed while Quirke and the other plainclothes detective waited. When the paramedics had finally finished with him Quirke said, "You'd better have a damned good explanation for that. Are ye off your friggin' head or what?"

Pascal took a long drink of water. His throat felt raw, parched, and perhaps it was burned as well. "He would have been dead," he replied simply. It came out as a tortured croak.

"Sergeant Carbage saw you come out. You were lit up like a Christmas tree. I'm surprised you got off as easy as you did."

Pascal touched the top of his head. Strands of his hair crackled between his fingers and broke away, dissolving into dust. "Is he alive?"

"Alive," the younger man said. "Drunk. Going to jail." He had an accent that sounded like the north of England, and big sad eyes.

"Drunk?"

"Oh yeah," Quirke said. "He crashed into the motorcycle. Poor bugger didn't have a chance. Killed on impact. At least it was quick." He scrutinised Pascal with his pitiless blue eyes. "You're an idiot. I don't know how they do police work in *la belle province*, but you just put a lot of lives at risk, including your own."

"He would have burned to death," Pascal snapped, "while the rest of you fucking Newfies stood around with your mouths open like dying codfish. Of course codfish is all you know."

"Here!" The Englishman stepped forward, dark eyes blazing. "Wind your neck in, you."

Pascal shrugged. "*Pardon*," he said, not meaning it in the least, "if I cause offence." He hopped down off the rear of the ambulance and pulled his jacket back on.

"You should let them take you to hospital," Quirke said. Something in his stance had altered; he was gazing at Pascal with interest. "Those burns might need further attention."

"Burns need only time to heal them." Pascal checked his pockets to make sure his phone and cigarettes were where he'd left them. "Not all wounds are fatal." He glanced back towards the transport truck, now reduced to a smouldering hulk thanks to the local fire brigade. "They certainly took their time." He pushed his sleeve back to check his watch, forgetting where he was and whom he was with. He saw Quirke's keen blue gaze dart to the scars on his exposed forearm, then away. The Newfoundlander was clearly dying to ask, but he was too polite, and besides, it had nothing to do with this investigation. Instead, he nodded and turned away, addressing some comment to a passing constable, and Pascal understood that he'd been dismissed.

Not that Quirke had the authority to dismiss him, but that was an argument for another time.

CHAPTER SIX

Wednesday

BOBBI LAMBERT arrived in Danny's office early Wednesday morning and took up a position near his filing cabinet. "Amalie Caron's car has blood in it, but none of it's hers," she said. She flapped a sheet of paper under his nose as Danny grunted to acknowledge it. He'd been awake since four, the pain in his knees nearly unbearable; he was unwilling to take a painkiller because it would make him drowsy, and he could hardly sleepwalk through his workday. "It's the boy's blood, which makes me uneasy."

Danny lifted his face from his cup of tea (Typhoo Extra Strong, brewed until it could probably support the weight of an iron bar) and peered at her. It had been raining since early that morning, which didn't help the pain in his knees. He'd only just received the list of library patrons who'd received materials from the bookmobile in the past fortnight, but most of them were people he knew, almost all of them elderly or disabled. As far as suspects went, there was nothing in it.

"Do you think she killed him?" he asked.

"I wouldn't rule it out." She picked a second slip of paper from the file folder she'd brought with her. "Organophosphate poisoning. Gerard Caron. I had a look at the report the *Sûreté* sent. Do you know where you get organophosphates?"

"At the organophosphate shop?" It was a feeble attempt at humour, and not surprisingly, Bobbi didn't laugh. A sudden gust of wind drove rain against the window and rattled the casement, and Danny found himself contemplating the bottle of Tylenol 3 in his desk drawer. Maybe he'd swallow one, just to take the edge off the pain. Surely one wasn't sufficient to make him sleepy?

"Flea collars." She gazed at him as if waiting for a response. "For *pets*," she added. "The Carons have never had a pet. According to his medical records, the boy, Joseph, is allergic to animal dander."

"I think I should promote you to detective," Danny said. He meant it, but Bobbi laughed.

"It's all there in the science," she said, but the compliment seemed to please her. "The markers are in the boy's blood. They couldn't have any kind of fur-bearing animal anywhere near him."

"So Amalie Caron was buying flea collars to put on her husband?" He'd heard of some weird kinks before, but this was really pushing it.

"She was probably buying them to poison her husband."

Nothing would surprise him. The more he learned about the Carons, the more it seemed their unhappy marriage was entirely to blame for their current troubles.

"Is there any chance Caron was poisoning himself? I mean, people do that. Maybe it was his way of getting the care and attention missing from his marriage." He couldn't imagine it, not really. From what he'd read, organophosphate poisoning was spectacularly unpleasant, with effects ranging from drooling to explosive diarrhea. "Would he do something like that?"

"I don't know," Bobbi replied. "He might. Oh and by the way, gasoline was the accelerant used in the fire. We ran some tests, and the particles from the fire confirmed it."

"Particles?"

"Gasoline burns hot—really hot—and consumes material more completely than other similar accelerants. If you look at the ash particles under the microscope, they're smaller." She shrugged. "Hotter fire, smaller particles."

"So, somebody did an experiment once and found this out? That's pretty—"

Whatever he'd been about to say ended abruptly as Kevin Carbage put his head round the door. "Sir—sorry, Bobbi—we just got a response to the APB we put out on Amalie and the boy. CCTV at the ferry terminal in Port aux Basques picked her up last night, but there's no sign of her son."

Danny's pulse quickened. "Did anyone there speak to her?"

"One of the ticket agents, briefly. Her name is Julie Squires. I spoke to her earlier this morning. She says Amalie asked for a one-way ticket to North Sydney, paid for it in cash, and that was it."

Of course. It wasn't likely Amalie would say anything to the ticket agent. Such scenarios only happened in TV dramas and bad novels. "All right. I want a look at that footage."

"I'll send it through," Kevin said.

"Thanks, Sergeant." Danny glanced at Bobbi. "Have we got Amalie Caron's car on site?"

"Yep. My guys are still working on it. Kevin found a piece of cardboard on the library bus. Tony Blake claims it came from something Amalie had, but he wouldn't say what."

"Have you had a chance to look at it yet?"

"I took a quick glance. There's not much to it, probably not enough to get anything conclusive." She offered him a sympathetic smile. "Sorry. The piece is about one centimetre square. It could have come from anything. It might not even be Amalie's. There's loads of people on and off that bus." She retrieved the lab results from his desk and tucked them back into the folder, preparing to leave.

"Thanks, Bobbi. Let me know if anything interesting shows up."

"You got it." She paused in the doorway. "You want this left open or shut?"

"Leave it open," he replied. "You might as well."

Danny opened his top desk drawer and took out the bottle of prescription-strength Tylenol. He'd only take one. Just something to cut the pain a little so he could work this case without distraction. He swallowed the tablet with the remains of his tea and opened the file Kevin had sent. The video was black-and-white, and there was no sound, but it was clear enough that he could make out the pattern on the floor tiles.

The interior of the Marine Atlantic ferry terminal was surprisingly busy for so late at night, with people forming an extensive queue in front of the ticketing desk. At the top right of the screen a pair of doors slid open and closed as travellers approached, some with luggage in hand. These would be the foot passengers, those leaving the island without a vehicle. He saw an older couple, both dressed in summer-weight clothing, the man carrying a knapsack, and then a trio of teenaged girls in crop tops and tight jeans. To the right of the ticket counter, a man sat alone at the end of a row of blue chairs, one leg crossed over the knee of the other. He seemed unable to sit still, his supporting leg jiggling constantly as he gazed around the terminal. Looking for someone? Danny wondered. Or just an anxious traveller? As he watched, the man took a mobile phone out of his hip pocket and peered at it, then put it back. Expecting a call, then, and noticeably jumpy about it.

You suspect everyone, Tadhg had said to him on more than one occasion, and it was true—but there was no room for sentiment in police work. Anyone was capable of anything at any time. Forget that and you ran the very real risk of making a grievous mistake. Danny had learned this the year before when he'd trusted that the Scottish criminal Martin Belshawe was who he claimed to be. By the time Danny realised that Belshawe was a psychopath, it was too late.

He wasn't about to make the same mistake with Blaise Pascal. From the very first moment the man arrived, he'd been behaving like someone with a lot to hide. The personnel file Danny had received from the *Sûreté* seemed to disclose a great deal, but when you read between the lines there was nothing there. Pascal was a *Sûreté* veteran; he'd started his career with the *Service de Police de la Ville de Montreal*. He was divorced, with one teenaged son. Fourteen years previous he'd accepted a position with the *Sûreté de Quebec* in Mont-Tremblant, a ski resort and tourist town located in the Laurentian mountains. His only listed next of kin was a Sergeant Louis Prud'Homme, a *Sûreté* coworker.

Danny had also been able to obtain a comprehensive list of the cases Pascal had worked, and it was impressive. The first big case of his career was the 1989 École Polytechnique massacre in Montreal, when Pascal was in his early twenties. The mass antifeminist shooting killed fourteen women. Pascal had also assisted with the capture and arrest of William Patrick Fyfe, the notorious serial rapist and murderer who'd terrorised Quebec and Ontario. He'd consulted on the Bernardo/Homolka murders and had worked many high-profile kidnapping cases. He was, according to the *Sûreté*, actively sought by several branches of the Montreal mafia for his interference in the drug trade. On paper he seemed to be the perfect police detective—smart, dedicated, thorough, and very, very good at his job. In person, however, he seemed like someone whose personal albatross was weighing on him, and you didn't need a dead bird around your neck to drag you down in this line of work.

Danny had done a little digging of his own and managed to unearth a copy of Pascal's work history—a précis of how he'd spent the past ten or fifteen years. Initially, it all seemed very ordinary. He'd graduated from the police academy at twenty-one and accepted a job with the SPVM shortly thereafter. Everything else progressed in an orderly fashion, except the closer Danny got to the present day, the more gaps appeared, periods of time when Pascal seemed unaccounted for. Two years previous he'd dropped out of sight for eighteen months, and before that he'd worked at a supermarket for half a year, stocking shelves. Where another person might take a sabbatical or a long vacation, Pascal stopped doing police work entirely and seemingly sought out undemanding work with very low pay. It didn't make sense.

Danny pulled his attention back to the video footage playing on his computer. Aware that he'd been lost in a reverie of his own that had no bearing on the current case, he backed up the footage to make sure he hadn't missed anything. He supposed it was only natural his mind had wandered. Pascal was a puzzle, and puzzles were something Danny loved to solve.

As he watched, the doors at the right of the screen opened, and he saw Amalie Caron walk quickly past the seated man to join the queue in front of the ticket counter. She was alone.

"Cillian," Danny called, and Riley appeared in the doorway quickly. "Have a look at this."

The Englishman crouched to peer at Danny's computer screen. "Kevin said the boy's not with her," he said. He straightened. "That's not good."

Danny let out a breath. "Not when you put it together with the blood in her car, no."

"Who's the bloke sitting down there?" He pointed at the man seated next to the ticket counter, the same one Danny had been watching. "Think he's something to do with it?"

"He's acting weird," Danny said. "Nervous." He shrugged. "It could be nothing."

They watched as Amalie moved up in the queue until she was standing in front of the ticket agent. As Kevin had reported, she purchased a ticket and paid for it. Nothing else appeared to pass between her and the agent at the desk.

"Which way do they go to board the ferry?" Riley asked.

"I don't know." It had been many years since Danny had taken the ferry off the island. Usually he flew. "The sign there says Vessels and has an arrow pointing straight ahead, so I assume that's the way they go."

They waited, watching as Amalie Caron turned from the ticket counter and moved to the right, then disappeared out of range of the camera.

"No idea if she got on the boat or not," Riley said.

"I don't think she'd buy a ticket and not get on." Danny turned in his chair to look at him. "Where's the sense in that? It's close to fifty dollars for a foot passenger. The Carons don't strike me as people with a lot of disposable income."

"I'll get hold of the passenger manifests, see if she boarded or not."
Riley thumbed his chin the way he always did when he was thinking.
"I'm more concerned about the boy. Where is he?"

Danny's desk phone rang—a rare occurrence. Most people
contacted him on his mobile. "Hello?"

The caller was a ticket agent from the international airport in St.
John's with a report that a Joseph Caron had boarded a flight for Toronto
earlier that morning.

"Which flight?" Danny asked.

"AC2064," the man replied. "It left at five this morning. He is
traveling as an unaccompanied minor."

Riley moved to leave, but Danny held up a hand. "Joseph Caron,"
he said to Riley sotto voce, "on a flight to Toronto."

"What? By himself?"

You had to be at least eight years old to travel as an unaccompanied
minor. He and Tadhg had sent Lily to see her mother in Ireland in July,
but she was sixteen, and Joseph Caron was what? Six? Seven? How had
Amalie managed to get him aboard a flight to Toronto? "Who checked
him in? Did you see any identification?"

He heard the clacking of computer keys on the other end of the
line, then, "Everything was in order, sir. The boy was taken to the
departures gate by his grandmother, who furnished his identification. A
birth certificate."

"I want a copy of it immediately." He glanced at Riley and shook
his head.

"I'm sorry, sir. That isn't possible. We don't keep copies. The
original identification travels with the child." The man did sound
apologetic, but Danny wasn't satisfied.

"Then send me the passenger manifest, for Christ's sake! What
time does the flight arrive? At what gate?"

"Seven in the morning, local time, at Gate 32."

"Arriving eight thirty Newfoundland time," Danny told Riley.
"Any minute, in other words." He turned his attention back to the man
on the phone. "Is he being met by someone in Toronto?"

"Of course. We would never allow—"

"Who?"

More clacking of the keyboard. "His uncle."

"What's his name?"

"Hubert Caron."

"Thanks." Danny hung up and turned to Riley. "Air Canada flight 2064, arriving in Toronto any minute." He tried to remember which Ontario police force was responsible for the airport, Peel Regional or the Ontario Provincial Police. "Get on to the Peel Regional Police in Ontario. See if they have anyone around Pearson Airport. Gate 32, and send them a recent photo of the boy. He's supposedly being met by his uncle, Hubert Caron." He pushed his chair back with such force it nearly fell over. "What the fuck is she doing? Goddammit, she could have sent him anywhere. And who's this Hubert Caron? Does he even have an uncle by that name? Who's this grandmother? Did she bring him to the airport?"

"I'm on it," Riley said, dialing the main communications centre for Peel Regional. "I've already gone through her social media once, but I might have missed something. I'll check the phone books too. He might be listed in one of the directories."

The secure door between the public part of the police station and the area where Danny and the other CID officers worked suddenly began rattling. Riley looked up from his computer, his phone pressed against his ear. "What the hell is that?"

A beep sounded, and Danny assumed someone had swiped their ID card. He glanced up and saw Blaise Pascal. "How did you get in here?"

Pascal presented a temporary ID. "The nice lady at the front desk made it up for me, on the orders of your… what is his name? Mallon?"

"Molloy." It was something the RNC's new Irish chief would do in the interest of inter-provincial police cooperation.

"She put him on a flight, didn't she?" Pascal glanced from Danny to Riley. "Hm? Amalie Caron? You think this is the first time she has done this?"

Something about the way the Frenchman said it suggested he knew more than he had previously said about Amalie Caron. The idea that Pascal and Amalie had history was gaining credence the more Danny thought about it—and the more he discovered about Pascal.

"Have a seat," Danny said. He indicated the chair by his desk. "How well do you know the woman?"

"We have had dealings in the past." Pascal retrieved an envelope from the inside pocket of his leather jacket and dropped it on the desk. "My… colleague in Mont-Tremblant forwarded this to me by overnight express. Go ahead, open it."

Danny took up the envelope and extracted its contents, a single sheet of paper. He scanned it briefly, then said, "It's in French."

"*Naturellement.*" Pascal wasn't quite smirking. "I will tell you what it says. 'Where I am going, you cannot follow. The boy will be quite safe.'"

"Is it from Amalie?" Danny leaned over to look at it. "What do you think it means?" The small, curly handwriting was clearly feminine, the written message positioned in the very centre of the page.

"Either it is from her, or we are intended to think this." Pascal shrugged. "It is the sort of thing she would do."

That statement implied he knew Amalie Caron on a personal level, which was worrying. How close an association did they have? Might it indicate Pascal was either corrupt or compromised?

"Know her well, do you?" Danny asked. "Are you in love with her? Is that it? You're going to save her?"

"I am not going to *save* her, Inspector." The scorn in Pascal's voice was nearly palpable.

"What, then?"

"I am going to stop her."

Riley placed the phone's handset back into its cradle with a discreet click as Danny turned to look at him. "Someone already alerted Peel about the flight. They've had officers at Gate 32 since early this morning."

"Someone alerted them…?" He glanced at Pascal. "You?"

"Yes."

Obviously Pascal had been closely monitoring the situation from the beginning. "Have they got the boy?" Danny asked Riley, who shook his head. "What?"

"Let me tell you," Pascal interjected. "He wasn't on that flight. And there is no Hubert Caron." He got to his feet. "I am going outside to smoke. If you feel you can make use of my assistance, come and get me." He smiled, and this time it was genuine. "I want to find her as much as you do, Inspector Quirke. If we are sensible, we can help each other." He nodded to them both, pulled out a pack of cigarettes, and headed for the door.

Riley waited until he had gone, then said, "Do you trust him?"

Danny shook his head. "Not completely. He's too much of an unknown quantity for me, and I don't know what his intentions are."

Danny had also spoken to Pascal's supervisor in Mont-Tremblant, and she'd had nothing but praise for him. She was, she said, prepared to forward all the necessary bona fides if Danny would allow Pascal to assist him on the case. Now that he thought about it, she'd been almost too happy to help. It made him suspicious. Was the *Sûreté* that eager to get rid of Pascal?

"Did you happen to notice the scars on his arm?" Riley asked. Danny gazed at him, confused. "When he looked at his watch yesterday," Riley added. "The road accident."

It had only been a fleeting glimpse, but the image of all those little red circles had been seared into Danny's memory. "Cigarette burns," he said. There had been a dozen or more.

"Yep."

"He doesn't fit the profile for self-injury," Danny said.

"Maybe," Riley countered, "he didn't do it to himself."

Danny thought about this for a moment. Women weren't always the victims in domestic violence cases, and even though it was comparatively rare, there were incidents where men were battered. It was a lot harder for men to come forward and report their wives or girlfriends as abusers, given the value society placed on perceived masculinity. "Could be," he allowed, "but let's leave that aside for the time being. We haven't got any evidence, and it's got nothing to do with the case at hand."

"You don't think being a survivor of domestic violence is going to skew his judgement?" Riley asked. "That's a lot of built-in bias."

"We're all biased," Danny said. He stood, putting an end to the discussion. "I'm going to get Inspector Pascal. Briefing in five minutes."

He found Pascal crouched against the side of the building, his coat collar turned up around his face, doggedly smoking despite the driving rain. He nodded when he saw Danny. "You people have shit weather," he said.

Danny laughed despite himself. "And you have a rare dedication to your addiction."

Pascal took the cigarette out of his mouth and regarded the lit end. "We all need a little something to get us through."

Through what? Danny wondered. "I would like your help," he said. "You have knowledge we can use. Please, come inside."

Pascal dropped the cigarette on the ground and stepped on it. The blatant littering annoyed Danny, but he decided to say nothing. Pascal was touchy, quick to take offence, and Danny wanted the Quebecois on his side. He held the door open for him and waited while Pascal shrugged out of his wet jacket.

"Here." Danny took it from him, subconsciously noting its unusual weight, and hung it on a hook in the entranceway. "Give it a chance to dry out." Pascal was wearing a long-sleeved plaid shirt in a subtle green-and-black pattern over a white T-shirt, and well-worn black jeans with a pair of Blundstone boots. He obviously didn't go in much for appearances. "Want a coffee before we get started?"

"*Merci*," Pascal replied. He moved to walk beside Danny but stopped and turned back. "*Un moment*, please. I must retrieve something from my jacket." Danny pretended busyness with his mobile phone but continued to watch Pascal with his peripheral vision. The Quebecois slid a hand into the leather coat's inner pocket and pulled out an automatic—a Glock 17 by the looks of it—before slipping it into the back of his jeans and dropping his shirt over it.

"We don't carry guns," Danny said when Pascal rejoined him.

"You do," Pascal retorted. "Sig Sauer, if I correctly recall."

"In St. John's, yes." Danny swiped his card to access the secure area and held the door open for Pascal. "But not here."

"Ah, *oui*." Pascal grinned. "Because there is no crime in small towns."

Danny made them both coffee from the Keurig in the kitchen before proceeding into the small interview room that doubled for briefings. The Kildevil Cove police station was not large. The contractor—Tadhg, in fact—had made the best use of the available space in the converted Loyal Orange Lodge building, which dated from the late 1800s. June Carbage and her twin brother, Kevin, along with constables Dougie Hughes and Sarah Avery, were already waiting when Danny arrived. Cillian Riley connected a laptop to the station's only projector and brought up a photo of the Carons' destroyed house.

"As you know," Danny said, moving to the front of the room, "Amalie and Gerard Caron's house exploded and burned on Monday morning. According to the fire department, the dwelling had been rigged to explode, and we believe Gerard Caron"—a photo of Caron appeared on the screen—"may have been responsible for this. He is a construction electrician by trade, currently working as a power-line technician." He gazed out over the assembled group and continued, "Apart from that fact, we have absolutely nothing to connect him to this crime."

He wished he had something more concrete to give them, but circumstantial evidence and supposition served no purpose here. Was Gerard Caron truly the guilty party? Or, as Pascal had hinted, was there more to it?

"In the wake of the explosion and fire, Gerard's wife Amalie disappeared, as has their son, Joseph," he continued. "We have put out an APB on Amalie and an Amber Alert is being circulated for Joseph, but so far we've heard nothing. We have CCTV footage of Amalie buying a ticket at the Marine Atlantic terminal in Port aux Basques. The boy wasn't with her. We received a report that Joseph was put aboard an Air Canada flight to Toronto, which was supposed to arrive at eight thirty our time." He glanced at his watch, which read quarter to nine. If Joseph had been aboard the flight, he'd almost certainly have landed by now. How long did it take to deplane and get to the arrivals area? Pearson was a big airport. If there really was a Hubert Caron, or someone using that name, coming to collect Joseph, then the boy was as good as gone. Once he arrived on the mainland, he could be made to disappear. "I've been in touch with Peel Regional Police. Just waiting to hear from them."

"It sounds like she did a fair bit of planning," Kevin commented.

"Shortly after the explosion, we were contacted by the owner of an autobody shop," Riley said. "Amalie Caron left her car at his garage for repairs on Sunday morning. She was supposed to pick it up on Monday but never did." He brought up a photo of the car's interior. "The back seat was found to contain some of Joseph Caron's blood."

A murmur ran around the room and Sarah Avery stuck her hand in the air. "Sir, do you think she hurt her own son?"

"We aren't jumping to any conclusions," Riley replied, glancing at Danny. "There could be any number of explanations for the blood."

"How much is it, though?" Dougie Hughes. "I mean, could it be from a nosebleed, like? Our little one's had those before, and she comes a gusher."

Several of the others fell into a discussion of this until Danny raised his hand for quiet. "We can only hope the child wasn't seriously injured. June, you have something?"

She nodded. "I've had a look at Amalie Caron's social media," she said. "It's pretty much what you'd expect. Recipes, photos of herself with the boy, that sort of thing. Something struck me as strange, though. I looked all through her Twitter and Facebook, and there isn't one single picture of her husband."

"None at all?" Riley asked.

"Not the one," June replied. "Worse than that? She's listed herself as single."

"Can you do a bit of digging?" Danny asked. "The usual places. And take a look at the social media history. I'm curious to see if she's always listed herself as single or if this is something recent."

"Absolutely," June agreed. "I'll get on it."

"The CCTV footage from the Marine Atlantic ferry terminal definitely shows her there, in plain sight," Danny continued. "But still no idea how she made it from here to the west coast, especially if she left her car in Heart's Desire."

"Isn't there a cross-island bus?" Riley asked.

"There is," Kevin said. "The DRL. It goes from St. John's to Port aux Basques every day. And yes, she could have taken that. Either she took the bus or had someone drive her."

Blaise Pascal cast an enquiring look at Danny, who nodded. He moved to the front of the room. "*Salut*, I am Inspector Blaise Pascal of the *Sûreté du Québec*. I have been investigating the Caron family for more than a decade. When your computer database flagged Amalie Caron, I was requested to come here. What I have to tell you about Amalie Caron will probably go against things you believe to be true." He fumbled in his hip pocket and brought out a handful of folded paper.

Not very professional, Danny thought, then chided himself. Every cop did things differently. Maybe Pascal was in the habit of jotting little notes to himself, as some people did.

"I have known Amalie Caron since 1987," Pascal continued, "when she worked as an exotic dancer in Montreal. Over the years, I have been involved in several missing persons investigations about her.

"Madame Caron has often reported her husband physically abuses her, but this is not the entire truth." Pascal raised a hand to his mouth, his shirt cuff falling away, and Danny saw again the livid red scars left by someone's burning cigarette. "She suffers from *la psychopathie*." Pascal turned to look at Danny. "What is the English word?"

"She's a psychopath." Uttering it aloud lent the word a startling validity. What proof did Pascal have? And why the hell hadn't he cleared this line of thought with Danny or Riley first?

"*Pardon*," Pascal said. "I realise this comes as a surprise, but this explanation is not baseless." He flicked through the handful of paper. "Her first arrest was in 1988, when she stabbed"—here he made a jabbing motion—"a woman she worked with, another dancer. She stated that the woman stole her boyfriend." He tucked that particular slip of paper back into his hip pocket and chose another. "In 1992, she was hospitalised and treated for *la depression*.

"Depression?" Danny asked.

"*Oui*. Doctors ran tests and found she had *la narcissisme*. She refused to take responsibility for things she did to others, and the depression occurred after she attacked a woman in the parking lot of a Provigo supermarket."

"Why would she be depressed about attacking someone else if she's a psychopath?" Riley asked. "In my experience, these people don't usually have a conscience."

Pascal fixed him with a cold stare. "She was not depressed because of what she did," he explained. "She was depressed because she was arrested and taken into custody. She cast herself as the victim." He selected another small piece of paper. "Amalie Caron follows a peculiar pattern. Her attacks on other people come at intervals, and there may be months or years in between when she does nothing at all."

"The mask of sanity," Danny interjected.

Pascal nodded. "*Oui*. Amalie Caron can exist for a time as a normal person, but eventually something will set her off." He consulted his little stack of papers. "Sometimes her quiet periods last for several months. Mostly she has behaved herself for the past fourteen years." He took out his mobile phone. "I will contact the *Sûreté* and have them send you the complete file on her so you have all the facts in front of you." He took out his mobile phone and moved off to one side. After a moment, they heard him speaking quietly in French, merely a handful of words before he rang off. "You will receive all the information by email," he said. "They are sending this material."

"Thanks," Danny said tartly. He wondered why Pascal couldn't have seen fit to divulge this information before now. Maybe he wanted the glory of bagging Amalie Caron all by himself, or maybe he was just a contrary bastard. "You're a pal."

Riley shifted uncomfortably in his chair, glanced around him. "Just because Amalie Caron hasn't been arrested in the past fourteen years doesn't mean she's behaved herself, though," he countered. "It just means she hasn't shown up on anybody's radar."

"That's what I was going to say," Dougie Hughes added. "Maybe she's been at stuff this whole time, but nobody knew nothing."

"That is also possible," Pascal agreed. "We should speak to her husband again. Where is Gerard Caron now?"

You'd know, Danny felt like saying. *You're the one who let him go.* "Kevin's been chasing him down," he said. "Any idea where he is at the moment, Sergeant?"

"He's staying at a friend's house on Belgium Road," Kevin interjected. "Max Belbin. He works in the offshore, so the house is empty. The Carons' young fella used to ride the school bus with Max's boy before Max and his wife split up."

Pascal was already headed towards the exit. "You know where this Belbin house is?" he called to Kevin as he went. "Can you take me there?"

Riley started up. "Hey, hold on a minute! This is our—"

"No, let him see to it," Danny said. "It's his case too. Kevin, you go with him. He'll probably need someone." Pascal's willingness—or foolhardiness—to plunge into the cab of a burning truck and his dogged dedication to finding Amalie Caron showed that he was serious. Pascal had been involved in the Carons' lives for the past fourteen years. However much Danny disliked Pascal's presumptuousness, it was only right that he have a hand in things. "Maybe we should bring Gerard in for further questioning, see how much he knows about Amalie's plans." He was already speaking to Blaise Pascal's retreating back. "Ask him if there's a pattern," Danny called. "We need to know what to expect."

BLAISE PASCAL had developed the unique ability to feel when something horrible was about to happen—or had already happened. Ever since he was a very young boy, he'd been able to sense emotional disturbances in those around him, a talent that had even saved his life a time or two. He'd spent six years behind the dark institutional walls of a Montreal orphanage, a grim building on rue Hochelaga where conditions were barely better than medieval. From the moment he arrived at the age of twelve, he learned that those who survived flew under the radar, out of the view of the nuns who ran the place and doled out vicious punishment whenever the mood took them. Pascal bore the marks of that punishment on his body, but the worst scars existed in places that couldn't be seen. He wasn't a Duplessis orphan—those horrific events had occurred before his time—but there were many similarities. He considered himself a survivor rather than a victim and had trained himself to forget.

He was experiencing that same feeling of incipient tragedy now. Something horrific had occurred or was occurring and there was nothing he or anybody else could do to stop it. A series of events had been set in motion, like a vast boulder rolling down a hill. He glanced across the interior of the police car at the young officer who was driving, a sergeant in his late thirties, *blond cendré*, and with the wide blue eyes of the true innocent. "Where is this rue Belge?"

"Belgium Road," the sergeant replied. What was his name again? A play on words in English, something about rubbish. Garbage? "Most people around here just call it Belgium."

"Are they Belgians?" Pascal asked, unfamiliar with Newfoundland naming conventions.

The sergeant—Carbage, that was his name—grinned. "No, Inspector. It's just a name."

The driving rain of earlier had stopped by now, giving way to a tentative sky with drifting clouds across a thick backdrop of pale grey. It would probably rain again, but for now the roads were dry and the air pleasantly warm. They turned off the main highway, passing a wooden bus shelter and a small school building with no children around it. The road was narrow, unpaved, and heavily potholed in spots, desperately in need of an overhaul. This seemed to be a poor district, or one without much political clout, and Pascal saw evidence of disrepair everywhere he looked. "What do they do, these people? To earn money?"

Carbage shrugged. "Everybody used to fish for a living, but that's all gone now. A lot of people have gone elsewhere, to Alberta or places like that, to look for work."

"What kind of work do they do in Alberta? Not fishing."

"No, not fishing." He pulled the car up in front of a small yellow house built in a vaguely Scandinavian style and shut off the motor. "He should be here."

"He does not do any work either?" Pascal opened the door and got out, waiting while Carbage put on his cap and straightened his uniform jacket.

"Let me talk to him," Carbage instructed, "sir."

Pascal moved with him to the front door and waited while Carbage knocked. The area around the small house was peaceful, quiet, and uncommonly beautiful, with a great many birch trees set around a space of green and a narrow stream running behind it. He drew a slow breath, filling his lungs with the clean salt air. He could easily see why they stayed, these people. If one wanted solitude, here it was right on the doorstep.

"Gerard?" the constable called. "It's Kevin Carbage. I'd like a word with ye."

The accent would take some getting used to, Pascal thought. Not quite Irish but not far off it, either, a broad brogue salted with a touch of… Poole, was it? Or Dorset? He'd studied linguistics at Université Laval, but that was years ago, and he couldn't be entirely sure. How did they even understand each other, these people? Carbage knocked again, a little harder this time.

"I think he is not in," Pascal said. "I'll go around the back."

The house had been built on a small plot of land with narrow margins on either side. At the rear of the dwelling, towards what he guessed was north, it was bisected by the stream, which emptied into a shallow fen. The west side was heavily shadowed by trees, fir and spruce. He found a narrow door set into the north side; it was unlocked and opened when he turned the handle.

"*Salut*, is anyone here?" So this was illegal entry, but what the hell, he thought. "I am a police officer. I am coming in." *I am already in.* He gave a mental shrug.

The interior of the house was sparsely furnished, the furniture and fixtures dating to perhaps the late 1970s or early 1980s. The carpet in the living room was a dull brown and owed much of its colour to dirt, and the sofa and single chair were dark green, of a style popular in the sixties. The kitchen appliances consisted of a small stove and bar-sized refrigerator, as well as a chrome set of two chairs and a table.

"Hello? Monsieur Caron?" He stood for a moment listening, but heard nothing, and the only movement was the irresolute twirling of dust motes in a sunbeam. Pascal went through to the front door and opened it. It too was unlocked. "He is not here."

Carbage stepped inside and glanced around him. "That's weird. He said he was staying here with Max."

A pinprick of anger flared in Pascal's gut. "And you believed him?"

"I know him," Carbage said evenly. "We used to play rec hockey together in the winter. He seemed like a good man."

Pascal weighed this opinion for a moment. "Well," he said, "good man or not, he is not here." Some impulse made him turn and go towards the kitchen sink. "Looks like nobody has been here for a few days."

The sink had been in use, that much was evident, and some drops of water clung to the shallow indentation around the drain. He pulled out the small flashlight he usually carried and flicked it on, pointed it at the sink plug, which had been placed upside down in the drainage hole. "*Merde.* You, come look at this."

Carbage leaned over to peer into the sink. "That's not Gerard's." He fumbled in his pocket and brought out a nitrile glove and a pair of tweezers, then deftly extracted the single long blond hair and folded it into a small evidence bag. "What do you think?"

Pascal snapped off the flashlight and stuck it back in his pocket. "I think Amalie Caron has been here."

Carbage's cellphone vibrated audibly. He swiped at the screen to accept the call. "Yes?"

A female voice reported that the man who owned the house was working on the oil rig Hibernia and had been for the past two weeks. "Gerard Caron wasn't staying with him at all."

Pascal, who had been standing close enough to hear this, asked, "Then where the hell is he?"

Carbage ignored him. "Does Danny know?" The female voice indicated he did. "We're on our way back."

THE STATION was in an uproar when Carbage and Pascal arrived. Carbage immediately handed off the hair to a small woman with a bright red punk hairdo that reminded Pascal of a rooster. "It's probably Amalie Caron's, but we need to be sure," he told her.

Pascal, impressed, said, "They do whatever you tell them?" He followed the sergeant towards the secure area of the station, pausing to swipe his card and usher them both through.

Carbage glanced back at him. "We work as a team around here."

Inspector Quirke was in his office. "I've got an APB out for Caron," he told Carbage. "Get on to that missus he's friends with up the shore. See if he's at her place. The fucker didn't just vanish into thin air." He picked up a cup from the desk and drank from it, then tapped the screen of his computer. "Bay de Verde," he said. "That's where she lives. Kevin, did you—" The phone at his elbow chattered. "Quirke."

The Englishman they called Riley entered the office. "Danny, we've just received some files from the *Sûreté*."

Quirke held up a hand for quiet, then punched the button to activate the phone's speaker.

"I've got a surprise for you." The voice was mechanical, distorted, high pitched.

"Who is this?" Quirke demanded.

There was a pause, during which Pascal could hear the caller breathing. There was a slight hitch towards the end of the exhale, almost indistinguishable.

"I hope you like it." A click followed, then the dial tone.

Quirke reached across to disconnect. He gazed at each of them in turn, lingering on Pascal. "Is that her?" he asked.

Pascal blew air through his lips, frustrated. "Impossible to tell. That voice sounded like someone sucking on a helium balloon."

Quirke's computer beeped, and he leaned forward to touch a key. "Email," he said, and after a moment, "Mother of God."

They all crowded in to look. The video was poor quality, grainy and out of focus, but the man on the screen was, without a doubt, Gerard Caron. He appeared to be in a confined space. "Is that a storage locker?" Riley asked. "You can rent them by the week or the month or—"

"It's a root cellar." Quirke's voice sounded flat, all the emotion sucked out.

There was something very wrong with Caron's face. The top half was relatively intact but obscured by a dark liquid that flowed over his forehead, obliterating his eyebrows, pooling in the empty sockets where his eyes should have been.

"Christ, it's blood," Riley said. "His eyes... his eyes are gone." A disquieted ripple of sound ran around the room.

"If anybody is listening," Caron said thickly, "you had better be quick. She's going to kill me." A gloved hand appeared, hovering in the air, holding a metal implement that looked like a shrimp fork. Someone near the back of the room whispered a curse. The metal utensil touched Caron's face, stroking his cheek. "Please," he begged, "I promise you, I will do whatever you want." The fork dug into the soft meat of his jaw, gouging deep, and he shrieked, a horrible noise. The video cut off suddenly with Caron's screaming face frozen on the screen.

"*Tabarnak*," Pascal whispered. "It's starting again."

CHAPTER SEVEN

Wednesday afternoon

"TELL ME again," Danny said. The Tylenol he'd taken earlier to combat the pain in his failing knees had worn off, and his joints were throbbing like a toothache. "And don't leave anything out."

He was sitting across the desk from Blaise Pascal, who sat slumped in his chair, head in his hands. The *Sûreté* officer looked exhausted, utterly defeated, but Danny had no pity for him, not in that moment. Pascal knew more about Amalie Caron than he'd said, and Danny wanted the rest. As of right now, Amalie was nowhere to be found, and neither was her son, Joseph. An officer from Peel Regional had called to say that no one matching Joseph's description had gotten off the plane at Pearson Airport. How Amalie had managed that was anyone's guess.

"As I have already told you, she is a psychopath." Pascal raised his head. "In 2006 she lured two teenaged girls back to her apartment on the rue St-Jacques in downtown Montreal, fed them an overdose of allergy medication, and strangled them in their sleep."

"And you didn't arrest her?" Danny asked, annoyed. "Why not?"

"Because she fled. We only discovered the bodies two days after the deed was *accompli*. DNA evidence at the scene indicated they had been killed by Amalie, but she herself? *Disparue*. I have been tracking her for fourteen years." He rubbed both hands over his face. "Why the hell you think I came all the way down here? For your shitty weather?"

Cillian Riley spoke up. "You lost track of her for fourteen years."

"It was like she had vanished off the face of the earth." Pascal took out his cigarettes, then seemed to remember where he was and put them away again. "The girls she killed, their eyes were also removed."

"What happened to the eyes?" Riley asked. It was a horrible question and a morbid one, but Danny was glad someone had asked.

Pascal raised his shoulders, hands lifted, and shrugged. "*Je ne sais pas.* I don't know. They were never recovered."

Eyes, Danny thought, goddamn fucking eyes again. He'd already been down this particular road with a case two years previous. A young mother, Deborah Harris, had been found dead in a bog with one of her eyes gouged out. "How is it that Amalie Caron has been on the run for fourteen years, yet there were no sightings of her at all?"

"Because she is good at hiding." Pascal stood up and began to pace around the confines of the office. "Do you think we have been sitting on our hands all this time? Every goddamn law enforcement agency on the continent has been involved. There was no trace of her. *Rien.*" He reached the far wall and leaned his back against it. "Shortly after the murdered schoolgirls, we discovered the body of Alain Goncourt. He was a man Amalie involved herself with. She was Amalie Belanger back then. His eyes had been gouged out, and he had been *éviscéré*—eviscerated. Guts everywhere."

"Is Gerard Caron alive or dead?" Danny asked. "In your opinion."

Pascal gazed at him steadily for a moment, his dark eyes fathomless and full of some emotion Danny couldn't readily identify. "Who knows," he said at last. "Perhaps his soul is with God. Perhaps he still lives. Only Amalie can tell us."

"And the boy?"

Pascal dropped his eyes. "Pray for him."

"How the hell is she doing all this if she boarded a ferry for the mainland?" Danny sounded as exasperated as he felt, and the pain in his knees wasn't helping.

Following a tap on the door, Dougie Hughes appeared. He looked like someone who had just endured a terrible shock. "Sirs?" He nodded at Danny. "A neighbour went by Gary Pretty's house just half an hour ago."

"Gary Pretty?"

"The man Amalie Caron was seeing on the bookmobile route," Riley said.

"Allegedly seeing," Danny said. No one acknowledged this.

"The neighbour had some groceries to drop off," Hughes continued. "Apparently Gary's not been well. She's the one who found him."

Danny glanced at Pascal. "Found him?"

"He's dead, sir." Hughes swallowed, his Adam's apple bobbing. "According to her, there's a lot of blood."

"*Calisse,*" Pascal hissed. He pushed away from the wall. "Where is this Pretty Gary's house?"

"You stay put," Danny said. "We can take care of this ourselves."

Pascal patted the gun at the small of his back. "Of course you can, but Amalie Caron is my investigation, and if this is her work...." He lifted his hands to shoulder height and let them fall.

Danny nodded. Pascal's intimate knowledge of Amalie Caron— if this was indeed her doing—could be useful to them. But he wasn't about to let Pascal run things unaccompanied in Danny's territory. "Me and you, then. Come on." He nodded at Hughes. "Take Sarah and get a cordon erected around the site. Let no one through. I don't care if they're Jesus Christ."

GARY PRETTY'S house was set on a headland overlooking the sea. If you stood in front of it and turned south towards the main body of the peninsula you might just make out the long shape of Baccalieu Island on your left. The island was a protected seabird sanctuary, most notable for hosting the largest known colony of Leach's storm-petrel in the world, but just now that was of no consequence. The first thing a casual onlooker would see was the line of yellow police tape marking out the perimeter of the property and the flashing red-and-blue lights of the two patrol cars positioned at either side of the house. Danny pulled up behind the nearest of these and parked, and he and Pascal got out. Sarah Avery was standing by the line of fluttering tape, and she nodded at their approach.

"Have you been inside?" Danny asked.

She shook her head, her dark ponytail swirling. "No, sir. Bobbi is on her way, and I didn't want to contaminate the scene."

"Good. That's good." He pulled out a handful of blue elasticated shoe covers and passed two of them to Pascal. "What about the neighbour?"

Avery consulted her notebook. "Mrs. Rice. She lives just over the road. Elderly, harmless. Somebody's nan. She said she came by just after nine this morning to deliver some fresh bread and homemade jam and found him. I took her information and told her we'll be in touch." No doubt Mrs. Rice was already on the phone to all 127 residents of Grates Cove, telling everything she knew. So much for confidentiality.

"You have stepping plates for inside the house?" Pascal asked, bending to slip shoe covers on.

"No budget for that sort of thing." And normally no call. Serious crimes were scarce on most of the island, with an average of one to two homicides per year. "Come on." He lifted the tape to allow Pascal to slip underneath. "I don't need to tell you to be careful where you're walking."

"No," Pascal retorted sharply, "you do not, and yet anyway you do." He seemed irritated, as if this were his patch and Danny was the one treading on it.

The house's storm door was open and banging in the wind. Danny slipped on a pair of nitrile gloves and caught hold of it to fasten it back against the clapboard with the attached hook. He stepped clear of the threshold and reminded himself to go out the same way he'd come in—not because of the old superstition but to minimise any further contamination. The less he tracked through the site the better, although the neighbour who'd discovered Pretty had most likely introduced plenty of her own DNA.

"The body is still in situ," Danny said once they were standing in the kitchen, "in the bedroom. Most of these older homes have that at the back."

Pascal gestured, a "go ahead" motion. "I will follow in your footsteps."

The interior of the house was dark, the windows heavily curtained, and the overcast sky cast the rooms in an eerie half-light. There was a mustiness to the air, typical of old wood, much of it harvested from decommissioned fishing boats and reborn as timbers or other structural elements. The scent was overlaid with the coppery odour of fresh blood.

"Down here, I think." Pascal tilted his head towards the northernmost wall. "You can smell it most here." He stepped aside to let Danny precede him into the room, a small sleeping chamber with a single window facing the sea. Someone—most likely the visiting neighbour—had opened the window. "This is a not good idea," Pascal murmured, "considering the wind today." He shook his head. "Your forensic people will have to allow for particulate matter."

"She probably did it for the smell," Danny said, "but I wish she hadn't."

Gary Pretty lay on a double bed in the corner of the room, fully dressed except for a shirt and with his arms and legs spread. His entire torso had been split wide open like the cracked chest of a game bird, the contents spilling out to either side. The bed was soaked with blood, some of it already beginning to congeal.

"*Calisse.*" Pascal drew near and leaned over the corpse. "She cut his throat as well."

"Do you think that killed him?" The question was ridiculous, but Danny felt compelled to ask all the same.

Pascal froze suddenly, eyes fixed on the wall above the bed. "*Regarde ça.*" Look at that. His expression was stiff, artificial, and altogether unreadable. He swallowed hard, his throat clicking audibly.

"Jesus." Someone had dipped a hand or a rag into Gary Pretty's blood and used it to scribe a message on the faded rose wallpaper: *Ma Jolie Louise.*

"I don't understand."

"It's from a song," Pascal explained. His gaze hovered on the macabre inscription and slid away. "Daniel Lanois, you know of him?" Danny nodded. "It's about a man who loses his job, and he drinks too much, so his wife leaves him."

"That old story."

The Quebecois turned to peer at him intently. "Your wife left you?"

"My wife died," Danny said. "Now I'm married to someone else." He stepped closer to the writing, pulled out his phone, and snapped a series of photos. "Our forensics chief will take some proper pictures when she gets here."

"Was he"—Pascal nodded at the dead man on the bed—"married himself?"

"No, we don't think so. He was… involved with Amalie Caron. To what degree, we aren't sure."

A female voice called to them from the front door, and then Bobbi Lambert appeared, dressed in a white Tyvek suit with the hood pulled up. A pale blue medical mask covered her nose and mouth, leaving only her wide blue eyes visible. "Good afternoon, sir," she greeted Danny. "*Salut, Inspecteur.*" Pascal inclined his head and smiled.

"You never told me you speak French," Danny said.

"*Juste un peu,*" she replied with a grin. "Only a little. Enough to get by in a pub in downtown Montreal. Maybe." Her gaze wandered to Danny's feet. "Good to see you're wearing shoe covers, but you should probably be suited up," she said. "You too, *Monsieur l'inspecteur.*"

Pascal gave her a dazzling grin, which was itself rather shocking, considering his usually sour mien. "*Pardon, madame,* it will not happen again."

"So the deceased is in here?" She moved farther into the room. "Oh, I see. Cracked him open like a spatchcocked turkey. Haven't seen that before."

"Spatch… cock?" Pascal's eyebrows had ascended nearly into his hairline.

"I'll explain later," Danny said. "Bobbi, the man's name is Gary Pretty. Possibly in an intimate relationship with Amalie Caron, but at this point that's merely hearsay. A neighbour came by with some groceries for him and found him like this." He indicated the writing on the wallpaper. "Left a message and all."

"A Daniel Lanois song," Bobbi remarked. She laid her forensics case on the bed and opened it, glancing back at Danny. "I assume there's contamination from the neighbour." A digital SLR camera appeared in her hand, and she fired off several quick shots of the corpse where it lay and the writing on the wall.

"The window as well," Pascal said. "She perhaps opened it for the smell. No doubt it introduced particulate matter into the room."

Bobbi made an irritated noise. "Bloody people." She waved an impatient hand at them. "Go on, the two of yez. Git. You're after tracking God knows what in here."

"Can you give me a time of death?" Danny asked. There was no way to be exact—that still lay beyond the power of modern science—but Bobbi's best guess would be accurate.

"Near enough," she replied. "Although he could have been here a while. I'll let you know what I find." She paused, camera in hand. "Do you want me to call Green's"—the local funeral home—"to remove the body?"

"If you don't mind," Danny said. "And maybe give Regan a call as well. Let her know we're sending him over to her. She'll have copper kittens if he just shows up unannounced."

"Will do, boss."

"I need to start a house-to-house," Danny said, when he and Pascal were back outside. He bent to remove the shoe covers and stuffed them into his pocket. "But both of my constables need to remain on site while Bobbi and her team are working inside." It was vital to establish whether anyone had been seen coming or going from the house in the previous twenty-four hours. Eyewitnesses were unreliable, but sometimes a casual observer might see something useful.

Pascal gazed at him for a long moment. "Why don't you do it yourself?"

"Yes, but I'm—"

"Come. You and I will do it together."

"You're serious."

"It is a tiny little village. How long will it take? Ten minutes?" Pascal pulled out his pack of cigarettes, extracted one, and lit it.

"I have bad knees," Danny explained. Pascal glanced down at them. "I do, really." The Quebecois raised his eyebrows. "All right," Danny huffed. "Fine. Come on."

It was policing the way Danny had done it at the very beginning of his career, when he was an RNC constable in St. John's and the island had yet to see the dangerous rush of prosperity that came ashore with the oil. Newfoundland was arguably safer back then, before the influx of petroleum revenue brought drugs and organised crime, and St. John's a city where you could walk the streets at all hours and encounter nothing even remotely dangerous.

The first two doors they knocked on remained closed, even though at one house Pascal insisted he had seen a curtain move in a front-room window. Several of the other residents had nothing to report, and one older lady, clearly suffering from dementia, asked them when Dr. Lockwood was coming to see about her eyes. Danny explained gently that Dr. Lockwood no longer practised in the area, having been dead for thirty years, but she insisted she'd had a phone call from him just that morning. "He called me and told me he was coming over to see me. I got a banana loaf baked for him and everything. He loves my banana loaf, he do, so."

"Poor old soul," Danny remarked when he and Pascal were outside. "Probably worked hard her whole life and raised her youngsters, only to end up like that."

"My *maman* went the same way," Pascal replied, looking wistful. "She raised all eight of us children."

"You have seven siblings?" He wondered what Pascal would think of his own family background—the bastard son of a mysterious Welsh nurse, herself dead mere hours after his birth, after which he was raised by his birth mother's best friend and led to believe he was their flesh and blood.

Pascal avoided looking at him. *"Non."*

Okay, Danny thought, there's an abrupt end to that conversation. "There are only three or four more houses," he said by way of changing the subject. "Let's see what they have to say." But their efforts yielded no further results. Gary Pretty's house was located at a distance from the rest of the community, set off by itself. It only made sense that no one had seen anything much, or if they had, they were keeping quiet about it in the way that people did in small villages.

On a road named Martin's Island they knocked at the door of a small white bungalow with a red pickup truck parked outside. A line of washing had been hung out to dry at the rear of the dwelling, but the recent rains had dampened it, and it swung listlessly in the breeze. "Do you know anyone in this town?" Pascal asked as they waited.

"No," Danny replied, "not anymore." A ginger-and-white tomcat appeared from around the corner of a shed and ran towards them, meowing piteously and rubbing himself against Danny's legs. The cat was so thin his ribs were showing, and he was missing patches of fur. "Poor thing." Danny picked the animal up and rubbed under his chin. "Are you hungry?"

"Put that fucking cat down." The male voice came from behind them, and both Danny and Pascal turned at once. "Dat's nothing but a fucking nuisance." He was perhaps in his late thirties, lean and stringy, but with a pronounced beer belly. The dark blue coveralls he wore proclaimed Dave's Autobody underneath a layer of dirt and grease, and he carried a wrench, which he brandished like a weapon.

"Maybe if you fed him once in a while, he wouldn't be such a nuisance." Danny put the cat gently on the ground and fetched out his badge. "Inspector Deiniol Quirke, Royal Newfoundland Constabulary. This is my colleague, Inspector Blaise Pascal, *Sûreté du Québec.*"

"What's a fucking frog doing around here?"

Pascal made a disgusted face. "Look in the mirror and ask yourself what kind of animal you are," he said sharply. "That house over there, where Gary Pretty lives. You see anyone go in or out of there?"

"I seen a lot of fucking useless cops over there," he said and spat on the ground.

Danny grimaced as the spittle just missed his boots. "Your name is…?"

"I haven't got to tell ye." He planted his feet and crossed his arms over his chest. "And yez can't make me."

The door to the house banged open and a woman appeared, wearing a quilted pink housecoat with an apron tied over it. She was short and wide, and her dark blond hair was pulled back in a sloppy ponytail. "Cyril, who's dat?"

"None of your fucking business," he replied without turning around. "Now get back in the fucking house or I'll fucking blind ye."

"You have an estimable vocabulary," Pascal commented. "Perhaps if you answer the question, we two will be on our way." The woman stayed where she was, watching them with a gimlet stare. "Did you see anyone coming or going from the Pretty house recently?"

"I seen Gary going—" The woman started to speak and was cut off by her husband.

"I told you to get in dat jeezly house!" He brandished the wrench. "I'll kill you."

"*Bon.*" Pascal whipped out a pair of handcuffs—from where, Danny didn't know; no one at the Kildevil Cove station had signed anything out to him—and caught hold of Cyril's left hand, twisting it neatly behind him, the wrist forced backwards at a painful angle.

"You can't arrest me!" Cyril struggled, but it was futile. Pascal was tall and thin, with a wiry strength.

"Have you seen anyone?" Pascal caught hold of the man's bound wrists and started dragging him towards the road.

"All right! Jesus!" He subsided, albeit reluctantly, and after a moment Pascal released him. "Mrs. Rice went in there, right?" He glowered at Danny and Pascal while massaging his wrists. "I'm going to sue the whole fuckin' crowd of ye for police brutality."

"You have not seen brutality," Pascal commented. "What is your full name and current address?"

"Cyril Brookings. I lives here."

"Thank you," Danny said. "Mr. Brookings, do you recall seeing anyone going into or coming out of Mr. Pretty's house in the past twenty-four hours?"

"I seen Mrs. Rice going in there this morning, bringing over bread and stuff. She treats him like he's frigging royalty, that one." Brookings lifted his filthy baseball cap and raked a hand through his greasy, thinning hair. "Then after she went, there was some fella in a pickup truck."

Danny pulled out his notebook. "What kind of a pickup truck?"

"One of them small ones. White, it was. Dirty. Of course, the roads around here are not fit. I don't know what we pays our taxes for."

"Did you see this man?" Pascal asked. "Or did he spring out of your imagination?"

"I seen him, all right?" Brookings replaced the baseball cap and tugged it down in front. "He was wearing a hoodie, though, with a baseball cap underneath it. Couldn't see his face on account of he had sunglasses on, them big ones."

"How tall? What age?" Danny glanced behind him to where the woman still stood on the doorstep, only now she'd produced a cigarette from somewhere and was struggling to light it from a book of paper matches.

"He was about your height," she called, pointing at Danny. "Skinny. He had raggedy old jeans on, and black shoes. Looked kind of dirty if you asks me."

"Nobody is asking you," her husband shot back. "Go in the goddamn house out of it."

"Had you seen this man around here before?" Pascal asked. He lit a cigarette and exhaled a long plume of smoke. "Is he a stranger to you?"

"He's not from here." Brookings glanced up at the sky. "I think you fellas should get in out of the weather. Gonna rain now the once."

Danny fished out one of his cards and handed it to him, although he had no doubt it would end up in the woodstove. "If you remember anything else, give me a call. That's my direct line."

Brookings squinted at it. "Oh, I heard tell of you. You're the one from St. John's. Married to a fella, aren't ye?" He leered. "Wonder how the crowd up in the Cove likes that."

Danny didn't reply to this. "Give me a call," he repeated, "if you see anything."

He and Pascal headed for the car, arriving just as the sky opened up. Danny unlocked the doors and they both tumbled in, grateful to have escaped a drenching. "I guess we'll put out an APB for this mysterious man," he commented, starting the car, "just in case anyone else saw anything."

"If he even exists," Pascal said. He glanced over at Danny while fastening his seat belt. "You are *homosexuel*?" His tone was casual, but Danny guessed the intention was anything but.

"Bisexual," Danny replied evenly. He wasn't about to get into a fight with Pascal about his orientation. "And yes, I have a husband. His name is Tadhg Heaney. Is that going to be a problem?"

Pascal gave another of his elegant Gallic shrugs. "Why would it be?" He gazed at Danny for a moment, as if wondering what else to say, and Danny sensed there was more the Quebecois wanted to add. In the end, Pascal said nothing.

JUNE CARBAGE met them both in the break room as Danny was making coffee for himself and Pascal. He explained what Cyril Brookings and his wife had said, but June wasn't convinced.

"I went to high school with him," she said. "Half of what comes out of his mouth is lies."

"Did Bobbi get back to you about the flash drive yet?" Danny asked. "The one you found in Amalie's car." The Keurig machine finished its business, chortling and gurgling, and he handed the first cup to Pascal. "Cream in the fridge there and sugar on the table."

"That's what I wanted to see you about," June replied. She glanced over to where Pascal was rooting through the fridge and said in a low voice, "How was he?"

"Good," Danny said. "Why do you ask?"

"I've some information for you." Her gaze swivelled to Pascal again. "But not here. In private." In a normal tone she continued, "She did. Apparently, everything on there is legitimate, but I haven't had time to go through it yet. There are a lot of individual files."

"How about we call a briefing and have a look through some of them?" Danny gestured at the Keurig, but June shook her head. "Just the ones you've seen so far. I want to see what the others think." He glanced up as Pascal approached. "Coffee okay?"

"Yes, it is very good. Listen, I am wondering if there is perhaps a small space you could loan me. Just enough to put a desk and chair? I have my own laptop computer, so that is no problem."

"I'm sure Marilyn can set you up with something. It might not be much, but...." Maybe the station should have office space set aside for personnel visiting from other jurisdictions. "Marilyn can set you up." He wondered how long Pascal was going to be with them. Did he not have other cases to pursue in Quebec?

"A little room somewhere, a *petit* desk and chair, you know, something like this."

"Marilyn can set you up," Danny repeated.

"But it's only a small matter. Even a broom closet would do." Pascal moved so he was standing closer. "Me, I don't need much. A room, a desk—"

"Yes, all *right*," Danny snapped. He turned away, intending to speak to June, and saw that Pascal was smirking.

The bastard had been baiting him on purpose.

The briefing yielded nothing much, which was as Danny had expected. The flash drive June had discovered in Amalie Caron's car contained more than fifty separate video files, each at least five minutes long. She'd only had time to examine ten, but "They're all alike: a young boy being threatened by the same male figure, who himself never appears onscreen." Even Pascal, who knew more about Amalie than any of them, was perplexed.

"I don't know why she has this," he said. "She appears nowhere in the films. Is it her boy?"

June had obtained a copy of Joseph's most recent school photo and projected it onto the screen. "It's difficult to tell. The boy in these videos is never in clear view, at least not the ones I've seen so far. The verbal and physical abuse is the same just about every time. It's like they're acting from a script."

"Could someone else have planted it in her car?" Kevin asked. "As deliberate misdirection?"

Danny sucked air through his teeth, considering. "Doesn't seem likely," he said finally. "We might be reaching."

"Agreed." Cillian Riley nodded. "That flash drive could belong to anyone at all. Maybe Amalie didn't put it there. Maybe she didn't even know it was there."

"I'll go through the rest of the videos," June said, "and see what else is there before I log it into evidence."

"Did we get anything else from Marine Atlantic?" Danny asked. "We have Mrs. Caron on camera in the departures area but no proof she even got on the ferry."

"I've been through the passenger manifest," Riley said. "Her name is there. It looks like she did board the boat for the mainland, but where she went after that isn't clear." He turned to Pascal. "Would she return to Quebec, do you think?"

"Not unless she is very brave," Pascal replied, "or extremely stupid. The *Sûreté* is looking for her also. She would be stopped no matter where she landed." He shook his head. "This woman is not stupid, okay? She is very intelligent, has a lot of what you call cunning. Anything she does is to confuse us and throw us off."

"The video I got on my computer"—he nodded at Constable Dougie Hughes—"any luck finding out where that came from?"

"Not so far, sir. No IP address, so I've no way of tracking down the provider. She could have used any public computer anywhere." Hughes looked apologetic. "It was shot on an older iPhone in Night Mode, which is no help at all."

"If she was torturing her husband in a root cellar," Kevin mused, "then presumably she couldn't be boarding a ferry for the mainland." He glanced around at the others. "Right?"

"She could have recorded that video anywhere," Hughes told them.

Constable Sarah Avery spoke up. "Sure, wouldn't you be able to tell from the video properties? All that information should be there."

"Not if she stripped out the EXIF data," Hughes responded, "and that's easy enough to do."

"EXIF?" Now Danny was really confused.

"Exchangeable Image File Format, sir. It's all encoded in the photo or video. You can click on it and see where the video was made and when."

"But it can be removed."

"Yes," Hughes confirmed. "Too easily, sir."

Well, he hadn't actually expected anything different. "All right, keep trying. Any little bit of information is useful, even if there's something encoded in the video file itself."

Hughes nodded. "Will do."

June caught hold of Danny's sleeve as he was leaving the room and pulled him aside. "I wanted to talk to you about Inspector Pascal," she said.

"Right, yes. You said."

"I did a little bit of checking up on him. Sir, he's not what he claims to be."

"He's not French?" He couldn't resist teasing her.

June refused to take the bait. "Of course the *Sûreté* wouldn't get into the finer details, but...." She glanced around to make certain they weren't being overheard. "He is under internal investigation by the BEI—the *Bureau des enquêtes indépendantes*—for corruption."

CHAPTER EIGHT

Wednesday evening

IT WAS well past six by the time Danny finally made it home. Lily heard the door open and came to meet him, Easter on her heels. In the past couple of years, she had grown out of the coltish awkwardness of early puberty and into a poised, inward-looking young woman. A lot of her natural ebullience—a quality Danny loved—had disappeared, been tamed into a more mature sensibility. He missed it, missed the old Lily, the one who liked to jump from the third or fourth stair up and land on him, giggling madly when they both fell over. Nowadays, she was apt to respond to his questions with a shrug, or worse, a cold stare.

"You're late," she said now. There were dark circles under her eyes, as if she hadn't been getting enough sleep. "You should have been home ages ago." She moved to take his laptop and car keys.

"I apologise." He toed off his shoes and left them on the mat.

"Dad's making fish and brewis. It's almost ready." She laid the keys and the computer on the little hall table and crossed her arms on her chest. "You look like shite, Danny." She peered at him, her head tilted to the side.

"Thank you very much." He wasn't in the mood for her scrutiny. "Don't you have homework?"

"I did it dinnertime." She was still staring at him.

"What, Lily?" He bent to scratch Easter behind the ears and was rewarded for his efforts with a flurry of licks.

"Dad will tell you." She turned and went back upstairs, leaving him puzzled and irritated. Bloody teenagers!

He went down the hall to the kitchen, which was located at the back of the renovated biscuit-box house he and Tadhg had purchased together shortly before their marriage. The house had been a point of some contention: Danny wanted it restored to its former glory, but Tadhg insisted on a complete remodel. After much wrangling, they'd managed a compromise. The sitting room and the bedrooms were returned to their nineteenth-century grandeur, while the kitchen was stripped to the wall studs and remade in the spare Nordic style Tadhg preferred. Since he did most of the cooking, Danny figured it was only fair.

He found his husband standing over the huge Wolf gas range, stirring something in a cast iron frying pan while the smell of seared pork fat filled the air. Scruncheons, Danny thought, the delicious little squares of rendered fatback that would be poured over boiled salt cod and softened hardtack to make fish and brewis.

"Glad you're home." Tadhg reached out an arm and pulled him close to his side, pressing his face into Danny's neck. "Christ, ye smell like detective work."

Danny laughed. "I'm tired and I'm starving and my knees hurt. Can ye behave yourself for once, bhoy?"

"Ye wouldn't love me if I did, sure." Tadhg turned his face to kiss him. "How's it going? Any luck finding that missus yet?"

"*Pfft.*" Danny made an irritated noise. "Mind, now, God only knows where she's after getting to." He pulled away and went to the liquor cabinet to fetch out a bottle of Glenfiddich and bring it back into the kitchen. "Give us a couple of glasses."

Tadhg frowned. "Sure we're going to eat supper now the once."

"Tadhg." It wasn't quite a whine. "For the love of Christ." He splashed a healthy measure of the clear amber liquid into a glass and downed it all at once, savouring the warm burn it made on the way down. "Lily said you had something to tell me."

Tadhg drew a slow breath. "There's a letter for you." He went to fetch it from the kitchen cubbyhole they used for bills and important papers and laid it on the table in front of Danny. It was postmarked in the United Kingdom, and the return address read Canolfan Rheidol, Rhodfa Padarn, Aberystwyth. Danny knew immediately what it was—a reply to his letter of enquiry from a couple of months ago, requesting information from the local registry of births, deaths, and marriages in Aberystwyth. He'd done a similar search of the Newfoundland records to obtain a copy of his own birth certificate, only to be told a recent computer virus had wiped it and thousands of others from the government server. The young female clerk who reported this to him in a phone call sounded genuinely sorry and told him they were working to retrieve the lost data and would he like a return call when his documents had been discovered?

"Aren't you going to open it?" Tadhg asked. He pulled out a chair and sat down. "Do you want me to do it?"

"No, I...." He picked up the envelope and turned it over. How many pairs of hands had it passed through in its journey across the sea? He reached for the bottle and poured another slug of whiskey into his glass, then necked the whole works at once.

"Are ye hoping to drink it open?" Tadhg nodded at it. "Go on, my love. Open it."

He held the envelope up to the light, then tapped the contents down and tore off the end. The single sheet of paper slid out easily, and he read its message with a glance. "A thorough search of the records shows no entry for an Angharad Davies at any time in the twentieth century." He had suspected it would be this way. The story his sister, Sandra, had told him about his birth mother was far too pat and contrived to be true. "She lied to me. Sandra lied."

"But... why would she?" Tadhg took the letter from his hand. "She'd have no reason to. It's nothing to do with her if you...." He glanced over the single sheet of paper. "I don't understand why she'd do something like that."

Danny stood up, walked a half dozen uncertain steps towards the dining room, then turned and came back again. "Neither do I." He pinched the skin above his nose with two fingers. "What reason could she have?"

"Why don't ye call her?" Tadhg got up and came to him, wrapped an arm around his shoulders, and pulled him close. "Instead of speculating, just ask."

"What time's it in Portugal?"

"Around ten, ten thirty, I guess." Tadhg's overseas travel had diminished since his earlier days, when he routinely flew between countries in search of business deals. His relationship with Danny and their recent marriage had turned him into a homebody, a man who preferred the life they'd built for themselves to anything the outside world could give him.

"I'll call her."

Tadhg steered him gently towards the table. "Have something to eat first. You've probably been running on fumes all day."

Lily was summoned from upstairs, but Tadhg had to call her three times, and they were a good twenty minutes into the meal before she appeared. The supper Tadhg had cooked was delicious. Danny fed tiny bits of hardtack to the dog under the table, while Lily sat in a contemplative silence, picking at her supper and seeming miles away. Danny was waiting for the kettle to boil for tea when his mobile phone rang.

It was Cillian Riley. "Danny, one of the local fishermen got something in his nets. They hauled it aboard."

"Got something?" Whales and other sea mammals became entangled in fishing gear. Best scenario, they were rescued by the Department of Fisheries and Oceans. Sadly, some of them perished. He really hoped the latter wasn't the case this time. But Riley wouldn't call Danny for a trapped sea creature, surely. "And?"

"It's a body."

THE TINY motel room in Winterton hadn't improved in the hours since Blaise Pascal last left it. The walls were still covered in the same dingy brown wallpaper with its barely discernible pattern of pears and branches; the bed still sagged in the middle; the filthy carpet still smelled like other people's feet. He propped the front door open to the sound of the rain and wondered about a visit to the extremely convenient liquor store just down the road. With a few belts of strong whiskey inside him, the room wouldn't smell, and the irritating noise of rubber tires on wet pavement wouldn't bother him nearly as much.

His mobile phone rang as he was digging in his pockets for his debit card: Prud'Homme. He thumbed the green circle to accept the call. "*Salut*, Prud'Homme. *Qu'est-ce qui se passe?*"

"There is plenty going on," Prud'Homme confirmed in English. "Not all of it is good, however."

Pascal fumbled out a cigarette and lit it. "*Quoi?*"

A certain investigator from the Bureau des enquêtes indépendantes had rung three times in the past two days, Prud'Homme told him, looking for Pascal. She was most insistent that he return her calls in the matter of an ongoing investigation. "She asked where you were, but I didn't tell her anything."

"*Bon.* That's very good. Keep putting her off. I can't be bothered with her at the moment." He drew on his cigarette. "Besides, her voice reminds me of my ex-wife."

Prud'Homme laughed. "I never met the lady."

"Then give thanks to *le bon Dieu*," Pascal said. "No, what I am doing here is too important to leave." He grinned to himself. "I bet no one even misses me."

There was a long pause. "I miss you," Prud'Homme said finally. Then, aware that his declaration had likely embarrassed them both, he hurried on. "Nathalie has been promising to have one of those parties where she will tell us the sex of the unborn child. Mon Dieu, you'd think it was the second coming of the Christ child." Nathalie was the departmental secretary; Pascal liked her, but a gender reveal party wasn't exactly within his purview. "I told her you have important work to do in Terre-Neuve, and she asked if you were catching fish."

"Keep me informed, will you?"

"*Oui, bien sûr*. Of course I will." He paused. "What makes you think you will find Amalie Caron?"

"I have to." The enormity of what he'd promised to do—to find Amalie Caron and bring her to justice—felt like a leaden shroud about his shoulders. "She cannot be allowed to escape this time. She has already killed."

"Someone there? In Terre-Neuve?"

"Yes."

"Fuck." Prud'Homme huffed out a breath. "Well, be careful. I will do my best to keep the BEI at bay, but I can't keep them off of you forever."

"I know." Pascal smiled. Prud'Homme was such a loyal friend. He was grateful to have him. "Goodbye, now."

He rang off and his stomach growled. When had he last eaten? There always seemed to be food in the break room at the small police station, but nothing appealed. Someone had earlier pushed a brochure through his door showing the menu and prices of the small restaurant attached to the motel, so he decided to chance it and went next door to buy a bowl of homemade soup with fresh bread. He'd left his mobile on the table; it was ringing when he returned.

The call was from the Centre for Child and Adolescent Psychiatry, and he answered it at once. Ignoring it was not an option. "Blaise Pascal."

"Monsieur, I am the charge nurse on your son's unit. I regret there has been an incident."

He froze, hearing nothing for a moment but the swishing of blood in his ears. "*Quoi?*"

"Your son, Théodore, has taken an overdose of his medication."

For a moment he wasn't entirely sure he was hearing her correctly. "Overdose." He sat down at the table and reached out to remove the plastic lid from the bowl of soup he'd bought. "My son." There was a spoon in a little clear sleeve, impossible to open one-handed, so he gave up and tossed it onto the table. "How...?"

"We think he has been saving his pills. He did not answer when we did room checks earlier today, and a member of staff found him unresponsive."

Mon Dieu.... Théodore. No point in asking the boy what had occurred because Théo refused to speak to him or anyone, ever. In the very early days after the fire, he had lain under heavy sedation in Montreal Children's Hospital, suffering third-degree burns over 70 percent of his body. "It isn't the pain, monsieur," the attending physician explained. "Third-degree burns don't hurt, because the nerves are destroyed." The outcome had been extremely uncertain, and for a long time he didn't know if Théodore would live. He'd sat vigil beside his child's bed, ignoring the pain of his own burns and refusing medical help until the staff had finally given in and treated him where he was. His own scars would never fade, but he didn't mind. Some things were worth remembering, if only to arm oneself against the future.

"Is he...?" He swallowed, his mouth dry as dust. "What did... *il est mort?*" Of course the boy was dead. Found unresponsive, she said. If not dead, then in a coma, perhaps irreversible. It was the normal outcome of such things, and he'd seen it before in his line of work. Too often. He'd picked them up off the streets downtown, on rue St-Jacques and Place D'Youville, those whom life had trampled under.

"*Non, monsieur.* He has pulled through."

The breath went out of him in a sudden gust. "Did he say anything?"

"*Non, monsieur.*" He nodded even though she couldn't see him. Went on nodding, his head bobbing like a demented Bonhomme, unable to speak, as willfully mute now as Théodore. "Are you coming to see him?"

Coming to see him? The boy refused to speak or acknowledge him in any way, as if the fire and its concomitant effects were his fault... as if everything was Pascal's fault. "What good will that do?"

He pressed the red circle to disconnect, ending the call. The bowl of soup sat in front of him, steam coiling up from its surface, but he had little appetite. He pushed it away and went to start the shower in the tiny bathroom, but the water was barely a trickle, and his scars itched and burned because of the cheap, evil-smelling soap. The red, inflamed skin existed always as a reminder of that awful morning, waking up after a double shift, exhausted, and smelling smoke. Then stumbling out of bed to find the small apartment engulfed in flames, and Théodore....

Well.

He shut off the pitiful stream of water and dried himself with one of two thin towels, the texture like sandpaper. Maybe tomorrow he would look around for somewhere better to stay, perhaps a tourist house or an empty flat to rent, someplace already fully furnished, with proper linens, and he'd cook his own meals. And a closet with real hangers where he could put his clothes instead of stacking them like *beignets* in a corner—

"Inspector Pascal."

The voice came from a dark corner of the room, and he startled violently, then saw it was the Englishman from the police station. "*Tabarnak*! What the hell do you mean, hiding over there? You could give me a heart attack."

The Englishman's eyes—what was his name, again? O'Reilly? O'Regan?—skated over his body, lingering on the burn scars, and Pascal realised he was only wearing a towel. *Fuck*. So much for his dignity.

"Danny asked me to come fetch you. We tried calling, but you weren't answering your mobile." He nodded at it, still on the table where Pascal had left it.

"I was in the shower." He held on to the towel with a death grip. "What do you want?"

"Some local fishermen found a dead body in their nets." The Englishman—Riley—came forward into the light. "Inspector Quirke asked me to fetch you on the off chance it might be Gerard Caron."

A LIGHT drizzle had begun to fall when Danny arrived at Kildevil Cove's government wharf. A single fishing boat, the *Silver Seas*, was pulled up alongside, its motor idling, while the crew gathered on deck. The net and its contents had been heaved onto the wharf, and Harry Dean, the boat's captain, stood looking down at it.

"Harry, good to see you again." Danny shook his hand.

"Not the best circumstances," Dean replied. He was about forty, stocky and handsome; his stoic expression didn't quite hide the evidence of his distress. "I'm after seeing a lot, but nothing like this. Lord Jesus, bhoy." He turned away, shaking his head.

"Where were you?" Danny asked. He didn't bother to crouch down to look, not trusting his painful knees to bring him back up again, but instead leaned over to examine the corpse.

"We was way down in the Flemish Cap, bhoy." Dean maintained his distance from the body. "Hauling our nets and one of the boys seen something in the water. First thing I thought it was a whale. They gets theirselves caught up."

"No." Danny pulled out a flashlight and trained it on the trussed bundle. "Not a whale." He played the light over what remained of the facial features, the nose and lips worn off, the forehead abraded due to contact with the ocean floor. It was impossible to tell if the corpse had been male or female. "Wrapped up tight, though." It wasn't unheard of for a body to be pulled aboard in a fishing net. He straightened and put the flashlight away. "How did you call it in?"

"We uses the ELOG," Dean replied, referring to the electronic log book system most commercial fishermen used to report their catches to the Department of Fisheries and Oceans.

"Do you know who it is?"

"What?" Dean gazed at him in stunned silence, and Danny realised how stupid it sounded. The corpse was barely recognisable as human. "No, bhoy," he said finally, "I don't know who that is, and I wants nothing to do with it. Now see here. I done you fellas a favour by calling this in—"

"Calm down," Danny said, interrupting him. "Nobody's accusing you of anything." He glanced towards the crew, still gathered on deck and watching the proceedings with interest. "Any of you know this person?" There was suddenly a great deal of mumbling and several men turned away, disavowing any knowledge of the corpse. "Anybody?"

Whoever the poor soul was, it probably wasn't Gerard Caron. The body was much smaller, didn't have Caron's height or breadth of shoulder. The remains appeared completely genderless, mediocre in size and shape, the face an empty, flat oval. He realised with a sinking feeling that identifying the body might be close to impossible, given its condition.

"That's nothing to do with we." A young, ginger-haired man hopped onto the wharf. "You wants to bring charges, ye can go right ahead, see?" He advanced on Danny, fists clenched. "It got nothing to do with we."

Danny wondered if he'd have to knock him on his arse or if the fisherman would see sense and back off before it was too late, but then one of the station's patrol cars pulled up and stopped, disgorging Cillian Riley and Blaise Pascal. Pascal looked angrier than usual, as if Riley had interrupted him in the middle of something important. He nodded to Danny as he approached but didn't speak.

"So this is the catch of the day?" Riley asked. He crouched beside the netted body and peered at it. "What's the story?"

"Nothing to do with these guys," Danny said. The man who'd been advancing on him dropped his fists and retreated. "Turn that engine off," he told Harry Dean. "This boat is now a crime scene."

DR. REGAN Lampe peered owlishly at the bloated, faceless corpse resting on her autopsy table in the morgue in Carbonear General Hospital and shook her head. Given what Danny knew of her, she was probably frowning underneath her blue surgical mask, but it couldn't be helped. It was barely seven in the morning, the day after the remains had been hauled aboard the *Silver Seas* by Harry Dean's crew, and nobody was quite awake yet.

"I didn't know where else to take him," he said defensively. "Her. Them. They don't do autopsies in Old Perlican."

"Who is it?" Regan asked.

"No idea," Danny replied. "There was no ID on the body, and they were hauled up in a fishing net just inside the Flemish Cap." Sarah Avery and Dougie Hughes had both gone over the list of missing persons for Newfoundland and the rest of the country, but their efforts were no help at all. The body was so degraded that it looked barely human.

Regan muttered something in Inuktitut that sounded suspiciously like a swear word. "All right," she agreed. "But don't expect miracles. Best case, I can give you a cause of death and any underlying disease, comorbidities, but that's about it. This body is so beat up it looks like it's been through a tumble dryer."

They stood gazing down at the corpse in silence. Who had this been, in life, Danny wondered? Did the person have breasts? If so, there remained no evidence of them. If the individual had been assigned male at birth, there would probably have been a penis, but there was no sign of that either. Regan picked a scalpel off the tray at her side and made a long, straight cut from the pubic bone to the base of the throat, extending the incision first to the left and then to the right, as far as the tips of the shoulders. A wet, turgid smell, not unlike raw meat, rose from the body, and Danny pressed his lips together beneath his mask, tongue firmly against the roof of his mouth. He wasn't necessarily squeamish where death was concerned, but the first cut always jarred him.

Blaise Pascal, standing a small distance away, gestured at the corpse. "What do you think killed them?"

She turned to look at him, then back to Danny, her dark eyes gleaming with scorn.

"Inspector Blaise Pascal," he told her, "*Sûreté du Québec*. He's involved in the investigation."

"Oh," Regan said after a moment. "I didn't think he was here for the poutine."

Pascal bristled. "Why it is always these joke about poutine with you people? Perhaps you eat too many codfish, you." Obviously he was angry; his English was taking a beating. It took next to nothing to piss him off, yet this guy was a career police officer. How the hell did he get anything done with such a hair-trigger temper?

"Maybe they drowned," she snapped. "They were found in the water." She turned her back on him and moved to spread the flesh of the chest apart, using her scalpel to slice through subcutaneous fat and muscle. "In good physical shape," she remarked. "Excellent muscular development and not much fat." She reached with her free hand to palpate the muscles of the shoulders and upper arms. "A rower, probably. Somebody comfortable in boats at the very least. Or comfortable in the gym."

"Perhaps," Pascal said, "he was not too fond of poutine."

Regan's eyes flashed. "Does he have to be here?" she asked Danny.

"He does," Pascal replied. He refrained from further comment, however, and watched silently as Regan's scalpel moved to free the skin from the underlying structures, scoring each side of the chest plate. She leaned in close, examining the pectoral muscles and the armpits.

"Whoa." Regan drew back, turning to gaze at Danny. "That's unexpected."

"What is it?" It all looked like raw meat to him.

"Right here." She pointed with a gloved finger to an area just inside the corpse's left armpit. "I can't be entirely sure, given the degradation of the body, but that looks like the remnants of a hemorrhagic tumour." Regan stepped back slightly and shook her head. "Mind you, I'm not certain. Think I'll biopsy the cells for pathology." She sounded as if she were talking to herself. "Definitely hemorrhagic. Stained the chest wall. Relatively intact too, so that's good."

"Regan?"

"Don't take this as a guarantee," she said, ", but...." She dropped the scalpel into a kidney-shaped steel tray and used both hands to gesture at the open section of the corpse's chest wall. "Breast cancer. Possible modified mastectomy. Maybe radical, but that's open for debate." She drew a slow breath. "Men can have breast cancer, of course, but this was probably a woman. Any missing women around here that you've been looking for?"

Danny stared at her. "A woman," he repeated. "Are you serious?" It wasn't so much that she'd washed up in a fishing net—body disposal at sea wasn't usually gender-specific—but most specimens found in such a manner were men. Unless, he amended silently, human trafficking was involved. He would never forget the young woman he'd found dead on a Kildevil Cove beach a year or so previous, tattooed with the ownership mark of her traffickers, another victim of monsters for whom human life had no value beyond that of a commodity. "Amalie Caron is missing—absconded, most likely—but I don't think this is her." The corpse was unusually beaten up, as dead bodies tended to get when exposed to sea water and tumbled about by ocean currents.

"A close-up look at the skull will tell me more," Regan said. "Men usually have bigger heads than women—not always, but it's a place to start. And the bones would be thicker. Either way, the pelvis will tell me for sure."

"So you think this person is *une femme*?" Pascal edged closer to the table, peering down at the flayed corpse.

Regan fixed him with a look. "It remains to be seen." She would not commit until she finished the autopsy, Danny knew. She gestured at the table with her chin. "Move back. You're in my way."

She reached for a small electric saw that reminded Danny of the immersion blender Tadhg used whenever he was making fancy soup. A touch of a switch and the room filled with a high-pitched electrical whine, rather like a dentist's drill. Danny knew by now to establish distance; even though corpses didn't bleed, a body that had been in the water for any amount of time was bound to have retained fluid in the pleural cavity, and he wasn't keen on being splashed. He and Pascal watched silently as Regan sawed through the ribs at either side, then reached underneath with her scalpel to free the structure from the underlying tissues. Finally, she lifted away the chest plate like someone taking the lid off a cooking pot. It wasn't the usual order of events for most autopsies—normally a medical examiner would open the skull first—but Regan did things her own way.

"Wow," she said after a moment.

"Now what?" Danny leaned closer. "What is it?"

"Excellent heart," Regan replied, "at least on initial inspection. I'll know more once I get it out of there. Lungs look great too." She glanced at Danny. "If this was a woman—and I really do think it was—then she was an athlete."

"Where the hell did she come from?" It was a rhetorical question. The woman was as much of an enigma now as she'd been initially. "How long was she in the water, do you think?"

A thorough soaking in the concentrated brine of the North Atlantic hadn't done her any aesthetic favours. It would take something like dental records to identify her unless her fingerprints were still viable.

"I'd say possibly a week," Regan said, pointing to the dead woman's hand, "maybe more. There's extreme gloving of the fingers and toes." The sloughing of skin from the extremities usually occurred when a body had been in the water anywhere from three to seven days, depending on water temperature.

"Any chance of getting a fingerprint?" Danny asked. From his vantage point it didn't look promising, but there had been numerous advances in thanatopractical processing in recent years, including the injection of fluids from other regions of the body in order to restore tissue tenseness and volume. The fingerprints in such a case would pop up, allowing investigators to take casts and identify the victim that way. There were even funeral homes that did it if they had a certified embalmer on staff.

Regan shrugged. "Hard to say." She lifted one of the dead woman's hands and peered at it. "Usually if there's penetration damage to the depth of one millimetre, the fingerprints are gone, and there's no skin left on this woman's fingers at all."

"If she's been immersed in sea water for a week—"

"I said *possibly* a week," Regan snapped, interrupting him, "maybe more. Adipocere takes at least five weeks to form in sea water, so if it was present—which it isn't—that would provide a useful timeline." She probed the heart with a fingertip. "Damn fine organ," she murmured. "Let's have a look at the skull." Moving swiftly, she traced a hemispheric cut from the left ear to the right, crossing the apex of the skull, and peeled the scalp down over the face.

Danny sensed Blaise Pascal shifting uncomfortably just behind him. "*Calisse de Tabarnak*," the Quebecois murmured.

"If you're going to be sick, do it over there." Regan pointed to the opposite corner of the room, where a drain was fitted into the floor. She gazed at the front portion of the dead woman's skull, then said, "Give me a hand to flip her over."

Pascal backed away, clearly unwilling to have any contact with the corpse, so Danny was left to do the work by himself. He got both hands under the dead woman, one on her back and the other beneath her knees and, while Regan pulled from the opposite side of the table, turned her onto her stomach. She was heavier than he expected, and for a horrible second or two, it seemed she might slip from his grasp, but with Regan's practised hand guiding him, she seemed to tumble effortlessly through space. Then Regan duplicated the process she'd performed on the front of the head, pulling down the flap of scalp to reveal the skull.

"Holy shit," she said.

Danny didn't have to ask what she meant. He could clearly see the two entry wounds made by gunshots in the back of the dead woman's head. "Cause of death," he commented. "Organised crime, most likely. It's typical." He stood to the side as Pascal approached the table.

"Can you retrieve these bullets?" Pascal asked.

"Shouldn't be a problem," Regan replied. "It won't get us any closer to identifying her, but you'll be able to tell what kind of gun they came from. I've got some other things to do here, so I'll courier them over to you. Or you can send someone to get them." She glanced at Danny. "Just don't ask me to bring them to you. I'm too damn busy."

"I'll see if Annie Turnbull can take a look at her mouth. Might get something from that, and we might not." He made a mental note to contact Dr. Turnbull, the only forensic odontologist on the Avalon Peninsula. If the stars aligned in his favour, there were dental records that could help identify the dead woman, and Danny had already taken a DNA swab. Regan would run a full toxicology screen on the blood, which would hopefully illuminate the presence of any drugs or poisons.

"All right," Danny said, stripping off the paper gown, "I'll wait to hear from you." There was no need to stay throughout the entire process, and Regan wouldn't thank him for hovering. She was extremely good at what she did, but she was not a people person. He could tell that having him and Pascal in the room while she conducted the postmortem was irritating her.

"Did you have breakfast yet?" Danny asked once he and Pascal were outside. It was a glorious day, warm and sunny, and he was starving.

"*Non.*" Pascal took out a cigarette and fitted it into the corner of his mouth to light it. The flame of his cigarette lighter flared up violently, nearly searing the tip of his nose, but the man didn't even blink. *You should see the scars*, Riley had told Danny after fetching Pascal the night before. *He's been badly burned, all down one side of his torso. House fire, I'd say, if I was a betting man.* "Are you hungry?"

"Famished," Danny admitted. "Gut-foundered." He grinned at Pascal's confused expression. "Local parlance," he said. "Never mind."

Fifteen minutes later they were seated at a table next to the window in the Famish Gut Diner and Pub on Water Street, waiting on a full breakfast—what Danny's Scottish grandmother called a fry-up. Pascal had gone outside to smoke and returned with his mobile phone held to his ear.

"A hospital in Quebec City," he explained once he'd ended the call. "My son, Théodore, he is not very well. I am checking on him."

"I'm sorry to hear that." Danny kept his expression neutral, worried about offending the Quebecois, who seemed to be offended by just about everything. "But he is being cared for?"

"*Oui*, he is." The waiter appeared with their breakfast, and Pascal didn't speak again until the man had set down the plates and gone. "He has been in there for a long time. The nurse called me last evening—" He fell abruptly silent, turning his gaze on the opposite wall.

"What is it?" Danny asked. He remembered Cillian Riley had tried to get hold of Pascal the previous evening, when Harry Dean's crew had reported hauling the body aboard, but he'd proven difficult to reach. In the end, Riley had gone to Pascal's motel room to find him. "Is he okay?"

Pascal pulled a handful of napkins out of the metal dispenser on the table, many more than he would need. "He has taken an overdose of his medication." One of his hands clenched itself into a fist, fingers so tightly curled that the knuckles shone white through the skin.

Oh, Christ, Danny thought. He wondered why Pascal was here and not in Quebec. "Is there anything I can do to help? Arrange your flight for you?" The moment the words were out of his mouth. he knew he'd really stepped in it.

Pascal pulled his dark eyebrows down until they met in the middle. "I am not going anywhere." He reached for the sugar dispenser and dumped a fair amount into his coffee. "I will not help him by being there. He does not speak. He will not speak to me." He stared moodily into his cup and then gulped some coffee. "My son was burned in a fire when he was ten years old. It destroyed both of his hands."

"I'm sorry." He seemed to be repeating himself.

Pascal didn't look at him. "Théodore was good at music, and he planned to study piano in New York City, but after that...." He waved his free hand in the air. "*Pffft*. All gone. He stopped speaking to me, to anyone."

Danny wondered how anyone could bear such a profound loss, but perhaps Pascal's work helped him to forget. "Does he speak to his mother?"

Pascal put down his coffee and picked up his knife and fork. "My ex-wife had to go away for a while." He ate a portion of his eggs, chewing savagely, then said, "A long while." A glance at Danny across the table. "Attempted murder carries a hard sentence in this country."

Mother of God. "Did she give a reason?" Burning down the family home while your husband and son were in it involved some high-level rage. Arson of that type was always deeply personal.

"I...." Pascal made a show of putting jam on his toast. "She never told me." He wouldn't meet Danny's eyes, probably realising that Danny suspected the lie. "But life, she goes on."

Danny started to say something, was interrupted by a call from Bobbi Lambert on his mobile. "Bobbi, what's on the go?"

"That body Harry Dean fished up," she said. "Regan sent over the personal effects, and we found something interesting in the pocket of her slacks."

"Oh?"

"Trust me." Bobbi sounded adamant. "You'll want to see this."

CHAPTER NINE

Thursday

THE HOTEL room in Montreal was smaller than Amalie was used to, but it would do for now, and anyway it wasn't like she was in a position to complain. The boy had been quiet all night, thanks to the strong cough syrup she'd given him, and she was confident he'd furnish her no trouble. He hadn't had one of his troublesome nosebleeds either. He'd had one the day she left her car off to have the tires rotated, but since she hadn't planned on returning for it, she'd decided not to try to clean it up. One more thing to confuse the police and put them off their game.

Her careful planning had, as always, brought them to where she needed to be with the authorities none the wiser. She had found an older woman who needed money and used a story about a daring escape from an abusive spouse to induce her to take the boy to the airport and escort him to the gate, claiming to be his *grandmère*. But then she had slipped him away while others were boarding and brought him to meet Amalie, who had made sure she was seen buying a ticket for the Marine Atlantic ferry in Port-des-Basques but also slipped away before boarding. She had driven a rental car to St. Barbe and taken the car ferry to Blanc Sablon, Quebec. Easy as that. For now, at least, *le flic* had no way of knowing where she and the boy were.

It was just after seven, but she had been awake since daylight, sleeping only in fits and starts for an hour or two at a time, always wary of footsteps in the corridor. She sat on the edge of the bed and shook him by the shoulder.

"Wake up, *mon petit*! Today we ride the big wheel."

The boy rolled onto his back and murmured something in his sleep. Were he a more attractive child, she might well be able to summon a particle of maternal love, but he was as ugly as he was stupid, and she bitterly resented being saddled with him. Hopefully that would no longer be a problem if all went according to plan. The previous night she'd gone to three separate Jean Coutu stores and bought as many packets of sinus medication as they'd allow her, then squirrelled them away in the bottom drawer of the hotel bureau against the day when she'd need them.

"Wake up!" She shook him more violently this time, and he hit out at her with his hands.

"Ow! *Maman*, what are you doing?" He scowled, scrunching his face up and trying to burrow back underneath the covers. She grabbed hold of the duvet and tore it off the bed, then flung it across the room. He stared at her, dark eyes like obstinate marbles in his pale face. She was reasonably sure he hated her as well.

"Get up, I said." She wasn't in the mood to put up with his nonsense, not today. This was too important. "Get out of that bed, you little bastard, and go take a shower. You stink." Children generally repulsed her, but small boys were the worst. She fancied they always smelled of spit and bubble gum, a certain odour that clung to them no matter how much they were bathed, and she'd bathed this one plenty.

He slid off the bed and went into the bathroom, and after a moment she could hear him pissing. "Make sure you flush, you fucking mongrel." Goddamn little *salaud*. What had she ever done to deserve him? Children were supposed to be a blessing, but this one was more like a curse. "And wash your shitty ass!" The toilet flushed, and then she heard him turning on the shower. "You stay in there ten minutes. I am going to set the timer." It was how she did things at home. She assigned tasks and gave him a strict time limit. If he failed to perform the task in the time allotted, he was punished. It wasn't cruel, but simply the way things had to be. He would learn when he got out into the wider world that he had certain duties and obligations—*if* he got out into the wider world. She was still undecided, had not yet written the ending to their story. Certain things depended on how matters progressed from here, this particular day. If all went well, she would be free of the child by nightfall.

While he washed, she set about firming up the day's agenda. Today they were going to the Old Port of Montreal, where they would visit the Science Centre and the clock tower before a picnic on the beach at lunchtime. After lunch she would take him to ride *La Grande roue*, the massive Ferris wheel overlooking the St. Lawrence River. Later, perhaps when her final piece of business was done, she would treat herself to a session at the Bota Bota spa, the perfect *denouement*.

She crossed to the small table set against the wall and picked up the stack of addressed envelopes she'd placed there earlier that morning, checking that each bore the proper amount of postage required to get it to its destination, and one other item—a padded brown envelope she had already filled and sealed. It was important to make certain everything was done that needed to be done. Where she was going, no one could follow; this last portion of her journey was a trip she needed to take alone.

Are you certain? she asked herself, holding the gaze of her reflection in the mirror. *There is no return.* Sometimes the most perfect revenge was not a dish served cold, but one served so burning hot that it seared both the palate and the soul. She saw things differently now, with new eyes, and understood what she had to do.

The bathroom door banged open, the handle slamming into the wall, and she suppressed a string of curses as the boy appeared in a cloud of steam. "I'm done," he announced.

"Then get dried and dressed, *petit salaud.*" Little bastard. It wasn't entirely correct, since the boy did have a father, just not the one he thought. Poor Gerard Caron, labouring all these years under the delusion that he'd sired a child. Even the silly local women commented on it: "Why, he has his father's eyes!" She giggled. The boy had inherited someone's eyes, just not Gerard Caron's.

"*Maman,* aren't we coming back here?" He was watching her fill the single suitcase she'd brought, tossing everything in haphazardly, not caring if the clothes were folded or the containers of liquid properly fastened. It didn't matter.

"Stop asking stupid questions, will you? Hurry up and get yourself ready or I will leave you behind." He had managed to dress himself and was sitting on the bed playing with a handheld video game, wasting his time as usual.

She wasn't nervous; it wasn't that. Perhaps it was a kind of madness, returning to Quebec when she knew they were hunting her, had been hunting her for years. Blaise Pascal had sworn that he would get her in the end, and he'd been looking such an awfully long time. He deserved something for his trouble, didn't he? A little acknowledgement of his efforts.

She had done this sort of thing before, many times, and the thrill of it had long since gone. That was the trouble with life: none of the real pleasures ever lasted. Even love was fleeting—not that she'd ever loved Caron, not truly. He was necessary and convenient, and perhaps she thought she'd loved him once, but that was before, and people always said—*Maman* said…. No, not *Maman*. *Grandmère* always said a woman never forgot her first love, even when he made himself unlovable. It was a conversation she would remember to the end of her days.

"WHY NOW?" she asked. He'd already gotten out of bed, was drawing on the uniform she despised, and far too quickly for her liking. She leaned across to the nightstand to retrieve her cigarettes and lit one.

"What do you mean?" He fastened the buttons of his shirt, fingers flying. "You knew what I was the very first time."

The "very first time" had been in a strip club on Saint Laurent Boulevard, and he'd come in after his shift with several of his cop buddies, *le flic*, all of them strutting up to the bar in uniform, laughing much too loudly, drowning out the quiet music and the murmur of conversation. She'd barely gotten warmed up on the pole and his eyes were all over her, looking and trying not to look, wanting and trying not to want. *Eh bien*, it was what they paid her for. Later, his pals funded the cost of a lap dance, grinning savagely when she shimmied up to him and slid down his body before settling her perfect backside into his lap, her face close to his. *Tell me what you want, handsome cochon.*

"Where are you going?" She slid out from under the rumpled sheet and pulled her dressing gown on over her nakedness. "Home to your wife?" She took a deep, savage drag off her cigarette, the tip glowing hot as hell.

"Yes. Home to my wife."

The slap caught him unawares, landing hard on the side of his face and rocking him backwards. He stumbled a pace or two and caught himself, staring at her. "What the fuck did you do that for?"

"Run on home, then, little boy. Run on home to your *maman* wife." Enough of his foolishness. She was twenty years old, young and beautiful, living in the most exciting city in the world, and she would waste no more time on him. "Maybe she likes your limp cock, even if I don't." She waited until he turned away, then leapt on him, driving the burning end of the cigarette against his forearm twice, three times, half a dozen. Something to remember her by.

THE BOY was still sitting on the bed. "Come on! *Tabarnak!*" She caught him by the arm and yanked him forward. He fell to his knees and began to cry, enraging her. "Get *up*." Still holding tightly to his wrist, she dragged him through the door and out into the corridor, the rubber toes of his sneakers catching on the carpet, the video game falling from his hands.

The rental car was waiting in the hotel parking garage, a BMW convertible. The day was warm for September, so she decided to drive with the top down. The boy climbed meekly into his seat, still sniffling, and fastened the seat belt around himself. "Where are we going?" he asked.

"We are going on *une grande aventure*," she replied. Maybe she'd let Pascal find her this time. Perhaps she could lure him from that goddamn little shithole of a town in Terre-Neuve where she'd left the dear old family home a smoking ruin. Of course she had the entire *Sûreté* out looking for her. Pascal wasn't stupid; he'd have alerted them already, unless the Newfies got there first. Yes, perhaps she would let him find her. Let him find her and fuck her. It had been a while, after all.

They stood in line for a long time at the Grande roue, the huge observation wheel located in the Old Port section of the city, but it was worth it. The boy shrieked as their car ascended, carrying them higher and higher into the sky, until they hovered some sixty metres above Montreal, with all of the surrounding landscape laid out before them.

"*Maman*, look!" he said, pointing to this or that structure and shuddering with delight. "*C'est merveilleux!*" It's marvelous. He yelled as it descended, curving them slowly back to earth, and when the great wheel stopped and they disembarked, he begged to be allowed to go again.

"There's no time," she said. They hurried to the Plage de l'Horloge, where they lay on the warm sand of the urban beach and watched ships passing on the St. Lawrence. The boy was well-behaved, and he didn't ask for anything or pester her with questions. She almost liked him.

At noon they ate the sandwiches she'd bought and drank fizzy orange soft drinks that left curlicues of dye at the corners of their mouths. He asked her where Papa was. "Papa has gone on a long journey, *mon fils*. A very long journey indeed." A filthy root cellar was an awful place to take one's final bows, but it couldn't be helped. For Caron she'd needed privacy and quiet. And Gary Pretty, whose eviscerated corpse she'd laid out on his bed like a fresh-carved October turkey for this year's *Action de grâce*. Grateful indeed for the blessings of the harvest. She was, and she was clever enough, too, to dispose of the knife in the sea. *These people, they always get caught*, Pascal had often told her. *They hang on to the murder weapon or they keep a souvenir.*

After lunch they queued at the entrance to the Science Centre, and she bought tickets to the IMAX theatre, where they watched first of all a film about dogs on surfboards and then one about ethereal golden bears living in a rain forest. When they went outside, she bought him a "steamie"—the delicious steamed hot dogs particular to the city—and he ate it sitting on a bench by the river. He was little, but he was growing, and so he was always hungry.

"*Maman*, I want to go home now." He turned his small face to her, his nose and forehead sunburned. "Are we going home?"

She didn't answer him immediately. The sun was warm, sparkling in a thousand tiny points of light on the little wavelets on the river, and the breeze smelled of happy people and delicious food and drink. It was important to savour such moments. Honestly, these were the sorts of memories one took with them to *paradis*.

"We are going," Amalie said finally. She stood and brushed crumbs from her skirt. "*Viens-tu?*" Are you coming? He clasped her hand, his earnest little sticky fingers in hers, and he was humming a tune as he skipped along beside her. Children, she thought, they lived always in the moment. The boy peered at a ladybug on the ground when they stopped at the crosswalk, his entire being consumed with looking, everything else forgotten. A city bus screamed past them, and it occurred to her that all she had to do was let go of his hand and step back. Step back and nudge him a little so that the weight of his bent head carried him forward into the street. A step, a nudge, and it would be all over. She would be simply the grieving mother. An ambulance would come, and the police, and Amalie would cry and be unable to answer their questions, overcome with grief. She could handle the police. She'd handled Blaise Pascal for all those years before he—

"*Maman*! The little feet. *Allons-y.*" The small figure—what he always called "the little feet"—had appeared on the Walk/Don't Walk sign, and he was tugging on her hand. The moment had passed.

She deliberately took a roundabout route back to where she'd left the car so he would be tired. If he wasn't entirely ready to nap, she had a remedy for that too: the little flat packet of sleeping tablets in her purse. It would be inconvenient to have to use them, but she would if the boy made it necessary. He was a human being, after all; it wasn't like drowning kittens. It wasn't like disposing of an adult. It was different. But he was nearly asleep when she bundled him into the rental car, speaking only once before they set off on their long journey. "Where are we going, *Maman*?"

"*Une grande aventure, mon fils.*"

Amalie smiled and started the car.

"BY THE way," Danny asked, leaning over the bench in Bobbi's lab, "did we get anything from the boat?" He'd stopped by the break room on his way to get another cup of strong tea, his fifth this morning. He hoped the eventual build-up of caffeine would numb the throbbing pain in his knees. He'd lain awake the night before, the pain sizzling along his nerves like a forest fire, while Tadhg snored peacefully beside him. Around 3:00 a.m. he got out of bed and went to the kitchen for a glass of water. It was a warm night, and they'd gone to bed with the windows open. He stood still for a moment, listening to the slow swish and scuff of the ocean on the shingle beach and the gentle susurration of the wind while he filled his glass a second time and drank. The constant ache in his damaged knee joints was beginning to cost him, and he wondered why it was taking so long to get the injections he'd agreed to. He'd heard nothing from Dr. St. Croix despite several phone calls to the clinic, and he was now desperate for sleep. Lately, any amount of rest beyond half an hour eluded him, the bliss of slumber falling prey to the lancing agony of his damaged joints.

Danny had been in pain before, but never like this, a pain with no end in sight and no way out. He'd quietly increased the dosage on his meds without telling anyone, thinking that at least he'd get some relief, but the side effects inevitably dragged him under. The Tylenol 3s contained codeine, which made him sleepy, so he tried to counteract that drowsiness with massive doses of caffeine. The drowsiness didn't extend to allowing him to rest at night, so he sleepwalked through his days. Even driving his car was proving difficult. Just this morning he'd dozed off on the highway and nearly ended up in a ditch.

"The boat was clean," Bobbi replied now. "Well," she amended, "as clean as can be expected. There was a fair amount of fish guts, but nothing suggestive of criminal activity. Any luck getting hold of Dr. Turnbull?"

He shook his head. "I called and got hold of her receptionist. Apparently Dr. Turnbull is on holiday for the next two weeks. I left a message."

"Two weeks," Bobbi commented. "Hopefully we'll stumble across something before then. God knows her face won't be any help."

"You found something on the body, though." He nodded at the portable light table set up on the bench. "Is this it?"

"It is." "It" was a scrap of paper the size of a mobile phone with some vague markings on it. "Doesn't look like much, I know, but we recovered some writing."

Bobbi was right. It didn't look like much. "Writing?"

"It's a list of names," she said. "Under ordinary circumstances I'd be tempted to say it's just random, but something about this isn't the usual. I've reproduced the contents, but it doesn't make any sense. Do you know any of these people?"

Danny glanced through the list but didn't recognize anyone. "Send me the names and I'll get one of the constables to run them through the database. It might be something, or it might be nothing."

"The names are French," Bobbi told him. "Maybe Inspector Pascal might be able to shed some light."

The mention of Pascal's name annoyed him. The woman Harry Dean's crew had fished out of the Atlantic had nothing to do with Pascal's pursuit of Amalie Caron. "I don't think we need to involve him, not at this stage. Was this the only thing she had in her pockets?"

"No. Hang on a sec." If his comment about Pascal affected her, Bobbi wasn't saying. She disappeared into her office and came back carrying a shallow plastic tray, which she placed on the bench in front of him. Danny took a pair of nitrile gloves from a nearby box and slipped them on before sorting through the disparate contents. There was a waterlogged packet of Juicy Fruit chewing gum, a quarter, a small piece of string with several knots tied in it, and a man's signet ring, its gold surface worn away with the passage of time.

"The ring was made in Montreal," Bobbi said. "There's a jeweller's hallmark on the inside. The rest of it?" She shrugged. "Your guess is as good as mine."

Danny held up the ring. "Can you make out an initial on this?"

"No. I'm going to run some tests on it now the once and see if I can bring something up, but usually if it's that degraded...." She let the rest of the sentence trail off. "We might be able to get fingerprints off the pack of gum."

"You can do that?" he asked. "Pull latent prints off a wet pack of chewing gum?"

"Oh yeah," she said. "There's reagent sprays we use. It's like magic. Never fear, if there are prints, we'll get them."

"Okay, thanks, Bobbi." He pulled the gloves off and binned them. "Did we get her clothing yet?"

"No yet," she replied. "I daresay Regan will send them over from Carbonear when she's ready." Regan Lampe usually retained a victim's clothing so she could check it for holes or burn marks, evidence relating to the cause of death.

He went down the hall to the small interview room that doubled as a briefing room, where most of the others were already gathered. June Carbage had requested the group meet because she had finally gotten through all of the files on the flash drive found in Amalie Caron's car and wanted to share her findings.

It was a short meeting. "I spent the weekend going through the whole Jesus works of it," she huffed, "backwards, forwards, and sideways."

"No joy?" Danny asked.

"Go 'way, for fuck sake." She brought up a list of the files, projected onto the screen behind her. "Every one of them has the same goddamn scenario over and over again. The only difference is some of them are shot from different angles." She clicked on one of the files and opened the video. A small boy, a rocking horse, a man's voice speaking French, demanding that the boy tell him "what you told your mother," and then the boy being beaten. In the second video, an identical set of conditions, except when the beating occurred at the end, the man was on the boy's left side instead of his right.

"Could it be mirrored, somehow?" Kevin asked. "Has the video been flipped horizontally?"

"Nope," June said. "I could be wrong, but I don't think this has been manipulated."

"It's like one of those 'spot the difference' games they used to publish in the newspapers," Riley said, "except the difference isn't that subtle at all." He glanced across at Danny. "I wonder if the dialogue is code for something."

"It could be," Danny said, "but how do we even find out? Maybe it's nothing, just people talking and a child being beaten, which is disturbing enough in itself. Are we sure the child is Amalie Caron's son?"

"I'd put money on it," Kevin said.

"I went back through the school yearbook," June told them, "and looked at his picture. I'm pretty sure it's him. Then again, it could be faked." The trouble was, the video never showed the boy's face, only glimpses of him from the back and from the side. "I can't see why she'd have this in the first place."

"Why does anyone have this sort of thing?" Blaise Pascal had slipped into the room unnoticed, holding a paper container of coffee from Strange Brew. "To consume it themselves—" He took a sip of his coffee. "—or to peddle it to other people." He nodded at the members of the team. "Good morning." Danny noticed the Quebecois didn't bother to apologise for crashing the meeting.

"Are you familiar with this sort of thing, Inspector?" June asked. Of all the team, she'd had the least amount of contact with Pascal, yet she addressed him with respect. Probably because of that, Danny thought sourly. Pascal was definitely an acquired taste.

"*Oui*, I am." He sat down in one of the empty chairs. "In Montreal we encounter this a great deal, probably much more than you do here in Newfoundland. It is a small place and not many people."

"Oh, they get up to all sorts round here," Riley interjected.

"Amalie Caron has no history of this, however," Pascal continued, "so it probably is not for the usual purpose."

Riley wrinkled his brow. "Sorry?"

"She was not *le souteneur*?"

"Pimp," Kevin offered. "She wasn't pimping her kid with these videos." He leaned forward in his seat to make eye contact with Pascal. "*C'est le mot juste, oui?*"

"*Oui, c'est le mot, vraiment*," Pascal confirmed. "*Vous parlez francais?*"

"*J'ai travaillé dans l'Estrie*," Kevin replied. "I used to work in the Eastern Townships."

"Can we speak English?" Danny snapped and immediately regretted it.

"Sorry, sir." Kevin sat back in his seat and pretended to be intensely interested in his coffee cup.

"*Le francais*," Pascal said slowly, "she is not a hard language to learn. Even for you."

You smug son of a bitch. Danny felt hot blood suffuse his face. *You wants your fucking arse kicked.* "I'll bear that in mind," he said, "for when the *Bureau des enquêtes indépendantes* comes calling."

A ponderous silence descended, and everyone in the room was suddenly at a loss as to where to look. Pascal held Danny's gaze, one eyebrow quirked. After several long moments he said, "I imagine you will be as useful as you always are, you."

"Sir," Dougie Hughes said. Danny's head swiveled towards him like it was mounted on gimbals. "There's a thing they can do nowadays. I've been reading about it. With video and such."

"Oh?" He kept Pascal in view from the corner of his eye. He'd have a word with the bastard later.

"It's called steganography. They're able to hide video inside another video." Hughes's hands described a complicated shape in midair. "You need special embedding software to do it, and another kind to decrypt it, but it can be done."

June straightened up and closed her laptop. The still frame of the video she'd been projecting disappeared from the screen. "That makes a lot of sense," she said. "Maybe we're looking at this the wrong way. Maybe it's not about child abuse as such."

"So the video files themselves are the point," Kevin said, "not their content. They're a carrier."

"Exactly," Hughes replied. Pascal glanced up from his phone and nodded but said nothing.

Danny drew a slow breath. "So if the embedded video is piggybacking on the original source files, the recipient of this material is... who?"

"Not piggybacking, sir," Hughes pointed out. "It's more like two strands of thread knit together."

"Knit or piggybacked, whatever, Constable." Danny was clearly out of his depth here.

"Of course, sir." Hughes sounded appropriately contrite. "The process uses... well, it's a bit technical, but it uses an algorithm to insert the hidden video into something else. For example, you could have a Disney movie for your kid, something like *Frozen*, and on the surface that's all it looks like."

"But it's not."

"No, sir. The technology is relatively new, but there are already reports of child pornography rings using it to transport illegal material via email and SMS, short messaging service. It's meant to stop anyone looking any deeper than the surface. Your average person on the street can't possibly tell if there's something else embedded. It's not noticeable by looking. Once you've acquired the software program you need, you can embed anything—pictures, data, executable files, sound recordings, other video."

"Is this readily available? This software, I mean." The idea that hidden bits of information in various formats could be floating around in his own digital files didn't sit well with Danny.

Hughes started to say something, but Pascal got there first. "It is everywhere," he said. "Simply everywhere. You don't even need to go to the dark web to get it. If she put it on this, she may have already uploaded to the internet, and good luck finding it."

A brief murmur ran around the room; then Danny said, "Hughes, can you decrypt the files on that flash drive?"

"Not without the software," the constable replied, "but Microsoft offers it for free. Shouldn't be too hard. Then it's just a matter of scanning through the videos." He nodded towards Pascal. "Would you help me with it, Inspector?"

"*Bien sûr*," Pascal replied as the meeting broke up. Danny caught up to him in the hallway.

"Amalie Caron," he said. "You say she wouldn't pimp out her own son."

"I said she was not known to do it." Pascal's dark eyes flickered over his features as if memorizing them. "This woman is capable of many things. What she does now, I have no idea. I have not seen her for seven years."

"You said fourteen."

"It was a very brief meeting, Inspector Quirke." Pascal patted his jacket pockets, probably looking for his cigarettes.

"And you didn't think to mention this until now," Danny said. "For Christ's sake! What else are you keeping from me?"

Pascal's features hardened. "I am keeping nothing from you. I arrested her seven years ago after a chance meeting on Côte-des-Neiges Road. She was going into a shop. I was coming out."

"And?"

"And nothing. *Rien.* She did not stay in custody. Insufficient evidence." His right hand went to his left wrist, massaging the flesh through his shirt, and Danny was reminded of the cigarette burns he and Riley had both seen there.

"That must have pissed you off."

Pascal uttered what might have been a laugh. "You don't know. But I am going to get her, Inspector, supposing it is the last—"

Whatever he'd been about to say was lost as Marilyn came hurrying up with an envelope in her hand. Her normally perfect coif was sticking up in improbable spikes and whorls, and she was sweating.

"Sir." She stopped in front of Danny and nodded at Pascal. "Inspector Pascal, a letter for you." She handed it across to him. The envelope was pale cream, greeting card sized, with Pascal's surname written on the front in pencil. There was no stamp or any other marking, not even a return address.

"Was this dropped off?" Danny asked.

"It was in the box when I went to collect the post this morning," Marilyn told him.

"We'll need to test it for trace," Danny continued, but Pascal had already torn it open and extracted the single sheet inside.

"*Sacrément*," he whispered. He held up the sheet so Danny could see it: *Tu es un menteur. You're a liar.* He looked more afraid than Danny had thus far seen him, and it was unsettling.

"What in the Jesus does that mean?" he asked, but Pascal wasn't answering. "Don't you think you should deal with it?" Danny persisted. "For Christ's sake, it could be a threat."

"It isn't a threat," Pascal said. He drew a breath and let it out slowly. "Not in the way you think."

"And," Marilyn continued, "Beatrice Pynn came in just now, all in a kerfuffle. She wants someone over to her place right away."

"Why?" Danny didn't know Beatrice Pynn well. She'd only recently moved back to Kildevil Cove after living in St. John's for a number of years, and from what he could tell, was trying to make a go of it as a hobby farmer on some family land she'd inherited.

"She found blood in her root cellar," Marilyn told him grimly. "None of it her own."

CHAPTER TEN

Thursday, mid-morning

BEATRICE PYNN met Danny and Pascal at her front gate. She was a strongly built woman about Danny's own age, pale-skinned and green-eyed, with wiry dark hair only partially confined by a headscarf. Her attire was practical for a hobby farm: a T-shirt, jeans, and rubber boots.

"Not a bad morning," she said. She glanced over both men from head to toe, then, apparently satisfied by what she saw, nodded and turned away. "Gonna be hot later on." She tossed this back over her shoulder. "Nice weather for this time of year."

"Why," Pascal asked Danny quietly, "do you people always talk about the weather?" Danny ignored him.

"Just down here," Beatrice called, leading them past a henhouse enclosure full of clucking Rhode Island Reds and one ostentatious British rooster. Pascal cast a wary eye over the fowl as he passed. *Some unfortunate history there*, Danny thought, although the idea of Pascal being chased by enraged chickens amused him.

"When did you discover the blood?" Danny asked. They'd arrived at the root cellar, a small structure dug into the side of the hill in the usual manner, with concrete walls and a wooden door. Danny and Pascal both paused to pull on gloves.

"This morning," Beatrice replied. "I've been trying to clean it up. The spuds are just about ready to come out of the ground, and the cabbage won't be far behind it." She had started inside with a bucket of sudsy water and a cloth but stopped as soon as she saw the small dark puddles on the floor. "I won't be setting foot in there now, I can tell ye that."

"So you did not go inside?" Pascal asked. He glanced over her attire with one brow arched, then turned back towards the cellar.

"No." She gazed at him in silence, obviously wondering who he was, but she didn't ask.

The interior of the cellar was cool and dark, the only light entering from the open door. Danny remembered his grandparents' root cellar, where the distinct smell of over-wintered vegetables mingled with the comforting odour of wood and soil. His grandmother—except she wasn't really his grandmother, he reminded himself—would give him an empty salt-beef bucket every Saturday evening and send him down into the cellar to pick out the vegetables for the next day's boiled dinner.

"It is right here, by the wall." Pascal crouched down and lightly touched the smallest puddle with the tip of a gloved finger. He held it up towards Danny. "Congealed. Almost no fluid left in it. If this were outdoors, it would be gone. Not that there is much of it to go."

He was right. The cool interior of the root cellar had preserved the little spots of blood and prevented the liquid serum from evaporating.

"You're right," Danny observed. "There's hardly anything. Strange." He moved past the first tiny puddle and towards the back of the little room, where the largest quantity of blood was located—a congealed spot smaller than the palm of his hand. Judging by the size and shape of it, it had dripped or trickled down from above.

"*Calisse*," Pascal hissed. "This is bullshit." His accent gave the final word an amusing lilt. "What the hell are you smiling about?"

"Nothing."

"She perhaps cut herself in here and forgot about it." Pascal nodded. "You think?"

"I'm not a blood-spatter expert." Danny pulled out his mobile phone, realised he probably wouldn't get much of a signal inside the root cellar, and stepped outside to call Bobbi Lambert.

"I think there might have been a chair here," Pascal said when Danny returned. "It has been removed." His guarded expression suggested he wasn't ready to entirely commit to this theory.

"A chair?" It would account for the size and shape of the blood droplets. If the victim was seated, most of the blood would have ended up on his clothes or the chair. "Are you sure?"

"*Non*. But, near enough, I think." He moved to stand with his back against the far wall of the cellar. "She would have stood here." He pressed his palms against the cement. "The camera would be over there, by the door."

"The camera?" It struck Danny where Pascal was going with this. "Amalie Caron."

"*Vraiment*." His expression was grim. "I think we cannot expect to find Gerard Caron alive." Based on the video, Pascal was probably right.

"Okay," Danny agreed, "but what did she do with the body?" He couldn't imagine someone the size of Amalie Caron sawing her husband into neat pieces and dropping him into the sea.

The Quebecois spread his hands. "*Aucune idée.*"

"I don't know either." Danny glanced around. "Well, Bobbi's team is on the way, and I'm going to get a couple of constables up here to keep people away. Beatrice isn't going to like this."

"Then she will have to put up with it," Pascal replied.

DR. REGAN Lampe finished weighing the unknown woman's organs and quickly dropped them into a viscera bag. She placed the bag in the abdominal cavity before replacing the chest plate, preparatory to closing the body. The whole thing felt horribly unfinished, and she couldn't escape the thought that she'd missed something. Danny said the way the woman had died was typical of organised crime, which meant whoever had fired those two shots into the back of her skull was mafia or similar. She knew, of course, that much of the island's drug trade was funnelled through organised crime, mostly biker gangs from the mainland, places like Montreal or Toronto. It was unlikely, however, that a local would have the kind of personal affiliation with them that ended in such a gruesome manner.

The door to the autopsy room swung open. "Dr. Lampe, the lab sent me down with the test results." One of the morgue assistants, a diffident young man named Darryl or Darren or David, advanced and offered a slip of paper at arm's length. "Thanks," he said, apropos of nothing, before turning to scurry towards the exit.

Regan scanned the page quickly, then again, just to make sure. "No toxins," she said aloud. "No drugs, no poison." So the two bullets to the back of the skull were the only cause of death. No surprise there. Two nine-millimetre slugs—she'd removed them from where they'd been deeply imbedded in the posterior portion of the brain—would have that effect on anyone.

Who had this woman been in life? How had she ended up in a fishing net? Regan came from people who understood every aspect of the natural world and who had an encyclopedic knowledge of the sea, including its tides and currents. If she had been killed north of the Avalon Peninsula, the cold Labrador Current would have brought her body south. She was found, Harry Dean said, just inside the Flemish Cap, an area of the Grand Banks nearly 600 kilometres away from Kildevil Cove, which meant her corpse had probably floated north courtesy of the warm Gulf Stream. If this was the case, then she'd been ejected from a ship or boat somewhere south of Newfoundland, approximately five to seven days previous to when Harry Dean's crew found her.

Regan abandoned the corpse, stripping off her gloves and reaching for her phone. Her initial call was to Danny Quirke, but it went directly to voicemail, so she tried Cillian Riley. He picked up on the second ring. "The Gulf Stream," Regan said.

"Sorry?"

"The woman in the net." She paused, waiting for his response, but he said nothing. "I've been thinking."

"What woman?"

"Don't be an idiot," she snapped. "The woman in the fishing net." She quickly outlined her theory to him. "Find out what ships were south of the island five to seven days ago and what they were doing there. That's where she was shot in the head and tossed over the side. I'm sure of it."

"I think we need to make you a detective," Riley said, clearly impressed.

"The two shots in the back of the head, that's organised crime. You can bet on it."

"Okay."

"She might have been involved with them."

"With who?"

"Oh my *God*, are you even paying attention?" She huffed out an irritated breath. "The woman has two bullets in the back of her head. She was shot by criminals and her body dumped over the side of a boat somewhere south of the island." A beat, then, "Are you listening?"

"I'd be hard pressed not to. Dr. Lampe, thank you." He sounded as if he meant it. "I think you might be onto something. I'll be sure and pass this on to Danny."

"Do that," she said. "Tell him to call me immediately, if not sooner."

Thursday evening

IT FELT like she'd been driving for days, following the curving mountain roads up, down, and around, while the boy slumbered in the back seat. It wasn't safe: he simply lay there, wrapped in a blanket, unsecured by a seat belt, and if she happened to hit a deer or run into a ditch, he would almost certainly be thrown clear of the vehicle and killed. All the effort she had thus far expended would be wasted, then, and the entire struggle for nothing, the game finished much too early. It wasn't yet time for the finale of this little tale, not with Pascal still in Newfoundland, still running around like an *imbécile*.

He could return to Quebec and hunt her here, but he knew the BEI was waiting for him. A quick telephone call to the *Sûreté* some months previous and she'd told them interesting things about *Inspecteur* Blaise Pascal. That he'd enjoyed lap dances from pretty girls during working hours; that he'd frequented prostitutes; that he'd fucked her in his patrol car in a back alley between rue Laval and boulevard de l'Hotel de Ville. She'd managed to weep a little bit as she confirmed that yes, he did all these things during his service with SPVM, but she had been afraid to come forward before. For all she knew, he was doing these despicable things still. How terrible, how shameful for a policeman to take advantage in this way, when she had been a single mother, only working in that profession so she could make the rent. Did they realise he was investigating a grisly murder that had occurred in the Côte-des-Neiges neighbourhood, just on the edge of the Summit Woods? They did? *Eh bien*, with public sentiment running firmly against the *Sûreté*, it certainly didn't look good for him.

She saw the lights of a Couche-Tard convenience store up ahead and slowed the car. A quick glance at Google Maps confirmed that she hadn't too far left to travel and would arrive at her destination with plenty of time to spare, so she parked and left the boy sleeping as she went inside. A single clerk stood at the counter, and a quick glance didn't show anyone else around the store. Still, it was risky. She had no doubt the dullards of the *Sûreté* had blanketed the entire province—no, the entire country—with pictures of her face and the news that she was a "person of interest," so even stepping foot inside a shop where she could be recognised was dangerous. But it couldn't be helped. She'd sipped water all the way from Montreal, and her bladder was full. If she didn't find a toilet, she'd end up pissing all over the seat of the rental car.

She found the bathroom towards the back of the store, went inside, and locked the door behind her. The toilet seat was clean but cold, and she shuddered as she sat down. The room's interior was painted a pale grey shade, with a faded wallpaper border of pink flowers up near the ceiling. The room smelled like lemons. An air freshener, probably piped in to mask the scent of piss and shit, riding atop the tortuous Muzak version of Céline Dion that was playing over the speakers.

She finished emptying her bladder and wiped herself with the pitifully thin paper, then washed her hands at the sink. The woman staring back at her from the mirror looked the same as always, but Amalie Caron wasn't the same at all. She drew a hand through her hair, pushing it back from her face. *I am finally myself again.* It was gratifying to live the way she wanted, a kind of renaissance. Indeed, she felt reborn. Having to hold herself together in the name of conjugal harmony had chafed at her. All these years of pretending to love Gerard Caron, of submitting to his caresses, his lovemaking, had sickened her. Acting the sweet, dutiful young wife and mother was equally bad because she'd had to bow to Caron's decisions, go along with whatever he thought was correct. He'd had the idea that they could settle in Newfoundland and be a regular family, that Amalie's past need not constrain her. As long as no one knew about her former misdeeds, there was hope for them.

"It can be our ancient history," he'd said. "We will forget about it, and no one will ever know. This is our new life now."

They attended the local Catholic church, where everyone could see them, and went regularly to confession. Amalie invented sins to tell the priest in the hope of shocking him, stories with no substance and little basis in reality, florid tales of sexual affairs with men from the village or the teenage boys who smuggled bootleg liquor from St. Pierre. It was a way of staving off the boredom that permeated every moment of the day ever since they'd come to the island. Thank God she'd gotten away at last.

She unlocked the door and went out. There was a cooler of fruit-flavoured drinks near the counter, and she paused, picked out an orange and a grape. On impulse she also chose a bottle of vodka. The young male clerk was skinny, pale, with a face full of pimples. He kept staring at her while ringing up her purchases, and finally, as she was reaching to give him the money, he said, "*Je vous connais. La police vous cherche.*" I know who you are. The police are looking for you.

The pulse and swish of blood inside her ears was deafening. She gripped the counter with both hands until her knuckles turned white. Say something, she thought. Tell him he is wrong. "*Mais non,*" she protested, forcing a laugh. "You have mistaken me for someone else."

He pointed to her picture, posted to one side of the cash register. "*C'est vous.*" It's you.

In that instant she fled, taking the drinks and the vodka with her. The boy was still asleep when she wrenched open the door of the car and fell into the driver's seat, shuddering with horror and fear.

"*Maman*, where did you go?" The *petit salaud* was awake, damn him.

"Nowhere at all, *mon cher*." She pulled onto the highway and into the wrong lane, forgetting to fasten her seat belt. A tractor-trailer roared by much too close, horn blaring, flashing his high beams, blinding her. "Are you ready? We'll go on again."

"Where are we going?" His small face was pale in the rear-view mirror, and he was still drowsy, his body flaccid in the aftermath of sleep.

"Not far at all. We'll be there soon. *Oui, vraiment*, so very soon."

THE LIGHTS were out in most of the compound when Amalie arrived an hour later, but she knew she was expected. She had dosed one of the fruit drinks with vodka and sent the boy to sleep again in the back seat of the car. At the entrance she passed the large blue-and-white signboard reading *Royaume de l'Amour Infini de Jésus Crucifié*, a great many fleur-de-lis, then the familiar statue of the Blessed Virgin Mary, and finally the first of the convent's outbuildings. She left the car running while she got out to ring the bell. She resented that her hand was being forced before she'd had time for the entirety of her planned scenario to play out, but it couldn't be helped. The rage in her—the stupid *salaud* who'd recognised her at the Couche-Tard—desperately needed an outlet, but there was no time. That would come later, after this part was over and done with.

A tiny nun, dressed in the blue-and-white robes particular to her order, appeared. "*Je suis attendue*," Amalie said. I'm expected.

"Of course," the nun replied. "I am Sister Claire Joseph." She held out an arm as Amalie came towards her. "It is difficult," she continued, sweeping Amalie into a one-armed hug, "but we must do as we are bidden by the Lord and His Holy Mother."

"Say a mass for me, then." Amalie held a crumpled tissue to her face so that it hid her grin. "That I may receive His infinite love." She opened the car's rear door and bent to retrieve the boy from the back seat. He was profoundly asleep, drooling, slit-eyed and puffy, with a gout of saliva clinging to his hair. Disgusting. Children were so completely disgusting. She bore him in her arms towards the chapel's open door and laid him down on a pew, then stepped back. An enormous emotional weight seemed to fall from her shoulders, and she allowed herself the luxury of a sigh. "I give him into your care and your infinite love."

"Infinite love," Sister Claire Joseph echoed. "It is the reason we exist."

From there it didn't matter where Amalie went, as long as there was a bed in the room and curtains at the windows and a door that locked. She required nothing more, but for nostalgia's sake she drove a little distance outside the town and found the quaint hotel where she'd stayed just once before.

Seven years ago she came here; seven years ago tonight her son was conceived with a man who had no idea he was even the boy's father. She had lured him in, let him think he'd caught her, that her arrest and conviction would be his great triumph, and when she bedded him, she did it with one hand tethered to the headboard, held fast by his handcuffs. The sight of her slim white wrist encircled by cold metal excited him, and he accomplished quickly what she'd brought him there to do. Men were so easily led about by their cocks.

When it was done—when she was certain she was already *enceinte* with his child—she slipped out of the handcuffs and left him sleeping, insensible, sated with sex and a little something extra she'd slipped into his coffee.

She asked for and received the same room now. This pleased her. It was a little piece of kismet, a bit of luck for this last stage of her journey. Now there were notes to write and telephone calls to make. That inquisitive inspector in the Terre-Neuve police force had probably already discovered the bodies; no doubt he and Pascal were beating themselves senseless trying to find her.

"Soon, *mes amis*," she murmured. "All things in time. All things in time."

Thursday evening

THE PHONE call from Regan Lampe bothered Danny.

Not because it was from Regan, but because the message she'd left on his voicemail was garbled, indecipherable. The only thing he could make out was "call me." He'd tried that but got no reply. When he rang the hospital's main switchboard, they told him she was in surgery and could not be disturbed. It was pointless to leave a voicemail. Unlike him, Regan never bothered to check her messages. He'd just have to keep trying and hope he could connect with her before too long.

"There has been a report," Pascal announced, coming into Danny's office. He carried what looked suspiciously like two flat whites from Strange Brew. "Just now I was on the telephone with the *Sûreté*." He set one of the cardboard containers of coffee down in front of Danny. "A night clerk at a Couche-Tard near Mont-Tremblant encountered Amalie Caron."

"Oh?" Danny picked up the coffee with a murmured expression of thanks.

"When he challenged her, she fled. Without paying for what she bought." Pascal sat down in the chair across from Danny and slipped out of his leather jacket. It was still badly singed from his encounter with the burning transport truck several days previous, but he didn't seem to notice. "He managed to get the number of the licence plate. A rental car."

"So she's in Quebec." He sipped the hot coffee gratefully. "What's she doing in Mont-Tremblant?"

Pascal gazed at him over the rim of his cup. "You think I should go there and pick her off?"

"Can't the *Sûreté* do that?" Danny asked.

"*Vraiment.*"

"And you're not too keen on going where the BEI can find you."

"You seem to think I am some kind of *flic repou*." Pascal removed the plastic lid from his coffee and laid it on the desk.

"Bent cop?" Danny guessed. Despite the bona fides from Pascal's immediate superior in Mont-Tremblant, he wondered if this were true. "I don't know if I can trust you. That's all I'm saying."

"You think I trust you?" When Danny didn't reply, Pascal shrugged and began to roll up his sleeves. "What about this?" he asked, gesturing at the photos spread out on the desk. "These are the things you found in the dead woman's pockets?"

Danny was no farther ahead in determining who the anonymous woman might be. The fact that she'd been hauled up in a fishing net meant nothing. Given the direction of the currents that regularly swirled around the island, she might have come from Ireland or Iceland or Greenland. She might have been shot and dumped off an ocean liner or a passing cruise ship.

"Yeah," he said. "None of it makes any sense." His gaze was drawn as always to the cigarette burns on Pascal's wrist. Sensing Pascal noticed this, he hastened to look away but was too late.

"I seem to have an unusual familiarity with fire," the Quebecois said and smiled. It was one of the few genuine smiles he had ever offered, and it didn't quite fit with his normally sour expression. "A woman did that to me several years ago. Bad idea to hook up with her again."

"Was it Amalie Caron?"

Pascal chose not to reply, saying instead, "So these items you found in her pocket. They are useful?" He drew the photo of the gum package towards him and examined it.

"Undetermined, Bobbi said. Her team is going to try and lift some latent prints."

"Which will only help if this person's fingerprints are already in the database system. So here we are. *Eh bien.*" He pushed the photo away and selected another, this one of the dead woman's clothes. "Perhaps my detective skills are not up to this task."

"Your superior in Mont-Tremblant speaks very highly of you." Her enthusiasm for Pascal had surprised Danny, to put it mildly. She was so ardent in her defence of him that Danny wondered if the two were having it off. Pascal wasn't conventionally handsome, but he was dynamic and interesting. That combination would certainly be attractive to a great many women—and not a few men.

"I assume you requested my complete dossier from her?" Pascal smirked but then tapped the photo in front of him with two fingers. "These are very expensive clothing. Like she had them handmade. *Couture.*"

"You think she was wealthy?"

"If not wealthy then certainly well-paid for whatever it is she does." Pascal paged through the series of photos, examining some closely while putting others aside in a pile. He plucked one of the pictures from the stack and turned it so Danny could see it. "You ever seen underwear like this?"

"Uhh...." Of all the questions he'd anticipated from Pascal, this wasn't one of them. "I've never worn it myself, if that's what you're asking."

The *Sûreté* detective rolled his eyes. "Don't be stupid." He waved the photograph. "You know what this is? My ex-wife, I gave her one of these things for our anniversary. It is La Perla. These little panties, just this bit of string?" He pointed to the thong bikini panty in the photo. "Two hundred and fifty dollars."

"Mother of God." Danny couldn't imagine paying that much for a pair of his usual boxer briefs, the cotton ones that came in a twelve pack and that Tadhg gave him every year for Christmas. "Two hundred and fifty? For that?"

"Whoever this woman was"—Pascal laid the photograph on top of the small pile he'd made—"she had money. A lot of money."

"Or a lover who doted on her."

"*Peut-être.*" He shook his head. "In which case, where is her lover? Why has he abandoned her to fall overboard and get pulled up in a net like fishes?"

"Well, we know she's not a suicide."

Pascal nodded thoughtfully. "*Bien sûr.* She could not shoot herself in the back of her own head."

"Maybe there was a spouse *and* a lover," Danny proposed.

"Always possible," Pascal responded. He fell silent, his gaze turned inward.

Danny wondered what Pascal's personal life was like. Did he go home to a spouse or a lover? Was there anyone who cared about him, who worried when his work kept him overlong and he hadn't been in touch?

"Does it bother you that I asked for your personnel record?" Danny asked. "That I requested the whole thing, nothing redacted?"

Pascal laughed. "I have no dirty little secret, if that is what you are saying, and you have to make sure. I requested yours also. So?" He nodded at the photos. "Maybe this Mrs. No One came off a fishing trawler, eh? A foreign boat. She would be out there looking for some codfish."

"Wearing La Perla undies?" Danny said. The notion struck him as hilarious. "Not bloody likely."

"Not bloody likely," Pascal echoed.

Danny's mobile phone vibrated, interrupting him. He pulled it out and peered at the screen: Regan Lampe. "Seems like we're playing phone tag today," he said.

"I don't have much time," she replied, "but I have a theory."

"Okay." He listened while she explained her idea about where the body had gone into the water, then summarized, "So you think a criminal syndicate killed her on a ship and dumped the body overboard where the currents would take her to where she was found."

"Yes, that's what I think. Can't be sure she was connected to the syndicate, although I think it's likely. But I am sure she must have gone into the water south of the island."

Danny glanced at Pascal as the *Sûreté* officer tapped his fingertips on the table and mouthed something Danny couldn't make out. "If that's the case, could she be Amalie Caron?" Danny speculated. But as soon as he said it, he knew it was impossible, and Regan's snort told him what she thought of that idea. He could hear Regan being paged on the hospital's PA system and knew she would have to go.

"Pay attention to the timing," Regan snapped, getting the last word as she so often did. Then she disconnected abruptly, and Danny turned to Pascal. "Dr. Lampe thinks the woman could have been involved with a criminal organisation."

"And she was in a boat, got herself shot in the head, and went overboard like that, *là!*" He made a sweeping motion with both arms.

"In which case we have to ask ourselves: What was she doing out there?" Danny pondered this for a moment, could come up with nothing concrete. Anyone could be on any kind of boat at any time and for any reason.

"Shipping traffic in this country is a matter of public record," Pascal offered. "How long did your doctor say she was in the water, eh? The fishermen already said where they were." Pascal took out his mobile phone and pulled up a web browser, navigating quickly to a page showing all the international shipping traffic. "Look here. Every one of these little marks is a boat of some size. Doesn't matter the bigness of it. It all gets tracked."

Danny leaned over to look. "I'm familiar with this site," he said. "I've used it myself." It had been invaluable to him during the investigation of human trafficking offshore. "Regan said the body was in the water maybe five days, a week at the most, and must have entered the water south of Newfoundland. We know she was found in the Flemish Cap area on the Grand Banks. If we backtrack a week, maybe give or take a day or two, we should be able to find out which ships or boats were in the right area." This was basically what Regan had proposed.

"So the fishermen tell you where they were and what they were doing," Pascal said. "Are they telling the truth? Who knows?"

"They'd have no reason to lie," Danny replied. "Nothing to cover up, as long as they were operating within the law. Remember, they use the ELOG system. Anything they do while at sea is supposed to be recorded."

Pascal swiped at the phone's small screen, enlarging the view. "All of these boats are colour-coded," he said, "according to their function, which is useful for us. We can rule out tankers, fishing boats, things like this."

"I'm not so sure," Danny replied. "Sometimes people book passage on tankers or cargo ships and work their way along." Tadhg had done this immediately after university, ostensibly to gain experience of the world but more likely to piss off his father, who'd imagined him working in the family business.

"No," Pascal said flatly. "She would not be on a tanker ship wearing couture clothing and fancy underpants. We are looking for a leisure craft, something of that size."

"Cruise ship?"

"Or a luxury yacht, one of these big boats they use."

Danny thought about this for a moment. The cruise ship season in Newfoundland often extended well into autumn, so it wasn't beyond possibility. Many cruise companies had home ports in Florida or the Bahamas, and if she'd gone overboard somewhere south of the province, the Gulf Stream would likely bring her body north, as Regan theorized it had. The trouble with that theory was the unpredictability of the current. The Gulf Stream flowed in a northeasterly direction towards the island, spawning whirls and eddies that spun off in disparate directions. It was difficult to predict where a floating body would end up.

"Why is it you are not home with your husband?" Pascal asked out of nowhere. He picked up another photo, glanced at it briefly, and returned it to the desk. "It is late enough now."

"He's working, and my stepdaughter is staying at a friend's house for the night."

"You don't have to go home and walk the dog?" Pascal had noticed the framed photo of Danny, Tadhg, and Lily the previous day, with Easter posed prominently in the foreground.

"No, she took the dog with her." He sorted through the photos. This was a waste of time. There was nothing here. The contents of the dead woman's pockets didn't reveal anything of value. Bobbi's team had managed to pull the initial P off the signet ring, but the discovery came without context. "P" could be anyone, or no one at all. She might have found the ring or purchased it in a thrift shop.

"All these photos are very well done," Pascal concluded, "but not much help." He raised his hands to shoulder height and let them drop. "We still know nothing about who this woman is. Or was. She could be the queen of fairyland, prancing around in her *bobettes*."

Danny had no idea what *bobettes* were, and he wasn't keen on asking. His mobile phone rang again, and he reached to retrieve it from his hip pocket. "Deiniol Quirke."

"*Salut*, Inspector. I believe you are looking for me?" The voice was feminine, husky; she sounded ever so slightly amused. Danny gestured to Pascal and quickly put the phone on speaker so the *Sûreté* officer could hear.

"Who is this?" Danny asked.

"Don't be an idiot. You know who." There was a pause. "Is he there? *Salut*, Pascal. *Ça va bien?*" Danny pulled a notepad towards him, wrote *How does she know you're here?* He showed it to Pascal, who shrugged. "Of course he is there. Pascal, *mon amour*! Have you missed me?"

"*Oui, vraiment*, Amalie." Danny started to speak, but Pascal laid a hand on his wrist, silencing him. "Amalie, where is the boy, eh? Is he with you?"

"What do you care about the boy?" Her voice sharpened. "He is nothing to you."

"Amalie." Danny felt compelled to intervene. "Madame Caron. I just want to know that the boy is safe."

"Why?"

June Carbage, passing by in the corridor, stopped to put her head round the door. Danny motioned her in, a finger to his lips. "Where have you taken him?" he asked. "If you tell us, we can come and get him. Then you can go on your way. No questions."

"He is with good people," Amalie said, "who will not do him any harm. He is safe in their care, but you will never find him." A long pause. "*Ne me cherchez pas.* Don't look for me."

"Madame Caron, I'm certain we—" But Danny was too late; she had already disconnected.

"I'll see if we can trace the call," June said.

"It's too late now," Danny told her. "She wasn't on the line long enough." Just their goddamn luck.

"It might ping off one of the cell towers where she is," Pascal interjected, "and perhaps we find her that way."

"It's at least worth a try." This was typical June, never quite willing to give up, no matter the odds. "I'll see if I can get hold of Dougie."

"No, he's gone off shift." Danny didn't feel like bothering Hughes at home. The young constable had done his due diligence and then some, and he had a wife and young daughter. "Get on to the RCMP in Harbour Grace. They've got a few more resources than we do. They might be able to help."

"I'll let you know if they find anything." June nodded at them both and disappeared down the hall.

"Ah, fuck," Pascal breathed.

"What do you think she meant," Danny asked, "when she said she'd left him with good people? Does she have any family? A sister, perhaps?"

"Who knows? She has no family left. Her parents, they are both dead, and her sister is—" He shook his head. "*Indisponible.* Unavailable."

"Meaning?"

"She is serving a lengthy prison term."

"So Amalie could have left Joseph God knows where." Something as simple as a boy abducted by his mother, and yet they were doing nothing, achieving nothing. Gerard Caron was likely dead.

"She will not stay long in any place," Pascal warned him. At a buzzing noise he broke off, reached into his hip pocket, and brought out his phone. He stood up. "This woman is very good at disappearing herself. *Excusez-moi.* I must take this." He stepped out into the corridor.

Danny got up from where he'd been sitting behind his desk and drew a deep breath. It hurt—his neck and shoulders were so tight they might have been wound by an expert watchmaker—and the coffee had left a sour burn in his stomach. What did they know for sure about this case? Very little. Amalie Caron was most likely responsible for setting fire to the family home, for killing her husband, and for abducting her child.

Where was she now? What had she done with the child? Could they trust her declaration that she'd left him with "good people" who would care for him? Likely this was mere manipulation. She and Pascal had history—perhaps of an intimate nature—but to what degree the Quebecois wasn't saying. Danny's request for information from the

Sûreté meant that any intelligence the Quebec police had would be filtered through Pascal, who was entirely capable of telling Danny only what he decided was enough. This was Pascal's case and had been for the past fourteen years, a case in which Amalie Caron had planned and executed a devious series of circumstances for reasons known only to her. Danny didn't care for it, didn't like being at the mercy of a psychopath whose motivations were entirely unknown. He would have to go back to the very beginning, re-examine the evidence and the sequence of events as they occurred. They must have missed something. *He* must have missed something. It was the only explanation that made sense.

From the corridor he could hear Pascal speaking in French to someone on the phone. Danny wished he spoke and understood the language better. Pascal's clandestine conversations made him uncomfortable. To whom was he talking and what about?

A movement at the door and Pascal returned. "That was Louis Prud'Homme from the *Sûreté*. I work with him. The car Amalie Caron rented has been found abandoned in a parking lot near Arundel. They have officers on site, and he will keep me apprised." He paused, clearly aware that something was off with Danny. "You are all right?"

"Yes." He gazed at Pascal, trying again to fathom who this man was. Some people were genuinely mysterious, while others made themselves into an enigma for personal, ego-driven reasons. Pascal didn't seem like the latter. He suspected that, like himself, Pascal had his own painful secrets, psychic wounds that he hid beneath a veneer of *sang-froid* and sheer bloody mindedness. Not so tough after all. Just a man like anybody.

"Where are you staying?" Danny asked. Pascal told him the name of the motel in nearby Winterton, a notorious roadside inn frequented by long-haul truckers who didn't care about the state of their temporary lodgings. "Jesus, bhoy. Sure ye can't stay there. That place is a shithole."

"I know," Pascal admitted.

"Come over to my place. Least I can do is feed ye while we're waiting to hear from that *Sûreté* fella."

"Why?"

Good Christ, Danny thought, the man suspected everybody. "Because Hiscock's isn't a fit place for anyone to sleep, and ye looks like ye haven't had a decent feed in donkey's ages."

"You are going to feed me a donkey?" Pascal's curled lip said it all.

They gathered their things and left after a quick word with June, who was about to leave herself. Sarah Avery and a new hire from Cape Breton, Joey Yeo, would staff the station throughout the night. More than likely they'd have a quiet time of it.

Danny took Pascal home in his car, the Quebecois uncharacteristically silent. When they arrived, Danny ushered him inside and got him a cold beer from the fridge. "I think we've both earned it," he said. Pascal took a seat at the counter while Danny dug through the contents of the fridge and brought out a thick stack of cold cuts and a loaf of crusty white bread Tadhg had baked earlier that day. "Sandwich okay?"

"It would be perfect, *merci*." Pascal raised his bottle in a salute. "So where is he, your boyfriend?"

"Husband," Danny corrected. "He's working late." He went to the sink to wash his hands. "You're married, yourself?" There was no sign of a wedding ring, but then, not everybody chose to advertise their union the way he and Tadhg did.

"Divorced," Pascal told him, "and I have not married again. My ex-wife, she did not like the job, the long hours I often work." He became very interested in peeling the label off his bottle of beer. "What does your husband do?"

"He's a property developer," Danny replied, reaching for a towel to dry his hands. "Real estate. He's got a project on the go not too far from here, renovating an old house and putting up some holiday cottages."

Pascal nodded. "Holiday cottages." His long fingers kept picking at the beer label, pulling away a corner. "You have a daughter."

"Stepdaughter, actually." Danny cut two slices off the fresh loaf. "Mustard? Mayonnaise?"

"Just butter if you have it, please."

"Yes, Lily. She's sixteen. She's my husband's daughter from a previous relationship." He spread the bread with butter and layered cold cuts and cheese between the slices, then neatly bisected the completed sandwich with a sharp knife before sliding it onto a plate and handing it to Pascal. In the cupboard over the stove, he located a bag of artisanal chips made from various root vegetables, confirmation that Tadhg still had expensive—and strange—tastes. He opened the bag and dumped the contents into a blue-and-white Sveinbjörg Hallgrímsdóttir serving bowl Tadhg had bought on a trip to Reykjavik. "Not sure what these are like, but you never know. Another beer?"

"I will be driving later," Pascal reminded him. He picked up his sandwich and bit into it, making various small noises of appreciation.

"Yes, back to that shithole in Winterton," Danny said. "Sure that's not fit. Stay here for the night, and I'll help you find something better tomorrow. That place is fousty."

"You are sure?" Pascal looked a bit uneasy, Danny thought, but he couldn't allow a fellow officer to stay at Hiscock's Motel. God alone knew what diseases he'd pick up from the place, and the bedclothes probably hadn't been washed in recent memory.

"You can stay in Lily's room. She's gone off for the night to a friend's place, her and the dog."

"I don't want to be any trouble to you." His cell phone pinged, the sound of an incoming text message, and he picked it up to look at it. "Prud'Homme says they are going door to door in the Arundel area, but there is no sign of Amalie herself. They are also bringing in scent dogs."

"Do you think they'll find her?" Danny stuffed a handful of chips into his mouth. After he swallowed, he said, "Quebec is a big province."

Pascal picked up his sandwich to take another bite. "It is a big province, yes, but Amalie will be found. There are only so many places she can hide."

"Yet she evaded you for, what…? Fourteen years?" As soon as the words were out of his mouth, he knew he'd made a grievous error.

"And you," Pascal said, bristling, eyes narrowed, "allow a dangerous criminal *de l'Écosse* go free. Yes, I heard about it. Everyone knows. *Sacrément*, do you want to sit here and give each other insults or drink more beer?"

A ridge of irritation rose along Danny's back, sharp as the blade of a saw. Forcing a civil tone, he said, "I think we should have another beer." He got up to fetch two more bottles from the fridge and handed one to Pascal.

"Everybody fucks up," Pascal said, and thanked him for the beer. "We have all done it. For me it was Amalie Caron. For you, this Martin Belshawe. We all have bones in the cupboard." He paused to sip his beer. "If you think you are going to be this Super Cop who never makes mistakes, *pfft*! Forget about it. Better to be *le bon flic* who does his best. Anyway, everybody has scars."

"Why…?" Danny gestured at Pascal's wrist. "Why did she do that to you? It was Amalie, wasn't it? She burned you."

"It is a long and complicated story."

Sensing he wasn't about to get any more from Pascal, Danny rose and began clearing away the remains of their late supper. Once that was done, he took Pascal upstairs and showed him where he could shower and change for bed, since it was now nearly eleven and they needed an early rise in the morning. "There's a new toothbrush in the medicine cabinet there. And toothpaste. Use whatever you need."

He loaned Pascal a pair of Tadhg's lounge pants and a T-shirt and directed him to Lily's bedroom. The *Sûreté* detective gazed upon Lily's massive collection of stuffed toys with genuine dismay. "She sleeps with all these things?" The animals had been arranged on top of the bed in rows, with the largest—a massive Ikea Djungelskog bear—at the bottom and the smallest on top. Danny reassured him it was perfectly all right to put the animals on the floor and wished him a good night. A few moments later he heard the shower running, and he lay listening to it for a while until he slipped over the border of wakefulness and into sleep.

He woke sometime later to glance at the clock, registering that it was after two in the morning and Tadhg was in bed beside him.

"Danny," Tadhg whispered, "there's a man in Lily's bed." Danny told him about Pascal. "I could probably put him up in one of the holiday cottages," Tadhg said. "The model unit is done, furnished and everything. It's a bit basic, but anything's better than Hiscock's." He snuggled into Danny and pulled the duvet over them both. "You can thank me later."

CHAPTER ELEVEN

Friday morning

"IF ANYBODY'S got the weekend scheduled off," Danny told the assembled group in the briefing room, "consider it cancelled." He waited while the assorted cries and murmurs of dismay died out. "Amalie Caron—at least we believe it's her—has been in touch with us. She called late last evening. You've all received a transcript of the call. Here's what we think so far: Amalie Caron rigged the family home to explode before fleeing and taking her son, Joseph, with her." Everything he and Pascal had been able to find pointed towards Amalie having skills of her own, including her participation in a government program to introduce women to the industrial trades. "Before she danced at Sexe Plus, she'd completed eighteen months of a four-year electrical apprenticeship. So she could have easily wired the family home to explode."

June Carbage waved a hand at him. "Are we to consider her our primary suspect, sir?"

"Don't rule it out," Danny replied. "Her husband, Gerard Caron, has also gone missing, and we believe he came to some misadventure at Amalie's hands." He'd transferred the disturbing video of Gerard Caron's torture to his laptop, projecting it onto the large screen at the front of the room. "It's likely the man in this video is Gerard Caron, and we suspect the woman is his wife, Amalie."

The reactions of the assembled group were about what he'd expected, and similar to his own. He, Pascal, Kevin, and Riley had already seen it, but even in replay it was horrifying, disturbing.

"Holy Mother of God," someone murmured.

June Carbage gazed wide-eyed at the screen, a hand clamped over her mouth. "My God," she said, after a moment, "that's fucked up."

He let the video run to its end, then closed it out, replacing it with Bobbi's photos of the scene in Beatrice Pynn's root cellar. "We found some pools of partially coagulated blood in a local woman's unused cellar. They may belong to Gerard Caron. If what you've just seen on the video is genuine, he was probably killed there."

"I'm after listening to the call," Kevin Carbage said, "and I'm a bit confused. What does she mean when she says she left the boy with good people? What good people?"

Blaise Pascal spoke up from the back of the room where he stood against the wall, nursing a flat white from Strange Brew and looking singularly well-rested. Danny was gratified that a night in a warm, clean bed and a decent meal inside him had produced the desired result. He didn't expect a change in Pascal's attitude or behaviour, but now the bastard owed him.

"She may not mean anything at all," he said. "This woman often says things that mean nothing. Or, she says nothing, and it means everything."

"Not helpful," someone murmured.

"That's enough!" Danny snapped. Unlike Pascal, his night of rest hadn't been so rosy. He'd fallen asleep but hadn't managed to stay asleep, the pain in his knees waking him at half past four. When one pain pill didn't do the trick, he brought the bottle back upstairs with him and took two more, and only when the codeine had loosened the agony could he slip into sleep. It hadn't been an easy rest but a repose fraught with nightmarish images and disembodied voices calling out for him. He managed to sleep through his alarm and only woke when Tadhg shook him, telling him it was after eight and he had better get up. Tadhg hadn't needed to ask how many of the codeine pills he'd taken; the grogginess that made him oversleep was quite evident at the breakfast table. "Mind your mouth. Inspector Pascal outranks almost every bloody one of ye crowd."

The offending party—Joey Yeo—was instantly contrite. "Sorry, sir." He was very young, blond, blue-eyed, and awfully sure of himself for someone who'd only just graduated from the police studies program at Memorial. Young bugger needed his arse belted. Well, if he kept on the way he was going, he'd find himself relegated to the filing room, or cataloguing nuisance calls on the night shift.

"Eventually we will find out what she means," Pascal said. "And then we will know all of it."

"Amalie Caron rigged her family home to explode," Danny continued. "That's one strike against her. She fled to Quebec with her six-year-old son, and as of now, the boy's whereabouts are unknown. He must be found. As Inspector Pascal has said, she is a psychopath. She might have harmed the boy, or she may have abandoned him. She was spotted at a Couche-Tard convenience store last evening, and the *Sûreté du Quebec* have located her rental car, which she abandoned in a parking lot in the town of Arundel. All of this points to her being in the Mont-Tremblant area."

"If she's in Quebec"—Yeo again—"then let the *Sûreté* handle her."

"This is a joint operation," Pascal told them. "Madame Caron, the *Sûreté* will find her, of that I have no doubt."

"It's not just a matter for the *Sûreté*," Danny said. "Gary Pretty was known to Amalie Caron, was probably sleeping with her until she killed him." He brought up Bobbi's crime scene photos, including those of Gary Pretty's corpse. There were several discomfited murmurs and someone near the back of the room muttered, "Mother of God."

"If she did that to him," he continued, "you can just imagine what she's likely to do to an innocent child. The boy is six years old. He is in grave danger, and this investigation is ongoing until we can locate him and his mother."

"Inspector Pascal." June spoke up. "Where do you think he is?"

"Myself, I think he is in Quebec."

"Have there been any sightings of the boy since his mother left Newfoundland?" Cillian Riley asked.

"No," Pascal replied. He paused to sip his coffee. "Everything we know of Amalie Caron, she always takes the boy with her. We assume she did the same thing this time, even if we do not see him."

"A colleague of Inspector Pascal's is keeping us informed," Danny said, "and we'll continue to work our end from here. There are two things I want you to concentrate on: Gerard Caron and the woman that Harry Dean's crew pulled from the sea."

"Still no luck identifying her?" Kevin Carbage asked. June's twin brother had been curiously quiet during the search for Amalie Caron, contributing little to the ongoing investigation and rarely offering input on the case.

"I'm hoping to get Dr. Annie Turnbull in to have a look at the teeth," Danny replied. "We're a bit short of the advanced equipment and techniques that other larger stations have, but we'll make do." His gaze sought Bobbi Lambert in the crowd, and he nodded at her. "Bobbi's team are equal to any in the country. I'd bet money on it. For now, however, we are no closer to identifying the dead woman. Judging by the quality of her clothing, we think she may have been well-to-do, perhaps a professional. Dr. Lampe thinks, given the cause of death, that she may have been involved with a criminal syndicate, maybe drug traffickers or the mafia."

Kevin nodded, murmured his understanding, but didn't say anything further. It was very odd the way he'd become so reticent of late. Perhaps a word with his sister might clear things up.

"I've examined the blood you and Inspector Pascal found in the cellar," Bobbi Lambert interjected. "Some of it's Gerard Caron's. We ran it against the DNA collected from the house."

"Only some of it is Caron's?"

"That's the thing." Bobbi shook her head. "A portion of what we recovered isn't blood at all."

"Not blood." It took a moment for what she'd said to register with him. "Then what the hell is it?"

"As far as I can make out, it's stage blood, homemade. A mixture of hair gel, food colouring, and what seems to be Astroglide."

Someone in the back of the room giggled. Joey Yeo.

"Astroglide?" Danny asked.

"Personal lubricant."

"I know what it is." He mulled this over for a moment. "So Gerard Caron didn't actually lose much blood in the cellar, which probably means the video we saw of him having his eyes gouged out is fake."

Pascal glanced up, his coffee forgotten. "She didn't kill him? She just made it look that way?"

"The genuine blood you found. How long has it been there?" Danny knew she couldn't give him a definite time, but Bobbi's best guess was better than most people's absolute certainty.

"Coagulation was affected by the environment of the cellar," she replied. "But I'd say no more than twenty-four to forty-eight hours."

"So he could still be alive and on the island." Danny wondered if this were true. What did Caron have to gain by staying hidden? Had Amalie really tortured him, or was the video part of some elaborate scheme they'd cooked up between the two of them? "Dougie, anything on the video files?"

"Yes, sir. If I could...?" He came forward with an open laptop computer cradled in his arms. Danny stepped aside so Hughes could connect it to the projector and waited while he clicked through to the now-familiar list of files. "Our suspicions were correct. There's more here than initially meets the eye."

"In what way?" Riley asked.

"Whoever made these videos was using them as cover material. What you see on the screen"—Hughes touched a key and the familiar scene of the boy, the man, and the rocking horse appeared—"isn't the whole picture."

He clicked something else and the image of a heavyset man of about sixty, wearing only boxer shorts and a singlet, filled the frame. He was seated on a straight-backed wooden chair, one hand tied behind him. The other held a large purple dildo close to his face. Someone gave a command in French, and he inserted it into his mouth, letting it rest on his tongue. Another short phrase, spoken by the same person, and he pumped it in and out of his mouth, his hand moving faster and faster until it was nearly a blur.

"Jesus," Kevin muttered. "Is that supposed to be...?"

"Just wait," Hughes instructed. "It gets better—or maybe worse, depending on your point of view." The screen faded to black for a moment. When the scene resumed, the man was on his knees, his buttocks to the camera, pumping the dildo in and out of his own anus while blood ran down the backs of his legs onto the floor.

"It's called 'hurtcore.'" Hughes shut off the video not a moment too soon. "I did some checking, and the man in the video is—"

"Jean-Guy Bonenfant," Pascal put in. "A member of L'Assemblée nationale du Quebec."

Hughes nodded. "Yes, sir."

"What's hurtcore?" June asked. She looked as shocked and horrified as everyone else in the room.

"It is a particularly vile form of pornographie," Pascal said, "for those who derive pleasure seeing others harm themselves or be harmed." His gaze flickered to the screen and away again. "There have been several notable cases in this country, many of them involving children. This sort of thing appeals to sadists, those who like to cause pain to others."

"You said children." June looked distinctly queasy. "But this is a grown man."

Pascal smiled, a weary smile all too aware of its own irony. "The latest *tendance* is with adults, especially public figures. The person making it is paid twice: once when their client accesses this material, and again when the subject of the film pays *une rançon* to have it removed from the dark web." He shrugged. "Of course, it is never removed, not really. It only migrates, *peut-être*, to another site, or is distributed in other ways."

"There's special software they use," Hughes continued, "to encrypt the hidden video. Like I said before, you could buy a Disney movie for your kids from someone on eBay, not knowing what's really underneath. If you don't have the decryption software, there's no way of unlocking it."

"But the people who consume this sort of thing," Riley asked, "they have the software so they can watch it?"

"Yes."

The room sank into silence. After a moment, Danny said, "So if this was found in Amalie Caron's car, she was making these videos?"

Pascal nodded. "The one she sent you, it's basically the same thing. So yes."

"Riley, can you take over?" Danny came to where Pascal was and said, "A word. In private." He waited till they were both in his office, the door closed behind them, then said, "You knew she was doing this."

"I did not." Pascal sank into a chair uninvited.

"You knew she was doing something, though."

"We suspected. We had no proof." His gaze was steady, unwavering. "I tell you the truth. From time to time, certain videos would surface from this deep dark web, and some of our officers recognised a particular landmark out of a window in a room. Later we identified it as Montreal or Mont-Tremblant or Laval."

"So someone in Quebec was definitely making this... hurtcore." It didn't rule out Amalie Caron.

"*Oui*. Then one day myself and Prud'Homme are going through some video ourselves." One corner of Pascal's mouth lifted, but there was nothing funny about it, any of it. "We see something that is not familiar to us." He laid his coffee on the desk and took his mobile phone out of his hip pocket. "I will show you," he said, swiping at the screen, then turning it so Danny could see. "This is a still frame from a video we recovered. Look at the background, out the window."

Danny leaned forward to look. The scene was of a bedroom with an unmade bed under a low ceiling and an undraped window. Some wooden houses, brightly coloured in shades of green, blue, and even pink, rose in the background. Beyond them was the familiar shape of—

"Jesus, that's Signal Hill."

"*Vraiment*. So these films are being made all over the place," Pascal confirmed, "not merely in Quebec."

"You're not just here after Amalie Caron." Standing behind his desk was excruciating, the pain in Danny's knees sizzling along his nerve endings like liquid fire. He lowered himself into his chair and began rifling through his desk drawers for the Tylenol. "Goddammit, why can't you just be straight with me? I don't understand all this cloak-and-dagger bullshit. We're on the same side."

Pascal watched him for several moments, then asked, "Are you looking for something?"

Before he could reply, there was a tap on his door, and Marilyn appeared. "Dr. Lampe called. She's been trying to get you."

Regan had actually called him back? This was surprising. Danny felt for his mobile phone, pulled it out of his hip pocket. "Sorry, Marilyn. I turned it off during the briefing."

"You'd better call her back. You know what she's like." Her head withdrew, and she pulled the door shut behind her.

Pascal stood up to go. "I will pass on the information about the video files to the *Sûreté*," he said and left.

Danny called Regan, who answered on the first ring. "I found something." She sounded positively elated.

"Oh?"

"Sending you the file now. Check your email." His ear was suddenly full of dial tone. He turned to his computer and opened the image file she'd sent. At first, he couldn't make out what he was looking at—a pale expanse of what might be skin with a small brown mark. It was only when he clicked on the enlarged view that he understood. It was a birthmark, located just under the shoulder blade. Whose?

His office door swung open, and Blaise Pascal stepped through. He spotted what was on the screen and stretched out a hand towards it. "Thinking of that for a tattoo?"

Danny turned to look at him. "Take a guess what this is."

Pascal gazed at the screen for a moment. "A birthmark, *non*?" He moved close to peer at the image, one hand on Danny's shoulder. "*Sacrément*," he said. "It looks like a little pair of wings."

"It does. Dr. Lampe found it on the dead woman's back."

"It is certainly what I would call a distinguishing mark," Pascal said. "Who does it belong to?"

"It's familiar," Danny replied. "I've seen it before. I know I have." He suddenly remembered the bottle of Tylenol was in his jacket pocket; his jacket was hanging behind the door. He all but leapt for it, retrieved the painkillers, and swallowed two with the remnants of his morning coffee, now cold and unappealing. "You have something you want to share? Or is your information for the *Sûreté* only?" He'd wanted to broach the subject earlier. Every time some new piece of evidence surfaced, Pascal appeared to have gotten there first—to have inside knowledge that Danny and his team weren't privy to.

"I share such information with you when and where I feel it is appropriate." Pascal's dark eyes blazed at him. "When it has nothing to do with your investigation, I keep it to myself."

"You arrogant son of a bitch." A wave of heat washed over him. "Were you ever going to tell me? And where do you get off? This isn't your jurisdiction. You had absolutely no right—" A sharp rap on the door cut him off mid-sentence. "For fuck sake!"

"Sorry, sir." Sarah Avery stood well back from the door, as if she expected it to attack her. "I've finished with that list of names."

"Names?"

"From the dead woman's pocket," Pascal said. "The one you did not want me to look at."

"That's right, sir." She stepped into the office and laid a sheet of paper on Danny's desk, then retreated to where she'd been standing. "They all turned up on our database. Th-the computer shows, erm, they've all g-got past convictions."

"For what?" He took up the sheet of paper and scanned it briefly.

"Distributing pornography, solicitation, forcible confinement, sexual assault, aggravated sexual assault, and...." She trailed off and gestured at the sheet she'd given him. "It's all there."

"All right, thank you." He couldn't look at her, aware that he'd made an arse of himself.

"There's one other thing, sir."

"Oh?"

"They are all from the province of Quebec—Inspector Pascal was a lot of help—and most of their crimes were committed in that province. I don't know if that has anything to do with what we're looking for, but there it is."

"Thank you, Avery." He'd track her down later and apologise for shouting at her. It wasn't her he'd been shouting at. "You can go." She fled down the hall, and Danny didn't have to wonder why.

"I am familiar with these names," Pascal said, smirking. "So I decided to help the girl with this list. Don't worry. When the case is solved, I will give you the credit. Is that what you are afraid of?"

Danny's mobile buzzed. He pulled it out and glanced at the screen. Tadhg. "I have to take this," he said, stepping out into the corridor and closing the door behind him. It wouldn't do much to dampen sound or provide any privacy—Danny's office having no ceiling—so he went through to the front office and out the door to the parking lot. "I'm going to kill him," he said, as soon as he'd accepted the call. "I'm going to kick the shite out of him—"

"With your bad knees?" Tadhg interjected.

"—and pull his fucking arms off." Danny was so angry he could hardly breathe. "He knows things, Tadhg. That bastard has got information that pertains to this case and he won't—" He stopped, drew in a breath. "He is trying to fuck up this investigation. He is."

"There's a parcel came for you," Tadhg said.

This was such an abrupt change in the conversation that it threw him off. "What?"

"A parcel, my love," Tadhg repeated. "I fetched the mail myself, just now."

"But I didn't order anything." He, Tadhg, and Lily all shopped online. "Are you sure it's for me?"

"It is. I had to sign for it." Tadhg chuckled. "Luckily that one at the post office knows me, otherwise I wouldn't be allowed to take it." He paused. "It's insured for five thousand pounds."

"Dollars, you mean."

"No, Danny. It's from the UK."

His scalp prickled. Who was sending him parcels from the UK? "Not from Ireland?"

"No. Wales. It's postmarked from Wales."

The bottom dropped out of his stomach, then rebounded violently. He was going to be sick. He closed his eyes, forced himself to breathe, and pressed his tongue firmly against the roof of his mouth. "Wales," he said, when he could speak again. "Insured for five thousand pounds. Does it say…. Tadhg, does it say who sent it?"

"No, my love."

"What's in it?"

"I didn't open it. It's not for me. It's for you."

"Okay." The urge to vomit had thankfully passed. Maybe it was nothing. Something he'd ordered for Tadhg or Lily and forgotten about, an intended Christmas or birthday gift. "I'll look at it when I comes home. Later. Dinnertime or whatever."

"Danny. My love, whatever it is, we'll deal with it," Tadhg said. "Together. All right?"

"Yes." He felt suddenly close to tears. "You knows I loves the bones of ye."

"And I loves you."

"I'll see ye when I gets home." He closed out the connection, ending the call.

Pascal was still in his office when Danny went back inside. He'd presumably moved at some point, because there was a cup of coffee in front of him.

"You were telling me about the list," Danny said.

Pascal nodded. "The names are all connected with each other." He didn't apologise or make reference to the argument they'd had, but at least he wasn't smirking anymore.

"And?"

"They are part of a group, you see?" He sketched an imaginary design on the desktop with his index finger. "They do business in this dark web as you call it, putting up bad films and drugs, sometimes women. We have been investigating them for many years, but they are extremely difficult to find. They find new members by word of mouth, in various places around, here and there. As far as we have been able to tell, there is a… *initiation*, you know? Then they are in the club."

"Who are they?" Danny asked. It wouldn't surprise him if the mafia had moved into Kildevil Cove; drugs had been shipped in and out of remote rural ports for decades. Back in 1987, Montreal mafia don Vito Rizzuto had moved 225 million dollars' worth of hashish into the eastern end of the country via Ireland's Eye, and in 1993 the RCMP intercepted twenty-five tonnes of the stuff coming ashore at Little Heart's Ease. Danny knew the island was no longer the safe haven it had once been. The Hell's Angels controlled most of the drug trade, importing cocaine and heroin from Montreal, along with sex workers masquerading as exotic dancers.

"They are a clandestine group that are known to us. More than that I cannot say because of several ongoing investigations. It is not wrong to suppose that this woman in the fish net, she was involved. These people, they do not trust easily, so she is perhaps a long-time member of the group. If she—what do you say?—pissed them off, they would dispose of her."

"So, what? They're bringing in drugs? Is that it?"

Pascal sighed. "If it were only drugs, this would be clear, *certainement*. What do you know about human trafficking?"

Danny stared at him. "A lot," he said. He told Pascal about the case that had started with a trafficking victim washing ashore and ended with him nearly losing his career. He would never forgive Moira Fraser for what she'd done to him, and the sour taste of his guilt by association still lingered. She had vanished without a trace some eighteen months previous.

The Quebecois shifted his gaze to the window behind Danny. After a moment he asked, "Have you ever seen this film, *La Matrice*?"

Danny sifted through his scant knowledge of French and came up with the answer. "*The Matrix*."

"That is the one. There is a character in this, and he says something about how deep the rabbit hole goes." Pascal reached across to tap the sheet of paper Avery had left with them. "This is the very lip of the rabbit hole."

Danny felt suddenly very cold. "How deep does it go?"

Pascal held his gaze. "You have no idea. And what is down there? It is the stuff of nightmares."

BLAISE PASCAL waited until he was alone in his office before putting a call through to the Joliette Institute for Women, taking care to use his mobile phone rather than the one on his desk. This part of the investigation had nothing to do with Quirke and his team but concerned

Pascal personally, and he wasn't interested in explaining the nature of the call when it showed up in the station's records. Quirke was all right in his way, but he was far too inquisitive when it came to personal matters. Even his attempts at friendship and conciliation were intended to prise more information out of Pascal than he was willing to give.

"I am looking for Louise Belanger," he said when the call was answered.

"One moment. I will see if she is available."

A loud clang resounded as the receiver dropped. Louise had been assigned to the kitchen at the beginning of her incarceration, so his call had been routed through there. "*Oui*, this is Louise Belanger." She sounded harried and out of breath.

"It's Blaise."

"I still remember your voice. I'm not entirely insane."

That was debatable. "I'm looking for information."

She laughed, a brittle sound like someone breaking hard plastic. "You know what you can do."

"I'll make it worth your while." He waited. It was true that everyone, almost without exception, had their price, and in his long years of service with the *Sûreté*, he had yet to meet someone who couldn't be bought.

"I need cigarettes. You can get me a new lighter, eh, Blaise?" A nasty cackle. "Maybe I'll burn this place to the ground as well." Those who supervised her were under strict orders: Louise wasn't to be within shouting distance of anything that could cause a fire. It amused him to think of her being employed in Joliette's kitchens and not being allowed to work the stove. He almost made a snide remark, but it was better not to antagonise her. She was the only one who could give him the help he needed now.

"You know I can't do that." He picked up a pen from the desk and drew a series of circles on a pad of paper. "What else would you like?"

"Have you talked to Théo?"

She would feign maternal feeling to get the things she wanted out of him. *Eh bien*, he'd go along for the ride. It wasn't so difficult. "Yes. I went to see him." No need to tell her their son had taken an overdose. Louise would place the blame squarely on his shoulders, insist that it was his fault, that Théo's mental problems were the result of bad Pascal blood. "He is doing very well. They think he will talk soon. The nurse told me that last week he tried to say something, so that's good news."

"You always were a shitty liar."

He said nothing, simply allowed that to sit between them for a moment. "What about some chocolate? I can arrange to have it sent. Lecavalier Petrone, I remember, in Pointe-Saint-Charles. It is your favourite." During their marriage, he'd made a habit of giving her a large gift box every Christmas. The chocolates were beautiful, miniature works of art painted in bright colours and abstract patterns with cocoa butter, each one unique and different from the others.

"You think you can buy me?"

"Lecavalier Petrone. Whatever you want. As much as you want." He drew a pile of circles, added vines and leaves so it resembled a bunch of grapes. Once, on their wedding anniversary, they had toured the Vignoble Ste-Pétronille winery, located in gorgeous Ile d'Orléans. It was a hot summer's day with scarcely a breeze to stir the vines, and they'd wandered hand in hand, hardly speaking. She had been almost civil.

"What about if I want you to come and fuck me?"

"Don't be crude." *I'd rather stick it in a rotting cabbage*, he thought. "Come on, what do you want?"

She agreed to a signature selection box of chocolates and some cigarettes, along with several books she wanted to read as well as spending money. The goddamn woman was going to bankrupt him if she kept on. "I want to ask you a question about your sister," Pascal said at last. He drew a caricature of a queen seated on a throne, with a kneeling man prostrating himself before her.

"About Amalie? *Pourquoi?*"

"Do you think she would hurt Joseph?" No reply. He could hear activity in the background, silverware being shuffled into a drawer and pots clanging as their lids were lifted. Someone coughed, the phlegm-ridden, chesty cough of a lifelong smoker, and he thought guiltily of the pack in his own shirt pocket. What was it the *foutu Anglais* said? 'Where there is smoke, there is fire.'

"Her brat?"

Louise had been unable to form a maternal bond with Théo when he was born, and for months and even years afterwards, struggled to relate to their son on his own level. She became enraged when he did things common to infants, such as soiling his diaper as soon as it was on or spitting up his milk. Breastfeeding was difficult and painful, not at all the natural process she had been led to believe, and when he did manage to latch on, he wouldn't suckle. She saw this as a rejection of her, assuming that his behaviour meant she was unsuited for motherhood. *He hates me,* she would say, raging at their son. *The petit salaud doesn't like the taste of me. I'm not good enough for him.*

"I don't know," Louise replied now. "Do you think she would? By the way, I saw your little boyfriend on the news, talking about how the *Sûreté* was going to arrest Amalie."

She probably meant Prud'Homme, who'd been interviewed by Radio-Canada about the disappearance. "Do you think she would injure the boy?"

"I told you, Blaise, I don't know. Look, I have to go soon—"

"Just one more question," he said and hated the note of pleading in his voice.

"What?" Someone in the background called her name, and she replied she'd be there in a moment.

"Where is she? Where is the boy?"

"That's two questions, *salaud.*"

"*Ben là*, Louise."

"The boy is where no one will ever find him, with good people who will take care of him forever." He could hear her smirk over the phone. "Amalie is, I hope, in hell." There was a click and the dial tone. She'd hung up on him.

"*Plotte*," he muttered, wishing she could hear him.

His mobile rang again as he was on his way to the breakroom for a cup of coffee. This time it was Prud'Homme. "*Salut*, Inspector."

"Prud'Homme, you have news?"

"Amalie Caron. She made several trips to *les Apôtres de l'amour de Dieu*. The Apostles of the Love of God, here in Mont-Tremblant. You have heard of them?"

"She made these trips when? Yes, I've heard of them." The break room door was open, and the woman sergeant was in there, sitting at a table with the Englishman and peeling an orange. She glanced up as he entered and smiled; she had managed to peel the fruit in one long, unbroken strip.

"July and August, around the middle of the month, and then at the beginning of September," Prud'Homme announced. He sounded proud of himself.

"Where did you get this information?" Pascal nodded at June Carbage and the Englishman as he passed by.

"I was inspired. Lying in bed one night, thinking about this case, I tried to put myself into her mind. I realised I didn't know enough about her to do that. I had to go back in time in order to understand." He'd done some searching through archived case files from the 1990s, he said, and turned up a former friend of Amalie's, Françoise Mathieu. Both women had worked at the same strip club on rue St-Dominique, GantVelours, until Mathieu found religion.

"What do you mean?" Pascal plucked a coffee pod off a neat pyramid of them someone had created on the counter and put it in the Keurig.

"She joined a… I suppose you could say it is a church, but not in the traditional sense."

"Let me guess: these Apostles." Pascal took a clean cup from the cupboard and placed it under the machine's spout.

"Correct. I did a little bit of checking. She is still there."

The Keurig hissed and gurgled, decanting a thin brown stream into Pascal's cup. "What?"

"She is still there, *Inspecteur*. And she has had visitors. To be clear, one visitor in particular."

His heart thumped uneasily in his chest, a jagged rhythm like a stutter. "Amalie Caron."

"On July 23, a photo radar camera in Mirabel caught an image of a red Toyota Corolla, which later turned out to be a rental car. Do you want to know who was inside?" He didn't wait for Pascal's reply. "On August 2, Amalie Caron ran a red light on route 327 near Brébeuf. Nine minutes later, her image was again captured by photo radar on route 323, just outside Mont-Tremblant."

Pascal set his coffee on the counter and went to the fridge. "You're sure it was her."

"If not her, then she has a twin sister we don't know about."

He let out the breath he'd been holding. "*Merci*, Prud'Homme."

"This is not all, sir. On September 2, she appeared briefly outside an elementary school on rue Charbonneau in Mont-Tremblant. A school custodian witnessed her watching the building from across the street. Later that day, a woman called, inquiring if her six-year-old son could attend. *Malheureusement*, there were no places left."

"How do you know this?"

"I went there," Prud'Homme replied. "I spoke to these people myself. I don't believe they are lying. Right now I am reviewing the CCTV footage from the school security cameras to see if she actually entered the building."

"Was the child with her? Could she have left him with these disciples or whatever they call themselves?"

"*Je ne sais pas*." I don't know. "But I am following up on everything, and I will tell you what I find." Prud'Homme drew a long breath and blew it out. "*Monsieur*, why would she be looking at schools in Mont-Tremblant? Could she be planning to move? Why Mont-Tremblant? What's here for her?"

"I am." It made sense, he thought, as he stirred cream into his coffee. No doubt Amalie felt they had unfinished business. "Prud'Homme, this is excellent detective work. I think you are looking to take my job."

"Speaking of which, *monsieur*—"

"The BEI? Prud'Homme, I am depending on you to keep them off me. I have work to do here. When it's done, I will deal with them."

"*D'accord, Monsieur l'inspecteur*. I'll be in touch."

"Wondered where you'd got to." Quirke had come up behind him. He nodded at the mobile phone in Pascal's hand. "You look like a man who's got information."

"I do."

"Feel up to sharing?"

"*Bien sûr que oui*. Yes, of course."

"Let's meet in my office."

IN A hotel room in Mont-Tremblant, Amalie Caron laid out a line of pills and smiled to herself. *Tout à l'heure*, she thought smugly.

All in good time.

CHAPTER TWELVE

Saturday morning

JUNE CARBAGE arrived back at the station bright and early on Saturday morning, glad to have something to do. Her partner, Amy, had decided the weekend was an excellent time to have a full-on clear-out. She'd even bought extra bin bags in anticipation, and the last thing June wanted to do was get in her way.

"So you're not going to stay and supervise?" Amy asked over breakfast. "Just to be sure I'm not tossing out your most precious possessions?" It was said with a vehemence that surprised June, and she wondered what dark emotion was at the back of it. Lately Amy had been wildly inconsistent in her behaviour, veering between her usual easygoing manner and something darker. She'd always been generous with her praise and showed her appreciation for June with flagrantly romantic gestures like unexpected flowers in the middle of an ordinary day. In recent months, however, she'd become critical and nasty, responding to June's overtures with sarcasm or jeering. What June couldn't figure out was why.

"I trust your judgement," June said mildly and left before Amy could respond.

"Good morning," Danny greeted her as she entered the station. The morning was cool and overcast, with a northeasterly breeze that seemed to presage the winter to come. "Up early, aren't ye?" He was standing by the front desk, sorting through a stack of files and checking the previous night's call log.

"I could say the same for you," she replied. "What's Tadhg think about you deserting the connubial bed before dawn, anyway?"

"He's at the construction site all day," Danny said. "Couldn't wait to shove me out the door. Cuppa tea?"

"I won't say no." She went to hang up her coat and check her email at her desk. It being a Saturday, there wasn't much there of any interest, mostly spam that contained special offers for anti-aging creams and Sex! Sex! Sex! with a hot Nigerian prince who wanted to transfer fifty

million dollars into her personal bank account. At the very bottom of the
electronic pile was a message from an unfamiliar address. She clicked on
it without thinking and was taken aback by the first two lines:

Please don't tell Danny.

I need your help.

It was dated eight days previous and came from Moira Fraser, the
former chief superintendent in charge of the Kildevil Cove station. Why it
took so long to be delivered, June couldn't tell. That it was from a woman
who'd turned out to be a sex trafficker was the biggest surprise. June
would be hard pressed to say why Moira Fraser had so readily jettisoned
a police career, but her ties to the psychopath Martin Belshawe, a Scot
who'd infiltrated the Royal Newfoundland Constabulary, might have
something to do with it. Belshawe had wormed his way into Danny's
good graces by masquerading as a detective working with Interpol. Like
most psychopaths, he was charming, and he seemed to know a great deal
about the cases he was supposedly investigating. Everybody, including
Danny and June herself, had been taken in by him.

It made sense that Moira would try to crawl back to the nest,
especially now that most members of the trafficking ring were in
prison. She was likely alone in the world, without help and hoping to be
welcomed back into the fold as if nothing had happened.

"Milky, and I left the bag in, just the way you like it." Danny
appeared at her elbow and passed her a mug of tea. "There's brownies in
the fridge. I didn't know if you'd want one." He leaned in and gazed at
her computer screen. "Is that…?"

June took the tea with a murmur of thanks. "From Moira. Well, it
says it's from her. It ended up in my spam folder."

"You check your spam folder?"

She lifted her shoulders and let them drop. "You never know.
Something important might end up in there. It's better to check, isn't it?"

"That's interesting. 'Don't tell Danny.'" His hand tightened around
the mug of tea. "Maybe she figures I'm still mad at her, the bitch."

"Aren't you?"

"You're fucking right I am," he said, so savagely that June was
taken aback for a moment. Of course, Danny had every right to feel the
way he did. Moira Fraser's involvement with the criminal organisation
that trafficked vulnerable young women had reflected badly on him. She'd
been his immediate superior, and those in power assumed that Danny was

complicit in her crimes. The result had been a demotion all the way back down to constable, probably because there was no lower rank and because he was enough of an asset to the Constabulary that they wanted him kept in. "That goddamn woman nearly cost me everything. I'd still be a constable, left behind doing everybody's scutwork, if it wasn't for Molloy. Wherever she is, I hope she's suffering the torments of the damned."

"Do you think I should answer it?" She wasn't even sure where she'd begin. What could she say to the woman who'd thrown such a monkey wrench into the everyday workings of their little station? "Sure, you knows yourself, come on back"? Not that such an invitation was even hers to extend in the first place.

"No. Leave it. Forward it to me. I'll see if Dougie can track down where it came from, and we'll find out where she is. There's a few people at Interpol still wanting a word with that... woman."

June pulled up the forensic photos of the woman who'd been caught in Harry Dean's fishing net and paged through them again. She had no real idea what she was looking for. June herself had searched all local, national, and international police databases for possibilities based on the little information they had and turned up nothing, which was only to be expected. Regan had taken cheek swabs for DNA analysis, but this would take another two or three weeks, and that was supposing the RCMP lab in St. John's wasn't particularly busy and the woman's DNA was on file—a long shot at best. Danny had been trying to contact Dr. Annie Turnbull, the island's only forensic odontologist, but she was on vacation and not due to return for another two weeks—two weeks longer than Regan was willing to let him take up one of her mortuary drawers. June suspected that an examination of the dead woman's mouth wouldn't yield much more than what they already had.

It was all so frustrating.

She looked up as Danny approached again. "What is it?"

"I've just downloaded Regan's autopsy report on Gary Pretty." He laid some papers on the corner of her desk. "Made a copy for you."

June paged through it, skimming the contents. "It says here that his spinal fluid contained high concentrations of cortisol."

"It's a stress hormone."

She read on. "And levels of prolactin were three times the norm in sampled cerebrospinal fluid. Hypoxia?"

"He was tortured to death," Danny said grimly, "and suffocated at intervals."

June felt suddenly cold all over. "Amalie Caron did this?"

"Yeah."

"She cut him open while he was still alive." The crime scene photos taken by Bobbi were numerous and explicit, showing Gary Pretty's injuries in intimate detail. "There must have been a hell of a lot of blood."

"Enough to leave a parting message."

June had seen the crime scene photos: *Ma Jolie Louise*. "What do you think she meant by it?"

"When we were at the scene, Pascal said it was a song lyric by Daniel Lanois." Danny shook his head. "His reaction said something else." He paused, probably recalling the day he and Pascal found Pretty's corpse. "It was like… he was shocked, you know? Really badly shocked. Like he'd seen something completely unexpected."

"He's a veteran *Sûreté* detective," June said. "Surely he's been at homicide scenes before." If Danny's recollection of events was accurate, then Pascal's violent reaction was telling. "It's just a song lyric."

"Not to him." Danny turned to go. "Were we able to get any additional info on him? Besides what the *Sûreté* supplied?"

"Don't think so, sir. He's divorced, so there's no mention of a spouse in the personnel dossier they sent us."

"Mm." Her reply clearly hadn't satisfied him. "Feel like having a dig around?"

"I'll try, but I don't know how much they're willing to disclose."

"They told you he was being investigated by the BEI."

"True, but that's got to be a matter of record anyway. They'd look bad if they didn't tell us and we went looking and found it. You want me to find out his wife's name?"

"Ex-wife." He grinned as he turned to go. "Thanks."

"Sir." June called him back. "The stuff in the dead woman's pockets. Do you think it might have been put there deliberately? To throw us off?"

"Possibly. Maybe not. Who's to say?"

"Do you think she could be someone local?" June asked.

"It's possible," Danny allowed, "but who could she be?"

"Someone hungry for a different life?" As if to emphasise the point, her stomach growled. Danny did say there were brownies in the fridge.

"A local woman involved in organised crime." He fell silent for a moment, clearly pondering the possibilities. "The only person I can think of is—"

"Moira." She tapped her computer screen. "And just like that, she pops up in my email. What are the odds? Almost like someone's been encouraging her."

"You're too young to be so cynical," Danny said. "Tell you what, I'll ring Molloy and see if he can request Moira's medical records. Might be worth a look."

"What about me?" June asked. "Got any important tasks for me?"

"Catalogue the things we found and enter them into evidence," he told her. "And for the love of God"—he grinned—"eat something."

June had helped herself to the brownies in the break room fridge and was busy scarfing down a slice of leftover pizza when Bobbi Lambert came in. Her bright red punk hairstyle looked like a woodpecker's feathered crest, and she was equally chirpy. "That piece of cardboard," she said by way of greeting, then, "What's that ye got? Pizza?"

"Leftovers from that staff meeting," June replied through a mouthful. "There's more there if ye wants it. What piece of cardboard?"

Bobbi went to the fridge and hauled out the pizza box. "Bookmobile. Remember we found a piece of cardboard in there? Tiny little bit. No bigger than your pinky fingernail." She plucked a slice of pizza and bit into it. "Jesus God, this is even better when it's cold."

"Well, tell me." June polished off her slice and went to flick the kettle on. She took a clean mug from the cupboard and dropped a Barry's teabag into it. Danny, tired of station personnel nicking his Lyons, had bought a case of strong, malty Barry's tea the last time he'd been in Ireland.

"I honest to God didn't think we'd get anything off it," Bobbi replied. "Tiny little piece. But this young fella from the university, goes with my sister, and him with brains to burn, so."

"He figured it out?" Now Bobbi would tell her to guess what it was, and June wouldn't be able to. "It's a pregnancy test. Am I right?"

Bobbi looked gobsmacked. "How the hell did you know that?"

"I don't know." She was being honest. "It just popped into my head. I suppose with women of childbearing age it's either that or tampons."

"You're a friggin' witch, you are." Bobbi scoffed. "Yes, it's a pregnancy test. One of them dollar-store jobbies. How accurate they are, God only knows."

The kettle came to a boil and snapped off, and June went to pour water into her mug. "You want a cuppa?"

Bobbi nodded. "God love ye." She finished the slice of pizza and wiped her hands on her jeans. "What we'll never know is if it was positive or negative. Oh well. Ours is not to wonder why." And with that, she was gone.

If Amalie Caron was pregnant… who was the father? June checked her watch: it was just past nine. She wondered if Inspector Pascal was in his office and went to find him.

To call the basement region of the station "labyrinthine" would be going too far, even if it was comprised of narrow, twisting passageways that sometimes led to the cells and other times led nowhere. Danny had reassured them all that nothing sinister occurred down below, and the narrow corridors were simply constructed in an era when people were smaller. The depth to which the building's cellar descended was at least eighteen feet—or five and a half metres—into the typically rocky Newfoundland soil, the space subdivided longitudinally to create a basement and a subbasement. She wasn't claustrophobic in the least, but the ceilings were rather lower than June would have liked, and she had to resist the urge to duck her head to stay clear of imagined obstructions. Pascal's "office" was little more than a closet, a narrow room about two metres wide and three metres long, the size of a prison cell, and the dank, airless space felt like one. He could have occupied the interview room, which at least had windows, but he'd need to vacate any time the space was needed. The break room was far too noisy, and the only other free space in the station was the external garage, where both patrol cars were kept. Marilyn had done her best to find Pascal somewhere to work, but the station was woefully short of habitable space.

She found him hunched over his laptop, typing furiously with both index fingers. "Inspector?"

He glanced up, his features set in a scowl, but relaxed when he saw it was her. "*Salut*, Sergeant Carbage. What brings you to this underworld?"

"I'm so sorry," she said reflexively. "It's a horrible place to try and work. I wish we had something better for you."

Pascal shrugged. "*Eh bien*, it serves my purpose." He closed the cover of the laptop. "You need help?"

"I wanted to ask your opinion."

"Oh." His dark brows rose and fell. "This is unusual. I am beginning to think I am invisible." He grinned to soften the remark, but she was embarrassed all the same. Nobody at the station seemed inclined to include Pascal in anything, despite the fact that he'd been investigating Amalie Caron for fourteen years. Danny regarded him as an annoyance at best, asking for Pascal's input only if it was absolutely necessary. There was also the small matter of the boss's ego.

I'm only human, June. This had been his defence when she'd called him on it recently. *That bastard is treading on my patch. I have my pride. And he's keeping things from us too.*

"The woman Harry Dean found in his nets. It doesn't add up." At Pascal's nod, she continued. "There were things in her pockets."

"I have looked at the photographs."

"Chewing gum, a piece of string, a series of names." A bizarre list indeed. "Why would someone carry these things about with them?"

"What do you think?" he asked, and she told him. "It is possible," he said, "but is it also probable? If you kill a someone and then tip her into the sea, why would you put such things into her pockets as might be destroyed by water? If you want to ruin her identity, you cut off the fingertips, you demolish the face."

"Of course." June felt distinctly like an idiot. "I knew that. I mean, I learned that in school." She blamed her currently addled state on her lack of sleep. Lately Amy had been absent from the supper table more nights than she was home or leaving at odd hours and for spurious reasons. The night before last she'd not returned to their bed until well after 3:00 a.m., and when June pressed her about her absence, she became angry and defensive.

"I know the names on that list. I helped *mademoiselle* Avery with them." Pascal opened his laptop and poked at a series of keys. "Come here. Look at this."

She came round to his side of the desk. He'd brought up a photograph in which two men—one older, grey-haired, and wearing thick glasses, the other young, fit, and muscular—were seen walking towards a waiting police car, flanked by *Sûreté* officers. "This man here"—Pascal indicated the older man—"he is Jean-Baptiste Roul, formerly a high-ranking person in Poussin Panto, a criminal."

"What's Poussin Panto?" June asked.

"It is a syndicate of organised crime."

"So he's in prison." She wondered where Pascal was going with this.

"No, he is in the ground. Or perhaps blowing in the wind. Burial, cremation, I don't remember, and I don't care."

June asked the obvious question. "So what about the woman we found in the water?"

"What about her?"

"Could she have been involved with organised crime as well?" The expensive clothes, the bizarre death so many kilometres from land, and the destruction of the face that could have been a side-effect of scraping along the bottom of the ocean but might have also been deliberate. Destroy the face and the fingerprints and there is no hope of making a positive identification.

He caught her gaze briefly, then looked away. "I don't know. Perhaps we will never know." His smile, when it came, was perfunctory and fake. "Was there anything else?"

"No." Was he trying to get rid of her? Perhaps her questions made him uncomfortable. June wished her French was better so she could speak to him in his native language, where even the most subtle nuance would come across clearly. "No, that's everything. Thanks for making time for me. I appreciate it."

At the foot of the stairs she stopped, one hand on the railing. Did Pascal know who the dead woman was? June had always relied on her instincts, and in this case Danny was right. There was something about Pascal's presence in Kildevil Cove that didn't add up. She turned to go back but stopped herself. Pascal outranked her, and he wouldn't welcome another impromptu interrogation, especially not from her.

AMALIE WAS surprised when she woke the next morning, still alive and undiscovered. If anything, the two sleeping pills she'd washed down with vodka had given her the best night's sleep she'd had in ages. She went into the bathroom and started the shower running in the huge glassed-in cabinet before stripping off the sweatpants and T-shirt she'd slept in. A long mirror took up one whole wall of the room and gave back an image of her naked self. She turned to face it, her hands at her sides. "I had a beautiful body."

Before Blaise Pascal, before Joseph, when she was still a pretty young thing. Before all of... this. The abdominal scar, a dark purple line decorated with dots at either side where the staples had gone in, travelled transversely from hip to hip. She'd screamed and sweated in labour for more than thirty-six hours, but the child refused to be born. Finally the surgeon came to cut her, flay her open like an animal carcass and pull Joseph from her, lifting the silent infant up in front of her face. *Your son, madame.* They whisked him away before she could even touch him. Perhaps that was the trouble. Maybe if she'd had time to bond with him....

Her reflection bared its teeth at her in a feral smile. Some animals ate their young.

She spent more than an hour under the hot water, letting the needle-sharp spray tattoo her naked skin. She scrubbed every inch of herself, even between her toes, and washed her hair with the hotel's lemon-scented shampoo before shutting off the water. There were things she had to do, still—letters she needed to write, loose ends that needed tying—before she could draw a line under all of this and move on. She had prepared a list of those she needed to contact, with Blaise Pascal at the very top of it. Hopefully he'd enjoyed the present she'd left him, poor dear old Gary Pretty, lying atop the bed where they'd fucked, with his guts hanging out. He was such a simpleton, but all men were, really, and she'd only given him what he wanted. *I wish you could open me up and crawl inside me.* He said this to her once, as they lay together after sex, their naked bodies slick with sweat. *Just open me up wide.*

My dear Blaise.... There was a stack of hotel notepaper and some envelopes in the desk drawer, and she had postage stamps in her purse. Affix the right amount of postage and you could send anything anywhere.

You wonder where Joseph is and what I have done with him. I haven't killed him, if that's what you're worried about. He is safe with people who love him, and he will never be found. Assurément, you've worked it all out by now. She folded the single sheet and stuffed it into an envelope, sealed the flap, and put a stamp on it.

On another sheet of notepaper she wrote to her husband, Gerard Caron, *I have taken the boy somewhere safe where he will never be found. I realise this is a huge big mess, but you would have never been completely happy where we were, mon ami, so this is a favour I have done you as well as myself. As far as everybody knows, you are dead and gone. Take the new life I have given you. This is an enormous debt, but I know you will find a way to repay all that you owe to me.*

Finally, she took her mobile phone from her purse and dropped it into a padded mailing envelope, sealed it firmly, and wrote the name and address of its intended recipient on the front. This she would leave in the room to be eventually discovered. She then dressed and went down to the hotel lobby, where she put both envelopes into a Canada Post mailbox, then took the elevator back to her room. Before going inside, she placed the Do Not Disturb notice on the doorknob and hoped that no overzealous chambermaid would disregard its warning.

CHAPTER THIRTEEN

Saturday

BLAISE PASCAL was out of his office as soon as the woman sergeant had gone, his mobile phone in hand. He slipped out the side door and into the parking lot and walked until he was hidden by a small stand of trees. He knew the number off by heart but had programmed it into speed dial so he could call with the touch of a single button. Today, for some reason, it seemed to take an inordinate amount of time until the call was answered. Pascal didn't waste words but got straight to the point.

"They found her," he said. "No… washed up in a fishing net … *bien sûr* … the body? Is in cold storage." He glanced back towards the police station, then out at the road. No one was coming, but it was a sunny Saturday in early autumn, and the local people were about. It would be better not to have to answer awkward questions. "I don't know. I have no answers. My intention is…." He drew a slow breath, forcing himself calm. This was not how it was to have happened. The situation had spiraled out of control, and despite all their best efforts, everything had turned to shit. "You are making a mistake. We need to go public with this as soon as possible. *Mon Dieu*, that goddamn woman, she destroyed so much." He forced himself to listen to the voice on the other end of the call. "I can still fix it. … No? *Vraiment*? … All right. *Bon*." He swiped the red circle viciously, ending the call.

Fucking idiots, every one of them. If he only—before he finished the thought, his phone rang again. "What?" The caller this time was Prud'Homme, who apologised for disturbing him. "No, it's all right, Louis." Pascal allowed himself the familiarity of using Prud'Homme's Christian name. "I am grateful to hear a friendly voice." His head was pounding. Time to get back on the blood pressure tablets, he thought, and maybe quitting smoking wouldn't be a bad idea either. "*Ça va bien?*"

"If you are asking about the Caron woman, no further sightings," Prud'Homme replied. It wasn't the news Pascal had been hoping for. "But we are still looking."

"Ah, *bon*. Anything else?"

Prud'Homme paused, then, "When are you coming home?"

The question struck him as so funny that Pascal laughed aloud. "Are you asking on behalf of the *Sûreté* or for yourself?"

"*Monsieur l'inspecteur*, for others I am asking this," Prud'Homme replied, pretending coyness, but Pascal knew him too well.

"I am gratified that you miss me," he said, "but there are some outstanding matters here that need to be tied up first. The man Gerard Caron is still missing without a trace, it seems."

He'd hoped his call to Louise might have provided some leads, but his ex-wife hadn't been helpful. If she'd spoken to Amalie recently, she hadn't bothered to share that information with him. Either way, his investigation into the other—arguably more important—matter had borne fruit: it was no secret who had killed the woman in the fishing net, and Pascal strongly suspected that she'd fallen afoul of the criminal syndicate. Either she had made a grievous misstep and put other members of the group at risk or she had simply lost her usefulness, so they'd killed her and dumped her body into the sea in an area where it was almost certain to come ashore. A sort of final "fuck you" to Deiniol Quirke and the Kildevil police force, and to Pascal himself.

"What about this other thing?" Prud'Homme asked. "Have you made any headway?"

Pascal told him about the body found in the fishing net, and how he suspected it might be exactly who they were looking for. "She has been one step, two steps, three, ahead of us all the time, and now she turns up here. What are the odds of that happening, eh?"

Silence on the other end as Prud'Homme digested this. "Do you think they knew you were there?"

"Of course I do, *niaiseux*! These bastards know everything." The plan he had so carefully tended all these long months was now in tatters. Somehow, the bastards at the back of it had found out Pascal was in Newfoundland and understood that only a small part of it had to do with Amalie Caron. "Someone might have leaked something, Louis. I don't know who, but it's fucked me up."

He'd intended that his target be taken into custody and offered a reward if she agreed to testify against the others. There had been no prior communication between them, but Pascal was familiar with her, knew her role in the organisation and what she was expected to do. He and Prud'Homme had even selected the appropriate bait, a young *Sûreté* constable who was street smart and could handle herself in the sort of setup he had in mind. Now all that was blown to hell. The woman in the fishing net was an important player in a sex-trafficking ring founded by the notorious Jean-Baptiste Roul, whose criminal organisation operated all up and down the eastern seaboard. The woman in the net—of course he knew her name, but you never knew who was listening in on the telephone—was a very big fish indeed, with a history that placed her at the very centre of several sordid sex crimes.

At least until the Roul family decided she'd outgrown her usefulness.

Jean-Baptiste Roul's darling son Andre—better known as "Petit Andi"—had been out of prison these past six weeks, and it was Andre who'd been directly responsible for the woman. Pascal suspected it was Petit Andi who'd ordered her death. He wondered how long he'd be able to keep this bit of information from Deiniol Quirke. The Newfoundlander would lose his mind when he discovered what Pascal hadn't told him, how he'd been hunting a much bigger fish than Amalie Caron, a fish that Quirke had business with, serious business. The man wasn't exactly stupid, and he'd clearly had his suspicions about Pascal from the beginning. Was it time to confess everything, now that it had all gone to shit?

The Roul family had a long history of settling scores with anyone who crossed them, so it wasn't surprising the woman had ended up where she did. But *calisse*, how the hell had they found out? The whole goddamn thing—an operation that had taken twenty-two months to plan—was about to come crashing down around everybody's ears. It was, as *les anglais* said, a complete clusterfuck. Worse, the goddamn target had gone ahead and contacted someone at Quirke's station, which she'd been expressly told not to do. That transgression alone was sufficient to bring their wrath. *Peut-être* she'd thought to crawl back to the nest and be forgiven, that she could worm her way back into Quirke's good graces. Idiot woman.

"Are you all right, *Monsieur l'inspecteur*?" Prud'Homme asked.

Pascal yearned to confide in him but knew he couldn't possibly take the risk. This was all going wrong, so very badly, and there was nothing he could do to stop it. "Fine, Prud'Homme. Don't worry about it. I will tie things up here and then return." He paused, wondering if it would be appropriate to add some personal sentiment. "Tell that woman from the BEI I will meet with her next week." He smiled even though Prud'Homme couldn't see him. "It will be the perfect ending to... all of this."

He tucked the phone away and decided to take a brief walk through the town to clear his head and perhaps breathe some fresh air into lungs over-burdened with frustration and tobacco smoke. Since arriving in Kildevil Cove he had done nothing but work, and *certainement* there was work to be done, but even he had his limits. Staying up late at night and staring at his laptop screen was no good for him, but perhaps if he stared long enough an answer to this entire *maudit* mess would suggest itself.

Pascal left the station car park and turned right onto the oddly named Secretary Road. There were hills directly ahead in the distance, their rounded tops furred with spruce and tamarack, their contours reminiscent of the Laurentides and Mont-Tremblant. It was time he left this place, went home to face whatever waited for him there—the BEI and his little office, Prud'Homme's questions and his endless cups of terrible coffee. He ought to visit Théodore, see how his son was doing, coax him into telling Pascal all the things he knew, no matter how awful. Whatever truth his son had to tell, Pascal needed to hear it.

It was a bleak Wednesday near the end of January when the doctors moved Théo from the children's hospital in Montreal and into his current set of circumstances. The same day Pascal was approached by two men in dark overcoats and told he needed to go with them, to get into a car and drive many kilometres up into the mountains where they took him into a pleasant room with plants and expensive pictures on the walls and explained—very clearly—what would happen if he did not go along with the things they had planned for him to do. *Votre petit fou...* your little lunatic, this boy with the burned hands whom you appear to love, isn't that so, *Monsieur l'inspecteur*? He would not be so happy in a hospital where they did not care about him. Your duty as a father demands you care for him yourself, and you do, correct? *Non, monsieur*, don't speak. You will do the listening.

At first he thought they were emissaries of the Roul family or some others of that crowd, the Montreal mafia who openly flouted laws left, right, and centre and did apparently whatever they pleased. They were pissed off with him, the Rouls; they and their associates didn't care for Pascal's forays into their downtown dens of iniquity, and when he engineered the capture and arrest of Jean-Baptiste and Petit Andi, everyone assumed he'd end up at the bottom of the St. Lawrence. But these men weren't working for the Rouls or any of their friends, and the truth was much, much worse. They'd showed up to recruit him. His consent was unnecessary.

I'm a Sûreté officer.

Yes, we know.

Then you realise I can't possibly do the things you are asking.

Of course you can, monsieur. We will even make it worth your while.

They knew everything about him: his current address and all the places he had lived before then; his wife Louise's whereabouts; the particulars of Théo's illness; the fire at their old Montreal apartment; how Pascal's brothers and sisters had died. They told him about little indiscretions he'd committed while in uniform and how he'd used his influence as a police officer to call in favours, that he was known to visit prostitutes and had carried on a long-term relationship with one particular *plotte*: Amalie Caron.

These two men didn't bother to remove their dark overcoats the entire time but sat with him in a very nice hotel room in an upscale resort close to Mont-Tremblant on a bleak Wednesday in January and talked. They explained how things would be if he refused, and what would happen to Louise, and Théodore. Certain details of his life would be made public, leaked to Radio-Canada and the *Montreal Gazette*, and not only would his career with the *Sûreté* be over, but he would most likely end up in prison.

Not a happy ending for him, and everybody knew how *le flic* were treated in such places. A shame, but it couldn't be helped.

"Who are you?" he asked. They showed their badges. "*Eh bien*," he said, and shrugged. A secret branch of the federal government that almost no one knew about, involved in high-level investigations of drug smuggling, human trafficking, child pornography, and the dark web. They answered directly to the prime minister and were given wide-ranging powers that extended to most countries of the free world.

"A wonderful little tale you have spun," Pascal mocked them. "You are like, what is it, James Bond? *Les super flics*?" He laughed at his own joke. When they told him what they wanted him to do, he laughed even harder. *Bien sûr*, he'd done undercover training, but that was years ago and he—

You will do it, Inspecteur Pascal. You will.

And he had.

He stopped in front of the coffee shop now, the one Quirke and his colleagues liked so much, and debated whether to go in. It was open—the sign in the window was lit up—but Pascal was restless, eager to keep moving, and coffee would only make him more jittery than he already was. Perhaps if he told Quirke what was going on, the Newfoundlander might help, or was it naïve of him to think so? He knew Quirke had been investigating him from the very beginning, the moment he stepped foot in Quirke's quaint little cove, but Pascal no longer cared. He had been doing this for so many years, and he was worn out from the subterfuge and the endless lies, the need to hide himself from even those who knew him best, people like Prud'Homme. He'd been forced to betray so many. Ultimately, he would end up betraying himself, and then he really would end up at the bottom of the St. Lawrence.

He passed the coffee shop, moving faster now, the sea on his left and the high cliffs of the coastal headlands on his right. The day was pleasant, the weather warmer than expected for this time of year, the sea breeze soft, redolent with salt and the smell of spruce and fir trees. The land rose sharply, following the curve of the road, and he accelerated, his breath coming hard in his lungs. Too many cigarettes, he thought. Too many smokes and too little exercise, too much bad food and sleepless nights in shitty motel rooms, alone. Fourteen years of chasing Amalie Caron across several provinces while she was always one step—no, hundreds of steps—ahead of him, and the business with the traffickers that never seemed to come to a satisfactory conclusion.

And you call yourself a detective. His mouth twisted in self-derision. It had always been a sore point between him and Louise, his career. Rather, his lack of mobility upwards through the ranks. They had met when he was a constable. Louise had come to the police station with her sister, who wanted to report an assault by a male friend. The way she said it, Pascal suspected the friend was actually a client, and that Louise's younger sister made her living the way a lot of beautiful young women did, but he was polite to her. Polite the way his mother had taught him to be, and wasn't that a lovely change, considering how some police treated girls like her. This apparently made an impression on Louise, and they began dating. He thought no more of the sister until much later, when he and Louise were about to marry and his pals insisted on taking him to the bar where Louise's sister worked. There he saw her in her natural element. Amalie. He had no idea back then what she was, the things she was capable of. If anyone had told him, he'd have called them a liar.

He crested the hill, still with the sea on his left, but now the cliffs melted away in the general undulation of the land, their edges smoothed off, burred to a gentler roundness. A narrow dirt road on the right led into the trees, and he took it, curious about where it led. Louise was right. He'd never had even an ounce of ambition in his work, assumed he'd eventually rise to some rank slightly above constable but nothing further. He'd never considered that he could amount to more than that, considering where he came from and....

A movement to his left caught his attention, and he turned, his entire body suddenly adrenalised, but it was merely a bird, a grouse or partridge, whatever they were called, a flicker of wings among the trees. He stood very still and breathed deliberately, filling his lungs with the soft salt air while his pulse slowed to normal and his sudden fear ran off the ends of his fingers. There was no one there; it was only a bird. There were birds in the country, and small animals. It was only natural to hear things, see movement, and sense their presence. Even people, hikers and picnickers, locals walking their dogs, a campfire.

A slow thread of smoke rose from a point about ten metres distant, within a stand of trees. The wind shifted, carrying the smell of it to where he stood, the unmistakable scent of burning. He started forward, running— *You won't get there in time. You never get there in time. You've had this same dream a thousand times, and it always ends the very same way.*

A sound like laughter, people talking. Pascal stopped abruptly. Four teenagers were sitting around a small campfire. They turned as one to stare at him.

"What's wrong with you, my son?" one of them asked. He was wearing jeans and a padded tartan shirt, had a scruffy beard and a ring in one ear. "Ye looks like ye seen a ghost, sure." He glanced back at his friends, as if wondering what to do.

A girl stood up and came towards him. "Are you all right?" she asked. She had long, straight brown hair and vivid blue eyes; she reminded him of Louise when she was young. "Is there someone I can call?"

Pascal blinked and began to back away. "No, *merci.* I... took a wrong turn." Glancing behind him, he saw that the road was still there, so it wasn't a dream, not this time. Easy to retrace his steps, find his way back to the main road, turn again towards Kildevil Cove. He'd lost himself in thought and the memories came back, the way they did when he wasn't paying attention. He remembered the conversation he'd had with Quirke the morning they had breakfast together. *My ex-wife had to go away for a while... a long while. Attempted murder carries a hard sentence in this country.*

She'd known about him and Amalie, of course. It was never even in question. Louise had figured him out. He'd been a fucking idiot, assuming that the sisters weren't close, that Amalie didn't confide in Louise. Of course she did. She'd have told Louise everything anyway, just to fuck things up, to rip the bottom out of his life, and Louise starting the fire at the apartment was bad enough on its own, but she had ruined all their lives, especially Théodore's. There was no need to destroy their son, but Louise hadn't given a damn. The boy had crawled into bed with him when Pascal had come home off the night shift and Louise, already awake, disabled the smoke alarms. *I want to sleep with Papa... I want to sleep in Papa's bed.*

Louise said nothing. She took a shopping list, said she was going to Provigo for groceries, and left them both to burn to death in that apartment. It had spread so fast, climbing up the walls and racing across the ceiling, devouring the cheap cotton drapes and the rugs, and he'd only just managed to escape with Théo. With Théo in his arms, screaming, the sound cutting through him like a blade—

His mobile phone was ringing: Prud'Homme. He fumbled it out of his pocket. "*Oui?*"

"*Monsieur l'inspecteur*, I thought best to tell you *immédiatement.*" Prud'Homme sounded like he'd run up a flight of stairs full tilt. "First of all. Before anyone."

"What?" Pascal had reached the main road. "Prud'Homme, tell me."

Prud'Homme took a long, slow breath. "Just before eight this morning, a chambermaid...." A long pause, during which Pascal fancied he could hear the hum of the mobile network between them. "L'Hotel Promenade, in Mont-Tremblant."

Pascal's face felt tight, the skin around his eyes prickling with heat. "Tell me."

"Amalie Caron has been found. Monsieur, she—"

"*Quoi?*"

"She is dead."

CHAPTER FOURTEEN

Saturday evening

DANNY ARRIVED home to find Tadhg in the kitchen, sleeves rolled up and elbow deep in the dish he was cooking for supper. The entire house smelled of fresh tomatoes, oil, and garlic, and Easter the dog was dancing attendance, criss-crossing between Tadhg's feet in the hope he'd drop her a delicious morsel.

"Mmm," Danny sighed, moving to kiss Tadhg. "Smells like pizza."

"It is," Tadhg replied. "Homemade pizza. I'm doing the sauce, and Lily is doing the crust." He returned the kiss with enthusiasm, holding his tomato-stained hands free of Danny's white shirt.

Danny caught hold of his wrists and examined Tadhg's hands. "Are you sure it's only tomatoes you've been chopping?" he asked. "Looks like a crime scene in here." He tilted Tadhg's left hand towards his mouth and sucked the tip of his index finger. "All right," he said, "I believe you. Where's Lily?"

"Her Ladyship is upstairs," Tadhg replied. "She's got the pizza dough proofing in the oven. Take a look."

Danny opened the door of the enormous Wolf gas range Tadhg had insisted on. A metal bowl with a tea towel over it bulged alarmingly at the back of the oven. "I think it'll be going up the stairs to meet her the once." He closed the door, leaving the dough to commune with itself in peace.

"Oh, it's supposed to do that, apparently." Tadhg lifted the wooden cutting board he'd been using and dumped a pile of chopped tomatoes into a pan on top of the stove. They hit the hot oil with a liquid sizzle, and he put the cover on. "'Aeration provides oxygen for the dough development.'" He smirked. "Don't ask me where she gets it. It'll be ready soon. You want a cup of tea?"

Lily called out from upstairs, and Easter sped away. The little dog loved Danny and Tadhg but was utterly devoted to Lily.

"You know I do." Danny sank into a chair at the kitchen table and picked up a pile of mail. There was the usual stuff—the light bill, an invoice for firewood they'd ordered from a local man, and an advertising flyer for free highlights with a haircut at Betty's HairTrap in Winterton.

And the parcel Tadhg had mentioned, the one from Wales that had arrived on Friday but which he'd avoided opening or even looking at, afraid of what it might contain. The box was small, perhaps the size of a cigarette packet, and tightly wrapped in brown paper tied with the kind of butcher's twine that could be readily obtained anywhere.

A cup of tea appeared in his field of vision, followed by a plate of cookies. They looked homemade. "A brown parcel, approximately ten centimetres wide and two centimetres tall, bound with kraft paper. String is unremarkable, of consistent quality with common twine. Note to self: have Bobbi dust for fingerprints and other trace evidence." Tadhg caught Danny's eye and smirked.

"You're some funny," Danny said. "I don't talk like that."

"Yes, I 'low you don't." He moved back to fetch his own cup of tea and took a seat across the table. "Are you going to open it?"

"What if it's dangerous?" It was small enough to hold in his palm, but an instrument of destruction didn't need to be large. The timer that had blown up the Carons' house had been the size of an old-style cell phone.

"I haven't heard any ticking," Tadhg replied. He reached out, laid a hand on Danny's forearm. "This could answer a lot of your questions," he said quietly. And when Danny nodded, "I'll fetch the scissors to cut the string."

In the end, it was Tadhg who opened the parcel, not Danny, and Tadhg who extracted its contents, a yellow gold locket and chain, somewhat battered and clearly showing its age. He held it out on his palm for Danny to see. "It's a lady's necklace."

"Oh," Danny said, the breath going out of him in a rush. "Is there a note?"

Tadhg shook out the box. "No note. Nothing but that."

"Aberystwyth. I've never been there." He glanced up at Tadhg, forcing a smile. "Maybe I *should* get Bobbi to dust it for fingerprints." The parcel hadn't answered any of his questions about his parentage; if anything, it created an even more vexing conundrum. Who had sent the parcel? There was no return address, nothing to indicate where it had come from except the postmark. The parcel itself had been insured for five thousand pounds sterling, which probably meant the necklace was real gold. He picked it off Tadhg's palm and held it as the metal warmed to the temperature of his skin. It was heavy, perhaps fifty grams in weight, or about two ounces, and engraved on the front with a rather elaborate drawing of a dragon and a castle.

"It's obviously Welsh," Tadhg pointed out, "given that dragon there and the castle. Is there anything inside?"

Of course: it was a locket. Danny managed to get a fingernail between the two halves and pried them gently apart, terrified of damaging it, but it yielded without protest, the tiny hinge completely intact. The interior had been fitted for photos, and it contained two, a man and a woman, both in Edwardian-era dress. The woman was unremarkable, her dark hair pulled back in a severe style that didn't flatter her plain features. The man was not so much handsome as compelling, with pale eyes and light hair. Contrary to the fashion of the era, his moustache was tightly groomed to follow the curve of his top lip, and his winged eyebrows gave his face a slightly mischievous aspect.

Tadhg stared at the photo, deeply shocked. "Jesus, Danny," he breathed, "it's you. It's *you.*"

It was the truth. Erase the moustache, for Danny was clean-shaven, and the face looking back at him from the old photograph was his own. The base of his stomach lurched, and he thrust the locket away from him, pushing back from the table.

"It's a joke," he said flatly. "Someone's idea of fun." Gathering up the locket, box, and paper, he shoved all of it at Tadhg. "Send it back where it came from. Put it in the mail. I don't care. That's… that's nothing to do with me."

There was a clatter from above and Lily came slowly down the stairs, Easter at her heels. "Dad! Danny, you won't believe what I just—" She stopped short when she caught sight of them, frozen in a weird tableau, Tadhg in the act of rising from the table while Danny crouched to retrieve the chair he'd knocked over in his haste. "What… the hell… is going on here?"

Danny spoke first. "Everything's fine, Lily." He righted the chair and pushed it close to the table. "Something came for me in the mail."

She hopped down the last three stairs, landing with a bang at the bottom, Easter close behind. "Is it the parcel that came from Wales? Oh my God, let me see!" She bounded into the kitchen, hair flying. "Is that it?" Her gaze lighted on the crumpled paper and string, and then she saw the locket. She seized it in both hands and held it up. "Danny, it's gorgeous. Oh wow." Holding the necklace against her collar bone, she asked, "Can I borrow it sometime? To wear to a dance?"

Tadhg moved to gently take it from her. "Danny isn't sure where it came from, my love." He laid the locket back in the box. "It might not have been meant for him."

"But it was addressed to him," she protested. "Someone sent it all the way from Wales, and maybe it's from his real family—" She fell silent, her cheeks reddening.

"Lily." Tadhg cast a warning glance in her direction. "Why don't you take the dog for a walk?"

"I hear you and Danny talking all the time," she said. "I'm not deaf, and I'm not stupid either." She gazed at Danny. "I know about your family… that they aren't your real family, I mean. You know that doesn't matter anyway, right? Me and Dad and Easter are your family now." Lily lifted her shoulders and let them drop in the manner of teenage girls everywhere. "That's why you got married to Dad, isn't it?"

"I married your father because I love him," Danny said but knew this wasn't what she was asking. Still and all, it would have to do for an answer. "Lily, I don't know where the locket came from, or if it's even meant for me. Until I find out who sent it and why, I'd rather keep it to myself." He reached down to ruffle the soft fur on Easter's head. "You'd better check on that pizza dough." He picked up the locket and the box it came from and started towards the stairs. The locket could live in his sock drawer until he decided to pursue the matter further.

He was halfway upstairs when a knock sounded at the door. "I'll get it!" Tadhg called. Danny paused where he was, one hand on the banister, waiting, while Tadhg spoke to whomever was there. "Danny?" Of course. No chance he'd get a quiet evening in. He sighed and started down the stairs again.

Blaise Pascal was standing in the front porch of their home, hands shoved into his pockets, examining the mat under his feet. He looked up when he heard Danny's approach. "I have news," he said abruptly. "You are not going to like it."

"Tell me," Danny said hollowly.

"The *Sûreté* have located Amalie Caron." Pascal glanced away for a moment, then back.

"Where?" Danny was aware that Tadhg had come into the porch, was standing just behind him.

"For God's sake," Tadhg said, "invite the man in, Danny. We're supposed to be civilised. Inspector Pascal, we're just about to—"

"Where is she?" It was like Tadhg hadn't even spoken at all.

"In a hotel room in Mont-Tremblant." Pascal glanced briefly at Tadhg. "She is dead."

"Dead?" Perhaps Gerard Caron was still alive, Danny thought. Maybe he'd caught up with her and killed her in retaliation for taking the child. Maybe he—

"By her own hand."

So it was over. Just like that, it was over, and he'd never even had a chance to.... He should have been the one to arrest her, goddammit. She'd committed her crimes on his patch, not Pascal's, and this was just bloody typical of him. Everything Danny had seen since the man had first stepped foot in Kildevil Cove, and now here he was saying.... Amalie Caron, her husband.... What about...? "What about the boy?" Danny asked. "What about Joseph?"

"He has not been found." Pascal wet his lips. "Early indications are she, Amalie, took an overdose of allergy medication."

"Jesus," Tadhg murmured.

Danny turned to him. "I need to book a flight," he said.

"Where do you think you are going?" Pascal asked.

"I'm going to Quebec," Danny assured him. "With you."

The *Sûreté* detective didn't bother to argue. "*Allons-y*," he said. "Let's go, then."

THEY HAD managed to find the last two available seats on an evening flight, which would see them land in Montreal near midnight. Pascal bought a paperback book from a stall in the airport and read for the duration of the flight, but Danny couldn't concentrate long enough to pursue a single train of thought, let alone digest the contents of a book. He must have slept, or something close to it, because he came to himself some time later to hear the arrival announcement as the steward came through the cabin to pick up their empty coffee cups.

"We have arrived early," Pascal told him as they stood to retrieve their bags from the overhead compartment. "Tailwind, perhaps."

"Blown all the way to Montreal," Danny quipped, but the joke fell flat. He sensed Pascal was just as tired as he was, only better at hiding it. The large wall display in the Arrivals area read eleven thirty, but it might have been several days in the past or even in the future. The sense of disorientation Danny usually felt when flying was compounded by grogginess, and he was still unsettled by what the gold locket from Wales had revealed. The man in the photograph looked too much like him for it to be mere happenstance, but photographs could be faked. Still, if it was a ruse, it was an expensive one, assuming the necklace was actually worth the five thousand pounds it had been insured for. That was a hell of a lot of money for its owner to give up.

Pascal had arranged for a rental car to be waiting outside, so there would be minimal delay. He accepted the keys from the driver, and he and Danny got in. "I am driving?" Pascal asked as Danny was fastening his seat belt.

This struck Danny as so funny that he laughed aloud. "It looks that way."

"This is funny?" Pascal adjusted the seat and then the rear-view mirror before pulling away from the curb.

"I don't know the way," Danny said. "Even with GPS or a satnav, I'm horrible with directions." He and Tadhg had taken a weekend trip to Nova Scotia the previous year and decided to explore the area around Lunenburg. They'd planned to stop in the beautiful historic old town for a lobster lunch before heading back to Halifax. Tadhg drove and put Danny in charge of navigation. They got to Lunenburg with no trouble, but the return journey was another story, and instead of going back the way they'd come, Danny had somehow led them to Annapolis Royal—on the other side of the province.

"Sit back and relax yourself," Pascal said. "Too bad it is dark. It is a very pretty drive."

"How long till we get there?"

"It usually takes about ninety minutes. It will not take that long for us."

Uh-oh. "Why?"

"You should know, in this province, posted speed limits are just a suggestion." Pascal's wolfish grin didn't reassure him, and he wondered if he'd make it back to Newfoundland in one piece.

They left the bright lights of the airport behind them, moving out of Montreal proper and onto Autoroute 15, heading north to Mont-Tremblant. Pascal, despite his threats about the speed limit, drove very well, accelerating smoothly to overtake slow-moving vehicles and only exceeding the posted limits on longer stretches of empty highway. He made no effort to engage Danny in conversation but kept his attention on the road.

"Do you know where the hotel is?" Danny asked. "I assume they've retained the body in situ."

"Yes." Pascal's eyes narrowed. "I am familiar with it." He blew air through pursed lips. "Perhaps too familiar."

"You know it."

"Mm."

"You've been there before." This was like pulling teeth, Danny thought.

Pascal turned to look at him. "Why are you interested in this?" he asked. "The woman is dead. I trust what Prud'Homme told me. You can go and look at her for yourself, and that will be the end of it."

"It's hardly the end of it," Danny replied. "We've still no idea where her husband is, or the boy." The boy who wasn't actually Gerard Caron's son, he remembered. Under Quebec law, the boy should have his mother's or his birth father's surname—their choice—but he had been called Joseph Caron in Kildevil Cove. No one would have questioned this if they had not seen the boy's birth certificate, and why would they? But still Danny wondered why the truth hadn't occurred to him before now. Gerard was blond, and the boy's hair was dark brown, almost black, to match his dark brown eyes.

Danny decided to change tack. "I bet it's beautiful here in winter," he said.

"It's fucking cold here in winter." Pascal lapsed into a sullen silence, his gaze fixed on the road ahead of them, and Danny abandoned all attempts at conversation. *To hell with you*, he thought, *you contrary bastard. Keep your secrets.*

The road rose and fell and rose and fell, careened sharply around unexpected bends and once narrowly missed what could have been a head-on collision with a tractor-trailer, during which Danny's entire life flashed before his eyes. Another man would have been cursing—or praying—but Danny's hold on his childhood religion had always been flimsy at best. He didn't even own a set of rosary beads anymore.

Pascal said nothing during the remainder of the trip, his gaze turned inward, focusing on some imagined vista only he could see. Not for the first time, Danny wondered what his connection was to Amalie Caron.

Quite apart from his long investigation of her, something tied Pascal and the dead woman together. It wasn't unknown for a police officer to form a bond or even a liaison with a suspect, and he'd been guilty of the same a time or two himself. Maybe it was more than that. Could the *Sûreté* officer have been in love with her? He couldn't imagine Pascal in love with anyone.

Eventually they turned off the highway and onto a narrow dirt road through a pine forest, at the far end of which Danny could just make out the revolving flicker of red-and-blue police lights. Pascal pulled up to the side and shut off the rental car. He and Danny both got out.

"This is where the body was found," Pascal said. He started towards a group of uniformed officers, calling something to them in French. A ring of police tape had been erected around the perimeter of the small hotel, and several *Sûreté* officers were stationed at intervals to keep unwanted observers away—not that anyone was there. The locals in this area must not be the curious type. There were no onlookers straining forwards to catch a glimpse of the crime scene.

Pascal held the tape aloft for Danny to step underneath as a blond man with the thick, muscular build of a rugby player approached. "This is Prud'Homme," Pascal said. "He is sometime my assistant."

Prud'Homme immediately moved to shake Danny's hand. "*Bonjour, Inspecteur Quirke.*" His friendly manner said he was the absolute antithesis of the dour Pascal. "It is good you are here, although this case have come to a *malheureuse* conclusion." His English was not as good as Pascal's, Danny noted, but it was still easily understood.

Danny returned the handshake. "*Salut,*" he said. It was the only French he knew. He hoped he hadn't said anything offensive.

He and Pascal accompanied Prud'Homme into the hotel, which was built along the lines of an Alpine château, albeit in miniature. The lobby was charming, a warmly decorated interior space situated around a spiral staircase. The hotel personnel were expecting them and had been positioned behind the reception desk in a row, like household servants in a British costume drama. The manager was a tall, thin man with a pencil moustache and a hairstyle belonging to the 1940s. He was impeccably dressed in the hotel uniform of red blazer and dark blue trousers. At Pascal's approach he stepped forward, wringing his hands. Danny couldn't understand what he was saying, but he was clearly distressed at the discovery of a corpse in one of the upstairs rooms.

Pascal listened for a moment, then nodded and stepped back. He tilted his head towards the staircase, beckoning Danny and Prud'Homme. "*Avec moi.*" They started up the stairs behind him and gained the upper floor in moments. Despite its small size, the hotel was luxurious, with a thickly carpeted corridor and what appeared to be solid oak doors leading to each of the suites.

"Seven hundred dollars a night," Prud'Homme murmured to him, grinning. "Can you imagine?" Pascal heard him and glanced behind to shoot the young officer a dirty look. "He is much too cheap to stay here, even on his wedding night," Prud'Homme continued, tilting his head in Pascal's direction. He rolled his eyes in a comical manner but fell silent as they approached the room inhabited by the former Amalie Caron, nodding at the uniformed officer stationed outside.

She had spared no expense for her final resting place. The room was beautiful and well-appointed, a deluxe suite featuring what looked like genuine Persian carpets over a solid oak floor. The furnishings appeared to be handcrafted in teak or mahogany—Danny couldn't be sure—and polished to a dazzling sheen. One small bag stood near the door, still tightly zipped, as if the owner was just about to pick it up on her way out, but the window shades were drawn, casting the room into semidarkness, and the still figure of Amalie lay supine on the bed. She was pale, her eyes closed, but a sardonic smile played about the mouth, as grotesque as the lipless face of a skull. She was fully clothed in jeans and a T-shirt, although her feet were bare. The toenails had been painted a vibrant shade of red.

Prud'Homme murmured something and crossed himself as Pascal moved forward. He stopped a foot or two away from the corpse and simply looked, saying nothing, but Danny fancied a shutter came down behind Pascal's eyes, closing him off. His features hardened, the mouth and cheeks losing their mobility, the forehead relaxing into the wan aspect of a mask. It was a decent enough façade, but the muscles at the hinges of his jaw bulged, and a nerve in his temple twitched. Amalie Caron had been more than just another case. Danny was certain of it, and even standing here in the presence of Pascal's grief felt like an intrusion. The *Sûreté* inspector swallowed hard. "*La cause vérifiée du décès?*"

Prud'Homme darted a glance at Danny. "*Elle s'est suicidée.*" He cleared his throat and continued in English, "A number of empty boxes were found in the bathroom. Allergy medicine, as I told you. What you call this, Benadryl? She have an overdose."

"That's not good," Danny commented. He wasn't a doctor, but he'd heard tell of people—usually teenagers responding to some social media challenge or other—deliberately ingesting overdoses of the drug in the hopes of procuring a high. It had led to several deaths.

"Sometime they take this, and it do not turn out the way one expect," Prud'Homme said. "She have been buying it in many different stores, because they will not allow someone to purchase—"

"*Sortez*," Pascal said quietly, interrupting him. "*Partez*. Go on, get out!" When Danny moved to go, he caught hold of his sleeve. "Not you. Prud'Homme, *s'il te plaît*." He waited until the younger man had left, then crossed the room to close the door behind him. "What I want to say is not for him to listen to."

"You want me to listen?" Danny asked. He wondered what he was letting himself in for.

"How is it you say in English?" Pascal made a soft noise that might have been a laugh but wasn't. "I want someone to bear witness. What I have to tell you does not belong in any official record or any police report."

"Is this why the BEI are after you?"

A smile flickered briefly on Pascal's features, then disappeared. He walked slowly towards the bed where the corpse of Amalie Caron lay flat on her back, her unseeing gaze directed at the ceiling. "What is it you are thinking, about me and her?"

"That you are—were—in love with her. That you've been in love with her for years." Danny came to stand beside him. "You probably thought you'd save her, something like that. If you loved her enough."

Pascal was silent for so long that Danny wondered if the *Sûreté* detective had even heard him. Finally he said, "*Non*. I was obsessed with her. She was one of those women who knows how to give a man whatever he wants."

"Did she give you want you wanted?"

"For a while." Pascal swayed towards the bed, perhaps thinking of sitting beside her, but held himself back. "Then she became like a devil from Hell." He looked across at Danny. "She was my wife's sister, you know?"

It ought to have shocked him, but it didn't. Amalie and her sister would have shared a surname in Quebec, but Danny knew Amalie only as Caron, and Pascal had never mentioned his ex-wife's surname. This news about the two women's relationship was part and parcel of the many secrets people kept, even to the grave, and Danny knew all about secrets. "Did she divorce you because of that?"

"I divorced her." Pascal paused, perhaps remembering. "She tried to burn down our home with me and my son in it." He nodded at the dead woman. "After Amalie told her we were having an affair, me and her. I had come off the night shift, and my son was asleep in the bed with me." The fire had destroyed the boy's hands, he said, as well as his mind. "You remember I told you my wife is in prison. Ex-wife. It was not the first time Louise tried to kill me and the boy."

"Your wife's name is Louise?" It all made sense now, Pascal's reaction to the message written above Gary Pretty's bed: *Ma Jolie Louise*. "You knew Amalie killed Gary Pretty. You knew she was the one who wrote on the wall."

"Why didn't I tell you?" Pascal asked. "We both knew it was Amalie. What other suspect but her? *Personne*. No one."

He'd probably figured Danny didn't need to know about his wife— ex-wife—and her connection to Amalie Caron. In truth, it was only of peripheral importance to the case, except... "Amalie was making specific reference to your wife, though."

"The message was for me. As I told you, I have been chasing her for many years. This is where it ends, all of it." He stepped away from the bed, making for the door.

"Wait." Danny followed on his heels. "So Amalie is dead, but what about the boy, Joseph?" Indeed, what about Gerard Caron? Was he dead as well? Or had the torture video been a ruse, the introduction of a disparate element to throw them off the scent?

Pascal yanked open the door and shouted for Prud'Homme. The young officer was just coming up the stairs. "*Monsieur l'inspecteur*." He was holding a flat brown envelope, one of the padded ones used to send delicate items through the mail. "This was left for you at the reception desk."

Pascal inserted his index finger under the flap and tore it open, reached inside to extract the contents. "*Sacrément*," he murmured as an ornate and very beautiful set of rosary beads fell out into his hand. Each bead was a different shade of red—burgundy and carmine, crimson and scarlet—like an individual flame. "*Je remets entre vos mains le ruban de ma vie*."

Danny recognised the engraved centrepiece of Our Lady, Undoer of Knots. "I entrust into your hands the ribbon of my life." Was Pascal religious? If so, his prayers sounded remarkably like swear words. The *Sûreté* inspector thrust a hand back into the envelope and brought out a slip of yellow paper, folded in half. He read it silently, then passed it to Prud'Homme, who read the note then translated aloud for Danny: "He is safe with people who love him, and you will never find him."

It struck Danny like a punch to the gut. "What does she mean?" The boy Joseph was gone, spirited away to God knows where and left with unknown people. Anything could have happened to him.

"I don't know," Pascal said. He shook his head, then handed the envelope and its contents to Prud'Homme. "Enter this into evidence. And anything else you find in the room. Look for her phone. There may be useful information in it." He turned on his heels and walked away, so fast that Danny almost had to run to catch up.

"Why a set of rosary beads?" he asked once he'd drawn level with the fleeing *Sûreté* detective. "I don't understand why she would tell you that about Joseph. You're not his fa—"

The penny dropped with an almost audible clang, and Danny suddenly understood. "Oh my God. It's you."

Blaise Pascal was Joseph Caron's father.

CHAPTER FIFTEEN

Sunday morning

JUNE CARBAGE woke early from a sleep so profound it felt as though she had been drugged. She rolled over and patted the place where her partner, Amy, should have been sleeping beside her. It was empty, so she cracked an eyelid to peer at the bedside clock: 7:05. Ridiculously early, even for Amy, whose career as a marine biologist often saw her out of bed before sunrise, especially if there was a boat involved.

June rubbed her eyes and groaned aloud as the sandpaper-dry lids pressed against her tender corneas. She'd been up late the previous night staring at a computer screen, trying to figure out where the message from Moira Fraser had originated. Danny had assigned Dougie Hughes to track it down, but Dougie's little girl was seriously unwell while cutting her teeth, and he and his wife, Lisa, had had to take her to the hospital. June offered to step in and help.

It was easy enough to create a fake email address under a false name, and June had no doubt that Moira's connections to organised crime gave her certain advantages. She had effectively disappeared the previous year, her whereabouts undetectable. No one, not even the RCMP or Interpol, knew where she was. Of course, the email might not have come from Moira at all, but from an imposter, someone who'd heard of her disappearance and thought to stir up a little trouble. Some people really didn't have enough to do.

She slid out of bed and put her feet on the floor, then stretched luxuriously, her arms above her head. The first rays of the morning sun had found a way through the blinds, and the ambient temperature was warm. Maybe she could coax Amy into a hike and perhaps a picnic later. There was something to be said for eating *en plein air*. She smirked. There was something to be said for making love that way too.

The house she shared with Amy was a barn conversion, constructed all on one level, with a minimal loft they sometimes used as a reading nook on rainy weekend afternoons. Tadhg Heaney's company had created a warm, welcoming space out of what had been an old cow byre, transforming its dim interior into a broad, light-filled space with plenty of windows on the southern-facing side and a large verandah that wrapped around the building on three sides. Both June and Amy had fallen in love with the house at first glance, but since June's salary was the larger, she had agreed to purchase it and taken out the mortgage in her name. The only downside was the open floor plan, which meant that sound travelled unhindered in all directions. If someone wanted to have a private telephone conversation, she had to go outside. Otherwise it was like living in a custom-built sound amplifier.

June could hear Amy speaking to someone now. It sounded as if she were on the telephone. She frowned in irritation. Hopefully it wasn't one of Amy's work colleagues. Those bastards had no common sense and tended to phone at all hours, regardless of the time. June was looking forward to a quiet breakfast with just the two of them, maybe on the verandah if the weather was warm enough, not sitting at the kitchen island with a bowl of cold cereal and the *Guardian* newspaper's online edition. She headed down the hall towards the kitchen, the wooden floors cool against her bare feet. Amy was on the phone, leaning against the french window in the dining room, and it didn't sound like a friendly conversation.

"… if you had any sense at all. … No, that's not what I'm saying."

June went to switch on the kettle and take her favourite bone-china mug from the rack by the sink. Who was on the other end of the conversation?

"Do not do that. … No, I'm serious. Listen, if you do this—" Amy glanced around and saw June and stopped speaking abruptly. She slowly lowered the phone to her side. "Good morning."

"You're up early." June nodded at Amy's mobile. "Finish your call. I've put the kettle on."

She went back into the kitchen, heard Amy say, "I gotta go," and then nothing further.

"That was Phil." Amy had followed her and now stood by the sink, watching as the kettle came to a boil. "I'm sick and tired of telling him not to call me on the weekends." She reached out and laid a hand on June's shoulder. "Did you sleep well? Hey, you know what we should do? We should take a picnic up the Ridge. It's a perfect day for it."

Everything from Amy's posture to the tone of her voice told June she was lying, and this knowledge chilled her to the bone. Amy had never, in all their years together, lied to her. It simply wasn't in her nature.

"Danny asked me to go in today." Now June was the liar. "There's some stuff related to an ongoing case that I need to clear up." She allowed herself to be pulled into the other woman's embrace, patting Amy's back awkwardly. "We'll do something later on, okay?"

"If that's what you want." Amy stepped away from her. "I won't have any tea right now. I'm going to get a shower." She left the kitchen, heading for the bathroom at the back of the house, and June watched her go.

The phrase "guilty as sin" occurred to her, something that her father used to say to her and Kevin when they were young. *The two of ye are as guilty as sin. Look at yez. Butter wouldn't melt.* Of course their guilt was all in his mind—he was obsessed with sin and salvation—but it didn't matter. The punishment was always harsh and unjustified.

If she had Amy's mobile, she could check the last number and find out who called, June thought, pouring hot water over the tea bag in her cup. What if it *was* just Phil from Amy's work? Then she'd feel like an idiot as well as a bad girlfriend. If there was only some way to check. She heard the shower start and then the noise of Amy pulling back the curtain. The hooks always grated on the rail like that, a nasty screeching sound. If she picked up the phone to have a quick look, it would set her mind at ease, and then she and Amy would be all right again and whoever had been calling would be none of her concern. She'd know when to put the phone back because she'd hear the curtain hooks scraping the metal shower rail again. It was like an early warning system, wasn't it? Besides, she was just going to take a quick look. Amy's phone wasn't locked or password protected or anything like that, not like June's. All it would take was a glance, nothing more, and she'd be quiet. Amy usually left her mobile on the bureau in the bedroom, and June needed to go there anyway to get dressed.

She needed to go there. She did.

Now she was staring at the unmade bed and the jeans and blouses tossed on the old rocking chair in the corner of the bedroom, the worn rag rug that Amy's great-grandmother had made, and her own pale feet with their purple-polished toenails. She was listening to the sound of the shower running in the other room, and Amy singing "The Galway Shawl" because she loved the old traditional tunes, she did, so. The bedroom window was still open because they both liked to sleep with fresh air coming in no matter the season or the weather. It was something they both liked, one of many things. *This is a mistake*, she thought—too late, however. The mobile was already in her hand, and she was tapping at the screen and scrolling through the list of recent calls to see who Amy had been talking to.

The call from earlier that day was inconsequential—Amy's coworker as she had claimed. June started to heave a sigh of relief, but the list of calls kept scrolling, as they tended to do, and suddenly a name flashed in front of her eyes that stole her breath completely. Moira Fraser. Her email might have been untraceable, but she hadn't called Amy from a burner phone.

Brazen, so absolutely brazen, and how long had it been going on? June was scrupulous about what she told Amy about her work, but everyone in the Cove knew Moira Fraser's legacy, how she'd been selling vulnerable young girls into sexual slavery and profiting from it and how Danny had paid a considerable price for his association with her. Just knowing that Moira Fraser had been his supervisor had been enough for the Constabulary to demote him all the way down to constable.

So many calls, the last less than two weeks ago.

"What are you doing?" Amy didn't sound angry or even surprised. "Checking up on me?" She was wearing her bathrobe and had a towel wrapped around her wet hair. June had failed to register the water being turned off or the scrape of the shower curtain hooks against the rail.

She startled violently, nearly dropping the mobile, but recovered quickly. She turned the screen so Amy could see it. "Why have you been talking to her?"

Amy's face hardened, eyes narrowing to slits, her expression cunning. "None of your business." She didn't even sound like the Amy that June knew—the Amy she'd loved for twelve years.

"This woman is wanted by the police." The anger began to build in her, burning like a white-hot coal at the back of her throat. "By Interpol, for Christ's sake. Lord God, Amy, she's a sex trafficker."

"Alleged sex trafficker."

If she had struck June across the face, it couldn't have hurt more. My God, she thought, who are you? "How long have you been in contact with her? Is this a long-term thing? Because if it is—"

"You'll do what?" Amy snatched the phone from her hand and continued across to the bureau, opened a drawer, and pulled out articles of clothing, throwing them onto the unmade bed as if she hated them. "Going to run and tell Danny?"

"Danny is in Quebec," June replied through lips that felt wooden. She watched numbly as Amy untied the belt of her bathrobe and let it drop to the floor. Normally seeing her this way, naked in the morning light, would have delighted June and filled her with desire. Now she felt sickened by the sight, revolted. She turned away. "I'm going over to Kevin's for a while. If I...." No, she thought, don't bother even saying it. Accusations would accomplish nothing, and Amy would probably deny it anyway. June moved to the bedroom chair in the corner to retrieve the clothes she'd worn yesterday. She'd slept in her underwear, and the bra was probably ready to be washed, but it would have to do. Her only thought was to get as far away from Amy Colbourne as possible.

"Run away and tell," Amy jeered, the childish phrase sounding crude and ugly coming from her twisted face. She didn't even resemble herself, and June wondered why she'd never noticed how cruel her mouth was, or how she could so readily extinguish the light in her eyes and replace it with naked hate. "Go on, ye makes me sick to me stomach." How could Amy be so horrible to her in their own home?

June suddenly remembered something. This wasn't even Amy's house. June had taken out the mortgage solely in her name, on the off chance that something like this would happen. She remembered what Amy said when she told her: *Think I'm going to turn on ye? That's not very romantic.* But romance had nothing to do with it. Growing up the way she had, June understood that self-protection was paramount and the only person you could ever truly trust was yourself.

"When I get back," she said, "I want you gone. Pack up your rubbish, all of it, and take it with you. Anything that's left is going on the bonfire."

Monday morning

BLAISE PASCAL'S apartment in Sainte-Agathe-des-Monts was so sparsely furnished that it resembled a prison cell, but Danny didn't really care. His flight had been inexplicably delayed, and Pascal had offered his spare room instead of a hotel, which Danny gratefully accepted. Normally he'd have stayed in rented accommodations—a B&B or similar—but he welcomed the chance to get to know Pascal a little better, if only to draw a line under their brief but tumultuous acquaintance.

The apartment overlooked a shimmering blue lake with a line of low hills in the distance, the Lac du Sables, Pascal told him. He assured Danny there were loads of fish in it, but he wouldn't know personally. "I have no time for *la piscine* like this. Too much work to do."

From the living room window, Danny could make out several luxury cottages settled deep into the trees that fringed the shores of the lake, along with power boats and other leisure craft intended for those who were accustomed to the best in life. Pascal's flat was large, and were it properly furnished, could have been a real home. But Danny got the impression Pascal was rarely there, and even when he was, it was only to shower and sleep before heading out the door again. He seemed to subsist on strong coffee and cigarettes.

Quite by accident they'd both risen early, and Pascal cooked them breakfast in his tidy little kitchen, whipping fresh eggs into an airy omelette and adding mushrooms and cheese in generous quantities. In his own environment, he seemed to relax and unbend a little, and the tense lines bracketing his mouth disappeared. To Danny's utter surprise, he actually had a sense of humour, dropping little jokes and sly puns into the breakfast conversation while he filled and refilled both their cups with good strong coffee brewed on top of the stove.

"I imagined you with a bottle of instant Nescafe," Danny said, "and some of that horrible white dust instead of cream."

Pascal grinned. "One time, I was doing tactical training up north. Way up there in the fucking cold. We had provisions but no liquid because it freeze solid real quick. Lots of coffee, which we make ourself on a little stove, but no cream, just powder." He feigned a shudder. "Horrible. I am astonish I survive." Since returning to his native province, his English had slipped a bit as he conversed with everyone except Danny in French, clearly reveling in his mother tongue. Danny was fascinated with he way it sounded and wished he'd taken the time to learn the language.

"About Joseph," he said, after a moment.

"What about him?" Pascal stirred cream into his coffee and added sugar, clinking the spoon loudly against the inside of the cup and avoiding Danny's gaze.

"He is your son, isn't he?" He waited. "Blaise?"

"I know this now," Pascal said. "I did not know before, but I thought it at times." He raised his eyes to Danny, frowning. "Why you always ask these question?" He sipped at his coffee, grimaced, added more sugar. "Always this kind of wanting to know with you."

"You'll find him," Danny said gently. It was a job for the *Sûreté* now, not the RNC. Wherever Joseph Caron—Joseph Belanger? Joseph Pascal?—was, it wasn't Newfoundland.

"*Non.*" He shook his head. "Wherever she have taken him, he is gone now, unless someone… trip across him by accident."

Danny wondered what Pascal had ever seen in Amalie. At best, she was narcissistic and unprincipled, liable to do anything to anyone at any time without provocation. At worst she was a dangerous serial murderer who killed because it suited her, because she could. Yes, she was beautiful, but beautiful like a wild animal that might turn on you in a heartbeat and rend your flesh to pieces.

"She would never have told me about the boy." Pascal's shoulders moved up and down. "Not until it fit into her *jeux pervers*, her wicked games." A faint smile appeared and disappeared. "I imagined myself in love with her, but it was never that. It was lust." He waved a hand like someone brushing away gnats. "Just nothing. *Rien.*" He rose from the table and began clearing away the breakfast things. "She gave me what I did not get, you know? Some people, their marriage is that of best friends. They go together, always have each other's back, like people say."

"You weren't in love with Louise?" Danny passed his empty plate across to Pascal, who stowed it in the dishwasher.

"At first, perhaps. In the beginning." Pascal rummaged in a nearby cupboard, brought out a box of dishwashing powder. "I think she get tired of me after a little while."

"Can't imagine anyone getting tired of you," Danny said, with a smirk.

"*Tais-toi.* You shut up." He bent to fill the receptacle with powder, then straightened, shut the door, and pressed a button to start the machine. "After Théo was born…."

Danny waited for him to continue, but Pascal was silent. "You can tell me." *You talk too much, and you don't listen*, Danny's late wife, Alison, once said. *Get better at listening, Dan. Don't be such a goddamn blabbermouth.*

"She was not always kind to me."

"And Amalie was?" He had trouble imagining it. Amalie Caron was a killer, a hollow woman with ice in her soul.

"Her unkindness, Amalie, it was a different flavour. This I did not know until much later. Too late." Pascal dumped the empty frying pan into the sink and ran hot water into it. "She make these demand on me, tell me to do things, degrade myself."

"Hurtcore," Danny said. "Was that it?" Was Pascal telling him the truth? He found it hard to imagine the proud *Sûreté* detective deliberately humiliating himself for a woman—for anyone, really.

"This is how they get you, people like this. First of all with this love, so much of it." Pascal seized a bottle of dish liquid and closed his fist around it, squirted it into the frying pan. "You do not know what to do with all this love, but you take it. They tell you these lies." He scrubbed the pan viciously, handling the brush like a deadly weapon. "Oh, you are *incroyable* in bed and just *formidable* and the rest of it."

"But—" Danny paused. Perhaps he shouldn't blunder into another man's pain this way. It was Pascal's private business, after all, and no longer relevant to the investigation, at least not Danny's part of it. "Surely you could see through her. You're smarter than that."

"Of course I could." He finished scrubbing the pan and dumped it into the dish drain face down. "Smart? Not so much when it come to that woman. You know how this goes."

It was your typical psychopathic "love bombing," Danny thought. Find some vulnerable person, tell him what you know he wants to hear, massage his ego, get him comfortable, and then after you have him completely in your control, take it all away. Watch your puppet dance.

"All this love have to be bought and paid for," Pascal continued. "But not with money. You know this, eh? She want to inflict damage, make me less of who I am in reality."

There must have been so little love in his life, and it made him vulnerable to Amalie Caron. It saddened Danny to think of this brilliant, complicated man being preyed upon by her, manipulated in a sick dance born of this twisted woman's darkness… and wouldn't a career cop know better? Surely he'd seen women like Amalie, knew what they were capable of. The way he told it, he'd succumbed immediately to her twisted charm. Danny remembered what June had said back home, when

Pascal first joined them from Quebec: *He is under internal investigation by the BEI—the Bureau des enquêtes indépendantes—for corruption.*

"It seem to me that we make vows," Pascal said. He nodded at Danny's empty cup. "More coffee?" At Danny's nod, he poured a refill. "Me and her, we almost get married to each other."

"What will you do now?" Danny stirred sugar into his coffee and added cream, watching as the pale swirls chased themselves around the circumference of his cup. He glanced up to see Pascal smiling down at him, something mischievous in the depths of his dark eyes.

"How about a trip to Montreal?"

A MAN waited in the early light outside Blaise Pascal's Mont-Tremblant apartment building. He had been there for a while, smoking cigarette after cigarette, crushing the spent butts out under the heel of his boot, then bending to pick them up, shred the tobacco between his fingers, and pocket the filter. Good thing he still remembered how to field strip a cigarette. It was the sort of skill one picked up on the battlefield. He just couldn't remember which one. It was either Afghanistan or Iraq. Almost certainly Iraq. He'd been in the Persian Gulf as well; he was almost certain of it. The Persian Gulf—that had been a bad war, a very bad war. So many were killed. Perhaps he had been killed as well. Maybe what came home wasn't what anyone expected. He could be forgiven for thinking he desired mercy for his sins. Deserved it.

He was having difficulty thinking about things in any ordered way.

Pascal had defiled his wife, and in doing so, the *Sûreté* officer had defiled him as well, and he was tired of feeling dirty. They'd made vows to each other, her and him, and for his part he'd always stayed well within the lines. He was her champion, her personal knight errant, and he would stand in the way of anyone who offered her an insult.

At 10:00 a.m. the building's front door swung open, disgorging Pascal and another man, the Newfoundlander, Quirke. They were talking amicably in English, laughing together as they moved towards a blue Ford pickup truck. As he watched, Pascal unlocked the vehicle and both men got in, Pascal on the driver's side. Now—now was the time to follow, to observe. He leapt for his rental car and slid behind the wheel, careful to keep his distance from them as their truck pulled onto rue Principale Est, heading south. The town and the surrounding area had changed a great deal since he had been here last, and certain familiar features of the landscape had been moved, he was certain of it. There was a massive stone church looming by the side of the road, and a coffee shop where he'd often liked to go was missing, stolen away, devoured. The air smelled to him of brimstone, like the sharp, acidic soldering flux his father had used working as a plumber. His father worked in small, confined spaces, crushed between several kinds of darkness, where there were no other voices but his own and nothing to listen to, no one who might speak. It would be horrible. Such things were often horrible. Such things could never be helped.

Pascal's truck was going by a Tim Hortons coffee shop, and he was close enough to see Pascal and the Newfoundlander talking and laughing with each other. He was careful now to stay far enough behind so Pascal wouldn't see him. Being seen would ruin all his plans, and he'd spent a long time making them. He didn't want to let her down, would not have her thinking any less of him. He was doing this for her.

Eventually they left rue Principale behind, merging onto the Laurentian Autoroute, still heading south. There were any number of small towns between there and here, he thought, but it was likely Pascal was going to Montreal, so he would go to Montreal as well. The air was warm, but the trees had begun to turn colours, shimmering through the entire spectrum until he felt sick with watching them. "*Voici l'automne arrive/les voyageurs vont monter/les canots dessus les dos.*" "Here comes the autumn/the travellers will carry/their canoes on their backs." It was an old folk song, one he shouldn't have remembered but did, something that was sung to him so many years ago when he first came to *l'hôpital*.

"We will make you well again, *mon petit*." This was what they promised him, and it was true. Their medicines and honest Christian care banished his illness. He left that place behind, forgot about it. He had tried his best to forget it, most of it, but sometimes it came to him in sleep or periods of stress, like now. But there'd been others in that place, and someone he remembered, or should have. *Je me souviens*, they said. It's even on our licence plates, he thought. I have no choice but to remember.

He almost lost Pascal at Sainte-Anne-des-Plaines, when the *Sûreté* officer pulled off the Autoroute du Souvenir to gas up. But he was able to locate the correct off-ramp and follow the pickup truck to a *dépanneur* and gas bar just off the highway. Pascal had parked at the pump closest to the door, so anything past that, looking towards the road, was out of his line of sight. So he now eased his own vehicle behind a dumpster, parking so that the bulk of the car was hidden, but he could still see what was going on by the pumps. *Do you even know I am watching you?* She had taught him the genius of hiding in plain sight, of making oneself so uninteresting to the naked eye that he might as well be invisible.

There was significant traffic flow along the divided portion of the highway, and the consistent roar drowned out any speech he might otherwise have heard. He watched as Pascal got out of the truck and activated the gas pump, one foot resting on the lip of a concrete abutment while he waited for the tank to fill. The *Sûreté* officer was wearing the kind of low-heeled boots he always associated with cowboys, and that's what Pascal was, a cowboy. He rode over the feelings of others, uncaring how much damage he caused. Too bad. *Quel dommage.*

As he filled the gas tank, Pascal looked around, turning to peer over his shoulder, eyes scanning the parking lot and the highway beyond. What was he looking for? Did he realise he was being followed? Perhaps he had the instincts of a wild animal who sensed danger on a primal level. That was a useful word for Pascal, primal. She had told him the detective was little better than an animal, and he believed her.

"Let me pour it over you," she said, and he had obeyed, tilting his head back so the blood could flow down over his face and drip into his lap, where he collected it in a shallow tray. The blood that ran onto the floor he'd supplied himself, from a small nick in his wrist that hardly hurt at all. They would come looking for it, the police, with their swabs and sample jars, and it needed to be placed where they could find it. "We must make sure there is something for them to collect." She obscured his eyes while she did it, so nothing would harm him, and the method was particularly clever, using a set of swimming goggles turned inside out to make it appear as if the orbs had been gouged out of his skull. Clever. She was so clever. She was so much smarter than him.

The Newfoundlander was coming out of the *dépanneur*, carrying several bottles of soft drinks and some slips of paper that fluttered between his fingers like the flags of a dying nation. Lottery tickets. Did he think he would have luck? Perhaps his luck would soon be running out. He watched as Quirke climbed back into the truck, followed after a moment by Pascal, walking quickly and shoving his wallet into his hip pocket as he went.

He remembered all the things she told him about this cop, this man who thought himself le bon flic but whose behaviour said otherwise. Did he think women were playthings to use and toss away? He waited while Pascal started the vehicle and pulled onto the highway, then followed, always keeping several car lengths between himself and the two policemen. He needed to know exactly where they were going in Montreal so he could go there too. The plan that had been forming in his mind had been given birth by her, but she was gone now, and it was up to him to carry on, to make the best of her gift to him. They were going to Montreal, and he would follow them. He would be waiting when they arrived.

He would be waiting.

PASCAL BOOKED them a double room at Hotel Yupik, Montreal, near the Notre-Dame Basilica in the old part of the city. He'd scoffed when Danny offered to pay half but allowed that Danny might buy him a beer at the Coldroom speakeasy later on. They'd arrived mid-morning but couldn't check in until three that afternoon, so Pascal took Danny on an impromptu walking tour of Old Montreal as long as his knees would allow. The weather was warm, but the light winds suggested the coolness of autumn, and it wouldn't be long before Montreal was in the grip of another frigid Quebec winter. They made a stop into the Basilica, where Pascal genuflected, crossing himself with a reverence that shocked Danny into silence. He saw Danny watching and said, "Perhaps if I die later, this is almost as good as seeing a priest, *non?*"

"Let's hope you don't die later on, then," Danny replied. He wasn't superstitious, but this particular topic made him uneasy, and he hurried to change the subject. "This is a beautiful place."

"A beautiful place to put your soul to rights before you meet your Maker, eh?" Pascal seemed to think this was hilarious and laughed loudly before a passing priest, his arms full of hymnals, shushed them.

"Messieurs, veuillez vous taire. C'est un lieu saint."

"He is correct," Pascal murmured, his voice a shade above a whisper. "We should be quiet. This is a holy place. Come with me. We go this way." He led Danny to where a life-sized statue of Christ languished in his death throes behind a bank of votive candles, their individual flames licking at the darkness inside the nave. "The artist who made him is Paul Jourdain," he said. "He died in 1769, so this is very old." Pascal dug into the pocket of his jeans, pulled out a couple of dollar coins, and dropped them into a nearby donation box. He lit one of the votives, holding the match in the flame for several seconds afterwards, then shook it out. "This is where we pray for the souls of our dead, and also for other prayers."

"I know," Danny replied. "I was raised Catholic myself." He had very few fond memories of it from childhood and little use for religion now. It seemed to be something people did for show so everyone else could see how holy they were.

Pascal turned from his contemplation of the flames. "Yet you don't pray?"

"No."

"Then I will pray for you."

Danny wondered who else Pascal was praying for. He knew so little about the man, except what he'd learned from Pascal's superiors in the *Sûreté* or managed to glean himself. He was divorced from Amalie Caron's sister, Louise, and apart from his son, Théo, Danny didn't know if the union had produced any children. He had mentioned his siblings only briefly, saying that he had come from a large family.

"I come here whenever I am in Montreal," Pascal said quietly. "To pray for my brothers and sisters, and also for my *maman*."

Danny remembered Pascal saying that his mother was deceased, but the implications of what he was saying now felt like a punch in the chest. "They're all... dead?"

"*Oui*. I am the only one left."

The shock of this revelation must have shown on Danny's face, for Pascal hastened to explain. "There was a fire in our house when I was twelve years old. It burned very fast, and...." He shrugged in that expressive Quebecois way that Danny was learning to appreciate. "The priest came to visit me. He explained it is God's will."

The paucity of this explanation must have been extraordinarily cruel for a twelve-year-old boy. "I'm so sorry," Danny said, wishing he were more articulate or had better words to offer. Tadhg would know what to say. Tadhg always knew what to say. "That must have been awful for you."

He moved away to allow Pascal some measure of privacy while he prayed. Fire. Pascal's life seemed to have been framed in fire, from his childhood family to the cigarette burns on his arm to the fire his ex-wife set that damaged him and his son and finally to the fire that destroyed the Caron house and brought him to Kildevil Cove. Danny didn't believe in fate, but it would be hard to argue that fire was not the demon Blaise Pascal had been fated to encounter all his life.

Shrugging off these uneasy speculations, Danny turned to examine the richly coloured ceilings overhead and the ancient building's striking Gothic architecture. His gaze sought out the confessionals, and he remembered many torturous Sunday mornings slipping into the narrow wooden box to ask forgiveness for his sins, many and various. As a young boy, he already knew he wasn't like other boys, even if he didn't yet have the language to describe the qualities that made him different. At puberty he indulged in the same covert games as all his friends did, but for him such dalliances were serious. By the time he reached high school, he'd fallen in and out of love with several of his male friends and with an equal number of the girls, something which alarmed him. You were supposed to pick one, weren't you? It was like being offered a choice of cake or pie for your dessert. You couldn't have both, and what did it matter, all those *I love you*'s murmured in the darkness of a classmate's bed if indeed it was a mortal sin?

He felt someone touch his shoulder: Pascal. "We will go now. There is much to see. We don't want to get mired in all this holiness, eh?"

They stepped out into the bright sunlight and spent the afternoon roaming the streets together. Pascal took him into the eclectic downtown neighbourhoods he had patrolled as a young constable, first with the SPVM and later with the *Sûreté*, regaling Danny with stories of sudden shoot-outs and near misses. He showed him the decrepit building that had once housed Sexe Plus, the club where Amalie worked and where his fellow officers had bought him a lap dance he didn't want the night before his wedding.

"You didn't want it?" Danny asked, incredulous. It was nearly three and they were headed back to their hotel to check in.

"Not my kind of thing," Pascal explained. "No, seriously. It's not how I think we should treat women, you know?" They rode up to the fourth floor together in the elevator, and Danny waited while Pascal operated the intricate door lock, which involved putting his palm over a sensor and then punching in a code.

"Don't know why they make it so complicated," Danny said, gesturing at the lock. "At least nobody can get in the room while we're gone." The door swung back on its hinges, and he wished he'd never uttered the words. The interior of the room looked like a tornado had come through.

"*Calisse!*" Pascal hissed. "What the fuck happened here?"

Both their suitcases had been upended, the contents scattered over the floor, and all the bureau drawers had been pulled out and flung across the room. The beds were stripped, the duvets and pillows tossed to one side, and there were clear imprints of somebody's booted feet on the bed linens. The word *merde*—shit—was scrawled on the wall above the nightstand in what looked like human faeces.

"Jesus," Danny said.

"Wouldn't be him." Pascal pulled a pair of latex gloves from his coat pocket and moved towards the wall. "He is much too holy to do something like this."

It took Danny a moment to realise the Quebecois was joking. "You're a queer hand," he said. "Half the time I don't even know what you're at." He watched as Pascal dabbed his index finger at the wall and brought the finger to his nose. "Is it shit?"

"*Non.* I think it probably chocolate, something like that." He peeled off the gloves and dropped them in the wastebasket, the one thing in the room that hadn't been upended. "I suppose we should inform the front desk, but I want to take a look around first."

They spent the next forty-five minutes searching the room for further evidence but, apart from the boot prints on the pillowcases and the bizarre writing on the wall, found nothing. Pascal informed the hotel manager, who insisted on moving them to another room. "I am so very sorry, *messieurs*. I cannot think how this happened. These rooms are very secure. No one should have been able to get in while you were out. I am so very sorry. *Messieurs*, please forgive what is clearly an oversight on my part." His bizarre obsequiousness reminded Danny of Peter Lorre's character from *Casablanca*, and he was relieved when Pascal finally shut him out the door.

"It seems like something Amalie might have done when she was alive," Danny remarked later when they'd gone down to the hotel restaurant for pre-dinner drinks.

"*Vraiment*," Pascal agreed, but he seemed determined not to talk about the incident.

Danny had changed into a pair of black jeans Alison had bought for him about a year before her death, and a navy-blue sweater he'd purchased in Inverness in April when he and Tadhg went there to be married. He probably looked all right, he reasoned, but part of him wondered if he mightn't be a bit more adventurous with his wardrobe. Tadhg's side of their bedroom closet was full of silk shirts and tailored suits in colours Danny would never consider wearing, not in a million years. If he found something he liked and which fitted him well, he'd buy several, but the Scottish part of Danny considered Tadhg's plethora of attire extravagant and wasteful.

Except you aren't really Scottish. Yes. It always came back to that. His grandmother—the woman he'd thought was his grandmother—had come from Scotland as a war bride, leaving behind her first daughter, Danny's aunt Maeve. *But Maeve's not really your aunt, and your mother wasn't even your mother, and you're the bastard son of a Welsh woman nobody knows.* Eventually he'd have to go there, to Aberystwyth, if only to track down the sender of the gold locket he'd received in the mail, and if only to find out whose picture that was inside—that of a man who looked remarkably like Danny.

After an excellent dinner of seafood, helped along by fine Quebecois wine, he and Pascal headed out into the warm evening to find a bar. He wasn't interested in a dance club or any modern iteration of Sexe Plus, and most of the popular places played music at a volume he found unbearable. Finally, Pascal steered him to the Coldroom on rue Saint-Vincent, not far from the Old Port of Montreal. In order to gain access, they had to ring the doorbell, and a barman came to let them in.

"Are you sure this is the right place?" Danny asked, following Pascal down a set of metal stairs and past a large black-and-white picture of a cartoon duck. "It looks like an underground car park."

"This is the right place," Pascal confirmed. "You will love it, believe me."

A white door opened into a cozy space with redbrick walls, warm ambient lighting, and the familiar gleam of glass bottles behind the bar. Two burly bartenders, both in tight-fitting jeans and black T-shirts, expertly mixed cocktails while chatting with the patrons. The music was instrumental jazz with a Latin flavour, the volume low enough to allow conversation. It had the feeling of the old Ship Inn, a pub Danny and Tadhg had often frequented in their student days at Memorial University. The punters were mostly younger people in their mid-twenties to mid-thirties, but there were one or two older people seated at the bar and three men Danny and Pascal's age occupied a banquette at the back.

"Let's sit down and see what we want." Pascal gestured towards an unoccupied banquette. "They have excellent draft beer in this place."

They did have excellent draft beer but also excellent tequila, and before too long Danny was matching Pascal shot for shot, licking salt and biting into fresh slices of lime, the flavour bursting on his tongue like an old and pleasant memory. Sometime after midnight, his mobile rang. The call was from Tadhg. He thumbed the green circle drunkenly to accept the call and roared about how much fun he was having. Further down the line he heard Tadhg laughing. "Ye're half-cut, are ye? What's that Frenchman after doing to ye?"

"*Il fait la fête!*" Pascal bawled. Like Danny, he was already three sheets to the wind.

"Lord Christ, bhoy, I'm half in the bag," Danny said. His face ached with laughing so much, but he couldn't seem to stop. He wondered what else was in the shots besides tequila. Cannabis was legal everywhere now, and it had crossed his mind during their spontaneous celebration that he was as free as anyone to indulge, without fear of legal repercussions. Would it be politic to ask Pascal if he wanted to smoke a little?

"I just wanted to check up on ye," Tadhg said. Danny could hear the smile in his voice. "When ye called to tell me your flight was delayed, I was wondering how ye'd get on all by yourself in the big city, but by the sounds of it, ye made out all right." He paused. "Lily says hurry home soon, and Easter is after taking your shirt and going in under the bed with it. She won't come out."

"Give them both kisses from me." It warmed his heart to think of the family he had waiting for him.

"And what about me?"

"You'll get what I got as soon as I'm home." Maybe romance was the province of the young, but right at that moment he didn't care. He yearned for Tadhg suddenly, a yearning coupled with the absurd fear that he might never see him again—that something horrible was about to happen, something that couldn't be prevented or averted. "I love you," he murmured, conscious of Pascal's gaze across the table. "You know that, right?" The heady, whirling exaltation of a moment before was gone. Now he felt only a cold dread. "Keep safe until I'm home. Keep Lily and Easter safe."

"My love, what's the matter?"

"I… it's getting late." He couldn't effectively articulate the fear that was pressing down on him. "I love you." It was important that he say it again, just in case. "Tadhg."

"Dan, is everything all right? Jesus, bhoy, you're scaring me."

"I'm fine. Just someone walking over my grave."

"Are you sure?"

He caught Pascal's eye and smiled; the Frenchman smiled back, but the smile didn't reach his eyes. *He feels it too*, Danny thought. "I'm sure." He murmured his goodbyes and rang off.

"Something is wrong." Pascal toyed with the empty shot glass in front of him, turning it in circles on the tabletop. "What did he say to you, your husband?"

"Nothing." Danny picked up his nearly empty pint glass and drank off the last of his beer. "We should leave soon. It's getting late."

Pascal turned his wrist to glance at his watch, and once more Danny saw the livid red circles left by cigarette burns. The *Sûreté* detective's gaze rose to meet his. "Amalie did that. Have I told you this? I have a long experience with fire, me." Danny shivered, thinking how Pascal's words echoed Danny's thoughts from earlier. Pascal attempted a smile but didn't quite make it. "Why am I telling you this? Perhaps because *je suis saoul comme une botte*."

"You're silly as a bottle?" Danny asked, taking a stab at it.

"I am drunk as a boot." Someone had left a cocktail napkin on the table, and Pascal pulled it towards him, began folding it diagonally. "I grew up in a institute for children who are—what do you call them—troubled?"

"Yes." Thankfully this wasn't something that happened anymore, but much of Canadian history was rife with stories of such places—warehouses for children nobody wanted because they were too much trouble. Treatment in such institutions was nothing short of horrific.

"When I was twelve years old, my father, he told me to go out of this house. You cause *trop de problèmes pour la famille*. I was always fighting with my brothers and sisters, making difficulty. Mostly I was bored in school and had to sit on my hands, as you say, while the others catch up to me." He turned the cocktail napkin around, folding it back upon itself. "You understand?"

The crowd huddled around the bar had begun to thin out, leaving only two diehards, older men who'd probably stumbled in at the tail end of the evening. A group of young women in their twenties rose from a crowded banquette across from where Danny and Pascal were and teetered out the door on their impossibly high heels, calling goodbye to the barman.

"Yes," Danny said.

"I decided I would do something to get back at them. I worked up a plan in my mind for what to do. We lived in a rural area, no neighbours close by, nothing. I waited until my family was sleeping, then I went out to the barn." His fingers worked the cocktail napkin, folding again and again, until it seemed he sought to compress it into some infinitesimal, impossible shape. "My father, he had gasoline stored there." He raised his head, seeking Danny's gaze. "I know what you are thinking. This man, he beat me every day of my life, treated me worse than an animal. I am nothing—*rien*—to these people. I never intended...." He fell silent, pressing his lips together. His fingers bent and folded the cocktail napkin once, twice more, until it achieved the shape of a swan. "Here," he said, sliding it across the table to Danny. "Something to remember me. Wait, I will give it an autograph." He took out a pen and scribbled something on the inside fold of one wing.

"What happened?" Danny asked. "With the fire." He reached across the table, captured the origami swan. It was meticulously done, every fold knife sharp and precise, an artwork in miniature that he would never be able to reproduce. He tucked it into the pocket of his jeans for safekeeping.

"I meant to set this fire to the door at the back... the kitchen, you know?" He shook his head. "There was dry grass, and it spread, the whole thing, so fast. So fast." He'd panicked and run to the road, hoping to flag down a passing vehicle. An off-duty volunteer firefighter had been passing by and saw the anguished boy waving from the middle of the road. She radioed a nearby station, but it was too late. By the time the trucks arrived, the house was engulfed in flames, and everyone inside was dead.

"My God." Danny couldn't think of anything else to say. Perhaps there wasn't anything. Pascal had been twelve years old, a child, doing something a child would think to do, not realising the harm it would cause.

"The police sent me to the institute, and I stayed there until my eighteenth birthday." The bartender appeared at their table and advised them the bar was closing soon. Did they want anything else?

"*Non, merci.*" Pascal stood, took out his wallet, and dropped a bill on the table. "We should go back," he said to Danny. "You have your flight tomorrow."

They made their way back upstairs, past the cartoonish illustration of the duck that Danny had barely glanced at on their way in. Initially he'd regarded it as whimsical, amusing, but now the image of the bird, its eyes crossed out, seemed to be mocking him; he realised it was supposed to be dead. *Don't drink tequila, Danny,* he told himself. *You know it makes you strange.* At the top of the stairs, he held the door open for Pascal to precede him outside. It had been warm inside the bar, but Montreal's September weather could be capricious, changeable, and the sudden gust of air that greeted him was significantly chillier than expected.

"I think it has cooled off," Pascal said. "Perhaps we should—"

Afterwards, Danny would wonder how the hell he hadn't seen the man emerging from the shadows with a gun in his hand. The double *pop-pop* of the weapon's discharge sounded like a firecracker going off. He watched, horrified, as Pascal stiffened and staggered backwards, his heel catching on a crack in the sidewalk and sending him down hard on his back.

"Jesus!" Danny surged towards him, too late to arrest his fall and too late to catch the gunman, who was sprinting off into the night, a shadow among shadows. He knelt by Pascal's side, but there was no need to search for the damage. Two dark stains gathered and spread across the front of his shirt. "Blaise... don't move, okay? Stay still. Christ, how do you say that in French?" Pascal coughed blood, reaching out with one hand to catch hold of Danny's shirt. "No, don't talk. Christ, don't talk." He shrugged out of his jacket, gathered it into a bundle, and pressed it against Pascal's chest. "Hold on to that." Pascal twitched, eyes rolling back in his head. "No, don't you dare. Stay awake. Fuck sake, Blaise!" Danny pushed the bundle of cloth hard against the wounds and fumbled his mobile out with his free hand. "It's 911 just like everywhere else," he commented. He wasn't sure if he was talking to himself or to Pascal. He hit the Call button, punched in the numbers, and listened for what seemed like an eternity as the rings went out and out.

"*Bonjour, neuf-un-un, urgence de Montréal. Quelle est votre urgence?*"

Oh Christ. "I-I don't speak F-French," Danny stuttered. "My friend has been shot. Police officer. *Sûreté.* He's shot."

"Where are you located, sir?"

"I'm in Montreal." *Idiot.* He glanced down at Pascal. "This would be so much easier if you could talk to them." It was gallows humour at its absolute worst. Pascal was shuddering, his body drawn in on itself. His face had achieved the sallow look of a corpse, and his eyes were rapidly losing their focus. "Blaise, stay with me. Come on! You die on me and I'll kick your fucking arse."

"I have located you by your phone," the 911 operator said. "An ambulance will be with you in three minutes, monsieur."

Three minutes. He hoped Pascal had three minutes to spare.

"*Écoute-moi.*" Pascal grabbed at his sleeve. "Danny." He coughed, a horrible rattling noise, and fresh blood trickled from the corners of his mouth. "My son Théo is in—"

"Stop trying to talk." He shifted his weight as his damaged knees began shrieking in protest at his position. "You are going to be fine. Just fine." Danny sank back, the sidewalk cold against his thighs and buttocks, and cradled Pascal's head in his lap.

"Want you to tell Théo—"

"Jesus Christ, would ye ever shut up? Tell him yourself." He pressed his wadded-up coat more firmly into Pascal's wound, hard enough to hurt. Pascal didn't make a sound. "Blaise?" Danny shook him gently. "Come on, bhoy." He leaned close, heard a noise like air escaping through the sidewall of a damaged car tire. "Oh no.... Blaise, come on. Come on, bhoy. Come on." He repeated it like a primal chant, like a prayer, was still repeating it as the ambulance's flashing lights washed his surroundings in a lurid cascade of red. The vehicle's back doors burst open, disgorging two EMTs who ran towards him and lifted Pascal from his lap.

"*Trop tard,*" one of them said. "*Heure de la mort?*"

"I don't understand you," Danny said as he was raised gently to his feet and guided to stand to one side of the waiting ambulance. "I don't speak French. I don't understand you, I don't." A young man shone a penlight into each of Danny's eyes, asked him where he was hurt, if he'd also been injured. "I'm not hurt. I'm not the one who's hurt. It's Pascal who's bleeding. He's bleeding."

They loaded Pascal onto a stretcher and then into the back of the ambulance. He was deathly pale and completely still. "Is he all right?" Danny asked. "Is he going to be all right?"

"Come with me, monsieur." An SPVM constable appeared and took Danny by the arm. "I will bring you to the station to make a statement."

"I have to go with him." He tried to pull away, but he was too weak. *I'm old and weak*, he thought. *That's why Pascal is bleeding. I've let him down. I'm too old for this. Too old and weak.*

"Let me help you," the constable said. He was about Kevin's age, similar in height and build, with short blond hair. "Come along with me, monsieur. We will talk a little, you and I."

"I need to help Inspector Pascal."

The constable leaned close and gazed at him. His nametag read Martin. "Monsieur, there is no one can help him now except *le bon Dieu*."

No one except the good God.

"I have to help him," Danny murmured. "I have to."

CHAPTER SIXTEEN

Wednesday

DANNY HAD taken the day off, exhausted from the events in Montreal, hours spent at the SPVM station answering questions that had no answers, and the return trip to Newfoundland on Tuesday afternoon, all without sleep save a few hours on the journey. Being neither family nor a close connection, he could do nothing for Pascal, and he'd desperately needed the solace of home. He and Tadhg had slept in, not rising until late and lingering over breakfast in the spacious kitchen while Easter dozed in a puddle of sunlight at his feet. "I think she knows what you've been through," Tadhg said, nodding towards the little dog.

"Dogs are sensitive souls," Danny replied. "I'm sure she picked up on my emotions." He leaned down to ruffle her velvety ears. "Darling girl. She knows she's loved."

Tadhg got up to flick the kettle on. "Another pot?"

"Always." Newfoundland lore about tea was the gospel truth. No matter the crisis or twist of fate, it kept you going. Danny's Scottish war bride grandmother—*she's not your grandmother and she never was*—swore by its curative powers.

"Have you heard anything this morning?" Tadhg took up the teapot and dumped the spent tea leaves into the bin, then rinsed the pot in hot water from the tap. "From Montreal?"

"No." All the horror of that night was still vivid in his memory, the images crowding into his thoughts unbidden. Pascal lying on a cold and dirty sidewalk as his life drained away. Where was the justice in that? "Louis Prud'Homme, the *Sûreté* man who works with Blaise, left a voice mail on my phone. They still haven't identified the shooter." The CCTV from outside the Coldroom didn't show anything much: a tall man in a hoodie stepping suddenly from the shadows, a gun in his hand. He could have been anyone.

"How's Pascal doing?" Tadhg gave him a diffident look. Danny had told him the previous day upon his arrival all he knew at the time, which was that Pascal had made it to the hospital but was in critical condition. "Do they think he'll make it?"

"He's in a medically induced coma. The prognosis isn't good." Prud'Homme had sounded more upset than Danny would have expected. What was his relationship with Blaise Pascal? Were they more than colleagues, more than merely friends?

The kettle came to its usual rapid boil, and Tadhg reached to flick it off. "I'm sorry, my love." He poured boiling water into the pot, swirled it around, and dumped it down the sink, then spooned fresh leaves in—enough to make a good, strong brew.

Danny gazed into his empty mug. "He's a good cop, you know."

"I liked him," Tadhg replied, filling the teapot with water and leaving it to steep. "I mean, I didn't know him like you did, but I liked him." He came to where Danny was and leaned down to hug him from behind, wrapping his arms around Danny's shoulders.

"He wasn't an easy man to like." The comment was petty, and he regretted it. Moreover, he was referring to Pascal in the past tense, as if he were already dead. "I should have tried harder with him."

Tadhg sighed. "Danny, my love, you didn't shoot him." He seemed about to say something else but was interrupted by his mobile phone. "It's Walter at the job site. Do you mind if I take this?"

Danny waved a hand. "No, go and do what ye got to do." He got up and wandered over to the teapot, wondering whether to give it a stir. It was bad luck, wasn't it? *Don't be stirring that teapot, now. Ye're just stirring up trouble, sure.* His grandmother again. There was a tap at the front door, followed by the sound of it opening and someone's feet scraping on the mat.

"Anybody home?" June Carbage's voice floated to him from the porch.

Danny went out to meet her. "What's on the go?" he asked, feeling a surge of anxiety in his chest and throat. "Is something after happening?"

"I didn't want to bother you on your day off," she started, apologetically, "but some information has come to light with regards to Moira." She toed off her shoes and followed him into the kitchen.

"Moira?" He pulled out a chair for her at the table and went to fetch the teapot and an extra cup. Easter stirred from her spot on the floor and leapt at June, wagging her whole body eagerly. June and her partner had looked after Easter the previous winter, when Danny and Tadhg had split up. Easter adored June, and the feeling was definitely mutual.

"You won't believe it when I tell you." June reached into her pocket for a treat to give the dog, tossing it high in the air so Easter would jump for it. Danny suspected this was a game they had often played before.

"Oh?"

"Moira had a contact here in the Cove." It took her no more than a handful of minutes to tell it. Amy and Moira had been involved years before and had kept in touch even after their intimate relationship broke up.

"Wait a minute," Danny interrupted her. "You mean to tell me that you knew about this?"

"No! My God, absolutely not," June said, hurrying to defend herself. "Sir, she was feeding Moira information, telling her things about you and the station. Twelve years," she said bitterly. "We were together twelve years. You'd think I would have known."

Danny poured hot tea into her cup and offered the milk jug, just as Tadhg reappeared from the front room. "I've got to go over there. They delivered the wrong fucking roof trusses," he said peevishly. He'd obviously been worrying at his hair, for it was standing up in spikes at the top of his head. "Hi, June." He came to where Danny was and kissed his cheek. "I'll be back when I gets back." And he was gone.

"Tell me," Danny said, quietly, when Tadhg had gone. "Tell me all of it. Don't leave anything out."

June's partner Amy—former partner now—had been in the habit of taking research trips and sabbaticals as part of her career. A marine biologist, she'd traveled far and wide, and as far as June was concerned, there had never been any cause for suspicion. She always arrived home when she said she would, and her demeanour towards June hadn't changed in the slightest. They enjoyed the same domestic and intimate closeness as they always had. Until a telephone conversation, which sounded suspicious but ironically turned out to be nothing, set June on the path to putting all the missing pieces together.

"I don't know if she was cheating on me with Moira," June averred, "and I don't want to know." She toyed with her teacup, not drinking the tea. "But she was passing information for months. I'm not sure how long, exactly. Maybe since Moira disappeared."

"And where did she get this information she's been passing?" June was a good cop, and Danny would hate to have to discipline her, but if she'd been discussing official business with Amy, he'd nail her to the wall. He'd have to.

"Not from me," she said emphatically. "Not from me."

"Okay." Danny got up and went to the pantry, brought out the tin of fancy biscuits. He opened it and set it on the table. As usual, Tadhg had been through it and snaffled all the custard creams. "Where, then?"

"I honestly don't know, sir. She has considerable computer abilities. Maybe she hacked into our systems."

"You know where Moira is?"

She shook her head, her dark hair swirling around her face. "No. The location was always encrypted. She's been very careful to cover her tracks. There's...." She trailed off, massaged her temples with two fingers. "My head aches like a bastard."

"I'm so sorry you've had to contend with this," Danny told her, "but I need whatever information you have." If Amy had hacked into June's work laptop, that was one thing. They could arrest her for that, no trouble. If June had left her laptop unsecured, it was a different matter altogether, and she was potentially to blame for the information leak. There would be an internal investigation and it wouldn't be pretty. Danny knew this from personal experience.

"Moira is being investigated by Interpol as well as CSIS," June said. "There's a global warrant out for her arrest. Apparently an Interpol agent has been shadowing her for nearly two years." This wasn't exactly news to Danny. It was common practice for Interpol to get involved when the crimes crossed international boundaries. He was getting irritated now. Didn't June have anything else of substance?

"I know." He heard the irritation in his own voice and didn't particularly care.

"I went through Amy's phone," June said, producing it out of her pocket. "There are dozens of text messages there, but this one"—she swiped at the screen—"is interesting." She passed the phone across to Danny. He took it from her and read the message on the screen:

AmyOh:> *That frog is looking in all the wrong places.*

Mosula:> *Good let him keep looking.* 😊

AmyOh:> *You better get this shit straightened out.*

Mosula:> *Don't tell me what to do.* 😞

AmyOh:> *Be more careful.*

"What frog?" he asked obtusely, then realised what it meant. *Mother of God.* "Blaise Pascal?" He checked the date of the message. "But this was weeks ago. Before Pascal came here."

June nodded. "Like I said, I've done some poking around, called in a few favours with the RCMP. I dated a constable there once, and she was able to point me in the right direction. Blaise Pascal has been working with Canadian Security Intelligence Service for a while. He might have come here to investigate Amalie Caron, but he was looking for Moira Fraser too."

BLAISE PASCAL had survived the surgery to remove two bullets from his chest, but hope for his recovery seemed premature.

"He is very sick, *monsieur*." The young doctor allowed Louis Prud'Homme to stay longer than was usual and had taken the time to explain Pascal's injuries. Both bullets had been fired at close to point-blank range, penetrating the chest cavity but thankfully missing the heart. "Either the assailant was in a hurry or he was a very bad shot."

"Or both," Prud'Homme commented. He wasn't trying to be funny, but the muscles of his face felt stiff and artificial when he tried to smile. Pascal was lying on his back, attached to myriad tubes and wires, while a bank of monitors kept track of his vital functions.

"We have a machine breathing for him right now," the surgeon continued, "until he is comfortable to breathe on his own." He examined Prud'Homme curiously, no doubt wanting to ask what relation Prud'Homme was to Pascal. Prud'Homme had shown his badge at the nursing station, and there were no questions asked, but he couldn't help feeling like he didn't belong. Pascal was very pale, and Prud'Homme had never seen him so still. "Your friend came very close to death."

Prud'Homme fixed him with the same stare that usually served him well during suspect interrogations. "I was told he expired in the ambulance and was revived."

"That is correct." The doctor pushed his glasses up on his nose. "He was dead and was brought back to life."

"Like Christ." Prud'Homme drew a breath. "Thank you for talking to me. I have no more questions at present, but I will be in touch. *Merci*." He turned his back, effectively dismissing the man, and drew close to Pascal. There was a chair by the side of the bed for visitors, but he doubted anyone besides himself had been to see Pascal.

"Well, *mon ami*," he whispered, "you have done it this time, eh?" He wasn't expecting a reply, and there was none. Even if Pascal had been awake, the tube in his throat would have prevented speech. A medically induced coma, the nurse had said, to allow him to heal. "He really got you good." Prud'Homme reached out and cupped Pascal's cheek, his thumb stroking the stubbled chin. "Don't think I am going to let this pass without comment. *Monsieur le docteur* says you were dead, and you came back, like Lazarus or Christ. I think that kind of miracle demands a comment, *non*?"

The monitor closest to Prud'Homme was tracking Pascal's pulse; it jumped a little before settling back into a regular sinus rhythm. Prud'Homme knew it meant nothing. Pascal wasn't conscious in any appreciable way, and the flicker of an electronic line on a computer screen was no indication that he'd heard. He was probably just dreaming.

"I will tell you what I will do, *mon frère*...." Prud'Homme leaned over and whispered into Pascal's ear. "Do you like this idea? I will do it, just for you. I make this vow." He lingered for a moment, then very gently placed his hand palm down on the centre of Pascal's chest. "Just for you."

He was smiling when he left the hospital—a dangerous smile. He stopped back at his hotel, an unassuming, pay-by-the-day shithole on Boulevard St-Laurent, with a bed that made him itchy and a room infested with mice. It wouldn't matter. After tonight he would never be back. The room, like his visit to the city, was merely the means to an end, nothing more. He had called in a favour from an informant who was relocating to Halifax, and for far too much money was able to buy a previously owned Glock pistol with its serial number conveniently removed. Once it had served its purpose, he wouldn't need it anymore, and it could find a new home at the bottom of the St. Lawrence River.

Prud'Homme had put the word out that he was looking for a certain someone who had capped a cop outside the Coldroom, and he spread some dollars around to encourage information sharing. A skinny goth girl with ripped tights and the persistently runny nose of a cokehead showed up at his door, offered him *une pipe*, which he declined—*le bon Dieu* only knew where her mouth had been. "I know where he is, this *mec*." She plopped down on the bed, looking around with disdain. "You live here?"

"No." Prud'Homme fetched out a pack of smokes and offered her one, lit it for her. "I wouldn't sit there if I were you." He leered at her, his eyebrows raised. "Lots of things could crawl up your *plotte* if you aren't careful."

"Don't be a pig." She scowled at him, wiped her nose in the sleeve of her black hoodie sweatshirt. "Got anything else around here?"

"If you mean drugs, no. You might find a chocolate bar in the fridge, but it's probably been nibbled at by mice. This place is crawling with rodents and other vermin."

"*Bien*." She stood up and held out her hand. "Two hundred, you said."

Prud'Homme eased his wallet out of the hip pocket of his jeans and opened it, counted out two hundred and twenty dollars. "You only get this when you tell me." He held it up between his fingers. "No information, no money."

Her eyes narrowed. "What are you going to do to him?"

"What do you care?" An ambulance passed by outside, the noise of the siren seeping through the paper-thin walls and into the room. "He's nothing to you."

"Curiosity," she replied with a shrug, eyes on the money. "He's only been back a little while. Everybody's wondering where he was, what he was doing."

"I'm only wondering where he's going to be tonight," Prud'Homme said dryly. "Either you cough it up or this goes back in my wallet and you can fuck off."

Le Cochon de Gaz, she told him, and he'd been there the past three nights, so there was a good chance, a very good chance, he would show up again. Prud'Homme handed her the money, catching a glimpse of a dirty bra strap as the bills disappeared inside. She moved closer, cupped one hand around his crotch. "*Beaucoup de mine dans ton crayon...* lots of lead in your pencil, eh?"

Prud'Homme pushed her away. "Get out."

She turned to go, pausing at the door to offer him a sleazy look. "We're good, you and me?"

"*Tiguidou*," he said. "Now go."

Fifteen minutes later, he had found his way to Le Cochon de Gaz, a dive bar of grim renown on the other end of Boulevard St-Laurent. Whatever else the girl had been, she wasn't a liar. Prud'Homme only had to wait twenty minutes in the parking lot adjacent to the bar before he spotted his quarry.

Gerard Caron hadn't changed a bit since Prud'Homme had seen him last. Seven years previous he'd turned up in Mont-Tremblant with his bitch Amalie, and they'd set themselves up in business, selling prescription opioids. He and Pascal had busted them, but the Carons had connections, and pretty soon their scumbag lawyer had both of them out on bail. Then the Carons disappeared off the face of the earth, so completely that Pascal suspected someone had taken out a hit on them. It was purely by chance that they'd pitched up in Newfoundland. They probably thought no one would notice them in a small village like Kildevil Cove, but their luck had since run out. Amalie Caron was dead, and Gerard Caron was very soon going to find out what happened when you shot a cop in Montreal.

Prud'Homme stationed himself close to the front entrance of the bar, walking up and down, smoking, and occasionally talking on his mobile phone so it would appear he was waiting for someone. The last thing he wanted to do was arouse suspicion, and if any of the bar's regulars suspected *le flic* was sniffing around, his chances of seeing Gerard Caron were miniscule. Now and then he went across the street and stood in an alley beside a run-down consignment shop with iron bars on its windows to safeguard the dazzling array of junk for sale. For the most part he had a clear view of the place, but now and then a bus or other large vehicle would block his sightline, and he worried that Gerard Caron would slip past him somehow.

At ten minutes past midnight, Caron came out of Le Cochon de Gaz with three other men and stood around smoking and talking for ten minutes. Prud'Homme stood a short distance away and fiddled with his phone while Caron spun some bullshit tale about being a *gros mec* in the local drug trade. His companions were all tall heavily built men, and Prud'Homme knew better than to take them on. He had no desire to get beaten to a pulp; he was here for Gerard Caron and nobody else.

Eventually Caron's buddies tired of his stories and, bidding him goodnight, went on their separate ways, leaving him standing on the sidewalk. Prud'Homme waited while Caron checked his mobile. Probably looking for the Metro schedule, he thought. The trains wouldn't be running too much longer. *Better hurry up and get home, salaud.* Caron stowed his phone in the inside pocket of his jacket and started off in a roughly southwesterly direction, towards Mount Royal Cemetery.

Prud'Homme followed. Just past Parc Jeanne-Mance, Caron stopped and looked around him. Prud'Homme sank back into the shadows, holding his breath. If Caron saw him, it was over. Caron would remember what Prud'Homme looked like, would recognise him immediately, and then any hope Prud'Homme had of netting the bastard would vanish like a fart in a jar of nails. But after a moment or two Caron turned on his heel and headed back in the direction he'd come, giving no indication he'd seen Prud'Homme or was even aware of his presence. Caron crossed Boulevard St. Laurent and continued down rue Rachael Ouest towards rue Saint-Urbain. He entered an art supply shop by the side door. Prud'Homme waited until Caron was inside, then followed, stepping over piles of trash and old clothing that spilled out of several burst bin bags and the body of a dead pigeon. He exclaimed in surprise when he nearly stepped on an old woman crouching on a lower step.

"*Tabarnak*! What the hell are you doing there?" She was dressed all in black, her scrawny figure swathed in an assortment of shawls and draperies. Prud'Homme had taken her for a pile of refuse. She swore at him, and he narrowly escaped the foul gobbet of spit ejected from her toothless mouth.

"Some people have no manners," she said. "Give me some money."

"Get a job," Prud'Homme retorted.

"What kind of work can I do at my age?" She held out a hand and nodded at the building's upper storey. "Give me some money and I'll leave you alone with your boyfriend."

Prud'Homme took out his wallet and fished out twenty dollars. "You know where he lives?"

"Ohhhh, is that all?" She reached for the money, but Prud'Homme held it clear of her grasp. "Just twenty?"

"What's the room number?"

"*Quel numéro?*" Her lips parted, and her toothless gums appeared. "No number, only one room up there on the top. Better knock, though, all *tiguidou*." Prud'Homme dropped the twenty-dollar bill into her outstretched hand and pushed past her. He went inside, making for the stairs.

The interior of the building smelled of piss and chemicals, but not the kind normally found in cleaning fluid. At the top of the stairs on the second-floor landing, a young woman sat propped against the wall with her head hanging down, her long hair trailing in a puddle of rancid-smelling vomit. Prud'Homme bent and put two fingers against the side of her neck, was astonished to feel a pulse beating beneath the skin. He shook her by the shoulder and spoke to her, but she didn't stir. Drunk, probably, or fucked up on some opioid that had sent her into dreamland. Maybe she'd wake up on her own, or maybe she wouldn't wake up at all. It didn't matter. She was someone else's problem.

He took the last set of stairs two at a time and emerged on the landing barely out of breath. Taking the Glock pistol out of its holster, he rapped on the door and waited.

"*Qui est là?*"

"*Salut*, Gerard." Prud'Homme's mouth stretched into a grim smile. "I've been waiting ages to catch up." He shoved the door open and fired two shots in rapid succession into Gerard Caron—one in the chest and one in the head.

Caron was dead before he hit the floor.

Prud'Homme went outside and caught a cab, directing the driver to take him to rue du Square-Victoria, where he paid the man and disembarked, then went down into the Metro station to board the next train that came along. When Blaise Pascal woke the next morning, Prud'Homme was at his bedside, showered, shaved, and dressed in clean clothes. His face was the first thing Pascal saw when he opened his eyes.

"*Bonjour, mon ami.*" Prud'Homme reached for his hand and held it tightly in his own. "It is good to have you back."

Epilogue

By the time his request cleared all the various regulatory bodies and the province's privacy commissioner, it was nearly three weeks later before Danny was able to examine Moira Fraser's medical records. He pored over them with Regan Lampe's help, the two of them holed up in Danny's office for an entire weekend while he sifted through a voluminous file folder encompassing every single doctor's visit, dentist's visit, gynecology screening, and mammogram Moira had ever had.

He felt a bit like a voyeur, parsing some of her most private history. When he expressed this to Regan, she fobbed it off. "For the love of God," she said, "the woman is probably dead. It's no odds to her what's in this file."

It was mid-October now, and the days were definitely cooler, the summer-blue sky fading to an autumnal grey, and the rain had a foretaste of snow in it. The most recent communication from Louis Prud'Homme said that Blaise Pascal was out of hospital and expected to recover completely, in time and with a little help. His mind was still fuzzy from the induced coma, but Prud'Homme would have him call Danny when he was able. No doubt they would have things to discuss, but in the meantime, as Prud'Homme's email put it, *I am looking after him my own self. He does not like this.* Danny wondered if Prud'Homme knew what he'd agreed to take on.

The young *Sûreté* officer also informed him that Gerard Caron had been sighted in the downtown Montreal area several weeks previous, but there had been no subsequent sightings. The SPVM made a thorough sweep of the area where he'd been seen, but no trace of him remained. *It is a mystery to everyone what happen to him*, Prud'Homme wrote, *but as for me, I think he have escaped.* Well, Montreal was a big place, and there were no doubt numerous areas where someone like Gerard Caron could go undiscovered for a very long time.

"You really think that was her in Harry Dean's net?" Danny asked.

"It's more likely than not," Regan replied. "Two bullets in the back of her skull and then dumped overboard?" She scoffed. "When's the last time we had an organised-crime execution around here?"

The answer, of course, was "never," but Danny supposed there was a first time for everything. Following Regan's suggestion that the woman in the net had been dumped at sea south of the island, he had Avery and Hughes compile a comprehensive list of all the vessels traveling in that area during the appropriate time frame and discovered two boats—a retrofitted sailboat and a so-called superyacht—whose position, speed, and intended destination made them the most likely candidates. The sailboat they were able to eliminate (it turned out to be a training vessel for Canadian naval cadets), but the yacht was of interest. Registered in Panama, it was carrying false identification when British port officials boarded it at Penzance several days later. The ship was taken under tow and impounded prior to being searched. Drug dogs found 1.5 tonnes of cocaine, all carefully wrapped and distributed throughout the vessel, and two young girls, approximately twelve to fourteen years old, bound and gagged in the hold.

"These buggers never give up," Adrian Molloy commented when Danny forwarded the information to him. "God only knows how many other ships and boats are out there, floating around with a similar cargo."

"Look at this." Regan held up a sheet of paper. "I was right." She handed it across to Danny, her smile just this side of smug. It was a surgical record containing information about a radical mastectomy performed under general anaesthetic by a Dr. G. Nugent at the Health Sciences Centre in St. John's.

"My God." He sat back in his chair. "Regan, do you know what this means?"

"Moira Fraser is dead."

"Moira Fraser is dead," he echoed. Amalie Caron was dead, Gerard Caron was in the wind somewhere, and Joseph Caron—Joseph Pascal, he silently amended—was still missing. His gaze fell on the little origami swan sitting on the corner of his desk. He'd kept it within sight ever since he returned from Quebec, a talisman of sorts. As always, he found himself marveling at the meticulous work of it, the multiple folds and angles, such artistry created out of something as quotidian as a napkin.

Regan's mobile phone rang; she picked it up and glanced at the screen. "I need to take this," she said, and rose to step out of the office, closing the door behind her. Danny picked up the swan and held it carefully in the palm of his hand while he examined it. The scribble Pascal had made that night in the Coldroom was still there, a hastily drawn *je me souviens*, the provincial motto of Quebec. It was a call to action, a reminder of Quebec's often bloody history and how the Quebecois people had fought to retain their unique language and culture. Pascal had said it was an autograph, but he hadn't signed his name. He'd written this instead: *I remember.*

What do you remember? Danny wondered. He would have liked to ask Pascal but knew he was hardly well enough for such a conversation, and there was no point asking Louis Prud'Homme. He didn't doubt that Pascal had meant the inscription as a sly joke, his way of telling Danny something without saying it outright. They'd been talking about the fire Pascal had set when he was a boy and how his simple action led to an unprecedented outcome. *I remember.* It told him nothing, and maybe that's all it was and he was jumping to conclusions.

He tugged at the wing where the motto was written and it gave way, unraveling in his hands. He'd ruined it. He shouldn't have touched it. There was no reason—

Moira Fraser. It was Pascal's writing, the same deranged scrawl as *je me souviens.* Moira Fraser, the woman responsible for so much damage, so many ruined lives, and Pascal was connected with her? Someone in the *Sûreté* must have known.

Danny dropped the origami swan and reached for his phone. What was the number? Of course he didn't have it close at hand because he'd never had to use it before now. Any interaction with the *Sûreté* was Pascal's purview; he'd always contacted his colleagues in Mont-Tremblant, not Danny. The call was answered immediately, and Danny asked to speak to Céline Tachereau. He wasted no time with politeness or small talk, diving straight in. "Tell me what else he was doing here. Inspector Pascal."

"Inspector Quirke. I should have known you would be in touch." She sounded amused and not at all surprised to hear from him. "*Oui,* Inspector Pascal is recovering very well. He has taken some time off work for this."

"He left behind a note referencing Moira Fraser."

"Referencing who, *monsieur*?"

"Don't be cute," Danny said. "I know he wasn't just here looking for Amalie Caron. You could have sent anybody, but instead you sent him, a career cop, to do a job a constable could have done."

There was a pronounced silence on the other end of the line that lasted for several seconds. He heard Tachereau draw a breath, and then she said, "I will send it to you as an encrypted file. You will destroy this as soon as you have read it. *D'accord?*"

"*Madame* Tachereau, thank you." He disconnected the call, then logged into his email. It had already arrived, a slender handful of words from Tachereau with an image file attached. He clicked on the image.

Mother of God.

His office door swung open, and Regan stepped in. "I'm going to have to—" She stopped short, gazing at the image on Danny's computer screen. "That's Pascal," she commented. The photo on the identification card was recent and displayed Pascal's usual sour expression, but it was the logo just above the photograph that caught and held Danny's attention.

"Interpol," he said. His heart thumped hard inside his ribcage. "He's Interpol. He wasn't down here just looking for Amalie Caron."

"He was looking for Moira Fraser," Regan said quietly. It all made sense. Pascal's secrecy, his reluctance to trust, his close-mouthed stubbornness, as well as his ability to turn up where he was least expected.

Amalie Caron was convenient insofar as Pascal needing a reason to come to the island, and it was true that Pascal had been pursuing her and her husband for fourteen years. But the Carons weren't the entire reason he'd turned up in Kildevil Cove. He'd come here hunting Moira, who'd conveniently disappeared after her role in a sex-trafficking ring was discovered and who had seemingly gone running back to her criminal compatriots. He'd probably deduced that Moira was the body in the fishing net, had been tracking her whereabouts ever since she'd gone off the radar. Danny knew the kind of work Interpol cops did and how dangerous it was. Pascal would willingly put himself in harm's way for the sake of others who would never appreciate or know what he'd done.

"Listen," Regan said, "I've got a situation. A boat overturned off Baccalieu Island—three drowned. I have to get back to receive the remains for autopsy." She hovered near his desk and gestured at his computer screen with her chin. "I'm thinking you have unfinished business with him."

"I do." Perhaps he'd meet up with Pascal again, apologise for being so arsy. Or maybe Pascal wouldn't want that. He'd probably see such an apology as an admission of weakness. "Thanks for this, Regan."

"I'll send you the bill." She collected her jacket off the coat tree near the door and left.

Danny did the same. Time to go home. Home to his family. Time to forget Moira Fraser, Amalie Caron, and Blaise Pascal and bask in the warmth of Tadhg's arms until the world turned and the next case came calling.

Keep Reading for an Excerpt from
Dark Souls
A Kildevil Cove Murder Mystery
by J.S. Cook

PROLOGUE

IT WAS ten-thirty on a Monday morning in January and full daylight somewhere above the clouds, but here, at sea level, it was nearly as dark as night. The few streetlights evident in the village tried valiantly to pierce the veil of blowing snow, but with little effect. Visibility was about one metre and closing fast. Anyone with any sense at all was safe at home, tucked up in their beds. It had been snowing for two days, with an ambient temperature of -25C, not including the wind that was freezing cold, straight out of the northeast, a sustained fury of 100 kilometres per hour, blown across the Labrador Sea from Greenland like a floating pall of ice.

A small open boat drifted on the waves, just inside the harbour of Kildevil Cove, a Newfoundland fishing village located halfway up the island's Avalon Peninsula. The boat rose and fell, rocking violently, unmoored and going nowhere. But it wasn't empty.

Its hapless occupant was swallowed in gloom, nearly forgotten, a frozen monument. She was a long way from home and close to death, deep in the final throes of hypothermia, her body too weak to shiver. Her jaw ached where one of her molars had been savagely torn out, but the flesh no longer bled, the wound stanched by the searing cold. It felt like she had been here forever.

THERE HAD been a party the night before, a belated New Year's celebration at the home of some friends. She wanted to make an occasion of it, so she wore the new silver cocktail dress ordered special from the States, and a pink faux-fur jacket and silver heels. She looked amazing. Afterwards, in the small hours of the morning, she'd said her lingering goodbyes and gone outside to wait for the cab she'd called when her expected ride fell through. Miracle it was that someone answered the call this hour of the morning, and she was some glad. Saved her from accepting a ride from Roy Fitzpatrick, who was a friggin' old perv. While she waited, she smoked a cigarette. She wasn't supposed to smoke, not in her condition, and God help her if Mam or Dad found out.

The night was clear and very cold, and she walked briskly back and forth while she smoked, the sharp toes of her inadequate shoes kicking up small plumes of snow. It should have taken no more than five minutes, but three cigarettes later there was still no taxi, and she was on the verge of going back inside when she saw the headlights piercing the darkness over Buckler's Hill.

"About time," she said when it appeared, a white passenger van with a red stripe and the taxi company's seagull logo painted on the door. "What took ye so long? Lord Christ, I'm froze, sure." All she could see was the back of the driver's head with its stringy dark hair. The rear-view mirror was tilted away from him, obscuring his face. "Burke's Lane, down past the shop. Big white house with the post office in front." He said nothing, put the car in gear, and pulled out onto the road.

She settled back in the seat and scrolled through some text messages on her phone. It had been a decent party, and everybody said she looked like a million in her new dress. All done up like a stick of chewing gum she was, so. Some fella working on the rig asked for her phone number and sent a picture he'd taken, the two of them together. He was tall and blond, blue-eyed, a Norwegian, the kind of fella you took home for the night and kept if you had any luck at all.

She glanced out the side window. "Hey! You're after missing the turn-off, bhoy. Pull your head out of your arse."

This was met with silence. The driver didn't even turn to look at her.

"Do ye hear me? 'Tis no good taking me the long way around, thinking you're going to get more money outta me, because you're not." What should have been a relatively brief cab ride was turning into something else. "Stop the car. I'm getting out." Again there was no reply. She slid across the seat and tried the door handle. It was locked. "I s'pose you thinks this is funny." The car was picking up speed, the driver taking the curves at a dangerous velocity. "Let me out!"

They crested Buckler's Hill and plunged down the other side, and the taxi slid dangerously on the icy road, skating across the double yellow line and bouncing off the guardrail. She had a momentary glimpse of a long embankment sloping down to the sea before the car righted itself, skidding onto the rumble strip before regaining the right-hand lane. Whatever game this man was playing, it wasn't funny. It was entirely possible that he meant her harm. She fumbled for her phone, swiped through to the keypad, cursed when she realised there was no mobile reception whatsoever. *Of course*, she thought, *the hills*.

The hills rose to the right, towering above her, dark, massed shapes, glistening with ice. Deadly. A boy she'd been at school with had fallen to his death clambering down the face of them, trying one summer's day to gain the patch of wild blueberries that lay some metres below. No mobile reception because the hills blocked radio signals, not only because of their size and position. No, there was something else. Iron. There was iron in the rock.

The taxi slowed, turned off the main road and onto a narrow lane that sloped down towards the sea.

"This is not where I wanted to be," she said. The loudness of her own voice shocked her, resonating like a shout in the profound silence. "This is the wrong place." He pulled the vehicle to the side and stopped.

I'll get out now. I will. She heard a click as the door locks disengaged, and then she lunged for the handle, forcing the door out and away from her. But she miscalculated the distance to the ground and tripped, falling to her knees in the snow. The shock of the cold took her breath away.

"Jesus." It came out as a whisper or a prayer. "Jesus."

She couldn't see his face as he came around the back end of the vehicle and grabbed her under the arms to haul her to her feet. A dark woollen scarf obscured his features, and he'd pulled a hood up over his head, leaving nothing bare except a pale space just under the eyes.

"Let me go." She struggled briefly, and he backhanded her savagely across the mouth, knocking her to the ground. "Please." It was hard to pull her body up into a sitting position; the cold had numbed her muscles and a queer lassitude tugged at her. Too much wine at the party, that was it. She liked a drink. Liked it too much. That was the trouble. "Please," she said again, and "Jesus." A sharp pain lanced the side of her neck, and she gasped. "No." Shaking it off was too much trouble. "No. Jesus."

The world went away.

SHE CAME to in a boat, and she was very cold, barely alive, shivering violently under a fall of snow as thick as shaken feathers. She managed with great effort to pull herself into a sitting position so she could peer over the gunwales. There was nothing around her but open sea. She had been set adrift and left in an open boat that was rapidly filling up with snow. Her muscles contracted, cramping violently, and her mouth opened to allow a small cry to escape, a tiny whimper no larger than the mew of a newborn kitten.

"Mam." How did she get here? "Ma—"

It was hard to breathe, and she needed to urinate so bad that it hurt. She opened her thighs and let it run from her, a welcome spill of warmth that swiftly vanished, leaving her colder than before. Her heart thumped in her chest, a slow and ponderous drumbeat'

Someone called her name; she raised her head. "Rose?" Her older sister. She was here. "Rose." So difficult to speak through split, abraded lips made raw by the cold. *Tell Mam*, she thought. *Tell Mam I'm here.* Christmas Eve, decorating the tree with Rose and Dad and Mam, waiting for Joey to come home from the offshore.

No—that was incorrect. Joey wasn't coming. The helicopter... something had happened to the helicopter. There was a monument put up, out by the war memorial, a metal plaque inscribed with all the names of those who'd died. Go back, remember it again: Christmas Eve, decorating the tree with Rose and Dad and Mam. *Some people like to pick the flowers.* She liked to pick the flowers too, but only in the summertime. Only in the summer.

"Mam."

It was better now to rest for a while. Just a little while. Just rest.

WHEN THE storm subsided, as it would eventually, the boat would drift ashore, coming to rest under an outcropping of rock inside the harbour mouth. In this stationary position, it would fill with snow until the slight figure lying in it was nearly obscured, as staid and motionless as one of the ancient dead.

CHAPTER ONE

FORMER ROYAL Newfoundland Constabulary Inspector Deiniol "Danny" Quirke stood at the window of the converted fishing room on a cliff overlooking the harbour at Kildevil Cove, watching the storm through binoculars and thinking of nothing in particular. It had been snowing quite literally for days. Several hours ago he had wrapped himself in his warmest clothes and ventured out, squinting his way through the blizzard to the shed for another yaffle of firewood to feed the Jøtul wood stove, which cheerfully ate everything he gave it and demanded more. At least it kept the room tolerably warm, or as warm as Danny liked it, which was about fourteen degrees Celsius, no more than that.

There was space on top for a kettle full of water, kept perennially near boiling so that a cup of tea was ready in a moment's time, and the frying pan he used to cook thick fillets of halibut or white puddings bought from Heaney's shop out on the Point, and the occasional fried egg cooked in pork fat, about as bad for his fifty-three-year-old arteries as anything you could eat. It wasn't something he cared too much about these days. He seemed to live on foods he could cook quickly: fish and potatoes, ham and eggs, the odd bowl of homemade soup dropped off by some elderly lady in the village who worried about his health.

Shocking what was after happening to him, they said. After letting himself go, he is, so, God love him. Good thing his poor sainted mother isn't alive to see it, although she's probably spinning in her grave, God rest her soul. He knew what they thought of him, saw it in the pitying glances that followed him in the shops, or on one of his rare trips to Strange Brew to get a coffee. To them he was a figure of considerable attraction, a tragic soul now relegated to the arse end of what had been a promising police career. Funny what happened when your former supervisor was into human trafficking and you got caught in the backdraft. Guilt by association, even though he'd always done his best to keep his hands clean.

Something was moving out there on the water, a slice of dark material moving on the swells, lifting and lowering at the behest of the wind. He took the binoculars away, adjusted the sights, then looked through them again. Yes, there it was, a small wooden boat, unmoored and drifting near the harbour mouth, the oarlocks empty. Who in their right mind would be out in a boat on a day like this? Was anyone in it? Or had it simply broken loose from the wharf? He stared at it until his eyes began to ache, straining to peer through the heavy veil of January snow, then put the binoculars away. No point in trying to see something that simply wasn't there. When the storm subsided, someone from the town would go out and retrieve the boat, haul it back ashore to safety. It was only an empty boat, nothing to concern himself with. Let some other fool take care of it.

He went back to the desk in front of the window and shuffled aside a pile of file folders, flicking through them until he found the one he wanted. The kettle whistled, briefly coming to a temporary boil, then fell silent. The wind baffled down the chimney, spat gusts of snow-flavoured cold into the woodstove, and the windows rattled. He was as alone as he had ever been.

He opened the file, paging through a stack of photographs he'd already seen a dozen times, looking for something new, some clue that probably didn't exist. It was a very old cold case—these being his only assignment at present—the murder of twelve-year-old Vanessa Tulk thirty years previous. The young girl disappeared one hot August day while hitch-hiking alone between Carbonear and Heart's Content; her body turned up two days later in a bog and was found by some berry pickers who had gone in there looking for cloudberries. The case was ruled a suicide and shelved, but the pathologist who did the autopsy reported the cause of death as a fractured skull. Danny wondered how she could have fractured her own skull, and did she do that before or after she turned up in the berry bog?

Without thinking he reached for the phone to call Tadhg, then remembered. Old habits and all that. Tadhg wasn't here anymore; he had shoved off for Ireland on a fool's errand, leaving only harsh words behind. Tadhg wasn't his anymore. The pain of it stuck into him, a jagged splinter, but he was used to it by now, and he allowed the sting of it to penetrate. It was time he was moving on, but moving on was difficult when you had nothing to move on to, when there was nowhere else to go.

He fetched down a cup from the shelf, dropped a teabag into it, and filled it from the kettle. How many cups was that today? At least a dozen. No wonder his heart was beating a mile a minute, fluttering underneath his breastbone like a netted bird. He poured milk into the cup from the carton he kept cold between two panes of the window and went to sit down at the desk again. Vanessa Tulk was still dead. She'd been that way for a very long time.

The jangling of his mobile phone startled him, loud as an air raid siren in the tiny flat. He picked it up from where it lay face down on the desk and turned it over. Maybe it was Tadhg. Maybe he....

No such luck. The caller was RNC Chief Adrian Molloy, his new boss, a transplant from Northern Ireland and Moira Fraser's substitute. "Hello?"

"Is that you, Danny?" Molloy's voice was slightly nasal and deceptively soft. Danny knew from recent experience it could cut like steel. "What is it you're at today?"

"The Tulk case, sir." He touched the corner of one of the autopsy photos with his fingertips. "I've been combing back through the original evidence, but I don't think we're going to get anywhere."

"Yes, well, put that aside for now," Molloy said. "There's been a report of a body found in a small open boat just inside the harbour. You need to take a look."

"Sir, with respect, I can't do that. I'm no longer in charge here. You'd best get hold of Cillian Riley at the station." Danny's suspected involvement with Moira Fraser's sex trafficking ring had seen him removed from his official position of inspector with the Kildevil Cove RNC substation while the whole mess was under investigation. The accusation that he'd been involved was a load of shite, but it was the kind of shite that stuck.

"I don't want Riley. I want you. Do you want to do this?"

Danny glanced out the window. "Dirty weather out there the day."

"Aw, but you're a hearty Newfoundlander, Danny." Molloy's voice was steeped in sarcasm. "Surely to God you don't mind a bit of snow?"

"I'll dress warm, sir." If Molloy wanted him looking at a body in a blizzard, he'd go—but privately Danny thought the chief inspector was out of his goddamn mind. He ended the call, then went to pull on heavy wool underwear and wool socks, a bulky pullover layered under thick wool trousers, and all of it topped off with a down-filled parka. He shoved his feet into a pair of Sorel boots, laced them tightly, and added a dark watch cap of Icelandic wool and a pair of "trigger mitts" his grandmother had knit for him many years before.

Is it cold in Newfoundland? Someone had asked him this at a police conference in Aberdeen back in the early 2000s. *Is the weather always bad?* He tried to remember how he'd answered them. *There are days in July when the light is long and the wind is warm and it's every bit as good as Heaven... and then there's days during the dead of winter when it's early dark and cold as hell and you wish you were anywhere else on earth.* That about summed it up.

He went outside, praying that the ancient Land Rover he was driving nowadays would start. With his demotion had come a pay cut, and he'd had to sell the Audi Quattro, was lucky enough to find the Rover for sale online at a price he could afford. The ad had stated only "it runs," but that was enough for Danny. As it was, the purchase cleaned him out, leaving little to live on for the foreseeable future, but his expenses these days were minimal. It went with not having a life anymore. The Rover was rusted all to hell, and the driver's side door had been warped in an accident and didn't meet flush with the frame so that rain and snow got inside the cab during inclement weather. It was a standard shift, which Danny hated driving, with a dicky clutch that sometimes stuck and sometimes did as it was told with no warning whatsoever. But today it started when he turned the key, and he was grateful. The rest he'd deal with later on.

He stopped by the station first, where Cillian Riley had been acting as supervisor and chief investigator in his absence. It was still snowing hard, and the wind was bitingly cold, shaking his flimsy vehicle, and he was glad to get into the warm. He stamped the snow off his boots inside the front door, took off his cap and gloves and stuffed them into the pockets of his parka. There was no one at the reception desk, so he rang the bell, feeling a little surge of gladness when Constable—no, he was a sergeant now—Kevin Carbage came to let him in.

"It's some good to see you, sir." Carbage didn't seem to know what to do with his hands. He leaned forward like he wanted to embrace Danny, then thought better of it, dropping his arms to his sides. Danny had already stepped into the anticipated hug, and Kevin's sudden capitulation left him hanging, his posture suggesting a lunge rather than an embrace. It wasn't Kevin's fault. No one knew what to make of him these days. He couldn't blame them for being awkward in his presence.

"Where's Riley?" Danny asked. He couldn't bring himself to say "Inspector Riley," even though that was the former sergeant's rank now. "Chief Inspector Molloy called. There's a body in a dory just offshore. He wants us to check it out."

"He's...." Kevin looked distinctly uncomfortable. He glanced away, wetting his lips. "He moved into your old office, sir."

"Good for him. Okay if I just go down?" Danny gestured towards the end of the hall.

"I'll have to let you in, sir." Kevin produced a white key card and motioned for Danny to follow him. "It's procedure." A bright red spot appeared on each cheekbone, and he ducked his head. *Christ*, Danny thought, *they're walking on eggshells around me.* He didn't like the feeling.

Inspector Cillian Riley was sitting behind Danny's desk, reading the contents of a file folder, when Danny appeared. He'd changed the office around, moved the filing cabinet to one side from its former position next to the bookcase and added some scenic posters of the local area. A stack of law books sat on the floor in front of the desk. Danny had heard Riley was planning to apply to law school in the fall.

"Well, Inspector Riley," Danny said with forced cheer, "you've done well for yourself."

"Oh." Riley dropped the file and stood up. "Sir. I didn't know you were coming." He glanced around. "We figured it was best if I moved in here... for the time being. Just until you're back." He came out from around the desk and grasped Danny's hand. "Are you back?"

"No, Cillian." Danny turned away for a moment, pretending interest in one of the posters. "I like what you've done with the place. It's nice."

"Sir—Danny—I can have this moved out in—"

"Cillian... it's fine." Danny reached out to squeeze his shoulder. "This is your office now. No, I'm here because Chief Inspector Molloy called me. There's a body in an open boat just offshore, and he asked me to check it out." He tried to smile, but his face felt frozen. Damn Molloy for tossing him into this! The entire situation was awkward as hell. "Thought I'd come by and see if you're up for it." He glanced pointedly at the coat rack set to one side of the desk. "Have you got any proper winter gear, or what?"

"Give me a minute," Riley said. "Got a heavy parka hung up in the break room."

THEY TOOK one of the patrol cars down to the harbour. It had been fitted with heavy winter tires, but even then the vehicle skidded and slipped. Riley, unused to driving in snow, was tight-lipped, his ungloved hands white-knuckled on the steering wheel. Danny pitied him. In order to drive in Newfoundland winter weather, you really needed to be born to it, and Riley, coming from Newcastle, had probably never seen a winter like this in his entire life.

"Just pull to the side," Danny directed, pointing at an abandoned fishing room a few feet up from the water. "We'll need the ambulance, so it's best to keep out of the way."

Riley stepped on the brakes, but the car continued on for some distance before finally coming to a stop. He shoved it up into park and sat quiet for a moment, hands trembling. "You can drive back" was all he said.

A second car pulled up behind them, and Danny was shocked to see Adrian Molloy climb out. He went to meet him. "Surprised to see you here, sir."

"I'm surprised to see anybody in this fucking weather," Molloy said. "What is it you fellas say around here? ''Tis not fit for chick nor child.'" He jerked his chin at the boat bobbing just offshore. "I believe in being hands-on, Constable. More than that bloody Fraser woman, at any rate. Come on. Let's go see what we've got."

Danny followed him down to the water's edge, squinting through the wind-driven snow at the small dory. There was definitely somebody in it, but the boat had filled with so much snow that it was impossible to tell anything much about its occupant.

"That's a nasty way to die," Molloy said. "Do you suppose he's frozen solid?"

"Wouldn't surprise me, sir." Danny yanked his watch cap on, pulling it down firmly over his ears, and tugged the hood of his parka over his head. "Think of me fondly," he murmured and waded into the icy North Atlantic.

Somewhere behind him he heard someone cry out, "Lord Christ, man, what the hell are you doing?" Molloy, he thought. Had to be.

The first shock of cold made him gasp aloud, but it soon passed. He knew he had mere seconds to reach the boat before the icy water stole the feeling from his feet. Already he could feel the chill of it, crawling up his legs, as far now as his upper thighs. For the first few steps, the bottom was sandy and relatively level, and he strode forward, confident that what he was treading on would hold him. But just before he reached the small craft, the underwater landscape dropped off suddenly and he stepped forward into empty sea. It closed over his head and rushed into the open places of his body, filling his mouth and eyes, his ears. His heavy woollen clothes were quickly soaked, immeasurably heavy now, dragging him under, and he kicked against the tide, clawed and freezing fingers reaching for the gunwale of the boat. He was so close he could see it. He slapped at the water, reached again, lungs straining with the effort of holding his breath. His vision was going, everything around him turning red, and then his right hand caught hold of something solid and he was pulling the boat towards him, rolling over the side, and falling into the relative safety of the little dory. "…of God!" Molloy exclaimed. "For the love of Jesus, are you all right?" He'd waded out up to his waist.

"Yeah," Danny managed to say, coughing and spitting out water as Molloy retreated back to shore. "Fine." He'd lost his gloves somewhere underwater, but it didn't matter now. He leaned over the frozen figure and scraped the snow away from the face, wondering what he'd see and hoping it was no one he knew.

A young woman, perhaps twenty-five years old, lying on her back with her head turned to the side as if she were seeing something over her shoulder. Long strands of her blond hair were frozen to her neck in complicated whorls, and her face was bone white, as if her body had been drained of blood. She lay with her hands clasped to her bosom, fingers tightly curled.

"Female," Danny called out. He touched her cheek and her lower lip, where a drop of blood clung, as perfect as a polished ruby. "She's not dressed for the weather, that's for sure." He ran a hand down the front of her body, brushing away the snow. The silver cocktail sheath and soaking-wet faux-fur jacket were no protection against the freezing temperature or the quickly falling snow. "Ah, ye poor young maid," he murmured. "You're cold enough to be prayed for, you are, so."

Her eyes opened.

J.S. Cook is a college lecturer who lives in St. John's, Newfoundland.

She grew up surrounded by the wild North Atlantic ocean in a small fishing village on the coast of Newfoundland. An avid lover of both the sea and the outdoors, she was powerfully seduced by the lure of this rugged, untamed landscape.

J.S. teaches communications and creative writing at the College of the North Atlantic. She makes her home in St. John's with her husband, Paul, and her two furkids: Juniper, a border terrier, and Riley, a chiweenie.

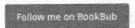

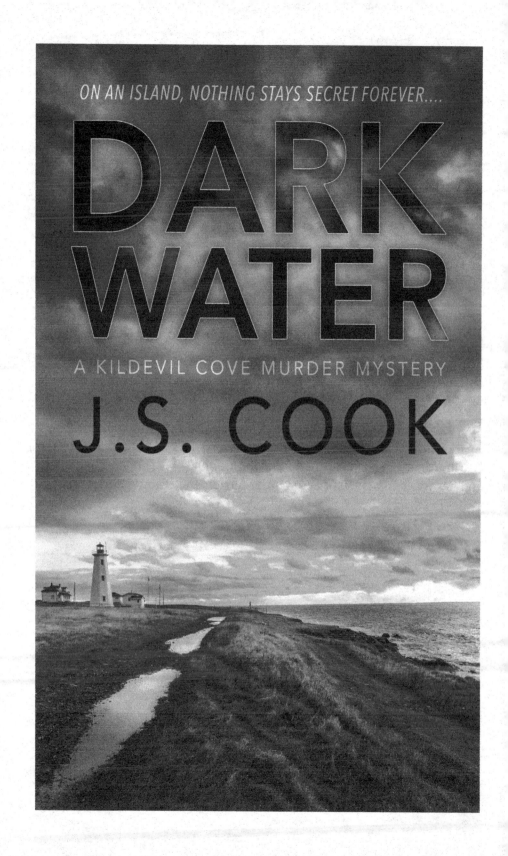

ON AN ISLAND, NOTHING STAYS SECRET FOREVER....

DARK WATER

A KILDEVIL COVE MURDER MYSTERY

J.S. COOK

A Kildevil Cove Murder Mystery

They say trouble comes in threes. Detective Danny Quirke is already mourning his wife and mired in an internal investigation that will likely spell the end of his career. Now he must return to the Newfoundland fishing village of his youth to bury his abusive grandfather. At least his three are up. Right?

Then the bones of local boy Llewellyn Single, drowned thirty years before, wash up on the beach, and secrets Danny thought were buried forever rise violently to the surface. Only two people know what really happened: Danny Quirke and his former best friend, millionaire Tadhg Heaney.

Danny and Tadhg have been bitter enemies for years. But when Danny is accused of Llewellyn's murder, he needs Tadhg's help exposing the truth—before those who believe he is responsible get their revenge.

After all, on an island, nothing stays secret forever....

Previously published by Dreamspinner Press as Wind and Dark Water, March 2020.

www.dreamspinnerpress.com

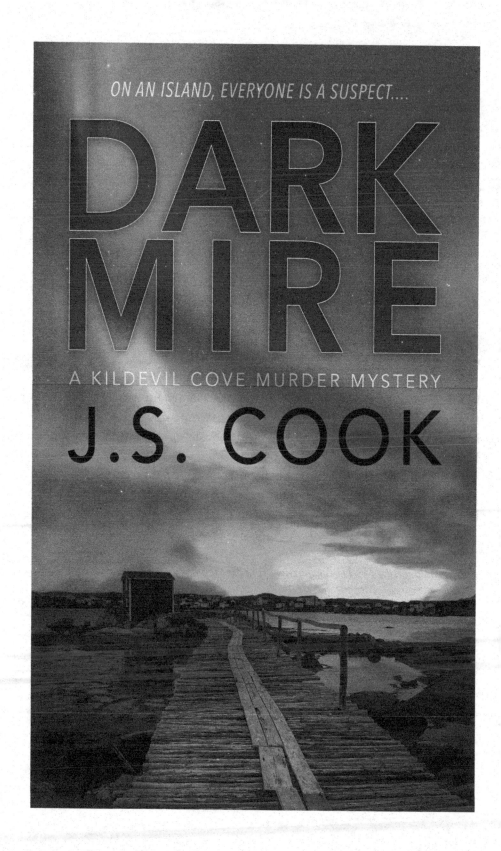

ON AN ISLAND, EVERYONE IS A SUSPECT....

DARK MIRE

A KILDEVIL COVE MURDER MYSTERY

J.S. COOK

A Kildevil Cove Murder Mystery

You never know what trouble will rise from the bog.

When the body of an unidentified woman is found in a Newfoundland bog, Inspector Danny Quirke must scramble his team of investigators to find her killer. But what initially seems like a straightforward case soon becomes mired in a tangled web of lies and deliberate obfuscation.

With the strange mutilation of the body—one eye gouged out completely—evidence seems to lead to a fringe religious group with bizarre beliefs. But while the pathologist indicates mushroom poisoning as the cause of death, Danny thinks circumstances point to something more sinister—especially when he begins to receive anonymous messages with links to horrific pictures of damaged human eyes.

Three more bodies join the first, with seemingly nothing to link them but a little girl in a yellow party dress who flits in and out of the mystery like a creature from the old legends. Then an old friend from his childhood reappears, and Danny is forced to confront uncomfortable truths about his own nearest and dearest.

On an island, everyone is a suspect…

www.dreamspinnerpress.com

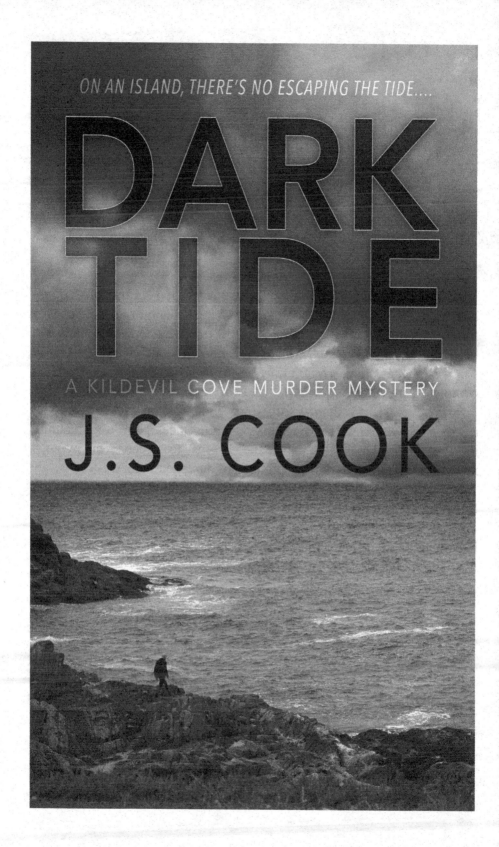

ON AN ISLAND, THERE'S NO ESCAPING THE TIDE....

DARK TIDE

A KILDEVIL COVE MURDER MYSTERY

J.S. COOK

A Kildevil Cove Murder Mystery

They say it never rains but it pours. Royal Newfoundland Constabulary Inspector Danny Quirke would have to agree.

First someone murders a vulnerable Kildevil Cove man and dumps him in an abandoned well. Then the body of a sex-trafficking victim washes up on a nearby beach. Danny has to get to the bottom of both deaths, but with few leads and little support from his superiors, he's spinning his wheels in a mud pit of a case. Vital resources go missing, witnesses disappear, and suspects proliferate.

Each step toward the truth brings him two steps back. Help comes in the form of Scottish investigator Martin Belshawe, but he may not be who he says he is, and someone in the highest echelons of the Newfoundland Constabulary is lying to Danny. Even Danny's lover, Tadhg Heaney, whom he looks to for emotional support, seems to know more than he should about the shady characters who keep popping up in the investigation.

With time running out, Danny must decide who, if anyone, he can trust—before the sex traffickers claim their next victims. But on an island, there's no escaping the tide.

www.dreamspinnerpress.com

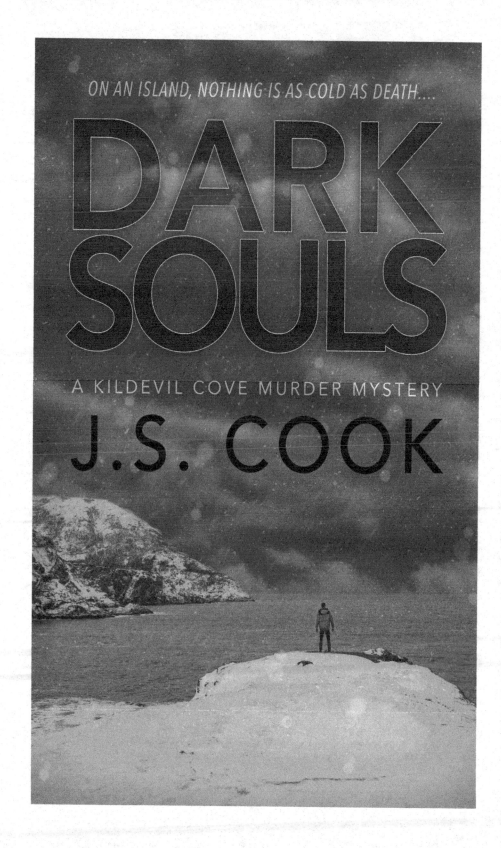

ON AN ISLAND, NOTHING IS AS COLD AS DEATH....

DARK SOULS

A KILDEVIL COVE MURDER MYSTERY

J.S. COOK

A Kildevil Cove Murder Mystery

There's trouble brewing in the cold waters of Kildevil Cove, and this time Danny Quirke may be hard put to stop it.

Due to his suspected association with his former boss's human trafficking organization, Danny has been demoted and is no longer in charge. To make matters worse, he's broken up with his partner, Tadhg… who may be in serious hot water himself. But then a faceless killer begins targeting Kildevil Cove's most vulnerable, and Danny can't refuse when his new boss asks him to take the case.

When Danny pulls a hypothermic young woman out of a small boat in the middle of a blizzard, she whispers a cryptic phrase about a man with no face. But who is he? What is his connection to the murders? And how is Danny going to solve the mystery while he's the subject of an investigation that could end his career?

www.dreamspinnerpress.com

J.S. COOK

GREATEST HITS

Enjoy J.S. Cook's best mysteries, with a side of lust and romance, in this collection.

In *But Not for Me*, gangster boss Nino Moretti rescues beautiful mob accountant Stanley Zadwadzki from a rival, but the consequences may cost them any chance at a relationship.

In *A Little Night Murder*, insurance investigator Frank Boyle may have escaped from danger once with help from detective Sam Lipinski, but a new investigation is turning up trouble once again.

In *Come to Dust*, Inspector Philemon Raft is set adrift among the deceitful ton of turn-of-the-century London, trying to locate the kidnapped Miriam Dewberry.

In *The Lovely Beast*, Jacob van Willingen is on a mission to exterminate the evil Caleb Donnithorn, but things aren't quite what they seem to be at this Romanian castle.

In *Skid Row Serenade*, novelist and war hero Tony Leonard visits his estranged wife only to find her beaten to death. On the run, he decides to fake his own death, with a little help from private investigator Edwin Malloy.

But Not for Me previously published by Dreamspinner Press, March 2013.
A Little Night Murder previously published by Dreamspinner Press, September 2013.
Come to Dust previously published by Dreamspinner Press, November 2013.
The Lovely Beast previously published by Dreamspinner Press, July 2014.
Skid Row Serenade previously published by Dreamspinner Press, August 2015.

www.dreamspinnerpress.com